CURSED BY THE STARS

MICHELE KHALIL

Cursed by the Stars. Copyright © 2026 by Michele Khalil

All rights reserved.

No part of this publication may be reproduced, distributed, or transmitted in any form or by any means, including photocopying, recording, or other electronic or mechanical methods, without the prior written permission of the publisher, except as permitted by U.S. copyright law. For permission requests, contact Michele Khalil.

No part of this book may be used or reproduced in any matter for the purpose of training artificial intelligence technologies or systems.

No AI was used during the planning, outlining, writing, or editing of this book because the author has watched far too many sci-fi movies and read far too many sci-fi books to contribute to the rise of oppressive robots.

The story, all names, characters, and incidents portrayed in this production are fictitious. No identification with actual persons (living or deceased), places, buildings, and products is intended or should be inferred.

Cover design by Khalil Covers

Map by Michele Khalil via Inkarnate

Illustrations by bellinnacraft (Etsy)

Set in Garamond and Cinzel

Edited by Victoria Jane (@editsbyvictoriajane | www.victoriajaneeditorial.com)

1st edition 2026

ISBN: 9781957467054

For the women who were never meant to be saved — only feared, desired, and remembered.

Let's burn it all down.

Cursed by the Stars is a dark romantasy about love, rage, and rebellion. It explores life shaped by trauma, grief, and fear. The story includes depictions of PTSD, depression, and anxiety-not as defining traits, but as lived experiences by an individual living with them. These conditions are deeply personal and look different for everyone, and this book reflects only one interpretation among many. But I do hope that readers who share similar experiences find moments of recognition or comfort within these pages.

It contains mature themes that may be triggering to some readers. To find the full list of trigger warnings, check out the website or use the QR code below.

Please take care of yourself as you read.

This story was written for the ones who have burned, survived, and still dare to love.

Glossary

Abaya — A long, loose-fitting robe worn over clothing, common in many Middle Eastern cultures.

Ambigua — A term given by the Imperium to those who deviate from the Zodiac paths, possessing powers outside the constellations. Considered a curse and hunted as abominations.

Aphelion — The great academy in Astrome where the Trials take place. A university and proving ground for Zodiacs, filled with ancient archives and secrets.

Araq — A strong distilled alcoholic drink, traditionally anise-flavored, consumed during social gatherings.

Astrome — The capital city, built in concentric rings with the palace (Qasr al-Nujūm) at its center. Known for its spires, domes, and marble villas.

Baghlahs — Heavy wooden cargo ships used across the seas, with wide hulls and lateen sails.

Blood Oath — An ancient ritual of binding sworn in blood. Originally sacred, used for peace, marriage, and sacrifice, but corrupted by the Imperium into an institutional tool of control for Trials and Aphelion entrants.

Crossborn — Zodiacs born outside noble Signborn lines, often from mixed or lesser-known families. They enter the Trials seeking opportunity or ambition.

Dhows — Traditional sailing vessels with slim hulls and triangular lateen sails, used for fishing, trading, and pearl diving.

Galabiya — A long, loose-fitting tunic or robe, usually ankle-length, worn by men and women.

Glaive — A polearm weapon with a long blade mounted on a staff, designed for sweeping slashes.

Howz — A shallow, decorative pool or fountain found in courtyards, often used for cooling air and reflecting light.

Khanjar — A curved, double-edged dagger, often ornate, worn as a symbol of honor or status.

Khallas — "Enough" or "finished" (Arabic: خلص). Used to cut off conversation or signal finality.

Kilij — A curved, single-edged saber of Turkish origin, prized for its sharp cut and distinctive forward-angled blade.

Kofta — Spiced ground meat shaped into balls or patties, often grilled or stewed.

Mashrabiya — Ornate wooden lattice screens used in Middle Eastern architecture, filtering sunlight and providing privacy.

Muqarnas — A honeycomb-like vaulting used in Islamic architecture, often in domes or entrances.

Naqus — A wooden or metal semantron (percussion instrument) struck to summon gatherings, used in temples or towers.

Qasr al-Nujūm — "Palace of the Stars," the central palace of Astrome.

Rohi — "My soul" (Arabic: روحي). A term of deep affection or love.

Sadekty — "My friend" (Arabic: صديقتي / صديقي depending on gender). A familiar, intimate term of trust.

Sarwal / Shalwar — Loose-fitting trousers tied at the waist, worn with tunics or robes.

Shokran — "Thank you" (Arabic: شكراً).

Signborn — Zodiacs born into noble bloodlines tied to a specific constellation, considered elite and powerful.

Tarha — A headscarf or shawl, often worn draped over the hair and shoulders.

Thobe — A long, ankle-length robe with long sleeves, commonly worn by men in Arab regions.

Waghl — "Intruder" (Arabic: وَغْل). A term of disdain for someone who enters without right or invitation.

Ziggurat — A terraced, pyramid-like structure. In the manuscript, it describes the grand architecture of Aphelion.

Zulfiqar — A legendary sword in Islamic tradition, recognized by its bifurcated (split) blade. It has become a symbol of power, justice, and divine strength.

The Zodiac Signs

Aries (March 21st - April
Superhuman strength, enhanced stamina, and the ability to manipulate objects using strength.

Leo (July 23rd - August
Biomorphing

Sagittarius (November 23rd - December 22nd)
Teleportation

Taurus (April 22nd - May
Atmokinesis

Virgo (August 22nd - September 23rd)
Healing

Capricorn (December 23rd - January 20th)
Invisibility

The Zodiac Signs

Gemini (May 22nd - June 21st)
Replication

Libra (September 24th - October 23rd)
Telepathy

Aquarius (January 21st - February 19th)
Telekinesis

Cancer (June 22nd - July 22nd)
Clairvoyance & Divination

Scorpio (October 24th - November 22nd)
Mind Control

Pisces (February 20th - March 20th)
Illusions

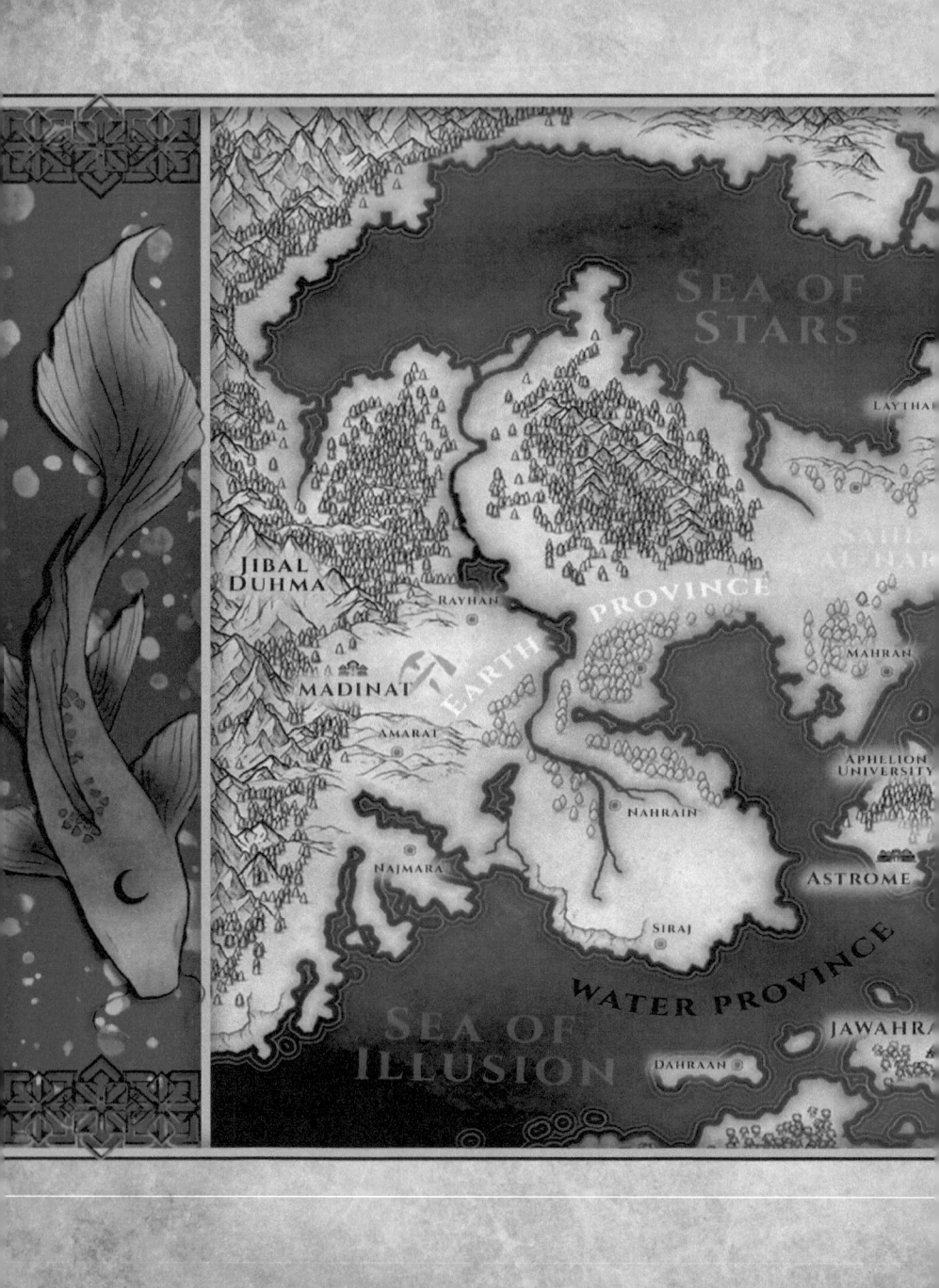

PRONUNCIATION GUIDE
PEOPLE

Talah bint Khalid [TAH-lah KHAH-lid]

Firas Soulinus/Iras Eldin [fee-RAHS so-LIN-us / EL-deen]

Mazin al-Sahri [MAH-zin al-SAH-ree]

Zayd Amir [ZAYD ah-MEER]

Adine Morad [ah-DEEN mo-RAHD]

Kamaria [kah-MAR-ee-ah]

Raven (like the bird)

Kamal Soulinus [kah-MAHL soo-LIN-us]

The Kaed [KAYD]

Saahira Khatri [sah-HEER-ah KHAH-tree]

Nadir Khatri [NAH-deer KHAH-tree]

Khalid Al-Rashid [KHAH-lid al-rah-SHEED]

Selene Amin [seh-LEEN ah-MEEN]

PRONUNCIATION GUIDE
PLACES

Aphelion [uh-FEE-lee-on]

Astrome [ASS-trohm]

Jawahra [jah-WAH-rah]

Qasr al-Nujūm [KASS-r al noo-JOOM] ("Palace of the Stars")

POWER GUIDE

Talah bint Khalid - Pisces
Firas Soulinus - Scorpio Ambigua
Mazin al-Sahri - Pisces
Adine Morad - Taurus
Zayd Amir - Gemini
Kamaria - Aries Ambigua
Raven - Sagittarius Ambigua
Saahira Khatri - Libra
Nadir Khatri - Libra
Khalid Al-Rashid - Pisces
Selene Amin - Pisces
Kamal Soulinus - Scorpio

FIRAS

Firas never imagined he'd return to the place that first took his freedom—and taught him what it meant to lose everything.

The sight of it twisted something deep in his chest. Aphelion was just as he remembered it. Maybe that was what hurt most.

The main hall was the first to greet them, with the ziggurat looming against the skyline. Its layered terraces stretched toward the heavens as if reaching for the stars that had once guided their ancestors. Made from sandstone and reinforced with veins of shimmering marble, its walls bore the subtle etchings of constellations. Golden afternoon sunlight bathed the stone in a warm glow, casting elongated shadows across the vast courtyard.

The high outer walls, formidable and unbroken, shielded the rest of the university from prying eyes. Intricate geometric patterns adorned them, and ivy and flowering vines softened the sharp precision of their lines, clinging to the stone like whispers of an older time. And beyond those walls lay the heart of the university. Firas knew it well.

This place had shaped him once. Now, it just reminded him how easily he'd been broken.

A labyrinth of interconnected courtyards and archways, where buildings of pale limestone and warm terracotta rose in elegant succession. Their domed rooftops shimmered under the sun, adorned with intricate mosaics of deep blues and emerald greens. Slender columns framed open-air halls, their pointed arches rippling across tiled courtyards. Windows, carved with delicate latticework, filtered the light into ever-shifting patterns.

Water flowed freely through the campus, winding through channels carved into the walkways, bubbling in elaborate howz pools nestled within open-air gardens, carrying the gentle murmur of running streams throughout the campus. The scent of jasmine and sandalwood drifted lazily on the breeze, mingling with the rich aroma of parchment and ink—an ever-present reminder that this was a place of learning, of power, of destiny.

And at the very heart of it all, the ziggurat remained unchanged. It was the gatekeeper of knowledge, its terraces teeming with verdant life—an oasis amidst stone, where carefully curated flora cascaded over the edges, breaking the rigid lines of the architecture with the softness of nature. It stood watch over the university, its shadow long, its presence eternal.

This was Aphelion.

A sanctuary. A challenge. A proving ground.

The beauty did its best to hide what it really was, though.

A death trap.

From the day he was born, Firas knew the true purpose of Aphelion—of the challenges that awaited here. It was a symbol of power, of privilege, of the future. While the rest of the world worked in turmoil and struggle, Aphelion granted its students everything they needed to be successful. Imperium councilors, diplomats, generals and more were molded here, opening golden doors for those that earned it.

And they *did* have to earn it.

"Are you sure about this?" Kamaria's sharp voice brought him back to the present. "What if someone recognizes you?"

Her eyes, dark as obsidian and twice as unyielding, scanned the courtyard like a hawk circling. She wore black as if it were armor, the sharp lines of her tunic and sarwal trousers a deliberate contrast to the loose, drifting styles of the others around them. Her hair was pulled back into tight braids, emphasizing the sharp angles of her cheekbones and the unwavering line of her jaw.

"No one is going to recognize a dead man," he reminded her.

"Don't be so quick to brush this off." Her words cut straight through him. "If this doesn't work…"

"It'll work." His voice carried more certainty than he actually felt, but that was the point. Doubt wouldn't get them anywhere. And if it didn't work… he wasn't ready to entertain that thought just yet. "If Samira didn't think this would work, she wouldn't have allowed me to come."

At the mention of their leader, Kam hesitated. Samira had been the head this rebellion far longer than either of them had been alive. She was the one who had taken them in, saving them from being hunted down. She'd given them a new life, a new purpose, honing them into perfect soldiers.

Kam said nothing more, but he could feel her disapproval rolling from her in waves. She'd been vehemently against this idea, and he couldn't blame her. The thought of walking these halls again…Firas suppressed the fear coiling through him.

There could be no room for error, or they'd all be dead.

Before, Firas had never thought much about why Zodiacs came from all over the world to this university just to potentially die. He never questioned the propaganda, the indoctrination— because that's exactly what this was. Zodiac children swarmed the Trials each year, hoping to earn those prestigious spots. For the Signborn, it was a symbol of their family's power, their lines. For Crossborn, it was ambition to build a better life.

Firas hated the words—Signborn and Crossborn. They carried both nothing and everything in their weight. Among the Zodiacs, lineage wasn't just pride. It was power. Families guarded their Signs with near-religious fervor, weaving generations of births into the same constellation as if chaining themselves to the stars would make them untouchable. The longer a line remained unbroken, the sharper their gifts became, until ability itself was treated like inheritance. Those families—the Signborn—sat as nobles over the rest, parading their constancy as proof of superiority. Parents planned their children with meticulous care, calculating dates, pairing unions with all the precision of a battle map. And when the plans went wrong… well, Firas had learned where those children ended up.

The Crossborn were the ones without legacy to steady their hands or sharpen their gifts. Their bloodlines tangled across Signs, producing children whose abilities rarely burned as bright, whose strength flickered rather than roared. To the Signborn, they were lesser—useful only as laborers, soldiers or servants. Entire generations of Crossborn bent beneath the weight of a world built on lineage, their toil the foundation on which every Signborn throne sat. But even they were not as bad as the Ambigua.

At least, that's what the Imperium believed.

No competitors had arrived just yet, still a few hours before the Blood Oaths would take place. They took the steps one at a time, neither in a hurry to enter the enormous double-doors of the Great Hall. Firas closed his eyes as they reached the top, memorizing the feeling of Astrome's sun beating upon their shoulders before they slipped into the darkness.

The entrance to the hall was dimly lit, with metal chandeliers hoisted high above them. Twelve pillars lined the entryway, one for each Zodiac Sign, leading toward two curved staircases that led to the second floor. Red carpet guided them over smooth marble, muting their footsteps.

Neither of them spoke a word as they climbed, knowing the chamber would echo any such secrets to those around them. Firas hated the place. There was no shadowy corner, no locked door, that could keep a secret here. Unless you were the Imperium.

"Hopefully, we'll get someone good," Kam said casually, eyes assessing the other mentors around them. Always watching.

He knew what she really meant.

Each mentor who volunteered had, at some point, passed the Trials. They were meant to give the competitors the best chance of getting through the horrors that awaited them. Without the mentors, it would be a bloodbath, and the Imperium hadn't set up the Trials as a way to cull the population—only to test those who wanted to study at the most prestigious university in their world.

"One could only hope," Firas replied. Though, that wasn't necessarily true. Their entire plan depended on keeping their little competitor alive. Whoever that may be.

Firas and Kam had survived their Trials…but they hadn't passed them. He wasn't exactly sure how Samira had done it, but she'd somehow forged their papers and greased some palms to let them in as mentors. It was risky, but Firas doubted many of the administrators at the school would remember every single student who had actually made it through.

The main office, nestled within the towering ziggurat, was a stark contrast to the grandeur of the university beyond. Not unlike the sprawling halls, this room was cloistered in shadow, its high stone walls lined with shelves of neatly stacked records and brittle scrolls. The scent of parchment, old ink, and the faintest trace of candle smoke clung to the air.

The ceiling, vaulted and inscribed with constellations, seemed to press down upon the room, its muted silver inlays catching the flickering glow of brass lanterns. A single narrow window let in a slant of light, illuminating dust motes that drifted lazily through the still air. Quills and ledgers were scattered haphazardly across the desk, a testament to the countless generations of students who had stood in this very spot, their futures decided with nothing more than ink on parchment.

Luckily, he no longer had to face those horrors as a competitor.

"Names?" A woman sat behind an imposing ebony desk,

her tone as uninterested as the sharp, calculating gaze she barely lifted from her records.

She was draped in the deep, somber hues of Capricorn. The stiff collar framed her neck like armor, and silver embroidery—subtle, almost austere—ran along the cuffs, the only concession to adornment. She exuded quiet authority, her presence as solid and unmoving as the stone walls surrounding her.

"Iras Eldin." He'd been lazy with his alias, but this would be the last place anyone expected him to be.

Especially when they all believed him to be dead for the past two years.

"Kamaria Elmissery," Kam replied, her tone softening slightly. She'd used her own name... a name no one knew. When she'd come as a competitor, she'd been a nobody. And had died a nobody all the same.

The woman did not bother to offer her own name. She shifted through the papers before her, coming up with two parchments before deftly handing them over.

"These are your room numbers and schedules," the woman instructed. "You will not know the name of your competitor until the Convocation. If you have any questions, please direct them to Khalias, director of the Trials this year."

Firas knew Khalias. He also knew he wouldn't be asking that man any questions lest he wanted to find himself in yet another grave. To Khalias, Firas was nothing but a dead boy rotting in the ground. That had been a few years ago, and Firas had changed since then—both physically and mentally. Khalias wouldn't recognize him.

Hopefully.

No, Khalias wouldn't be the biggest threat to his undercover identity. But his father would.

"Shokran."

Without a backward glance, Firas led the way back out into the hall. They veered right, winding through the labyrinthine halls until they reached an unmarked door. Beyond it, a spiral staircase descended into the depths, each step cool beneath their feet. At the bottom, another door awaited—this one bathed in a slant of golden sunlight, spilling through the cracks.

The vast, sprawling courtyard of Aphelion University stretched before them, a maze of colonnades, shaded archways, and meticulously arranged gardens. Stone pathways wove between fountains and howz pools, their still waters reflecting the rays of sunlight.

Firas and Kamaria moved with purpose, slipping past the towering pillars that framed the main hall's entrance. The air carried the distant murmur of the wind rustling through palm fronds, mingling with the faint echoes of voices drifting from the dormitories beyond. It seemed as if nothing had changed.

And yet... it had changed immensely.

He could still picture the first time he'd stood here—barely twenty, still believing that victory meant survival. That if he was clever enough, fast enough, ruthless enough, he could claw his way into freedom. Instead, Aphelion had stripped him bare, layer by layer, until all that remained was the truth: freedom here was an illusion, bought with obedience and blood. He would never again be able to look upon what the Imperium had built in the same way. The truth had torn him free of everything his father, the Imperium and their world had taught him. People like him weren't meant to exist in a place like this.

They navigated the covered walkways with practiced ease, their footsteps muffled against the smooth, timeworn stone. The corridors led them deeper into the heart of the university, where the buildings stood older, their walls thick with history. At last, they reached their destination—a discreet wooden door set into the stone, nearly indistinguishable from the surrounding architecture.

Firas placed a hand against the cool surface, exchanging a brief glance with Kamaria. This was where they had told Raven and Rami to meet them. But whether they had made it there remained to be seen. He took a slow breath, steadying the flicker of unease in his chest. Once, this place had tested him. Now, he was the one returning to test it.

Pushing the door open, they found themselves in a storage room. Firas had found it when he'd first arrived at Aphelion, ready for his own Trials. It had been a quiet place to escape to, away from his father's prying, disapproving eyes. Now, it would serve their purposes in other ways.

A familiar voice cut through the shrouded darkness, stark with relief. "You made it."

Rami slipped from the shadows, his movements quiet but edged with urgency. The dim light caught the soft curves of his face—thinner than Firas remembered when they'd separated weeks ago, yet still framed by the same unruly strands of straw-colored hair. His gray eyes simmered with a mixture of wariness and relief, shifting between Firas and Kamaria as if assessing the weight of this meeting. His clothes were neatly pressed but worn at the seams, a shadow of the clothes he'd worn before he was ripped from this world.

"Of course they made it." Raven leaned casually against the stone wall, arms crossed over her chest, though the sharpness in her gaze betrayed her feigned nonchalance. The flickering torchlight cast shifting shadows across her angular features—dark eyes brimming with mischief and calculation, a contrast to the silver-streaked strands of her cropped hair.

She was dressed in her usual black; the fabric fitted for movement, blending her seamlessly into the dim corridors of Aphelion. A dagger rested against her hip, half-hidden beneath her cloak, though Firas knew she didn't need it to be dangerous.

Rami exhaled, shoulders easing just slightly, though the tension never fully left his stance. "You took your time," he muttered, his voice low, but not without the familiar bite of dry humor.

"Glad to see you're still breathing," Firas said, gripping Rami's shoulder before pulling him into a firm, back-clapping embrace.

Raven smirked, pushing off the wall with effortless grace. "You really thought I'd let anything happen to him?"

"Knowing you? I wouldn't have been surprised if I found

you both hanging from the city's walls," Firas teased. Raven scoffed.

She'd chosen the name herself, shedding the one she was born with the night they found her, darting through the rain-slicked streets, breath ragged, boots splashing through the filth of the back alleys as Imperium soldiers closed in. When Firas and Kamaria pulled her from the chaos, she'd refused to speak her real name, as if it were a chain she had broken, a weight she would never wear again. And that was that.

"Have you found out anything else since we split?" Firas asked. He'd been hoping for more detailed reports from Samira and her general, Rafiq.

Rami pinched the bridge of his nose, a habit he fell into whenever his thoughts ran too deep. "Samira wasn't able to give us much. I know we're searching for older records—the kind they don't just leave lying around. They'd be in the Archives. You know, the restricted sections—the ones only Imperium councilors are allowed to access."

"Which I don't really understand why they'd be *here* and not at Qasr al-Nujūm," Raven cut in, nose wrinkling. Her voice was low, barely above a whisper. "Not that I'm super eager to break into the Palace of Stars, but still."

"This supposed knowledge… the Imperium wouldn't want to keep it in a place so obvious," Rami replied. His gaze darted toward the narrow window slits along the wall. Dusty shafts of late afternoon light spilled across the floor, slicing through the gloom. "Locking them away here—where only specific people have access—makes more sense."

Firas leaned back against the wall, the cool stone pressing through his shirt, grounding him. Beyond the door came the faintest echo of footsteps—guards, maybe, or students returning to their dorms. It made them all pause for a moment. No one would look for them here. Not in a dusty supply closet. Still, they needed to be careful.

He let out a sharp breath, folding his arms. "And that's all the information you have?" he asked, keeping his tone quiet but edged with frustration. "Samira or Rafiq didn't give any more information about what, specifically, we're looking for or where?"

"That's the only information I could get," Rami said defensively, his fingers worrying the hem of his sleeve.

"At least it's a start," Kam said, glancing toward the door, as though she could will the footsteps to fade. "Now we have a better idea of what we're after."

"But that's not the only reason we're here," Raven cut in, her gaze sharpening with intent.

Firas met her gaze, his expression unreadable, but the weight behind his words was undeniable. "We have two missions, sadekty—uncover whatever truths the Imperium is so desperate to keep buried... and make sure no one else is left behind."

Rami exhaled, glancing between them before nodding once, a smirk ghosting across his face. "For the lost, for the hunted... for those who refuse to fall."

A beat of silence, then—stronger, unshaken—they echoed him in unison.

"For those who refuse to fall."

"Have you seen any sign of...?" Rami trailed off, looking unsure.

Firas shook his head. "No, he isn't here as far as I can tell. But with all our little... distractions in place, he might be a little busy."

Rami's brow furrowed, gaze flicking between them as if weighing the logic. Whatever conclusion he reached didn't sit well. He'd known Firas's father since they were children, had seen his ruthlessness, his anger. It was Rami who had tended to the wounds his father had inflicted—both physical and emotional.

"Were you able to find out any information about the competitors?" Kam asked, turning to Raven.

"Not much... I was hoping to try to find out more before we met, but it got a little crowded." Raven shrugged. "But from what I've heard around the city, it's mostly Crossborn kids signing up. Not as many Signborns wanting to risk it this year." There was a hint of disdain within her words, her eyes darkening slightly.

The Imperium claimed the Trials weren't influenced by privilege, that it was a testing ground equal and open to all. But that wasn't necessarily the case. The Signborns, those who come from long lines of powerful families, risked their lives to not just prove themselves, but to garner connections that would further improve their family's standing. They didn't *need* whatever benefits came from being accepted into Aphelion. Crossborns, on the other hand... just passing the Trials would open doors for them they never would have been able to unlock in the first place.

"What if you two don't get someone who makes it through the first trial?" Rami asked nervously.

Kam and Firas exchanged a glance. "We'll try everything in our power to not let that happen."

"But if it does?"

Firas tried to suppress the flare of irritation that ignited in his chest. "That's the best we can do."

"And if that's not enough?" Raven asked quietly.

For a moment, no one spoke. The weight of their mission hung heavily on their shoulders, settling like dust in the stale air. Firas could feel the ghosts of the past pressing in from the walls—the screams from the Trials, the faces of those who hadn't made it out. Every step they took now was built on the bones of the ones they'd lost. Failure wasn't an option. Not again.

A quiet breath escaped him, steadying the storm clawing at his ribs. "It'll have to be enough," he said, the words soft but weighted like an oath.

TAIIAH

Talah's first taste of true freedom came on the very day she would surrender it.

She shouldered her pack, careful to avoid jostling Mazin beside her. Her best friend shifted from one foot to the other, blue eyes never leaving the row of Imperium soldiers that lined the docks ahead of them. His dark hair was tousled from the wild ocean winds, his skin the color of sun-warmed sand from the amount of time spent on the top deck these past few weeks as they traveled to the capital city.

Astrome was nothing like she'd ever imagined. The docks, sprawling and teeming with life, were a cacophony of voices and movement. The salt-laced air mingled with the scent of spice-laden cargo and the heavy musk of wet wood. Towering baghlahs and sleek dhows bobbed gently against the stone piers, their vibrant sails adorned with the emblems of the four Provinces. Merchants shouted their wares in a mix of dialects, voices rising above the gulls that circled hungrily overhead. The water itself, an inky blue, rippled with the reflections of sunlight, casting golden streaks that danced across the hulls of waiting ships. Crates of rare silks, polished gems, and jars of exotic oils were hauled ashore by brawny sailors, their backs glistening under the midday sun.

Along the piers, people haggled over goods, while street performers spun mesmerizing tales of constellations and ancient warriors in the shadows of Astrome's towering city walls. Talah watched as a Libra used their telepathic abilities to influence their audience's emotions, making their stories even more compelling. She felt its influence, even this far down the pier, the power drifting in the wind like the scent of newly baked bread. Two Aries sailors hefted crates over their shoulders as easily as one would sling a rucksack across their back. Closer to the water, Water Signs guided ships in one-by-one, forcing the sea to their will.

It was so different from Jawahra, yet so similar. Where their island was calm and steady, a paradise separated from the rest of their world, Astrome was chaotic and thriving. Jawahra's canals were cradled by the sea, weaving between brightly painted homes, their rhythm slow and familiar. The city moved at the pace of the tides, the people warm, unhurried, woven into the fabric of the water and wind. Even the floating markets, with their bursts of color and sound, felt intimate. But Astrome… Astrome pulsed with energy.

And all that separated her from this new world was a line of Imperium soldiers checking identification papers.

Talah's fingers tightened around her satchel strap, pulse quickening with every step forward. Freedom was right there—close enough to taste. The air even felt different here, lighter somehow, as if the world beyond the checkpoint carried a promise she'd been chasing for years. And yet, something in her chest stayed coiled, waiting.

She told herself the soldiers were only doing their jobs. She knew it was for their safety. The Imperium hadn't been all that diligent in covering up the Ambigua attacks that had been on the rise over the last few years. It seemed there was a new raid or skirmish every few weeks now. Even far from the mainland, Talah had heard about the attacks. But as the line crept forward, that familiar unease pressed harder against her ribs. Safety had always come with a cost under the Imperium—and she couldn't quite shake the feeling that the closer she got to freedom, the less it would belong to her.

"This was a terrible idea," Mazin muttered. "Your parents left before us to get here on time for the Trials, which means we can still make it back to Jawahra before they do." Light shifted around him, as it usually did when he was nervous, the illusion-casting flicking in and out.

"We're already here," Talah pointed out, trying to keep the slight tremor of irritation from her voice. "And I already know what you're going to say. My parents aren't going to kill you."

His jaw ticked as he clenched his teeth, eyes never leaving the line of soldiers ahead of them. "Your parents *are* going to kill me."

"Stop being dramatic." But guilt pricked her conscience. They both knew he wasn't exaggerating. If—when—her parents found out she wasn't locked safely behind their villa's walls in the south…

She'd be even more of a prisoner than she had been before.

He glanced over his shoulder at the ship that had taken them across the sea to the capital's island. "The boat's still here. We could still go back."

"With what money? We spent everything we saved already."

"We could—"

"And risk the wrath of my parents for no reason? You sure about that?" she asked, voice dropping dangerously low. Despite the fact that he had a good few inches on her, it never felt that way. Mazin's eyes narrowed; his hesitant step back told her all she needed to know.

He'd always been this way. The caution to her impulse, the logic to her daydreams. Not that she listened to him, much to his never-ending exasperation. Ever since they were children, Mazin had rarely stood up to her. Which is why she was able to drag his ass halfway across the world despite the fact that her parents would definitely string him up by his neck if they found out.

When they found out.

The line moved forward an inch, with both Talah and Mazin moving with it. Mazin moved stiffly beside her, eyes flicking over the crowd. He hadn't relaxed since they had left Jawahra.

"Is there anything I can say to change your mind?" he asked quietly.

"Nothing you've said so far has," she replied, fingers curling at her side. "And nothing else will."

For Talah, this was the only way she could earn the freedom she so desperately craved. Ever since she was a child, she had been locked away, like some fairy-tale princess. Only her prince never came...and never would. The Trials were deadly, yes, but it was the only way she could finally be released from her parent's shackles. To prove that she wasn't someone weak that needed protecting. It might have been a vain, shallow reason to risk her life. But it was a risk she was willing to take.

The Trials did not care whose blood it spilled, only that it flowed.

"We don't have to do this," Mazin whispered, voice dropping as they neared the line of soldiers. They were just feet away now. "We can talk to your parents. You just turned twenty—maybe they'll see things differently now."

"They won't," Talah replied firmly. "And you know that. Coming of age changes nothing for them."

His fingers raked through his hair. "There's got to be another way. This is... madness. People don't always survive the Trials, Tal."

"I know that." She tried to ignore the rising irritation.

Mazin didn't even seem to notice. "You weren't trained for this. And I heard that fewer Signborns are entering this year, anyway. They don't need to."

"*They* don't need to," Talah bit out, whipping around. She stood her ground, despite the fact that he towered over her. "But I do." She could see that Mazin didn't fully understand. She knew him too well.

In their world, power was everything. It was why Signborn noble families carefully planned their children's births to continue their Sign's lines. It was why they started training their children as soon as they hit puberty, when their abilities started to manifest. And her line? They'd been Pisces since their beginnings. Her father, mother, grandparents—all of them building that power generation by generation.

Still, even then, her parents had locked her away for nearly twenty years.

Talah never knew why. Whenever she'd asked, they'd given her some bullshit answer. It was for her protection. The world they lived in was ruthless, and she was the only child in a family of powerful people. But it always felt... off to her. She'd spent the majority of her teen years defying them, trying to prove that she was fully capable of fending for herself.

But none of that had mattered.

"Nothing I did ever showed them that I could be strong, Maz," Talah explained. "But this? The Trials? It'll force them to see me for who I really am."

"You don't have to prove that to them," he replied.

"I do when they've controlled every aspect of my life so far."

He fell silent. Being the youngest of five, he never had to face the same obstacles as she had. Mazin was a spare, just another safety net in case the others failed the family name. He didn't face the same pressure.

"You don't have to do this with me," she said softly. "If anyone is putting their life on the line for nothing, it's you."

Mazin shrugged one shoulder as they moved forward again. "I'm here for you. And that's enough of a reason for me."

She hoped that was true. Because selfishly she couldn't imagine facing this alone. The Trials were deadly, but together, they might stand a chance.

A soldier held out his hand abruptly as they finally stepped up. "Papers."

Mazin handed over both of theirs, shifting from one foot

to the other as they waited. The soldier glanced over the names, pausing on Talah's. With one brow rising, he slowly handed them back.

"Good luck, Ya anisa bint Khalid."

Talah's lips thinned. She had figured her name would be well-known. With a man like her father, it was almost impossible not to be.

Leaving the docks, Talah tried not to think about what that could mean for her in the Trials. Sure, her name would help, undoubtedly. But that was exactly what she wanted to avoid. She wanted to prove her worth based on her merit alone—not because her father was important. She'd never be able to step out from his shadow otherwise.

She wouldn't be able to prove her worth.

Her whole life had been built like a fortress—designed to protect her, yes, but also to contain her. Guards at the gates. Tutors instead of classmates. Rules for how she walked, spoke, smiled. Her mother's polished silences. Her father's quiet, unyielding expectations. Every part of her existence had been curated to preserve the image of what she should be: the perfect daughter, the perfect bloodline, the perfect Pisces. But that wasn't what she wanted anymore.

Because if she failed on her own terms, at least it would be hers. If she succeeded because of them, she would never know if she was enough.

"One last chance to change your mind?" Mazin offered hopefully.

Talah scanned their surroundings, taking it all in. Here, she could almost feel that hope like a tangible thing. She could feel it in the way the sea breeze carried laughter across the waves, in the swirl of color from merchant sails overhead, in the barefoot children darting between fish crates as if the world were still theirs to shape. Astrome's docks buzzed with the kind of chaos that didn't feel threatening. It felt alive.

Vendors shouted over each other in a dozen dialects. Spices wafted from food stalls, thick with cumin and citrus. Sailors sang as they unloaded crates, some off-key, others perfectly harmonized. Everything moved—ropes, gulls, hands, tides—and yet it all felt in balance.

This was the kind of place where people *became* something. Not through birthright or bloodlines, but grit and movement and choice.

Talah closed her eyes for a heartbeat, breathing in the scent of brine and sweet tea and sun-warmed stone. *Yes*, she thought. Maybe there was still a world where she wasn't just Khalid al-Rashid's daughter. Maybe there was still a version of her that could stand on its own.

She turned to Mazin, a small, defiant smile curving her lips.

"I'm not going anywhere."

TALAH
III

The carriage rolled to a stop before the towering ziggurat, its shadow stretching long across the stone courtyard. The weight of Aphelion loomed above them, its walls swallowing the light, the entrance yawning open like the mouth of a beast waiting to be fed.

Talah stepped down onto the worn cobblestones, her breath catching at the sight before her. Competitors crowded the courtyard. Their flowing abayas, embroidered kaftans, and belted thobes, dyed in the colors of their Signs, rippled in the breeze—a spectrum of deep reds and golds for Aries, earthy greens and browns for Taurus, the flowing silvers of Cancers, and the stark blacks of Capricorns. They stood in clusters, shifting like constellations in motion, their faces a mix of hardened resolve and reluctant fear.

Some were stone-faced, the way Scorpios often were, their gazes roaming over the crowd, already calculating their odds. Others, Geminis and Sagittarians, filled the air with last-minute jokes, their voices forced but defiant. Virgos adjusted their cuffs with meticulous precision, Aquarians observed with unreadable expressions, and Leos stood tall, their presence demanding attention even in a moment like this.

But not everyone hid behind bravado. Across the courtyard, tearful goodbyes unfolded like silent tragedies.

A young Taurus, broad-shouldered but trembling, pressed his forehead to his mother's, whispering words neither could bring themselves to say aloud. The scene played out over and over, in gestures both grand and quiet—hushed prayers, whispered promises, fingers gripping just a little too tightly, as if holding on long enough could change what was coming. Talah swallowed against the sudden tightness in her throat. They weren't just saying goodbye. They were preparing for the possibility of never coming back.

The weight of it pressed against her chest like an iron chain. She had spent her whole life imagining this moment—how it would feel to be chosen, to finally belong to something greater than herself. To prove she was more than the quiet girl locked away behind the villa's walls. But as she watched tears streak faces that might never see one another again, that dream began to hollow out. Belonging didn't look like glory. It looked like a sacrifice.

Is this what it takes to matter? To be seen? The thought repeated itself over and over in her head. And for the first time, she wondered if stepping into her birthright meant losing everything that made her *Talah*.

Their parents were allowing their children to risk their lives because they knew it would lead to a better one. Or hoped, anyway. The Signborns expected it—to prove their lineage. To gain even more power. The Crossborns dreamed of that life... and the Trials allowed them to think it was obtainable if they could just prove themselves worthy enough.

But her parents... they'd drag her back to her prison if they knew she was here. There was no support, no comfort in knowing she was doing what her family needed or expected her to do.

A nudge at her side pulled her from the thought.

Mazin. Ever her anchor. His eyes, full of quiet worry, searched hers. He didn't speak—he didn't have to. The tension in his shoulders, the way his fingers twitched at his sides, said enough.

She inhaled sharply, pushing the weight of doubt deep down. She had come here for a reason. She had defied everything—her parents, her safety, the life they had built for her—because she refused to be caged. She was meant to be here, meant to prove herself. There was no turning back now.

"Are you ready?" Mazin had stopped asking if she was sure back in the city when it had become clear she was never turning back.

"As ready as I'll ever be," she said, willing her voice to sound steadier than she felt.

They moved through the throng of competitors, their presence drawing more than just passing glances. Talah could feel their eyes trailing her and Mazin, assessing, calculating. Not just curiosity—hunger. A flicker of challenge in a Leo's smirk, the sharp edge of a Scorpio's stare, the quiet, knowing glance exchanged between two Aries, as if already deciding how best to eliminate them when the time came.

It's what they'd been trained for.

She recognized a few of them, all from noble families. Talah noticed Rayen, an Aries from one of the most feared bloodlines—his muscular frame stood stiff with a militant posture, a silent warning to anyone foolish enough to underestimate him. Their names and faces blurred together. Talah had only known most of them through the hushed gossip of her parents' servants, or brief glimpses during council banquets when she was made to sit still and silent beside her mother. They were shadows in silk and gold, part of a world that had watched her grow up behind glass.

Talah and Mazin fell in step behind the line of competitors who had already pried themselves away from their escorts, moving steadily toward what appeared to be an administrative office. There behind the desk sat a woman whose very presence felt like another fixture of this place—unyielding, indifferent, built into the stone of Aphelion itself.

She didn't ask for their names.

Her gaze flickered up only briefly, her dark eyes assessing, weighing, dismissing. Then, without ceremony, she pushed forward the parchment. The Blood Oath. The binding contract that ensured their loyalty to the Imperium's laws, to the Trials, and to whatever awaited them beyond this room.

In the beginning, the Blood Oath had been reserved for the most sacred of promises—used only in moments of grave consequence: to seal peace between warring bloodlines, to swear allegiance before the stars, or to bind soul to soul in ancient rites of marriage and sacrifice. It was not meant for institutions. It was meant to tell the truth.

But power corrupts even tradition.

Over time, the Imperium twisted it into something institutional—rebranded it as a tool of control rather than conviction. Now, it was used to bind those who entered Aphelion's gates, Signborn and Crossborns alike, to a rigid loyalty: to the Trials and to the Imperium.

Talah stepped forward, her pulse steady despite the gravity of what lay before her. Her name. Her signature. Her essence pressed into the worn paper beneath her fingertips.

Her freedom inked in blood.

The irony didn't escape her. She'd spent her life wrapped in silk and silence, guarded by marble walls and her father's name—safe, yes, but suffocatingly so. Every decision had been made for her. Every risk filtered, every path paved in advance. A gilded life, a caged one. But now? Now she was choosing danger. Bleeding for it. And somehow, it felt more honest than anything that had come before.

This cut—this Oath—it's mine. Not my parents'. Not the Council's. No one can walk me through the fire this time. No one can pull me back if I fall.

Because if pain was the price of freedom, she would pay it a thousand times over.

The woman wordlessly reached for the dagger resting on the desk. The blade was slim, its hilt simple, practical rather than ornamental. This was not a weapon meant for war, nor for defense—it was for ritual. For binding.

She held it out, expression free of any emotion.

The pain will be temporary… the price for freedom will last forever.

Talah took it without hesitation.

The metal was cool against her skin, a stark contrast to the warmth of her blood as she pressed the tip to her thumb. A sharp sting. A single drop. The bead of red welled and trembled before she pressed it to the parchment, her blood sealing her name among countless others who had come before her.

No turning back now.

Mazin stepped forward next. Talah didn't miss the way his jaw tightened, the flicker of hesitation in his eyes before he took the dagger and did the same. His gaze flicked to hers, as if seeking reassurance.

She didn't offer it.

She couldn't.

Not when her chest tightened every time she looked at him. Not when she knew—deep down—that he wouldn't be here if it weren't for her. He didn't belong in this room full of knives and politics and blood-bound promises. He belonged in the sea-salted quiet of their late-night talks, in the warmth of his illusions, in the gentle safety they'd built together when the world felt like too much. And now she'd dragged him into its center. Into her fire.

What if he died for her mistake?

What if she lost him just to prove something—to herself, to her father, to a world that didn't even know her?

The guilt coiled in her stomach like smoke, thick and choking. But she swallowed it down, forced her eyes forward, and pretended she didn't see the hope in his. Pretended she wasn't breaking apart, just trying to hold herself together.

The woman behind the desk was already moving, pulling out

another scroll, her movements mechanical, methodical, as she turned to a stack of assignments.

"Dormitory C." Her voice was crisp, clipped, as unfeeling as the ink that scrawled their names into record. She handed over the paper without another glance, already moving on to the next competitor.

And just like that, Talah belonged to Aphelion.

For now.

The dormitories of Aphelion were carved deep into the inner rings of the building beyond the main hall, hidden away behind thick stone corridors that muted the noise of the world beyond. Each door was a heavy slab of carved limestone, inset with latticed windows, allowing only fragmented slants of golden light to pierce through, painting intricate patterns across the cool tiled floors.

Inside, the room was simple but refined—a pair of narrow beds draped in deep indigo linens, a small wooden writing desk positioned between them, and a howz-style basin in the corner where fresh water trickled softly into a stone reservoir. The air was cool, perfumed faintly with the remnants of old incense and the sharper scent of fresh parchment stacked neatly on the desk.

Talah lingered in the doorway, taking it all in. *So this is where I'm supposed to belong.* The thought carried both awe and disbelief. The quiet hum of the place pressed against her skin, unfamiliar and strange. *It doesn't feel real.*

She set her pack down on the nearest bed, fingers brushing over the smooth fabric. *I should feel grateful. Lucky.* But all she felt was the weight of the silence, heavy and watchful. *What if I don't deserve this?*

The door swung open before she could chase the thought away—a breath of energy sweeping into the room like a desert wind before a storm.

A girl strode in with effortless poise, a rustle of fine emerald silk trailing in her wake. She was put together in a way that wasn't natural—it was intentional, curated. Her dark curls were meticulously coiled into intricate braids, pinned with delicate gold charms that caught the light with every step. Her jewelry was subtle but carefully chosen—thin golden bands stacked on her fingers, a delicate chain resting just below her collarbone, the kind of adornments that spoke of wealth without the need to flaunt it.

Her eyes, a sharp shade of green, flicked over Talah in an instant. Cataloging. Assessing.

A slow, relieved sigh escaped the girl's lips as she placed a delicate hand over her chest.

"Oh, thank the stars," she exhaled dramatically. "I was worried they'd put me with someone completely unsalvageable."

Talah blinked, thrown off by the sheer boldness of the statement.

"Excuse me?"

"Adine," the girl offered, sweeping past her. She smiled, but it was the kind of smile that radiated charm and self-assurance in equal measure. A smile that had probably smoothed over countless arguments and secured unspoken favors.

"No offense, of course," she said breezily, stepping further into the room and giving it the same scrutinizing once-over she had just given Talah. "But if I'm going to make an impression at the Convocation, I can't have my roommate looking like she just washed up from the docks."

Talah arched a brow, crossing her arms. "I did just wash up from the docks."

Adine paused—just for a beat—then let out a soft, knowing laugh, a conspiratorial smile curling at the edge of her lips.

"Then lucky for you, I can fix that."

Without waiting for a response, she set her hulking trunk onto her bed and flipped it open with practiced ease. The scent of expensive perfume and the faintest trace of rosewater drifted into the air as rich fabrics shifted inside—silks in deep emerald and sapphire hues, delicate embroidery catching the light, the unmistakable glint of polished brass buttons sewn onto tailored tunics.

But it wasn't just luxury tucked neatly away in her belongings.

Beneath the layers of finery, Talah caught the edge of something more pragmatic—sturdy leather, reinforced seams, the unmistakable weight of practical combat gear folded with the same care as the silks. And next to them, resting at the bottom of the trunk, a sheathed dagger, its hilt wrapped in dark, worn leather. She moved through her belongings with ease, sorting through fabrics and cosmetics with the air of someone who was used to being listened to, used to commanding attention without asking for it.

"There are two kinds of people who survive the Trials," she mused, flipping through a set of gold bangles, inspecting each one before selecting the perfect fit. "The ones with power and the ones who align themselves with power."

Talah toyed with the end of her braid, considering the words. "And which one are you?"

Adine smiled—not coy, not arrogant, but assured. "The kind that doesn't die."

She moved to the ornate mirror on the wall, adjusting the pin in her hair with practiced precision. "The mentors will be everything in these Trials. You get a good one? You live. You get a bad one?" She shrugged as if the answer was obvious. "You become a cautionary tale."

Talah frowned, her pulse steady even as her mind raced. *Mentors. Survival. Cautionary tales.* Words that made the Trials sound like a game—but Adine didn't speak like someone who'd ever lost. "Like who?" she asked, voice quiet but even.

"The Kaed's son."

Adine's words fell like stone between them.

Talah didn't have to ask who that was. Even sequestered away in her own little safe haven, she knew exactly who Adine was talking about. The Kaed, the general of the Imperium military. Ruthless, brilliant, and as cold as the steel he was known for wielding. *And his son—the one who was supposed to be untouchable.* The memory surfaced unbidden: the stories of a prodigy who'd died during the Trials, erased from record like he'd never existed.

If someone like that could fall, what chance do the rest of us have?

Adine watched her reaction in the mirror. "Something tells me you don't want to end up like him."

She's testing me.

Talah held her gaze. *I don't even know who I'm supposed to be yet.* But she didn't let that show. "I won't."

A flicker of something—*approval? Respect?*—passed through Adine's sharp green eyes before she gave a small, approving nod. "Good."

She turned back to her trunk, pulling out a delicate glass vial and dabbing a touch of perfume onto her wrists as if the conversation had already been settled. "Now, let's get ready. The Convocation won't wait for us."

Talah frowned. "It's just an introduction."

Adine snorted, tossing her a knowing look over her shoulder. "It's *the* introduction." She waved a hand in Talah's direction. "First impressions matter. If you look like you don't belong here, you won't last long enough to prove otherwise."

Talah narrowed her eyes. "I didn't realize appearances decided who lived and who died in the Trials."

Adine turned, leveling her with a smirk that held just a trace of steel beneath its polish. "They don't. But they do help you get noticed. And getting noticed could mean everything." Her head tilted slightly. "The Signborns like to bet on the Trials. For us, that money doesn't mean much. But it's not just money they like to toss around, but connections and influence."

It took Talah a few seconds to understand. "So they bet… on us?"

Adine gave a curt nod, turning back to her things. "For

Crossborns, that money could pay their whole way through Aphelion. It could mean money to send back home, I guess. Or whatever they need it for. But for us? It could mean getting a fast track to being the next councilor or Kaed. There's a reason why the elite still send their children to risk their lives." Adine shot a quick, loaded glance over her shoulder.

The weight of it sank in slowly, like cold water creeping under skin.

Talah had always known the Trials were cruel. Brutal. A performance dressed in tradition and sanctity. But this—this made it feel personal. This meant they weren't just being tested. They were being gambled on. Lives laid bare like pieces on a board, their pain turned into entertainment… all in the name of obtaining that better life. That power.

Adine reached into her trunk and pulled out a folded sapphire-blue kaftan, the rich fabric edged in silver thread that shimmered under the dim lantern light. With a casual flick of her wrist, she tossed it onto Talah's bed. "Wear that. You don't have to be the strongest person in the room yet, but you should at least look like you could be."

Talah eyed the kaftan warily, the weight of Adine's words settling in her chest. She wasn't wrong.

The Trials hadn't even begun, and already, they were fighting for something—perception, control, influence. If she wanted to stand a chance, she couldn't afford to look like someone who would be forgotten.

Outside, the deep toll of Aphelion's bells rang through the air, signaling the gathering of competitors.

Talah exhaled, grabbing the kaftan.

The Convocation awaited.

FIRAS IV

Stepping into the Great Hall was like stepping into a nest of vipers.

The ziggurat was a marvel of ancient craftsmanship, a testament to the power and prestige of the Imperium. The vast chamber stretched high, its ceiling an intricate masterpiece of celestial constellations carved into obsidian stone, glowing softly with embedded silver and lapis inlays that mirrored the skies above. Twelve towering pillars, each etched with the sigil of a Zodiac Sign, lined the hall, their bases wrapped in bands of shimmering gold. The walls were adorned with tapestries depicting the storied history of the Zodiac people, their colors rich and deep, illuminated by the flickering light of hundreds of candelabras.

Firas tried to shake the dark feelings creeping along the edges of his memory. He needed to focus on the task at hand. They knew the Convocation would just be one of many complications to their plan. It wasn't just the competitors and their mentors that attended. The elite, the professors, all were vying for the first chance to see the new potential students.

Including the Imperium.

At the far end of the chamber, a raised dais dominated the space, its marble steps leading to a semicircle of twelve ornate chairs, where the Zodiac councilors sat as equals. There was no single throne, no ruler elevated above the rest—only the twelve, their positions dictated by bloodline, legacy, and the weight of their collective decisions. The dais was flanked by gilded braziers, their flames casting flickering shadows across the polished floors, a reminder that the Imperium's authority burned eternal.

Firas wasn't sure who would remember him or how many. His best guess would be very few, but he couldn't afford to be wrong. The risk was always there. He either slipped beneath their notice or he'd be captured tonight in this very hall.

A bead of sweat slid down the side of his neck despite the cool air. His hood shadowed most of his face, but the faint scar running along his jaw caught the light when he turned his head. It was one of many reminders Aphelion had left him. His hair, once neatly trimmed, now curled loosely against his temples, longer than it should've been for someone trying to disappear.

He kept his head down as footsteps echoed somewhere deeper in the corridor. *Breathe. Blend in. Look like you belong anywhere and no one will stop you.* The thought had kept him alive before; it would have to do again now.

It had taken him months to convince Samira to allow him to go on this mission. He could still hear her voice in his head, questioning his control. *You're too close to it, Firas. Too tied to what happened there.*

Maybe she was right. But if there had even been an inkling of doubt that it would fail right away, he doubted the Ambigua leader would give her final approval. Still, he had to be careful. If he were found out, Kam and the others would be in danger as well.

And that's not a mistake I get to make twice.

His gaze swept across the chamber, cataloging everyone of significance. The room was a sea of silks, jewels, and finely embroidered tunics, each attendee's attire proudly displaying their Sign's colors. Many of the councilors were among the crowd rather than retreating to their assigned seating on the dais. Asad's voice echoed across the room as he animatedly conversed with fellow Aries Signborn, his crimson robes swaying with his emphatic gestures. Near him stood Amina, draped in an elegant silver and pale blue kaftan, her expression poised as she murmured to a group of Water Signs. Firas had always known the Cancer to be kind to him.

Until she wasn't.

Clusters of Signborn families gathered in their respective groups, their bloodlines traced back to the earliest Zodiacs. They watched the competitors around them, already mentally placing their bets. Some of the competitors were young heirs of prestigious lineages, their training evident in their controlled postures and barely concealed confidence. Others were less privileged, yet no less determined—wildcards hoping to carve their own legacy. Their eyes flicked across the room, sizing up potential rivals, gauging strengths and weaknesses even before the first test had begun.

A strange ache tugged at Firas's chest. *I used to stand where they're standing.* He could almost feel his father's hand, heavy on his shoulder, the weight of expectation pressing harder than any chain. He'd worn pride like armor then, mistaking it for purpose. *I thought I mattered. I thought winning meant something.*

The pity curdled into something darker, heavier. Disgust—not just for them, but for himself. For ever believing any of it. He turned away, jaw tightening, stomach twisting as the sound of laughter and murmured prayers filled the space behind him.

He knew the truth now. And it was far uglier than the lies he'd once built his life on. *How many did I step over to survive? How many believed the same lies I did?*

When he'd been a part of this world, he'd believed the lies, the propaganda. Everything his father and the Imperium fed him, he took without questioning. He'd been blind to the privilege, to just how predatory the Trials were. They gave the people hope when, in reality, they were a show. And if they happened to prove themselves powerful enough, then they were nothing but pawns.

The air crackled with tension, an electric charge of ambition, expectation, and the unspoken promise of what lay ahead. It was a room full of power—some inherited, some earned, and some still waiting to be claimed. Firas turned away in disgust to regain his composure, stomach churning.

He knew the truth.

There was only one positive to this whole thing—the one person Firas had braced himself to face was nowhere in sight. His pulse quickened from the gnawing unease that came with uncertainty. If his father was here, lurking just beyond his line of sight, it meant everything they had set into motion would fail before it even began. But Samira had assured him that she would keep his father busy. He just had to have faith in her, at least.

He exhaled slowly, forcing his shoulders to remain loose, his stance casual. Blend in. Be nothing more than another face in the crowd.

"Have we met before?" A voice slid through the murmuring chamber like silk drawn over a blade.

Firas stilled. Too smooth. Too intentional.

He turned, already schooling his expression into one of polite curiosity. And there, standing just a step too close, was Musa al-Asmar.

The Scorpio Councilor was everything Firas remembered—elegance draped in shadows, his dark robes accentuated with blood-red embroidery, a silver scorpion brooch pinned at his collar. His presence was suffocating, a subtle kind of pressure that made the air feel too thick, as if his very existence was meant to test the boundaries of one's mind.

Firas met his gaze evenly, careful, guarded. "I don't believe we've had the pleasure."

Musa tilted his head slightly, his blue-green eyes flickering over Firas's face, taking in every detail. Searching. "No?" He made a soft, thoughtful sound, tapping a finger against the rim of his goblet. "Perhaps I'm mistaken. It's just... something about you seems familiar."

Firas kept his posture relaxed, though every instinct screamed otherwise. His lips quirked in an easy smirk, as if amused by the idea. "I'm sure it's just a coincidence, Councilor. I'm not exactly memorable."

Musa's lips twitched at that—a predator's smile.

"Mm," he mused, swirling the wine in his cup. "No, I don't think that's true at all."

There was a pause; the moment stretched too thin.

A high-pitched clanging rang through the hall, courtesy of the small brass plate hanging from the ringer's fingers. As the sound of the naqus faded, the room fell silent. Musa gave him one last measured look before slipping away toward the dais like the snake he was. Firas watched him go, trying to calm his racing heart.

Musa might be a problem.

The Libra Councilor rose to her feet, pulling him back to the present. Firas remembered Saahira Khatri all too well and, in the two years he's been gone, it seemed as if she hadn't changed. The room fell silent as if her presence alone had stilled the very air. She was draped in soft silks of pale pink and silver, her deceptively delicate appearance belying the sharpness in her gaze. The head of the Libra bloodline, a master of telepathy and diplomacy, Saahira was never one for warmth—and tonight, her voice was as cold and unyielding as stone.

"The Trials," she began, her words crisp and unwavering, "are not a game."

Her eyes swept across the chamber, pinning each competitor under the weight of her gaze. "Many of you stand here tonight, believing yourselves strong, prepared. You have trained, studied, mastered your abilities. But let me tell you this—none of you truly understand what awaits you."

Firas's jaw flexed. *We didn't either.*

A murmur of unease passed through the room, but no one dared to interrupt. Firas had heard this speech before. Not word for word, but close enough—the same measured cruelty beneath the formality, the same promise of glory twisted into a warning.

Saahira continued, her tone like a blade cutting through false bravado. "Each year, we watch as the finest of your generation step into the maze. Each year, we see arrogance turned to terror. Power reduced to nothing. Some of you will be carried out broken, some never at all. The Trials do not discriminate. It does not matter if you come from a long line of Signborns, if your name is whispered in the halls of Aphelion, or if your family has spent fortunes to prepare you." Her lips curled, amusement flickering behind her sharp eyes. "The Trials do not care who you are."

No—they don't. They never did.

A tense silence settled over the crowd, competitors glancing at one another, some standing straighter while others swallowed hard. A memory, sharp and uninvited, flashed through his mind: *the sting of smoke, the fear constricting his lungs, the sound of someone screaming his name as the gates closed.* He blinked it away, but the chamber seemed to shift around him, its polished stone walls closing in, the scent of incense souring into something darker.

Firas exhaled slowly, letting the words wash over him like old ghosts. *And still, they'll walk into it. Just like we did.*

"The competitors will have four weeks to prove themselves worthy of Aphelion and everything it can bring them. Status, money, power—four weeks to show not just the university, but the world, just what you can do and how you can contribute to our great society." Saahira paused, eyes scanning the room. "That is why the Trials exist."

Lies. His fists curled at his sides, nails digging into his palms. *All lies.*

"We'll start with matching our competitors with their mentors," Saahira announced. "Your mentors will not just train you to survive, but they will help you thrive. It will be their job to help you show your true power in the Trials… and hopefully succeed." She glanced at the mentors huddled in the corner.

Kam sidled up beside Firas, arms crossing. "Finally," she

muttered. "I didn't think I could get through much more of that bullshit."

He cut her a warning glance.

Firas barely listened as names were called, the polite applause of those in attendance doing nothing to break his concentration. He let his gaze drift over the competitors as they lined up, watching the way some stood too tall, their shoulders squared with arrogance, while others shifted anxiously, their fingers twitching at their sides. He made note of every flicker of doubt, every forced display of confidence. Most of them were predictable—the heirs of old bloodlines standing stiff-backed and sure of their superiority, the ambitious Crossborns shifting on their feet, feigning confidence.

Firas was used to this. It was second nature at this point, ingrained in him from childhood. He had trained himself to read people like an open book—to recognize fear in the set of a jaw, to measure strength in the way a person carried themselves. Still, as the mentor assignments were announced, something in him coiled tight, instinct flaring like a blade catching light.

Then he caught sight of *her*.

The torchlight caught on the dark waves of her hair, deep auburn streaks barely visible in the flickering glow. Her skin was burnished gold, sun-warmed, a stark contrast to the cool silver of her eyes—too sharp, too knowing. She wore the elegance of her lineage effortlessly, but there was something underneath it, something raw. It was in the tension of her shoulders, the way her fingers flexed slightly at her sides as though bracing for something unseen.

As if she had felt the weight of his scrutiny, she looked up. Their eyes met.

Firas felt it in his chest—something sharp, a brief flicker of recognition that shouldn't exist. He had never met her before, and yet, in that moment, he knew her. Not in name, not in title, but in something deeper. Something instinctive.

Her gaze didn't waver, didn't dart away in deference or intimidation the way most did when they realized they had drawn his attention. Instead, she held it steady and unflinching, studying him as much as he was studying her.

Firas blinked, suddenly aware that the names had continued being called, the procession had continued moving—and he had missed all of it.

"Iras Eldin." Firas fully snapped back to the present just as the next words left the announcer's lips. "And his competitor, Talah Khalid, daughter of the Pisces Councilor."

The words landed like a blow to the ribs—sudden, breath-stealing, and sharp.

His body remained still, but the slow coil of tension in his chest tightened, constricted.

For a moment, the chamber froze. A silence heavier than any that had come before settled over the crowd, pressing down on the gathered competitors and mentors like a dense fog. The crackling of torches, the distant clink of a goblet being set too harshly on a tray—every small sound seemed amplified against the hush that followed Talah's name.

Then, the first murmur. A whisper, barely audible, but sharp with disbelief.

"She's actually competing?"
"I thought they'd keep her hidden forever."
"She has no chance."

Firas didn't need to turn his head to feel the wave of attention shift toward her. It rippled through the room, a slow-building storm of scrutiny, curiosity, and something darker—resentment. Whispers turned into hushed conversations, darting glances became pointed stares. Some were assessing, some skeptical. Others barely concealed their disdain.

Everyone had heard of her—a Signborn daughter, hidden away like a secret. A girl who should have been raised in the heart of their world, yet had spent her life a shadow in the distant waters of Jawahra. No one knew the reason her father had kept her from society. Firas himself had never cared for the gossip—he'd had bigger things to worry about. But now?

Now he would have to worry about it all.

Firas made a note of every reaction. The tightening of aristocratic mouths, the narrowing of sharp eyes. Some of the competitors exchanged looks—some mocking, some wary. And then there were those who looked at her with something closer to intrigue. The ones who knew there was always a reason behind secrecy. The ones who wondered what made her different. A few of the mentors shifted where they stood, their thoughts clear. She did not belong here.

Had her father even prepared her for this?

Signborn children spent years training to gain access to Aphelion and all of its benefits. He would know. But Firas couldn't imagine that her father had locked her away all these years only for her to risk her life here in the Trials.

Her gray eyes flickered once toward the dais, where the councilors sat like gods watching mortals play their games. The Pisces Councilor—her father—sat perfectly composed, his expression unreadable. But Firas saw the way his fingers curled against the arm of his chair, the way his chest rose and fell in a deliberately measured breath. The way he tried to hide the look of surprise in those piercing blue eyes.

Some of the other councilors merely watched, indifferent. Others leaned toward one another, exchanging quiet words. Amina studied Talah with a measured gaze, her silver robes pooling around her like mist. Saahira was expressionless, though the weight of her stare lingered longer than the others. But it was Musa, the Scorpio Councilor, whose lips curled into something almost amused. Almost cruel.

He'd already decided she wouldn't last.

The whispers continued, threading through the hall, an undercurrent of skepticism and thinly veiled amusement. She was garnering too much attention—attention they couldn't afford.

"Firas…" Kam's warning slid right through him. She didn't have to say a word. He already knew.

They had hoped to be paired with a competitor who would pass under the radar while still staying alive. One who wouldn't garner too much attention but last as long as they needed to complete their mission here. They needed to stay under the radar as much as possible… and having a competitor such as Talah meant that very anonymity was put at risk.

Everyone would be watching her.

Measuring her.

Judging her.

Samira is definitely not going to like this. Firas clenched his jaw, fingers flexing at his sides.

For the first time in a long time, he felt a slip in his control. This wasn't supposed to happen. Yet here she was, stepping forward toward him. His to mentor. His to train. His to keep alive.

And perhaps, the greatest threat to everything he was planning.

TAVAH

T he second her name was called, she knew she'd severely underestimated her plan.

An uneasy hush settled over the gathered crowd, like a storm rolling in on a windless sea. Her father's face had twisted from confusion to pure rage faster than a storm gathering over the ocean. He hadn't noticed her blending into the crowd before. But now… now there was no hiding.

There was a sharp rustling of robes. The heavy sound of a chair scraping against marble.

"This is a mistake." Councilor Khalid's voice, usually controlled and diplomatic, now carried an edge of authority that cut through the sudden stillness in the room. He descended from the dais in measured, purposeful strides, his presence parting the gathered spectators as if the very air bent to his will.

Talah took a deep breath. She knew he'd be upset. Surprised. She had braced for it. Even then, standing there made her feel like a child all over again.

A flicker of familiar movement caught her eye, briefly pulling her away from the dais. Her mother watched her from across the room, eyes dark with not just worry, but something deeper. Fear? Guilt snagged at the edges of Talah's consciousness. They hadn't even known she'd been missing, having left for Jawahra themselves just a few days before Talah and Mazin had.

All part of her plan. They would have tried to stop her had they known what she wanted to do.

"She will not be competing." Her father's words drew her focus back to the dais. "My daughter's name should never have been submitted."

Talah's throat tightened. He was stripping her of her choice, right here, in front of everyone.

She'd known he would object, but part of her had hoped he'd wait until they were alone. He'd always told her that image was everything, that control meant knowing when to speak and when to stay silent. Especially as a councilor's daughter. For a moment, she'd let herself believe he'd follow his own advice.

She had clearly misjudged him.

A low murmur rippled through the crowd, hushed whispers traded like secrets in the dim light. The weight of their gazes pressed down on her, sharp with curiosity, doubt, and something dangerously close to amusement. They were waiting. Watching. Judging.

Her pulse thundered in her ears, drowning out everything but the frantic beat of her own heart. Heat coiled in her chest, her palms slick with sweat as her mind scrambled for a response—any response. But for a breath, for a moment too long, she could only stand there, caught in the suffocating silence between expectation and action.

"That is not how this works, Councilor."

Every head in the hall turned.

The man who was to be her mentor—Iras—stepped away from the rest of the group. His posture was deceptively relaxed, hands folded behind his back. But his gaze—his gaze was locked onto her father's like a predator sizing up its prey. The woman behind him reached out, as if to pull him back, before thinking better of it. Talah's head tilted slightly.

Something about Iras seemed familiar, though she couldn't place it. She was sure he'd never been to her parent's villa in Jawahra. She would have remembered someone like him.

Her father shifted, his expression sharpening.

Iras took another step forward. "Once a competitor takes the Blood Oath, they cannot withdraw." His words were precise, deliberate, designed to leave no room for argument. "It is written in the Trials' laws. You, of all people, should know that."

Talah swore she saw a muscle tighten in her father's jaw.

"I forbid it. Not only as her councilor, but as her father."

"This decision isn't yours to make. Unless of course our esteemed Councilor wishes to challenge the laws he swore to uphold?"

Her father's gaze turned glacial. "She is my daughter—"

"And now she is a competitor." Her mentor cut him off, his tone even, unwavering. Unmovable. "And respectfully, competitors are bound by the rules."

Talah barely breathed.

She wasn't sure what shocked her more—the fact that someone had challenged her father in public or the fact that this complete stranger was standing up to him for her.

But her father was not so easily bested. He squared his shoulders, his gaze darkening. "You are out of your depth. And I suggest you choose your battles wisely."

A slow, deliberate smile tugged at the corner of Iras's mouth. "I always do."

Before her father could respond, Saahira Khatri stepped between them, the shimmering pink of her robes catching the flickering candlelight as she surveyed the tense chamber. The weight of the moment was heavy, tangible.

"This is highly irregular," Saahira announced, her voice carrying smoothly over the stunned silence. Talah didn't miss the sharp look she sent the Pisces Councilor. "Never in the history of the Trials has a councilor's child entered the competition under objection. Competitors are not required to seek parental consent—but no parent has ever denied it." Her tone was carefully measured, but her words sliced with precision, each syllable laced with layered intent. "To question the Trials is to question the very foundation of our honor. And such defiance, if left unanswered, invites others to believe they may do the same."

Saahira turned to her. "But I want to hear from you, Talah dear. Why enter the Trials? Why do you believe you should compete?"

Talah fought the urge to shrink under the scrutiny. Instead, she straightened her spine and met Saahira's gaze. She would not cower. *Not here. Not now.*

"I've spent my life behind gates I never chose," she said, voice steady. "Told who I could speak to, where I could go, what I could become. I was sheltered in the name of safety—kept away from the world, from the truth, from myself."

A murmur passed through the room, but she didn't falter. *Let them talk. Let them see me.*

"I don't know what my parents were protecting me from. But I know this: protection without purpose is just a cage. And I'm done living in a cage, no matter how nice it is. The Trials may be brutal, but at least they're honest. They don't pretend you're free while quietly deciding your life for you."

Her chest felt tight as she spoke, each word scraping raw against the part of her that still wanted her father's approval. *He'll never forgive me for this.* And yet, she couldn't stop.

Her gaze didn't leave Saahira's. "I want to compete because I need to know what I'm capable of. Not what others say I am, but what I choose to become. You ask why I believe I should be here?" She exhaled, voice low but unwavering. "Because this is a way for me to show that I am capable. That I'm strong enough to survive in this society we've built. Because I want to fight for my place in it."

Something close to respect flashed in Saahira's eyes, the corners of her lips tilting slightly.

Did I just win her favor—or seal my fate?

"And why should we not respect a warrior who wishes to prove their power?" Saahira turned to the crowd, putting on a show. "Our society is only as strong as its weakest link. Power brings prosperity. Our abilities are tied to the world around us, harnessing the elements. Common-born or noble, we are tied by these powers."

Khalid's nostrils flared. "You ask me to stand by while my daughter is thrown into the jaws of something she is not prepared for? That she hasn't *trained* for?"

Talah's throat tightened. She wanted to turn toward him, to say something—anything—that would make him see she wasn't that frightened little girl anymore. But the words she'd just spoken had already drawn a line between them.

I can't take them back now.

Saahira lifted a hand, silencing further argument. "I ask you, Councilor Khalid, to stand by the very laws that govern our people." Her gaze shifted across the dais, taking in the reactions of the other councilors. "It is clear we have a dilemma. But there is a way to resolve this. The Imperium is nothing but fair."

Talah's breath caught, a cold weight settling low in her chest. *No.* It couldn't end like this—not after everything she'd risked to get here. The edges of the room seemed to blur, her pulse roaring in her ears as Iras's expression shifted—derision flickering across his face before he stepped back among the other mentors.

The woman beside him shook her head slightly, casting him a look of quiet disapproval, but Talah barely saw it. *Please don't take this from me.* Every word she'd spoken, every ounce of courage she'd scraped together, hung in the balance, fragile as glass.

She forced herself to stand still, though every part of her wanted to reach forward, to speak, to beg. *If they send me away now... I'll never get another chance.*

"A vote," Saahira declared, her voice smooth but unmistakably commanding. "Before the people. Before the mentors and the competitors alike. Let the Imperium decide whether Talah bint Khalid may compete."

"After all," she added lightly, "the law applies to everyone." She didn't need to look at Khalid for the jab to land.

It took Talah a moment to figure out what Saahira was doing. If they allowed Talah's father to use his power to influence the Trials, it would shatter the very image they were trying to sell to... well, everyone. The Trials were a chance for the Crossborns to obtain the unobtainable. For the Signborns to further their own power. It was a way to level out the privilege, to make it accessible to anyone who was daring enough to risk their lives for it.

After all, the Trials did not discriminate.

And Saahira, ever the tactician, wouldn't let the Pisces Councilor break that farce without making him *bleed* for it.

Her father's expression darkened, his hands clenching into fists at his sides, but he didn't dare to protest. Even he knew that to fight a vote was to fight the very foundation of their government.

Saahira gestured toward Talah. "Step forward."

Talah forced her feet to move, feeling every eye in the room follow her as she crossed the chamber floor and stood at the base of the dais. She hated this. Being paraded like a spectacle, the weight of their judgment pressing down on her like a heavy tide.

Talah studied the eleven remaining councilors. Some she'd met before, when she'd been barely old enough to remember. Others, she knew only from the painstaking lessons drilled into her within the towering walls of her parent's villa. Their names had been inked into the histories she had studied, their legacies whispered in the corridors of power. Yet, seeing them now—flesh and bone rather than words on parchment—was an entirely different matter.

She glanced at her father, but his gaze was fixed ahead, his jaw tight. He wouldn't look at her.

The Libra Councilor turned her piercing gaze to Talah, assessing, measuring. "I vote yes. The law is clear, and the Trials will determine her strength, as it has done for every competitor before her."

A ripple of murmurs spread through the hall, the weight of the decision settling over the gathered crowd like a shifting tide. Saahira lowered herself gracefully into her seat, her sharp gaze never wavering from its mark.

Talah's pulse pounded in her ears as her eyes flicked to the Cancer Councilor, Amina, who rose next.

Her expression was troubled, but her voice carried with quiet certainty. "I vote yes. A competitor is a competitor, regardless of name or bloodline."

The room exhaled, another wave of hushed whispers rolling through the assembly. One more vote in her favor. A step closer to sealing her fate. One by one, the other councilors gave their verdicts. Some hesitated, clearly uncertain about allowing someone with such little known training into the Trials. Others saw it as an opportunity—a way to uphold the law, or perhaps to see her fail spectacularly.

Talah's hands curled into fists at her sides as the votes fell against her father's wishes.

"I vote no." Her father's face was the carefully constructed mask of a politician, a man who had spent his life navigating power. But Talah knew him too well to be fooled.

Musa, the Scorpio Councilor, was the last to speak.

A hush settled over the room as all eyes turned to him, waiting. Expecting.

He did not rush, did not react to the pressure of the moment. Instead, he let the silence stretch, savoring the anticipation like a spider spinning silk. Always in control. Always in command. Slowly, he leaned forward in his chair, fingers tapping idly against the carved armrest as if this decision was nothing more than an afterthought.

His lips curled into something resembling a smirk, a hint of amusement flickering in his dark eyes. "I think we all know how this will end," he mused, voice smooth, deliberate—a man who enjoyed watching the pieces of a game fall into place.

The words sent a shiver down Talah's spine. There was no

hesitation in them, no real curiosity about whether she would fail or succeed. He had already decided.

There was something chilling in the certainty of his tone.

"But," he continued, rolling the thought over in his mind like a gambler weighing his odds, "if she is so eager to prove herself, let her try."

Saahira turned to Atticus. "The Imperium has spoken."

A muscle ticked in his jaw. His hands remained steady, his posture composed, but Talah knew him. Knew that beneath the impassive exterior he was seething. Not just because he had lost—but because she had forced him into this. Forced him to watch, powerless, as she defied everything he had ever wanted for her. Still, he did not protest. A nod. Stiff. Final. A silent acceptance of his defeat.

Talah swallowed hard. She had won.

But as she turned, with the weight of the room pressing down on her, she felt the shift in the air. The whispers swirled around her like a rising tide—curiosity, speculation, doubt. The competitors eyed her differently now, some with barely concealed delight, others with silent speculation. They weren't just looking at her anymore. They were sizing her up.

She had forced their hands. Forced them to acknowledge her.

But in doing so, she had made herself a target.

"With that, the matter is settled," Saahira announced, her voice smooth, effortless in its authority. "The competitors will meet with their mentors starting tomorrow morning at the coliseum. Your training begins then. For now—" a small, knowing smile curled at her lips as she gestured toward the still-lavish spread of food and drink, the soft music that had been swallowed by the weight of the vote, "enjoy the rest of the Convocation."

A final murmur rippled through the chamber, the tension loosening just enough for the air to shift. Conversations resumed, hesitant at first, but soon flowing freely once more, as if the gravity of the moment had been just another spectacle to be observed.

Talah barely heard any of it.

Her eyes instinctively sought out the one place they shouldn't.

Her father stood rigid, still a figure of authority even in defeat. His expression remained unreadable as he stepped away from the dais, his posture never faltering. Beside him, her mother followed, face composed but tight at the edges, her hands clenched into the folds of her deep blue robes.

Neither of them looked at her.

Not once.

Her chest constricted, something sinking and hollow forming in her ribs. She wasn't sure what she had expected—rage, disappointment, even a quiet warning. But nothing?

Somehow, that was worse.

They disappeared into the arched entryway without a single glance back.

TALAH VI

Talah was moving before she could stop herself.
She darted through the crowd, shoving past robed officials and glittering nobles, ignoring the startled gasps and disapproving stares. Her footsteps slapped against the marble as she slipped through the same gilded doors her parents had disappeared behind seconds before.

The hallway was colder here, lined with towering pillars and flanked by flickering braziers that cast dancing shadows against the stone. Her parents were already halfway down the corridor, their cloaks swishing with each brisk step, the sound of their footsteps echoing like accusations in the silence.

"Mama," she called out, her voice cracking under the weight of everything she hadn't said. "Baba. Wait!"

Her mother faltered. Selene's hand reached instinctively for Khalid's sleeve, fingers curling in the fabric like she always did when uncertain. Khalid turned toward her, his jaw clenched, lips drawn into a grim line. Talah couldn't see his expression, but whatever passed between them made him stop.

Talah caught up to them, breath shallow, heart pounding in her throat. Her chest ached, not just from the sprint but from the years of silence pressing down on her.

"I'm sorry," she said quickly, urgently, before the door to them could close again. "I wanted to tell you. I wanted to—"

"Don't you see?" Khalid cut her off, spinning to face her. His voice was low but sharp, as if every word was a blade he hated to use. "It doesn't matter what you wanted."

The lamplight caught the silver beginning to thread through his dark beard, accenting the hard lines carved by years of command and worry. His eyes—Talah's eyes—burned with a stormed bronze hue, but now they flickered with something she hadn't noticed until this moment. Not anger. Not disappointment. Terror.

"We've spent your whole life keeping you out of sight," he continued, hands curling into fists at his sides. "Not because we didn't believe in you. Not because we wanted to smother you. We did it to keep you alive."

"Alive?" Talah reared back. "That wasn't living."

"It kept you safe," Khalid corrected himself.

"Safe from *what*?" Talah stared at him, trying to comprehend. "You won't be around forever… and then what?"

Her mother stepped between them, a vision of composed grace even with worry shadowing her face. Selene's beauty was a quieter reflection of Talah's—olive-toned skin that gleamed faintly in the lamplight, eyes the pale blue of morning over water, and hair like midnight silk braided and coiled at her nape. Her gown of soft gray shimmered faintly with threads of silver, and the faint scent of jasmine lingered as she reached for her daughter's hands. "You need to be careful, Rohi. This world…" She glanced over her shoulder, as if afraid the marble columns themselves might be listening. "This world isn't what it looks like from behind the glass."

Talah's breath caught.

Selene's grip tightened. "The Trials are not a game, no matter how polished the floors or how noble the cause. Behind the emblems and speeches and banners, there are eyes everywhere. Watching. Measuring. Waiting."

"I'm not afraid of being watched," Talah said quietly.

"You should be," her mother whispered. "Because the moment you show them something they don't understand, something they can't control—they will find a way to break you. Or worse, to use you."

Talah's voice trembled. "Why would they want to use me?"

Her mother hesitated. Her gaze dropped for a heartbeat, then rose again, fiercely protective. "Because you're more than what they expect. Even now, even when you barely know yourself. Your father and I—we've *seen* the way people look at difference in this world. We've been forced to play the game ourselves. They will call it strength when it serves them, and a threat when it doesn't."

"What does that even *mean*?" She couldn't keep the frustration from her voice.

Behind them, Khalid had gone still. Silent. Watching the exchange with eyes that had already seen too much. She turned to him, desperate.

"You're a councilor. You uphold the law. Govern this society. What is it you have to protect me from?" she demanded.

Khalid didn't answer right away. Talah's mind raced. *Protect me from what? From who?*

For a moment, the hallway held only silence—heavy, breathless. The kind of silence that preceded a storm. She thought of all the years she'd been told to stay within the villa walls, to study privately, to keep her head down at gatherings. And beneath those memories lurked something stranger—those fleeting sensations she'd never learned to name.

How her skin would prickle when standing too close to someone of another Sign. How the air around her sometimes felt off, thick with a static charge that wasn't quite fear but wasn't harmless either. She'd once thought it was imagination. Then later, shame. Her parents never spoke of it. They'd only grown more careful. Now, looking at her father's expression—his jaw locked, his eyes dark with something that looked like regret—she wondered if those moments hadn't been strange at all. Maybe they had been warnings.

Her father exhaled through his nose, slow and measured, as if trying to leash something untamed behind his composed exterior. "You think being a councilor means I'm safe from this world?" he said finally, voice low. "I see what lies beneath the laws, Talah. I see who they're really written for. And who they're written *against*."

Talah stared at him, searching his face. The marble mask of power and duty cracked just slightly, enough for her to glimpse the man beneath it—the father who had carried her on his shoulders, who used to whisper stories about stars and destinies before bed.

If even he is terrified for me... what chance do I have to survive?

"There are things we can't explain," he said. "Not yet. Things we've only...suspected. But suspicion alone can be enough to end lives in our world. Even the slightest of difference can spark fear."

Selene touched Talah's arm again, drawing her attention back. "We've kept you close because we had to, not because we didn't believe in you. You think we don't see your strength? Your fire? Of course we do. That's what terrifies us."

Talah's throat tightened. "Then tell me why. Tell me *what* it is you're so afraid of."

Asha's expression shattered into something softer, pained. Her eyes shimmered—but no tears fell. "Because if we say it out loud, Talah... it becomes real."

She cupped Talah's face, palms warm against her cheeks. "I need you to live. I need you to outlast this, whatever it is. Not for glory. Not for them." Her voice broke slightly. "For you. You're the best thing we've ever done. And we've already lost too much to gamble you."

Khalid stepped forward then, more hesitant than she'd ever seen him. His hand rested briefly on her shoulder—awkward, but real. "There are forces in this world that will offer you power, Talah, only to chain you with it. We don't know what you are yet, but we know enough to be afraid. And so should you."

Talah stood rooted, every part of her trembling. From anger. From love. From the ache of being half-seen and half-silenced.

"I don't want to be afraid," she said quietly. "I came here to show that I wasn't."

Her mother pressed their foreheads together. "Then be wise. Bravery without caution is just another way to bleed."

"Keep your guard up," her father cautioned, refusing to look at her now. "We've done all we can. But now you've forced our hand. Chosen your own path. And we cannot stop you."

Talah didn't know how to reply. She wanted answers—answers they clearly weren't willing to give.

"That mentor of yours..." her mother trailed off, head tilting slightly, her brow furrowing as if studying a puzzle with pieces just out of reach. "Iras, is it?"

Talah stiffened at the name, uncertain whether it was the subtle emphasis or something else that unsettled her.

Selene continued slowly, as if sifting through a memory buried too deep to grasp fully. "There's something about him. The way he carries himself. The way he watches. He's young, yes—but not unformed. He reminds me of someone, though I can't quite—" She shook her head, dismissing the thought like a whisper she couldn't catch.

Khalid let out a harsh breath. "Familiar or not, he's reckless."

Talah turned to him. "He stood up to you because he believed I deserved to compete."

Khalid's eyes snapped to hers. "He *challenged* me in front of the Imperium. That's not belief—that's arrogance. And arrogance in the wrong hands is dangerous."

"But he wasn't wrong," she said, defiant now.

"That doesn't make him trustworthy." His voice was cold, clipped. "I don't care how charming he plays it—men like that always have another agenda."

Selene stepped between them again, a quiet wall of calm. "He stood up for her when he had no reason to. That alone tells me that he'll be somewhat competent as a mentor."

"He's watching her, like they all are," Khalid muttered. "Whether to protect her or study her, I don't know. But don't mistake proximity for loyalty."

Talah swallowed, unsure whether to defend Iras or not. She didn't know him just yet and, even if his first impression did help her with her plan, she still didn't know what to make of him. But he'd stood up to her father—a *councilor*—and that meant something. He had shown no fear. No reservations. Talah realized a second too late what it was she felt about him.

Respect.

Her mother turned to her again, softer now. "You'll need someone, *rohi*. If he's offering help, take it—for now. Just don't give him more than you're willing to lose. Not yet."

"And not just him," Khalid added, gaze narrowing. "Trust no one completely. Not even those who seem to fight for you. Especially them."

Talah could only stare at them. "You think he's lying to me?"

"We think you're walking into a world where lies wear beautiful faces," her mother said gently. "And where even the truth comes with a cost."

Her father exhaled, stepping back. "We've done what we could. Now it's yours to face."

Her mother's hand lingered on her cheek for a moment longer, warm and trembling. Then it dropped away.

Without another word, they turned, their footsteps echoing down the corridor—two sharp, retreating heartbeats that grew softer with each step.

Talah didn't follow.

She stood there alone in the silence, the torchlight painting wavering shadows across the stone walls. The cold of the floor seeped through her shoes, anchoring her in place even as her thoughts spun loose and directionless. She wrapped her arms around herself, suddenly chilled, even though the air wasn't cold.

They hadn't told her anything. Not really. Not the truth. Not the *real* reason they'd kept her locked away, not the meaning behind their fear, not what they saw when they looked at her and didn't speak.

Only warnings.

Cryptic half-truths dressed up as love. Hints at something dark and dangerous—inside her, their world—but no names, no answers. Just more silence.

She dug her nails into her palms, fighting the heat rising behind her eyes. She hated that it hurt. Hated that she wanted to believe they were trying to protect her. Hated that she still ached for their approval, even after everything.

Talah leaned back against one of the pillars, pressing her head to the cool stone. Her mother's words repeated in her mind like a prayer—or a curse.

This world isn't what it looks like behind the glass.

Even now, even after everything, a part of her still burned with the need to prove them wrong. To prove that whatever she was, it wasn't something to be feared. That she was not a mistake to be hidden or a secret to be kept.

But a part of her felt small in this moment. Small, and alone.

Talah straightened. She couldn't stay here. She couldn't fall apart now. She pushed off the pillar, shoulders squared, spine tall. Her mother had told her to be wise. Her father had told her to trust no one.

But neither of them had told her who she was.

And if they wouldn't... she'd find out on her own.

FIRAS VII

Firas tried to ignore the look Kam was glaring into his soul. "We were told to lie low," Kam snapped, hauling him off to a shadowed corner, away from eager ears. Her boots struck the floor like gunshots. "What part of *blend in* didn't translate?"

Right, as if I had any choice in who my competitor would be, Firas thought bitterly.

Already their plan was going off the rails. He'd known there would be a chance of getting a child of importance, from an important family, but how could he have known he would get a *councilor's* kid? Irritation flickered beneath the flash of fear—fear of being found out, of failing his mission.

She's going to ruin everything.

"If she hadn't been allowed to compete, I would have been kicked out before we even had a chance to search for answers," Firas argued.

She caught his arm, yanking him into a side alcove veiled by hanging crimson banners embroidered with gold. Hidden enough.

"You challenged a councilor. *Her father*," Kam hissed, voice low and taut with fury. "Do you even understand what you just did?"

Firas exhaled, steadying the storm inside him. "I did what needed to be done."

"She didn't ask you to."

"I didn't do it for her." He met Kam's glare, jaw clenched. "I did it for the plan."

Kam scoffed. "Don't give me that martyr crap. You felt something. I saw it all over your face."

He didn't respond. Not right away. Because she wasn't wrong.

She ran away from the only privileged life she'd known to enter the deadliest tournament in our society and faced her father like it was nothing. He couldn't help but feel at least an ounce of respect.

"What?" Kam demanded, her hands moving to her hips. "Please don't tell me you actually felt *bad* for her."

"It's not that," Firas replied shortly, turning away.

"Then what is it?" Kam asked. "What made you risk your own life and go against everything Samira ordered us *not* to do?"

He drew in a slow breath, jaw tight. "It's... hard to explain."

Except it wasn't.

He knew exactly what had happened. The second her father tried to shut her down—to use his name, his status, his place in the world to silence her—something in Firas had cracked wide open. It wasn't pity, but recognition.

The fire behind her words, the way she stood alone in that room and didn't back down—even when it would've been safer to fold. He'd seen that before. Not in her. In a version of himself that had once believed the system could be challenged if he just stood his ground. Something old and raw had risen in him before he could stop it. Not emotion. Instinct.

Something dangerous.

"All eyes will be on her now," Kam warned. "And you. Samira won't like that."

"I don't care what Samira likes. She put me in charge of this mission."

"Then you better not screw it up before it even begins," Kam snapped.

A couple drifted past without slowing, their laughter echoing off the marble, dulled by the heavy velvet of the banners. Kam and Firas turned away, hiding their faces on instinct as the couple moved away.

"We need to separate," Kam muttered.

Firas nodded, adjusting the embroidered sash at his waist to appear more like any other overeager competitor. "I'll meet you at the closet tonight."

"Just stay out of trouble until then," Kam said, eyes lingering on him like a final warning. "And remember, she's not yours to save."

With that, she slipped away, melting into the current of Aphelion's veiled politics and silken lies.

Firas waited a beat before stepping out into the corridor. He needed a break from the suffocating facade. The pressure of holding it all together—his name, his face, his history, all packed tightly behind the mask of *Iras*—was beginning to split at the edges, and the mission had barely started. Every breath inside Aphelion felt like it had to be filtered through control, measured for danger. One wrong word, one wrong look, and everything he was hiding—who he was hiding—would collapse around him like glass.

He ran a hand through his hair and exhaled. Kam was right—this wasn't the time to feel anything. His mission was to watch, report, and intervene only if necessary. He wasn't supposed to care.

But he did.

He hated that he did. And for the stupidest reasons—because he saw a part of himself in her when he didn't even really *know* her. It was an illusion, just like everything else in this stars-forsaken world. And before he could get his thoughts in order, fate shoved him straight back into the chaos.

Because as he rounded the corner, he nearly ran straight into her.

She looked like a storm that hadn't yet broken—shoulders tense, eyes distant, lips pressed into a line that was holding back too much. Her steps faltered when she saw him, surprise flashing across her face, followed by something more guarded.

"You."

He didn't like how that word dropped from her lips—soft, measured, but heavy enough to lodge beneath his skin.

She tilted her head, studying him as she stepped closer, just enough to make the hallway feel smaller. The scent of her—salt and smoke and something faintly floral—hit him before her voice did. A shiver ran down his spine, electricity that had no right to his body, threading heat into his pulse.

"You didn't have to say anything back there," she said. Her voice was steady, but there was a roughness to it—like the edge of a blade that had already tasted resistance. "But you did."

Firas didn't flinch. He met her gaze, his own face carefully blank, the muscle in his jaw ticking once. "I didn't do it for *you*."

The tiniest hitch in her breath betrayed the hit. She folded her arms across her chest, posture stiffening like a drawbridge rising. "Right. You just enjoy provoking powerful councilors for fun?"

"It's not about fun," he said, voice low. The words scraped against his throat. His eyes flicked back toward the doors leading to the Great Hall, but it didn't help—he could still feel her, the faint warmth of her body cutting through the cool marble air. "Some things are worth the risk."

"But not me." She unfolded her arms slowly, one hand coming to rest on her hips. The movement drew his eyes before he could stop himself. He looked away just as quickly, the heat crawling up the back of his neck betraying him more than any words could. "That's what you're really saying."

He exhaled sharply, the sound caught between annoyance and something heavier. The scent of incense from the Great Hall still lingered in the air, sweet and suffocating. He didn't know if he wanted to step closer or turn and walk away before he said something he couldn't take back.

"I'm saying you stepped into a game you don't understand," he said, more clipped now.

Talah stepped in, closing the distance by a fraction. Just enough to make him feel it.

"Then enlighten me."

His eyes narrowed, the shimmer of heat behind them no longer entirely from frustration. He could feel his heartbeat in his throat, heavy and unsteady.

"You grew up behind pearly gates, didn't you? Fed. Educated. Guarded like gold. Maybe you *think* this is about ideals—about fairness and honor. But this world doesn't care about any of that. It cares about *power*. And people like you?" He leaned in slightly, just enough for her to hear the words meant to wound. "You've always had it. Even if you didn't realize it."

Her expression faltered—something like hurt, quickly smothered by pride. She straightened, spine stiff, chin lifting with practiced grace. But it wasn't the careful elegance of nobility that caught him—it was the defiance curling beneath it. The *fire* that lit behind her eyes, storm-blue and unflinching.

Firas hadn't noticed their color before. Not really. But now, in the low golden light filtering through the carved windows, he saw that her eyes weren't just blue—they were deep and strange and stormy, like the sea before it turned violent.

Her hair was dark, threaded with copper under the light, braided back in the traditional Pisces style—but not too tightly, like she'd rushed. A few strands had escaped, clinging to her temple with sweat, and one curled stubbornly against her cheek.

He hated that he noticed that.

Hated the way his gaze dragged lower—how the tension in her jaw only made her look fiercer, how even her stillness felt like it was coiled, ready to strike. She looked like someone born of salt and flame—raw, unpolished, real.

She was supposed to be soft. Sheltered.

But there was nothing soft in the way she looked at him now.

Nothing safe.

"You think you know me?" she asked again, her voice steady, but her eyes dared him to lie.

And Firas—traitor to the plan, to himself—wanted to.

He wanted to pretend she was just another rich girl playing soldier. Wanted to shove her into a box, close the lid, and walk away. But that look in her eyes made it impossible. Because in that moment, she didn't look like someone who'd been protected from the world.

She looked like someone who had survived something, at least. And had survived it alone.

He snapped his gaze away. Forced the wall back up.

"I know your type." It was the only thing he could say. The only thing that might stop him from saying more.

She stepped closer.

Close enough now that he could feel the heat, unrelenting, like a sandstorm rising across a quiet plain. The space between them shrank to nothing but breath. He caught the faint scent of her skin—salt and something like jasmine scorched by flame—and it hit him harder than it should have. His pulse kicked, betraying him.

Every instinct screamed at him to step back, but his body refused to listen. The air around her shimmered faintly, the same way it did before a storm; charged, alive, impossible to ignore. He could almost feel the hum of her energy brushing against his own, a quiet ache beneath his ribs.

"And what's *your* type?" she challenged, voice quieter now, more dangerous for it.

He didn't answer.

Wouldn't.

Because the truth was too complicated—too dangerous.

His jaw flexed. The air between them felt heavy, suffocating. He could see the flecks of light in her eyes, the faint rise and fall of her breath. For one dizzying second, he wanted to forget everything—who she was, what she represented—and just close the impossible distance that had been growing between them since the moment they met.

So instead, he turned. A single step, deliberate. A retreat disguised as indifference.

"Watch your step in the Trials, Councilor's daughter," he said, voice cool and distant now. "The arena doesn't care whose blood it spills."

"Neither do I," she threw back.

He paused mid-step, the weight of her words catching him like a sudden drop. His hand hovered at his side, tension drawn tight across his shoulders. For a second, he almost didn't look back. Almost.

When he did, her eyes were still locked on his—unapologetic, unwavering.

And stars help him, she *meant* it.

Good. Let her burn.

It would be easier that way—easier to keep his distance, to remind himself she was just another privileged girl playing at rebellion with no idea what war really was. Her arrogance would be her own undoing. All he needed to do was make sure she didn't get in his way.

But as he walked away, pulse hot and chest too tight, Firas realized with a sick twist of instinct that she wasn't going to be easy to ignore. And worse—she wasn't just dangerous to the mission.

She was dangerous to *him*.

TALAH
VIII

Talah didn't move until Iras was gone. Not until the sound of his footsteps faded, swallowed by the stone and silence.

He hadn't looked back. Not even once.

The burn in her chest wasn't anger—not *exactly*. It was something messier. Something she didn't have a name for yet. He'd stood up for her when no one else had dared… and then turned around and reminded her that she was still alone.

Straightening her spine, she forced her shoulders back and walked.

The golden doors to the Great Hall loomed ahead, still open, still blinding with torchlight and ceremony. As she stepped through them, the hum of voices quieted—just enough for her to feel the weight of every gaze flicking toward her. Not quite stares. But sharp enough to sting.

"You certainly know how to make an impression."

Talah turned and found herself staring into the mischievous face of a young man she'd never seen before. The boy's eyes glimmered with the kind of quick wit she already suspected would get him in trouble. He wore the unmistakable robes of a Gemini, the soft yellow tones vibrant against his tanned skin. His energy felt restless but oddly comforting, like a breeze chasing away the tension.

The boy leaned in slightly, his voice dipping to a mock-conspiratorial whisper. "I'm guessing public humiliation by your own father in front of the entire Convocation isn't exactly the most intimidating first impression."

"That's none of your concern," she snapped.

He gave a low whistle. "Well, you're either going to kill me, ignore me, or take me under your wing, so it kind of is. But I should warn you—I don't go down easy."

Talah arched a brow. "And you are?"

He grinned, quick and fox-like. "Zayd. Your friendly neighborhood underdog."

"Are you really an underdog if you have to announce it?" she asked.

"I guess you'll just have to find out," Zayd replied, shrugging.

Talah gave him a once-over, taking in the way he carried himself—cocky, but not arrogant. He moved with an easy, almost lazy grace, like a panther that knew it didn't need to chase its prey. His dark eyes slid over her expression, cataloging every shift in her features. His dark hair, tousled just enough to suggest he either didn't care or wanted it to look that way, framed a face built for deception. He was trouble.

And that was the last thing she needed.

"Tell me, did you really think your father wouldn't have stepped in?" Zayd asked, though there was no malice in his voice. He truly sounded curious. "If it were anyone else..."

He left it open, but she knew what he meant.

Talah set her jaw, forcing herself not to react. "I didn't ask for his help."

Zayd let out a low whistle. "That's rough then. Daddy dearest ruining your big moment? I wish my parents cared that much."

Her nails dug into her palms, but she refused to give him the satisfaction of a reaction.

"I mean, I get it." His smirk deepened, eyes dancing. He gestured to himself. "Third son and all—I understand. Living under all that power, all those expectations... no wonder you ran off to the Trials. From what I hear, he didn't exactly let you out much, did he? And then announcing to every single competitor that you hadn't trained for this? That's rough."

Talah's head whipped around, her glare sharpening. He was too perceptive for his own good.

She hated how it sounded like pity, even if it wasn't. Hated that part of her still burned with the truth of it. She *had* been caged—behind marble walls and polite smiles, beneath her father's shadow and her mother's gentle warnings. And when she'd thought she'd finally clawed her way free, it still wasn't enough.

"And here I was thinking you'd joined just for the adventure," he added. "Unless you're like every other Council kid who joined to prove themselves to parents who just don't care."

The words landed like a slap. Her hands curled at her sides, nails digging half-moons into her palms.

"I joined for myself," Talah snapped. "Not for him. Not for anyone else."

Zayd tilted his head, feigning deep contemplation. "Sure. We all heard your little speech. Very brave of you, by the way. But that's what everyone says, though, isn't it?"

She bristled. "You don't know anything about me."

"Not yet," he admitted easily. "But you're interesting. I might stick around just to find out."

"Talah!"

She turned just in time to see Mazin pushing his way through the shifting crowd, eyes flashing with exasperation. Right behind him, Adine followed, looking far too entertained by whatever disaster Talah had gotten herself into.

"There you are," Mazin said, breathless. "Are you alright?"

"I'm fine," she assured him, though she wasn't entirely sure if that was the truth. The sting from her parent's clear rejection of her decision sliced through her.

Mazin's gaze flicked to Zayd, suspicion clear in the slight narrowing of his eyes. "Who's this?"

"Zayd," the Gemini said smoothly, flashing an easy grin. "Your new best friend."

Mazin crossed his arms. "I highly doubt that."

"I grow on people," Zayd promised, unbothered. "And from what I can tell, your friend here might need someone like me around."

Mazin's frown deepened, his expression laced with clear disapproval. "She has me."

"Exactly my point," Zayd quipped, his gaze lazily trailing up and down Mazin's frame deliberately.

"Are you always this arrogant?" Adine asked, arching a perfectly manicured brow.

Zayd placed a hand over his heart in mock offense. "I'm a Gemini. It's a biological possibility."

Mazin ran a hand down his face. "I can already tell this is going to be a disaster. Your father is definitely going to kill me for this."

Talah ignored him. It wouldn't be the first time she'd dragged him into trouble and, hopefully, it wouldn't be the last. Instead, she took her time to study those in the room. She hadn't had much of a chance to do so before, when all she could focus on was how her father would react when her name would be called.

All around them, Signborn nobles drifted like jeweled vultures—cloaked in embroidered finery and false smiles, their gazes sweeping over the competitors like merchants inspecting wares. Conversations were quiet but direct, voices dipped low not out of politeness, but because they didn't want to be overheard speaking of odds.

Talah caught sight of a heavyset man in violet murmuring to a woman adorned in gold and emeralds. He gestured subtly toward a stocky boy near the dais—broad-shouldered and already holding court among younger competitors. A parchment was exchanged. Gold ink glinted in the torchlight.

"They're already wagering on who will survive the first cut," Mazin muttered, his voice tight beside her. "Disgusting."

Adine folded her arms, expression cool and detached, but her tone betrayed the bite beneath. "It's tradition. One of the oldest. Noble families make their bids, securing alliances before the Trials even begin. The smart ones use it for political leverage. The arrogant ones just want bragging rights. If you're smart, you'll play the game. If not..." She didn't need to explain further.

Zayd made a low sound of mock disgust. "A whole room of walking bank accounts pretending this is still about glory and not blood." He leaned closer to Talah, lowering his voice so only she could hear. "That's what they don't tell you in the welcome lectures. This isn't about merit. It's about spectacle. About whose win makes the best story."

She didn't respond. Because it was starting to look like he was right.

And it made her want to scream.

Mazin's lips thinned. "And we're just supposed to pretend this is fair?"

Zayd smirked, motioning to the lavish spread of food no one was touching. "In case you missed it, fair doesn't wear velvet and sip imported tea while children die for *power*." The derision basically dripped from each word.

Talah's gaze swept the room again, this time more aware. Of the subtle nods. The exchanged glances. The weight behind every stare.

"They don't think we're people," she said quietly. "We're just entertainment. Even if it's their own children."

Zayd nodded once. "Now you're getting it." He tilted back, stretching. "Firstborns don't have to worry about this sort of thing. They get all the attention. But the rest of us? We have to fight for it. Make our parents proud, yadda, yadda. I mean, which one of us hasn't heard the whole spiel about how sacrificing our lives would lead to glory and respect and everything else our parents want to add to their vast collection of privilege?"

Adine's lip curled as she shot Zayd a sideways glare. "Some of us are here because we don't have a choice."

Zayd raised an eyebrow, grinning. "What, did your parents' favorite die or something?"

The air shifted.

Her painted lips parted in disbelief—just for a heartbeat—before flattening into a line sharp enough to draw blood. When she spoke, her voice was cold steel.

"He did actually. My brother."

The words dropped like a blade between them.

Talah's breath caught. "I'm so sorry," she said quietly, the weight of it pressing hard against her chest.

Adine didn't blink. "Don't be." She tossed her long hair over one shoulder, eyes locked on Zayd like he wasn't worth the dust on her shoes. "He died defending civilians during an Ambigua attack."

Her voice didn't waver—but the fury beneath it gleamed like fire beneath ice. "A hero," she added, chin high. "Something you wouldn't recognize if it stood in front of you and bled."

Zayd's smirk faded, just slightly. He opened his mouth, but Adine was already turning.

She didn't wait for a reply.

The crowd parted around her without a word, without resistance—like a tide pulled by moonlight. Heads turned. Eyes followed. Even the nobles gave her space. Talah watched her go, struck by how effortlessly Adine commanded a room without even trying.

Maybe someday...

Zayd rocked back on his heels, lips still curved in that ever-present smirk. "Well, if nothing else, this is going to be fun."

Talah didn't respond.

Because *fun* wasn't the word for any of this.

The fire in Adine's voice still rang in her ears. The weight of the nobles' stares still clung to her skin like ash. And somewhere beneath it all, a darker truth churned in her gut.

She was going to have to kill someone.

Maybe not today. Maybe not tomorrow. But the Trials weren't won with clever words or noble speeches. They were won with blood. With blades and strategy and decisions you couldn't take back.

She knew that. She'd always known it.

And still, something in her recoiled.

Not because she was afraid of violence—but because part of her still wanted to believe there was another way. A cleaner way. A way that didn't ask her to become what this world had made of so many others. But if she wanted a place here—if she wanted control over her life, her choices, her future—she would have to be willing to stain her hands.

She'd have to be strong enough to live with it.

Even if it hollowed her out from the inside.

That was just how their world worked.

"Tal?" Mazin's voice pulled her back into the conversation. The worry in his eyes annoyed her.

"I'm fine," she replied, a bit sharper than she'd intended. Talah shifted, feeling uneasy. The enormous hall suddenly felt too small, too crowded.

Mazin noticed. As always.

"Are you—"

"If you ask if I'm alright one more time, the Trials will be the least of your concerns," Talah snapped, shooting him a dark look.

Mazin's hands went up defensively. "I'm just looking out for you."

"I never asked you to do that," she bit back.

"You don't have to," he replied just as quickly. "We've been a team since we were kids, Tal. Entering the Trials isn't going to change that." He studied her a bit too closely, gauging her reaction.

Talah stepped away from Zayd, knowing Mazin would follow. "I came here for a reason," she whispered fiercely. "For years, my dad treated me like a child. This is my one and only chance to prove that I am not. And I cannot do that if you're just going to act exactly as he did."

Hurt flashed in Mazin's eyes. "That's not what I—"

"It is, though," she said quickly. "I don't need you to watch out for me. I don't need you to take care of me. I can do this on my own. Being an ally doesn't mean you treat me like a child and do everything for me—it means supporting me while I do it on my own."

Mazin's lips thinned, the hurt still written across his face. "Fine. I'll respect that."

"Will you, though?" she asked quietly, not needing an answer. When he said nothing, just looked at her like he was still waiting for her to change her mind, Talah stepped back.

"I'm going back to my dorm," she said, her voice cool but frayed at the edges. "Today was... exhausting."

This time, he didn't try to stop her.

She turned and moved into the tide of bodies, slipping through clusters of silk-clad nobles and restless competitors like a current carving its way through stone. The air inside the Great Hall had grown thick with perfume, smoke, and the unspoken weight of expectation. Talah kept her eyes forward, refusing to flinch beneath the stares that clung to her like dust.

She didn't come here to be gawked at or wagered on. She wasn't a Council pet playing at rebellion. And yet that's what they saw: the daughter of Khalid, out of place among the bloodstained ambitions of the Crossborns, the privilege of the Signborn. Another pretty face in fine silk who would break the moment things got real.

Talah's fingers curled into fists as she approached the wide, gilded doors leading out of the Hall. Just a few more steps and she could be alone again—free of the games, the eyes, the *mask*.

"Leaving so soon, Miss Khalil?"

She turned, heart thudding, to find Councilor Khatri standing in the archway, watching her with a curious expression. The Libra Councilor was as composed as ever, her pink galabiya draped effortlessly over her thin shoulders. She exuded the quiet power that Libras were known for—diplomatic, deliberate, but dangerous in ways that didn't require brute force.

Talah forced herself to stand tall. "It's been a long day," she said carefully, measuring her tone.

"Indeed," Saahira mused, stepping closer. "But I imagine your journey here had been long as well. And yet, I find it... interesting that you chose to come at all."

"I don't understand what you mean, councilor. It's fairly common for the children of councilors to enter the Trials," Talah replied truthfully.

Saahira tilted her head slightly, her gaze sweeping over Talah like she was some puzzle that had yet to be solved. "You should," she said lightly, yet her words carried weight. "The children of councilors don't need to seek out the Trials—they already have the power, the proof, that their lineage is worthy. They do so only because it's just another way to showcase that power. They spend their entire lives training for it. But you... you did not."

The air felt thicker suddenly, heavy with the incense and the unspoken challenge buried beneath Saahira's poise. She could feel the councilor's eyes on her like a scalpel, stripping her bare.

"I trained on my own," Talah replied firmly. The words were steady, but her pulse wasn't. "I don't want to just be handed anything I didn't earn myself."

The councilor's eyebrow rose gracefully. "That much is clear. A girl raised away from society by her father, now in the open... one might wonder if she truly understands what it means to be seen."

The words sent a cold ripple down Talah's spine. *What it means to be seen.* She felt suddenly too aware of the polished marble beneath her boots, of the way her reflection shimmered faintly in the obsidian columns around them—as if the entire room was watching.

"I understand enough."

Saahira's lips twitched at the edges, the ghost of a smile. "Then I suggest you keep your wits about you, Ya anisa bint Khalid. A competitor who dares to challenge the Trials without years of training? And a girl, no less? Not everyone will take kindly to such ambition."

The words pressed into her chest like the slow tightening of a fist. She wanted to speak—wanted to throw the insult back—but she could feel her father's voice echoing in her head: *Control is power.*

Before Talah could respond, Saahira stepped past her, leaving only the faint scent of jasmine in her wake. Talah stood frozen for a moment, the eyes of so many weighing on her shoulder. She didn't have to look up to know that the councilor's words rang true—deep down, she knew what others would think. Would assume.

She would just have to prove them all wrong.

TALAH
IX

Morning dew clung to the blades of grass as Talah made her way to the coliseum. The campus was quiet this early. Most of the students wouldn't be arriving until after the Trials were completed. The coliseum was quiet at dawn, the air cool and laced with the scent of stone and dust. Talah took her time crossing the archway, her boots whispering over the damp ground. Morning light spilled through the towering columns, golden and soft, but it did little to warm the sharp gaze waiting for her.

"You're late."

Iras stood inside the arena, leaning against the stone wall, arms crossed. His dark hair was slightly damp, curling around his ears. His hand drifted down to the curved sword at his hip, fingers flexing around the pommel. He wore traditional sarwal trousers, the material loose around his thighs and tightly wound around his ankles. His tunic looked a size too big for him, though the material clung to his chest from the damp humidity that hung heavy in the air.

They were the first ones there. The coliseum arena stretched wide and open, a vast expanse of packed sand and trampled dust, darkened in places where the morning dew had long since seeped into the earth. The walls of the coliseum towered around her, their sunbaked stone etched with ancient carvings of Zodiac symbols and past champions. Though the arena was empty now, it still hummed with energy, the weight of centuries of battles pressing down on the still morning air.

Above, banners hung limply from the highest points of the coliseum, their rich colors faded from years of sun and storms. A faint breeze stirred them, and for a moment, Talah imagined the stands filled with roaring spectators, the air electric with expectation. Soon, the arena would be alive again. Soon, the sand would be disturbed by the footsteps of those who would fight for a place among the elite.

You're really here, she told herself, though the thought felt unreal.

All the years of being told *no*—no to training, no to leaving the villa, no to becoming anything other than what her father's name dictated—and somehow, she'd still made it to the one place he'd sworn to keep her from. But now that she was here, now that the wind off the arena walls whispered her name into the open air, she couldn't quite tell if what she felt was pride or the edge of something far more dangerous.

"Are you waiting for an invitation?" Iras called over his shoulder, his voice cutting through her thoughts.

Talah bristled at his tone. "Just waiting for some instruction," she bit back, slowly making her way down the rest of the stone steps.

"You won't have that in the Trials," Iras replied, shaking his head slightly. He pushed away from the wall, the movement fluid and precise. "I want some laps to start."

Talah's mouth parted in response before she thought better of it. She took off, feet struggling to find purchase in the sand. It didn't take long before her muscles were screaming, burning through her skin. Though that wasn't the only thing burning. She could feel his eyes tracking her every movement, watching as she struggled around the ring. Talah purposely ignored him, focusing on avoiding the tangles of vines in the earth section, the pools of water, and scorched sand.

Just as she passed him for the fourth time, just as she thought her legs would fail her, he called her name.

"Good enough," he called out.

Talah bent over, hands on her knees as she struggled for air. The stitch in her side cut across her abdomen. The early morning sun filled the arena, as the temperature of the sand rose. She'd been so focused on trying to stay on her feet, she hadn't even noticed the time passing. The others would be here soon enough.

"Get up," Iras barked.

Talah's head snapped up, her glare instinctive. Sweat stung her eyes, but she didn't look away. Stubbornly, she straightened, forcing her shoulders back as she tried to steady her breathing. Iras watched her, lip curled, dark eyes assessing. There was something in that look that made her skin prickle.

She hated that look. She'd seen it before, in the eyes of councilors, instructors, even her father's guards—people who'd already decided what she was capable of before she ever opened her mouth. But Iras wasn't just another skeptic. He was her mentor. Her judge. Her first obstacle.

Part of her wanted to earn his approval, to make him see that she belonged here as much as anyone else. The other part wanted to prove him wrong so thoroughly that he'd never dare look at her like that again.

Her lungs still burned, but she lifted her chin. "I'm up," she said, voice low, even.

"Then let's see how long you stay that way." The faintest smirk tugged at Iras's mouth.

"The first trial forces competitors to master their abilities in extreme conditions," he began. "You'll be thrown into this very arena, cycling through the four extreme elemental sections: fire, water, earth, and air." He motioned to the four parts of the arena

Talah had just been forced to run through.

"Not only will you have to fight the elements," Iras continued, "but you'll also be fighting your fellow competitors for tokens in order to advance to the next section. No token? You don't make it to the next section."

"Tokens?" Talah asked, nose scrunching as she tried to understand.

Iras gave a curt nod. "These tokens are linked to Libras, who will teleport you from one section to the next. This arena will look completely different—impenetrable walls separating each part. No way in and no way out, unless you get those damn tokens."

"Sounds reasonable," Talah mumbled. Iras shot her a dark look.

"You're going to be exhausted in the Trials. There will be times when you'll think you can't continue. Times you'll want to give up." His fingers curled around the hilt of his blade. "But if you give up, you die."

"Noted," Talah replied dryly, irritated when her words came out just a little too breathy.

His eyes narrowed. "Do you think this is a game?" The sharpness of his tone struck like a whip. Iras stepped closer, and the air between them seemed to shrink. His voice dropped, low and unrelenting. "You will be trapped in this maze. The only way out is either with those tokens…or on a stretcher to carry your dead body. The first trial can last hours or even days. And you'll need to be able to survive with no servants, no cooks, no soft bed to lay your head. In every single element."

The image he painted—alone, lost, powerless—sent a cold thread of fear down her spine, but she refused to let it show. Her palms prickled, the urge to clench her fists burning through her fingertips. The air felt too thin, too hot, but she held her ground.

Talah lifted her chin, forcing her voice steady even as her pulse thundered in her throat. "You don't think I can do this, do you?"

His expression didn't change. He was careful—too careful—

not to reveal his thoughts. But she knew it anyway. "The elite train their children for years for the Trials. They're given the best tutors, the best trainers, in order to survive this. Were you?"

She wanted to say yes—to throw something sharp and clever back at him—but her throat locked up. The truth pressed against her chest like a bruise. No matter how hard she tried, she couldn't erase the years she'd spent caged behind her father's walls, dreaming of this moment but never truly ready for it.

"Zodiacs who didn't have that privilege have still made it," Talah pointed out.

"Very few," Iras corrected, bitterness lacing his words.

"Then why did you stand up for me at the Convocation?" she demanded. "Why bother risking my father's wrath?"

His jaw flexed, but he said nothing.

"I'm here because I want to be," Talah continued. "I'm here because I'm willing to risk my life to prove to everyone that I'm not just some sheltered councilor's daughter."

"Why?"

The question caught her off guard, though it shouldn't have. Still, something about the way he asked it... the rough edge in his voice, the slight furrow between his brows... made her pulse trip. His expression had gone unreadable, but his eyes—dark, steady, searching—held her like a blade against glass. She noticed how he'd gone still, the restless energy he usually carried drawn tight inside him, as if he were holding back something he didn't want her to see.

She opened her mouth to answer, but for a heartbeat, nothing came out. *Why?* Because she was tired of being protected? Because she wanted to matter for more than her father's name? Because she needed to feel alive in a world that had decided her fate before she could choose it?

All of it. None of it. She didn't even know where to begin.

Her fingers curled at her sides. "Everyone has their reasons," she replied quietly. "Whether they're the spare heir to a long line of warriors who'd already proven themselves, or they're common-born and vying for a better life. But me? I'm neither of those. I have nothing to prove to my family. I don't have to fight for connections or power or money."

"Then why are you here?" Iras asked again.

"Because I need to prove it to myself." Talah's chin lifted higher. "Because my entire life, I'd been told I needed to be careful. That this world was dangerous. That I had no idea what it was truly like—because I didn't. And I was tired of other people telling me what I couldn't do."

Iras turned away, disgust slipping across his face. "So you risk your life for... what? Validation?"

"I'm risking my life because I wouldn't have one if I didn't," Talah snapped. The words came out sharper than she meant, but she didn't stop them. "A gilded cage is still just that—a cage. And the only validation I need is my own."

His eyes met hers then, and she felt the world narrow to that single, impossible look. There was no disdain in it now—only the barest flicker of something that felt too much like recognition. As if he saw the same hunger in her that he'd once seen in himself.

It unsettled her.

Because the way he looked at her wasn't pity, or doubt, or even challenge. It was something deeper—an acknowledgment she wasn't ready for. Like he understood the shape of her defiance because it mirrored his own. And for that single breath, she hated that he could see her so clearly when she barely understood herself.

The air between them thrummed with something taut, unspoken. She thought—just for a moment—that he might say her name differently this time. But before either of them could speak, a ripple of movement in the stands caught her attention. Competitors were beginning to filter into the arena, some with the stiff unease of first-years, others striding in like they already owned the sand beneath their boots. Iras immediately stepped back, creating distance between the two of them as he moved toward the other mentors gathering along the far wall.

Talah watched Iras go, her gaze lingering on his retreating

figure longer than she meant to. A strange mix of exhaustion and something sharper churned beneath her ribs. She wasn't sure if she wanted to hit him or thank him—or maybe both. Every muscle in her body ached, her skin slick with sweat and grit, but her pulse still hadn't steadied. The morning's training had left her raw, stripped of the thin layer of pride she'd walked in with.

Drawing a breath, she forced herself to look away. The small crowd in the stands had thickened, shadows moving between sunbeams. Then she spotted Mazin, perched on the edge of the stone bench, waving her over with that familiar grin that always managed to look half-worried.

"Sleep well?" he asked softly as she stepped from the arena and climbed the steps to his side.

"Well enough," she said, shrugging. Her throat still felt tight, her breath uneven from the drills.

He studied her for a moment too long, eyes narrowing in concern. "You look like you've been through hell."

"Thanks," she muttered, tugging the tie from her wrist to pull her hair back again. "That's kind of the point, isn't it?"

He didn't answer, but she could feel his worry radiating off him, thick as the heat still rising from the sand below. It was always like this—his quiet watching, his half-voiced questions, the way he hovered at the edges of her pain like he could absorb it for her. Once, that had comforted her. Now it made her skin itch.

She'd just spent an hour fighting to prove she could stand on her own, and the first thing Mazin did was look at her like she might break.

A resounding clap echoed across the arena, cutting through the tension.

"Gather around," a woman called out, motioning for the competitors to huddle before her.

She was tall and commanding, dressed in a deep maroon tunic cinched at the waist with an ornate leather belt. Her bronze skin gleamed under the torchlight, smooth and unlined despite the streaks of silver woven through her thick, black curls. There was a stillness about her, a presence that made the air seem heavier in her wake. Her dark eyes, nearly black, swept over the competitors with an unnerving sharpness, like she could strip them down to their bones with a single glance. A thin scar ran from the corner of her left eye to the edge of her jaw—a reminder, perhaps, of a time when she had been in their place.

Talah couldn't look away from her at first, but then her gaze flickered to the others standing behind her.

To the woman's right stood a tall, sharp-eyed figure who carried themselves with an air of quiet authority. Beside them, another mentor stood with practiced elegance, surveying the stands. A third lingered slightly apart from the group, their posture rigid, gaze cutting through the crowd like a blade. They stood together, some with arms crossed and stern expressions, others relaxed with indifferent expressions. But they all had one thing in common—an unspoken bond from their years spent here as students when they were younger.

Talah swallowed, unease curling in her stomach. Each of these mentors had once stood where she was now. And each had survived the Trials.

Her eyes flicked toward Iras as he took his place beside another mentor standing slightly apart from the crowd. Her dark skin gleamed beneath the early morning sun, her braided hair cinched with beads of bronze. She carried herself differently than the others—not stiff with arrogance like some, nor jittery with nerves like most. She was still, quiet, a predator waiting in the dark, studying her surroundings without a hint of wasted movement.

There was something effortless about her presence, something restrained but heavy, like she was holding back the full weight of who she was. It was a presence that demanded attention without asking for it. And yet, Talah wasn't sure if anyone else even noticed her, as if she had perfected the art of slipping between the cracks of awareness.

"Is that one yours?" Talah whispered, leaning against Mazin.

He blew out a sharp breath. "Yeah. She looks absolutely

terrifying."

"Welcome to your first day of training," the woman in front started. "My name is Azira. Each of us have been assigned to help you through the Trials this year. Not only will we help hone your skills over the next few days, but we'll also be responsible for mentally and physically preparing you to face whatever challenges await you."

"This first trial, as we all know, will be the maze," she continued. "Each of you will be dropped in a different elemental sector, specifically designed to test your abilities. In order to beat the maze, you will need to search out a single token in each quadrant. These tokens will teleport you to the next sector until you complete all four elements."

Her eyes roamed over the group of competitors, missing nothing. "The only way for you to leave will either be with those tokens… or to die."

Whispers broke out in the stands, a ripple of sound that moved through the crowd like wind across dry grass. Everyone knew of the maze. It was the only Trial to remain constant each year—the one whispered about in corridors, described in half-truths and warnings.

She'd seen sketches in old textbooks, heard the stories of those who'd barely made it out—bodies found days later, drained, burned, frozen. But none of it had ever felt real until now. The arena that had always seemed so distant, so legendary, suddenly felt like it was closing in around her.

"You will need to be prepared to stay in the maze for days," Azira warned them, forced to raise her voice over the crowd.

The words struck like stones—*days*. The idea of being trapped, of fighting for survival while the walls themselves turned against her, sent a cold shiver down her spine. She swallowed hard, forcing herself to stand taller, to hide the way her pulse fluttered wildly at the base of her throat.

This was it. No guards. No servants. No protection. Just her—and whatever waited in that labyrinth. Her palms went clammy. She curled her fingers into fists until her nails bit skin.

You wanted this, she reminded herself. *You fought for this.*

"How many tokens are there?" someone asked.

"Great question," Azira replied, nodding approvingly. "There are a limited number of tokens. Each one is linked to a Libra who uses that to teleport you to a different sector. We do not know for sure how many there are...but there is not enough for everyone."

She didn't have to explain further.

Talah glanced around, stomach tightening. She'd spent months—no, *years*—mentally preparing for what she would have to do here. She knew she would have to fight for her spot at Aphelion. To kill. But telling herself that she was ready to take lives was one thing.

Would she actually be able to do it?

It's either them... or me, she thought, trying to shake the seedling of doubt before it could take root.

"Now, find your mentor. Training starts now." Azira motioned toward those standing behind her, taking a step back.

"I'll see you after?" Mazin asked, forcing a lopsided grin. It didn't quite reach his eyes.

"Yeah," Talah replied. "I'll find you after."

She watched him jog down the steps, heading toward where his mentor waited. Iras was already moving through the crowd, his head jerking to the side as soon as she caught his eye.

Talah pushed her way down the steps, weaving through the crowd of competitors until she reached Iras. He didn't wait for her to catch her breath before turning sharply and striding toward the far end of the arena.

"Come on," he said over his shoulder, voice clipped. "We don't have time to waste."

She glanced back once at the sparring circles starting to form near the center. Weapons clashed in sharp bursts of sound, competitors parrying and lunging beneath their mentors' watchful eyes. One girl already had a dagger pressed to her opponent's throat.

"Shouldn't we be... doing that?" she asked, jogging to keep

up. "You know, teaching me how to face the others?"

Iras stopped abruptly and turned to face her, his expression unreadable. "You won't be any good in a fight if you're starving or dehydrated," he said. "Or dead because you froze to death your first night in the maze."

The words landed like a stone in her chest. "I know that," she said, folding her arms. "But—"

"No buts," he cut in, his voice dropping lower. "Everyone out there is going to focus on fighting. They'll run themselves into the ground before they even reach the real dangers waiting for them. You're going to be smarter than that."

Talah felt a flash of irritation. "Then why have me warm up with laps if we weren't going to do anything physical?"

Iras glanced back, with something that almost looked like amusement in his eyes. "I wanted to see how well you'd listen."

She bit the inside of her cheek, frustration burning in her throat. Glancing over her shoulder, she watched Mazin sparring with his mentor, sweat darkening the collar of his tunic as he swung a short sword in tight, practiced arcs. Every strike made her feel more and more behind.

Iras knelt suddenly and pointed to the dusty ground. "First things first. Fire. You're going to show me how you think you'd start one without flint. And how to hide the smoke so you don't make yourself a target."

Talah blinked at him. "What? I don't even—"

"Exactly," he said, cutting her off again. "That's why we're starting here. You'll thank me when you're not shivering to death on your first night out there."

Talah pressed her lips together and dropped to her knees, the grit of the arena floor digging into her skin. Iras crouched nearby, silent but watchful, as if he expected her to figure it all out on instinct.

"I've never done this before," she muttered, glancing at the dry twigs he'd placed in front of her. "I don't even know where to start."

"That's the point," he said simply. "You'll fail a dozen times before you get it right. Better now than when it's your life on the line."

The words stung more than she wanted to admit. Around them, the sounds of sparring rose; shouted instructions, the crash of bodies hitting the ground, the clash of steel. She couldn't stop herself from looking over her shoulder. She wanted to be over there, actually sparring with those she'd be facing in the maze—not rubbing sticks together.

"Wet or green wood produces thick white smoke. Dead, seasoned wood burns hotter and cleaner," Iras explained. "Large logs tend to smolder and create more smoke. A small, hot fire is much harder to spot. You'll want to feed it slowly. Dumping a lot of fuel on at once can smother the flames and create smoke."

She tried. And failed. And tried again. By the time a fragile spark finally caught, the sun had risen overhead, heat blazing. The tiny flame flickered to life, fragile and uncertain—just like she felt.

Iras leaned closer, smothering the fire with a sweep of sand until only the faintest thread of smoke curled up from the ashes. "Hide the signs," he said, brushing the dirt from his hands. "Or someone will follow it straight to you."

Talah stared at the smothered fire, her chest tight. She'd learned something important—she knew that. But the sound of swords clashing in the distance still echoed in her ears.

Iras stood and offered her a hand. "You did better than most would on their first try," he said, almost softly.

She took his hand and rose, brushing dirt from her knees. "I just... feel like I should be doing more," she admitted quietly.

"You will," he said softly. "But surviving the maze comes first. If you can't do that, none of the rest will matter."

FIRAS

Keeping her alive was turning out to be a lot harder than he'd thought.

Firas had thought he'd end up with another privileged Signborn kid who'd be somewhat prepared to face the maze at least. Instead, he'd gotten a girl who naively believed training herself would be enough. Stars, it was almost *insanity*.

She was leagues behind the others—a novice among warriors, a child stepping onto a battlefield she wasn't ready for. The Trials were merciless, designed to break even the strongest contenders. If the tasks themselves didn't devour her, then the competitors would.

Because here, survival wasn't just about outlasting the Trials—it was about proving you were strong enough to belong. And weakness? Weakness wasn't just preyed upon—it was completely eradicated.

He should never have defended her right to compete.

Still, he couldn't completely ignore the feelings of guilt that plagued him as he made his way toward the storage room. From everything he'd heard about the Pisces Councilor's daughter, her lack of preparation wasn't entirely her fault. But believing she could simply waltz in and compete? That was. It was bold. Reckless. A kind of audacity that teetered between bravery and sheer stupidity.

That, or ego, he thought grimly. *I still haven't decided which.*

He scrubbed a hand over his face, the heat of the morning pressing down against his skin. Every step toward that door felt heavier than the last. The scent of the training grounds still clung to him—sweat, dust, and the faint tang of blood—and it mingled with the sharper sting of guilt that refused to fade.

He should have walked away the moment he saw her. He should have kept his distance, focused on the mission. But there was something about her—the fierce defiance in her eyes, the way she stood her ground even when she was shaking—that crawled beneath his armor. She wasn't supposed to matter. She was just another piece on the Imperium's board.

And yet, the thought of her stepping into that maze without knowing what waited inside made his stomach twist. She didn't belong here—and, gods help him, a part of him respected her for coming, anyway.

Bold, he told himself again. *Not smart.*

Samira was definitely going to kill him for this. She'd given them one chance—just one. His plan to infiltrate the Trials and save unsuspecting Ambigua was a huge risk for them and for the rebellion. One slip-up, one mistake, could set them back and destroy everything they were trying to build.

He couldn't afford distraction. Especially not the kind that looked like her.

Firas knocked on the storage room door in a quick, familiar sequence—two sharp raps, a pause, then three lighter taps. A silent code, one he and Rami had used since they were kids sneaking around the markets in Jawahra.

On the other side, there was a brief hesitation, then the sound of a lock clicking open.

"Ready?" Rami murmured, stepping outside with the quiet

ease of someone who had long since learned to move unnoticed. His expression was taut, alert, though a flicker of hesitation passed over his face as he took in Firas's still-tense posture. "You look like you'd rather be fighting than sneaking into archives."

Firas exhaled sharply, running a hand through his curls. "We don't have time to waste. We only have an hour or two for the lunch break."

He didn't wait for Rami's reply. Without a word, he turned and strode down the dimly lit corridor, his movements fluid and precise. Time was slipping away.

The soldiers still patrolled, their presence a quiet reminder that Aphelion was never truly unguarded. But with so few people left on the grounds, their watchfulness had dulled—routine replacing urgency, familiarity breeding carelessness. It wasn't complete freedom, but it was enough.

Enough to get in. Enough not to get caught. And most guards wouldn't expect anything to happen during the daytime.

Firas and Rami moved quickly, their boots soundless against the polished stone floors as they moved in tandem. They couldn't afford hesitation. Every second wasted increased their chances of getting caught, and getting caught meant more than expulsion.

It meant exposure—and exposure meant death.

The library stood at the opposite end of the ziggurat, a sprawling architectural marvel that whispered of ancient grandeur and scholarly reverence. It was a place that seemed to belong to another time, its stone façade intricately carved with calligraphic inscriptions, each delicate curve of script honoring wisdom, knowledge, and the unyielding pursuit of truth.

The entrance alone was a testament to the university's craftsmanship—a towering horseshoe arch, rimmed with geometric tile work in deep cobalt and gold, forming constellations that seemed to shift under the flickering torchlight. Above the arch, a muqarnas ceiling, a honeycomb of carved niches, cascaded downward like a frozen waterfall of stone, each crevice casting shadow and depth, as if the very architecture guarded the secrets within.

Inside, the library opened into a vast hall, its ceiling soaring high into the darkness, upheld by rows of slender marble columns, their capitals adorned with intricate arabesque patterns. Ornate wooden mashrabiya screens covered the upper levels, allowing filtered sunlight to stream in during the day, casting latticed shadows onto the polished floors. Firas paused just inside the threshold, his breath catching for reasons that had nothing to do with the chill air. The grandeur pressed down on him like a physical weight. A reminder that he didn't belong here. Not really.

The floor itself was a mosaic masterpiece, depicting celestial constellations and forgotten maps, outlined in lapis lazuli and mother-of-pearl inlays. The centerpiece—a circular fountain of carved alabaster—sat in the middle of the room, its water flowing in a silent, endless cycle, the gentle trickling sound a melody against the hush of the library. He stopped by the fountain's edge, running his gloved fingers along the rim. The water was cool, startlingly pure. He wondered how many years it had flowed like this—uninterrupted, unbothered by the chaos outside these walls. *Everything in Aphelion endures,* he thought bitterly. *Everything but the people who serve it.*

Lining the walls were towering wooden bookshelves, dark cedar and walnut carved with sacred verses, their edges gilded in gold leaf. The books—ancient tomes bound in leather and silk, their spines embossed with gold calligraphy—rested behind delicate brass lattice doors, locked to all but the scholars who had earned the right to their knowledge. He caught sight of the locks and felt the familiar sting of resentment. All that knowledge—hidden behind barriers and titles, guarded from the people who actually needed it. How many lives might have been spared if the Council's truths weren't buried under so much gold and secrecy?

Above, wooden balconies curled along the perimeter of the chamber, supported by slender columns, giving scholars an elevated view of the vast collection below. Small hanging lanterns, crafted from colored glass and brass filigree, dangled from the high ceiling, their dim light casting warm amber glows across the parchment-covered desks and scroll-laden alcoves.

There were hidden reading nooks, tucked into arched recesses in the walls, where ancient scholars had once lost themselves in their studies. The scent of aged parchment, spiced ink, and old cedar filled the air, mingling with the faint traces of sandalwood incense still lingering in the stone. It should have felt sacred. It only felt heavy.

This is what they protect, he thought. *While people starve in the outer provinces, this is what they build to worship their own brilliance.*

But deeper still—beneath the library, past hidden doors and winding staircases—lay the restricted archives.

They slipped between the unattended stacks, their shelves ladened with tomes and scrolls, books from all over the world. It didn't take them long to reach the first checkpoint: a long, winding staircase leading to the lower levels, where the real secrets of Aphelion were buried. The air grew colder here, the scent of parchment and aged stone thick in the silence.

At the end of the hall, two guards stood at their post, arms folded, expressions lax but alert.

Firas pressed a hand to Rami's chest, signaling him to stop.

"We can't fight them," Rami whispered, barely a breath of sound. Firas nearly rolled his eyes at the obviousness of the statement.

"We won't have to," Firas murmured back.

Closing his eyes, he reached outward, feeling for the sharp edges of the guards' thoughts. His mind brushed against theirs—two distinct pulses of awareness, flickering with the sluggish boredom of an uneventful shift.

It was all he needed.

You're tired.

The suggestion slithered through the space between them, invisible but insidious.

You've been standing here for hours. Your limbs are heavy. Your thoughts are slow. Just for a moment, close your eyes…

One of the guards shifted, rolling his shoulders. His

companion let out a quiet sigh, rubbing a hand over his face.

"I hate this shift," the first one muttered.

The second one barely responded—his eyelids drooped, his posture slumping slightly against the wall. Firas pressed harder, weaving the exhaustion deeper into his mind.

Just a little rest. Just for a moment.

The guard blinked heavily. His stance loosened, fingers twitching as if his body was seconds from giving in. Firas thanked the stars that neither of them happened to be Scorpios. Or this would have been a hell of a lot harder to pull off. Then again, the Imperium wouldn't have wasted a Scorpio's ability on guarding a door.

The first guard stiffened slightly, his head tilting as if something didn't quite sit right.

Firas held his breath, pushing harder.

The guard's head nodded forward before his body relaxed against the wall. Both bodies slowly slid to the floor.

Rami snorted softly. "They deserve a raise."

Firas shook his head, starting for the door the two useless guards had been protecting.

The entrance to the restricted archives was hidden behind a thick iron-bound door and sealed with a mechanism designed to keep out even the most persistent intruders.

But they hadn't come across a lock they couldn't pick.

Rami immediately dropped to one knee, pulling a small set of tools from within his tunic. He set to work, his fingers moving swiftly, eyes narrowing in deep concentration.

"This is almost too easy," Rami muttered.

"No one's ever tried to break into the archives before because nobody believed they needed to," Firas noted dryly, though his words were laced with tension. "Why would they? When you've been conditioned never to question the councilors and their word?"

According to the Zodiacs, the history books were complete. The public records were transparent. The councilors were just.

That was the illusion the Imperium had woven into the

fabric of Aphelion, stitched into every lesson taught in the academy, every document carefully curated for public access. The archives were restricted, yes—but only to protect the sanctity of knowledge, or so the Council claimed. Not to hide the truth, but to preserve it. To shield the masses from dangerous misinformation, from unstable and unverified histories that could lead to unrest.

And the people believed them. Because why would they lie? Why question what had always been? And that was the brilliance of it. The greatest way to keep a secret was to convince the world there was nothing to hide.

Firas had seen the cracks in that illusion firsthand. He'd walked through villages erased from the maps hanging in the Council chambers. He'd seen Ambigua children taken from their homes. He'd smuggled ledgers and scrolls out of burned storehouses—records that didn't match the histories every student was forced to memorize.

He clenched his jaw, forcing his hands to stay still as he passed a wall of gold-lettered tomes. *Sanctity of knowledge*, they called it. But he'd seen what the Imperium did to those who dared to speak truths that didn't fit their version of history. He'd buried the ones who tried.

It wasn't preservation. It was control. Beautiful, gilded control—knowledge locked away so only the right people could wield it. That was what drove him here, beneath the marble and stained glass—to see it for himself. To find proof of what they'd buried. Proof of what they'd done.

His gaze lifted toward the darkness of the lower level ahead. The air down here smelled different—older, untouched by the incense and polish above. He could almost feel the weight of what was hidden pressing up from the stone, as if the truth itself was waiting for someone reckless enough to dig it out.

And maybe, for all his careful planning, that was exactly what he'd become.

"How long?" Firas whispered.

Rami didn't answer at first, his fingers working with a delicate precision that belied the urgency of the moment.

Finally, a soft click echoed in the silence. Firas and Rami shared a glance before Rami eased the heavy door inward, revealing a narrow stone staircase spiraling downward into darkness. The air shifted immediately—colder, heavier. The door groaned slightly as they slipped inside, but Rami caught it, pushing it closed without a sound. No hesitation. No turning back.

Firas moved first, stepping onto the worn stone steps, his senses flaring as they descended. Unlike the grandeur of the main library above—with its gold-leafed shelves and celestial mosaics—the archives beneath Aphelion were carved from the bones of the ancient building itself, the walls rough-hewn stone, the ceiling low and oppressive.

The flickering glow of brass lanterns lined the walls at irregular intervals, casting warped shadows that danced like specters. There was no sound but the whisper of their footsteps against the cold floor. Firas exhaled through his nose, steadying himself. He had studied the blueprints of Aphelion for months, traced its corridors in his mind over and over—but maps meant nothing when you were inside the belly of the beast.

At the bottom of the staircase, the hallway split in three directions. Firas froze, going over the map in his mind. And that's when they heard it—voices. Faint, distant, but approaching fast.

Rami turned to him, voice tight. "We don't have time to get lost."

Firas silenced his frustration. He needed to think. The records they needed would be in the deepest section—the oldest part of the archives, hidden within the foundation of the library itself. His gaze flicked toward the corridor on the right, where the floor sloped downward ever so slightly.

"There."

Firas grabbed Rami's sleeve and yanked him left, disappearing into the nearest corridor just as the echoes of boots carried down the stairwell. It almost felt like the good old days, when they'd just been kids avoiding his father's guards as they ran through the villa.

They moved swiftly, weaving through the maze-like halls, their fingers trailing against the rough stone in case they needed to double back. Then, at last, they found it. A final set of doors, flanked by two towering stone pillars, carved with inscriptions so weathered and worn that even the torchlight struggled to bring them to life. The doors themselves were massive slabs of blackened wood, bound in iron, their surface marked with sigils.

The old language.

Firas knew enough to recognize its meaning—barrier, knowledge, sacrifice. The Imperium never just hid knowledge. They buried it. Rami wasted no time, kneeling before the secondary lock, his fingers working swiftly to undo the final obstacle between them and the truth. Firas stood guard, every muscle taut with unease.

Something about this place felt wrong. Not just hidden. Dead. The silence here was absolute. No dripping water. No scurrying rats. Nothing. Like even time had been swallowed whole.

Click.

Rami exhaled in triumph. "Got it."

He pushed the door open, and the scent of decay and parchment long undisturbed rushed over them.

FIRAS
XI

Firas stepped inside first, his eyes adjusting to the deep, cavernous chamber.

The air was thick—damp with time itself, heavy with the weight of knowledge that had been sealed away for centuries.

There were no shelves. No meticulously cataloged records or neatly arranged tomes.

Instead, chaos.

The chamber was a graveyard of knowledge—stone tablets cracked and crumbling, scrolls half-unraveled in forgotten corners, leather-bound books stacked haphazardly atop one another, their spines splitting from age. Some had rotted away entirely, reduced to dust on the cold stone floor. Others remained eerily intact, their bindings still strong, as if time had simply refused to touch them.

A forgotten burial site of history.

Firas stepped carefully between the wreckage, the air thick with the dry scent of parchment and ash. His fingertips brushed across the nearest table, leaving trails in centuries of dust.

The silence felt heavier here, oppressive, as if the room itself resented being disturbed.

He swallowed hard. Once, these had been voices—hundreds of them—recording the truth of their world before the Imperium rewrote it. How many lives had been spent to carve these symbols, to preserve what mattered, only for it to be sealed underground and left to rot?

This is what they fear, he thought. *Not rebellion. Not even death. They fear remembering.*

Rami let out a low breath, barely above a whisper. "This…" His fingers brushed against the spine of an ancient book, the lettering faded beyond recognition. He swallowed. "They weren't just hiding this knowledge. They were erasing it."

Firas crouched beside a pile of tablets, running his fingers over the engravings. The text was archaic, almost unreadable, but he recognized enough to feel the tension coil in his chest. Names. Dates. Mentions of people and places that no longer existed.

His voice echoed against the cold stone walls, swallowed quickly by the vast chamber of forgotten knowledge.

He had been fighting with the Ambigua rebellion for two years now. Planned. Strategized. Fought. Slowly gaining the trust of Samira and Rafiq, their leaders, just to run missions like this. He'd learned all he could about what was really going on. But the truth?

They knew nothing.

Not really.

Everything they understood about who they were, what they were, had come in fragments. Pieces gathered from those like them—people who had lived in fear, in secrecy, who had discovered their abilities through accidents or suffering, through exile or near-death. They shared experiences, exchanged whispered theories, but there were no records. No teachings. No histories.

Even their name—Ambigua—had been given to them by the Imperium, not by themselves.

A curse, not an identity.

Samira preached that the Imperium had taken their origins, their legacy, and buried it so deeply that even those who carried the power had no idea where it came from. That was why they were here.

They needed answers.

Rami had already moved to a pile of half-crumbling scrolls, his fingers skimming across the fragile parchment. "We don't even know what we're looking for," he muttered, frustration lacing his words.

Firas ignored him, stepping toward a low stone table, half-covered in shattered tablets, ink-stained manuscripts, and a book so old that its leather binding had cracked along the edges. He traced a hand over the dust-caked lettering, his pulse quickening when he saw a familiar phrase—

A power beyond the stars—one that bends, shifts, and defies the constellations themselves.

His breath hitched. It was the closest thing to a definition he had ever seen.

"Rami," he called, his voice sharper now. "Here."

Rami abandoned the scrolls and hurried over as Firas carefully flipped open the brittle pages.

They scanned the text, eyes devouring the words, but frustration curled in Firas's stomach as he realized that even this was incomplete—torn pages, ink smudges, deliberate redactions.

A deviation from the Zodiac path, neither bound nor aligned. The Imperium sought to eradicate such chaos, for to exist outside the constellations was to exist beyond their control…

Firas's hands tightened around the edges of the book.

They already knew the Imperium feared them. Hunted them. But this confirmed what he had always suspected. The Imperium had been studying them…

And then, they had tried to erase them.

"They're trying to wipe it all out," Rami murmured, his expression darkening. "Everything. We're not just missing records. We're missing an entire piece of history."

Firas clenched his jaw.

The Ambigua hadn't always been a disorder to be corrected, a sickness to be purged. They had been something once. Something the Imperium had seen as a threat so great that they erased even the memory of it.

His mind flashed to the rebels—the people who depended on him for answers he didn't have yet. The ones who had joined this fight because they were willing to fight back, to search for hope, even if that hope was built on sand. If they had ever stood a chance of changing things, of surviving—then this was the key.

But it wasn't enough.

He slammed the book shut and shoved it aside, his pulse thudding harder now. "Keep looking."

They needed more. Something that told them where they had come from, what their abilities meant, why they were hunted so viciously. Something that showed they weren't the abominations everyone believed them to be. Because right now, all they had were questions.

And questions weren't enough to win a war.

Firas was about to turn away when a glint caught his eye. At the center of the room stood a pedestal of obsidian, smooth and polished, utterly untouched by the decay surrounding it. A single journal rested atop it. Unlike the other books, it was pristine—as if it had been placed there recently, or perhaps, preserved deliberately. The cover was dark leather, supple with age, but unmarked by time.

Firas's pulse kicked up.

He stepped forward, drawn toward it, his fingers hovering just above the book's surface before finally pressing against it. The second he touched it, he felt a chill roll down his spine. He lifted it carefully, his hands sure but reverent, as if the weight of the secrets within had already settled onto his shoulders. It was old—far older than anything else in the chamber.

But it was the cover that made his breath catch.

Embossed in faint gold script was a sigil he had never seen before.

A constellation, twisted and fragmented, interwoven with a symbol that sent ice lancing down his spine. A symbol that had been erased from history. It was shaped like an oval, cut in half, a wave crossing its center. A thirteenth Sign.

This was it. This was proof.

He could feel the tension in Rami beside him, his breath shallow as he peered over Firas's shoulder.

"This isn't a history text," Rami muttered. "It's personal. A journal of some sort. Someone wrote this." He glanced back toward the door, nervous. "We have to go."

Firas forced himself to move, shoving the journal inside his tunic and securing it against his chest. But before they could turn back, his gaze flickered over the scattered wreckage of knowledge around them. There was more here. More they couldn't leave behind.

"Grab whatever you can carry," he ordered, voice taut with urgency.

Rami shot him a look. "We're already risking too much."

"We might not get another chance."

Rami muttered a curse under his breath but didn't argue. Time was slipping through their fingers like sand, but if they left with only one book, it wouldn't be enough.

They moved fast, sifting through half-crumbling scrolls, brittle parchment, and forgotten ledgers in search of anything still intact.

Firas grabbed a bundle of scrolls wrapped in deteriorating silk, the edges barely holding together. His fingers skimmed the wax seal on one—an unfamiliar sigil, but one that didn't belong to the Imperium. A lost province? A hidden faction? He didn't know, but if it had been locked away down here, it meant something.

"Who's there?"

The voice snapped through the air, freezing them in place.

Firas whipped around, heart hammering, just as footsteps pounded from the hallway. A distant clang rang through the corridors, followed by the unmistakable scrape of a sword being unsheathed.

Firas reacted instantly, spinning toward Rami. "Move."

They ran.

The chamber blurred behind them as they tore through the maze of the archives, dodging fallen manuscripts and shattered remnants of history. The moment they burst back into the hallway, they heard a shout from behind them.

"Intruders!"

Firas gritted his teeth, pushing himself faster as they rounded the first corridor, taking a sharp turn down a narrow passage. A flash of movement in his peripheral vision—a guard turning the corner behind them.

Too close.

He reached out without thinking, his mind gripping the edges of the guard's thoughts—pushing, twisting.

You saw nothing. No one was here. This hallway is empty.

The guard stumbled, his body jerking like a puppet whose strings had been abruptly severed. Confusion twisted across his face. His grip on his weapon slackened. Firas couldn't control minds. Not entirely. But he could persuade them... if they were weak enough.

Firas yanked Rami forward, using the smallest window of distraction to put distance between them. They sprinted toward the staircase, taking the steps two at a time. Firas's lungs burned, the journal pressing hard against his ribs.

They crashed through the upper level, back into the grand halls of the main library. The moment they emerged into the towering space, Firas barely had time to register movement ahead.

Two more guards.

Rami grabbed his wrist. "Left!"

They darted into an alcove, slipping between rows of towering shelves. The scent of parchment and burning lantern oil wrapped around them. Footsteps thundered past. Firas pressed himself against the cold marble pillar, his breath locked in his throat. Rami did the same, clutching the stolen records against his chest.

A moment stretched.

Two.

The footsteps faded.

Rami glanced at him, eyes flashing. "We need to get back to the storage room."

Firas nodded, letting out a slow breath, already moving. The guards would sweep the area soon. They needed to disappear before that happened.

They slipped out of the library unnoticed, vanishing into the quieter halls of the university. By the time they reached the storage room, Firas's hands were still trembling from the rush. He knocked in a quick, familiar sequence—two sharp raps, a pause, then three lighter taps. The lock turned, the door cracking open.

Kam's dark eyes met his first, sharp and unreadable. Raven stood just behind her, arms folded. Neither spoke as they stepped inside. Firas finally exhaled, his grip loosening on the journal just slightly.

Then, he looked up, meeting Kam's gaze again.

She lifted an eyebrow. "Well?"

Firas pulled the journal from his tunic, the gold-embossed Sign catching the dim light. Kam's expression shifted.

Raven leaned forward, eyes narrowing. "What is that?"

Firas swallowed, the weight of the stolen knowledge settling over him.

"Proof," he said. "Hopefully."

Silence hung in the storage room, thick and heavy. The dim lantern cast flickering shadows against the stone walls, but it wasn't enough to dull the sharp tension settling between them.

"I just don't understand something," Rami said, studying the scrolls and papers he'd grabbed. "If they wanted to erase us completely, why keep these around? Why keep them here of all places? Why not just burn them?"

"Maybe they just hadn't gotten around to it yet," Raven scoffed. "Why does it matter?"

"Because I think it means something," Rami replied slowly. "Even if these are in a bad state, they kept them for a reason. Which means they're important. Whether these hold important information they needed to know about us, or... something."

"Makes sense," Kam said. "They care enough to learn from them, but not enough to take care of them. Then there's definitely got to be something we can use in these."

Firas placed the journal on the wooden crate beside him, but his mind was still racing, still back in that archive, still flipping through the words that had changed everything.

Kam was the first to break the silence.

"There are more of us."

Firas's head snapped up, his exhaustion momentarily forgotten.

Kam crossed her arms, leaning against the opposite wall. "Raven and I saw at least two others during training. I don't think they know what they are—not yet—but we saw it."

Rami straightened, his expression darkening. "You're sure?"

Raven nodded. "They slipped up, just barely. Small things—too small for their mentors or the other competitors to notice. But we did."

Firas sat back, exhaling slowly. Two more. Two more Ambigua hidden in plain sight. And they had no idea what they were. How they'd gone so long without knowing, he didn't know. But that was how it always was—not ignorance, but refusal.

People knew about the Ambigua. They whispered about them, feared them, spread stories of cursed bloodlines and dangerous powers. But to consider that they might be one? That the oddities in their own lives—the inexplicable moments, the flickers of power they couldn't explain—might mean they were the very thing they had been taught to fear?

That was too much. Especially with one of them being a Signborn—probably from one of the elite families as well. He would have grown up hating Ambigua, fed the endless propaganda they all were. So they ignored it. Looked the other way. Convinced themselves that what they had seen, what they had felt, was just a trick of the mind.

Because believing meant admitting the truth.

And the truth was dangerous.

Rami swore under his breath. "The Imperium is watching these Trials closer than ever. If they slip up again—"

"They're dead," Raven finished bluntly.

Quiet settled over them, the weight of that truth pressing against them all.

Firas knew what they had to do. They couldn't let these two get discovered. But before he could voice that thought, Kam's gaze hardened, and she took a step closer.

"And speaking of getting killed," she said, her voice like tempered steel, "let's talk about how you spent the entire training time to teach Talah how to light a measly fire."

"You and I both know it's important to know those skills," he said flatly, though even as the words left his mouth, they felt hollow.

Kam let out a sharp, humorless laugh. "A fire won't do much if she can't hold her own against the other opponents. She'll be dead before she can even light one."

Raven raised an eyebrow but said nothing, watching the exchange like a predator waiting to see how the fight would play out.

Firas straightened. "She has to learn some things on her own. She can't just expect to show up here and have everything handed to her."

Kam's eyes narrowed. "At what cost?"

Silence.

She took another step forward, her voice quieter but no less sharp. "If she gets killed, you get sent away. And we lose one more person on the inside to help us. Our plan would be that much more complicated if you're gone."

Firas knew that. He had known it the second he had walked away from Talah today, but hearing it aloud made it feel heavier.

He clenched his fists. "I'm not going to let her die."

The words were plain, practical. He left the rest of it—why

he could not bear the thought of her dead—unsaid. He could feel it, though: a small, hot fist of panic that tightened whenever he imagined her alone in that ring, eyes wide, reaching for something she couldn't name. That fist pulsed under his ribs like a second heartbeat.

Kam scoffed. "Is that so? You let her look weak in front of people who already see her as easy prey today. You think that makes her stronger? It doesn't. It makes her dead."

Firas's jaw tightened, frustration curling in his chest. "She needs to be prepared. If we coddle her, she'll never survive the Trials, Kam. You know that as well as I do."

Kam's expression didn't change. "What I know," she said coolly, "is that you're thinking like a soldier, not a competitor."

Firas stiffened.

Kam held his gaze, unwavering. "You think throwing her into the fire will make her stronger. Maybe it will. But not if she burns before she gets the chance to fight."

Silence stretched between them, thick and suffocating.

Kam didn't flinch. "You don't have to like her. You don't even have to trust her. But if she goes down, we all go down. So start acting like it. Train her to fight the others and teach her the survival skills outside of training times."

Firas wanted to argue. Wanted to push back, to tell Kam that he knew what he was doing, that he was preparing Talah for what was coming.

But he didn't.

Because she was right.

And that was the worst part.

Her words pressed on something raw and private—his longing to fix, to shield, to be the thing that makes other people's fear go away. He felt it then: how personal all of this had become, how much of his calm was a bargain he'd made with himself to keep from being consumed. He stiffened, because admitting any of that would make him soft where he needed to be sharp, exposed where he needed to be a blade. He drew a breath and let it out with the sound of someone bracing for a blow, not with the confession he almost wanted to make.

His shoulders dropped slightly, but he didn't speak. Kam studied him for a moment longer, then finally stepped back, folding her arms.

"Good," she said simply. "Now that we're clear on that, we need to figure out what we're going to do about these two new Ambigua before the Imperium finds them first."

Firas exhaled, shoving a hand through his hair. "We need to watch them first. See if they realize what they are. If they don't, we move before the Imperium does."

Rami nodded, but his expression was still grim. "We don't have much time."

Firas looked at the journal sitting on the crate beside him.

No, they didn't.

Because if they had learned anything tonight, it was that the Imperium didn't just want the Ambigua dead.

They wanted them forgotten.

And Firas would be damned if he let that happen.

T A L A H
XII

A ripple of silence spread through the mess hall as Talah entered, broken only by the low hum of whispered curiosity. Forks paused mid-air, conversations slowed, and more than a few eyes tracked her every move as she crossed the threshold. She could feel it all. The curiosity…the judgment. It hung in the air like humidity before a storm.

The mess hall sat at the heart of the student dormitories, a central artery in the living pulse of campus life. Towering archways framed its entrances on all four sides, allowing the midday sun to spill through and cast soft light across long communal tables of polished stone. High ceilings stretched above with open latticework, allowing a breeze to drift through and stir the fragrant mix of roasted spices, fresh bread, and charred meats.

It was nearly as big as the Great Hall, and could probably hold just as much. Yet, without Aphelion's students to take up room along their narrowed benches, it felt empty. Talah noted how the competitors had already separated into different groups, each taking up their own space throughout the hall. There were around forty-four of them this year—clean, balanced. Easy to whittle down over time.

It hadn't even been a full day, and already the lines had been drawn.

Talah scanned the room as she walked toward the buffet at the other end, seeing it for what it really was. Not just a gathering of competitors, but a map of loyalties and quiet divides. The Signborns had staked their claims early, clustered at the far tables beneath hanging lanterns and banners stitched with gold. They lounged with practiced ease, their laughter low and unbothered, as if they already owned the space.

She recognized a few of them—familiar faces from the rare times they'd visit Jawahra with their families on business with her father. Aarif El-Najjar, son of a prominent Leo family, still carried that same sharp grin and even sharper arrogance. Soraya Basara, a Virgo, sat straight-backed and severe, her dark eyes scanning the room like she was cataloging weaknesses. Talah caught the eye of Nadir, grandson of the Libra Councilor. He did a good job of hiding his sharp ambition beneath a courteous smile, giving her a slight nod. Raised under Saahira's shadow, Talah assumed he viewed the Trials as a proving ground to secure his grandmother's approval.

And then there was Rayen Al-Dahhak.

Heir to the most feared Aries bloodline. He sat at the center of the table, arms slung over the back of his chair as if he owned the hall itself. His eyes were already on her—assessing. Amused. Talah hadn't known him personally, but she knew of his family. They were etched into her memory like a warning: the lot of them were ruthless, ambitious, and bred for this thing. The Al-Dahhaks had built their legacy on providing the Imperium with soldiers for generations.

And Rayen looked every bit the part.

"Tal." Mazin's voice pulled her from her thoughts. He'd stepped into line behind her, offering a quiet presence against the rising buzz of the mess hall.

"Hey," she said, voice low. After their morning training session, she'd gone straight back to the dorms, craving space from the other competitors. From the stares. The whispers. She'd worried about running into Adine—worried about what she might say, or worse, what she wouldn't. But Adine hadn't returned, and Talah had been left with her own torturous thoughts for the past few hours.

Her roommate was here, however, already at a table with a few others Talah didn't recognize besides Zayd. Adine waved her over, patting the empty seat beside her.

"How was your training?" Mazin asked, keeping his voice just above a whisper. "Were you... making fire?" He tried to keep his tone even, but she heard his unspoken concern, anyway.

Talah let out a sharp breath, turning away from Adine. The thought had been circling her head all morning about whether her so-called mentor would even bother to actually train her. They only had five days before the Trials began. Not even a week to prepare for something designed to break them.

To kill them.

Her fingers twitched at her sides, the ghost of heat prickling along her palms. Every time she thought of the arena—of standing there with the world watching—her pulse stuttered in her throat.

"He says it's important to learn," she admitted. "But being able to light a fire won't matter if I'm dead before nightfall."

The words came out sharper than she meant them to. She could hear the bitterness in them, could feel it clawing up her throat. Because what she didn't say—what she couldn't—was that she wanted Firas to care enough to push her. To see her as more than a liability or a fragile thing to be handled carefully. He talked about patience, about control, about *understanding the flame*. But she didn't need philosophy. She needed to *survive*.

And yet... when he looked at her with that steady calm, when his voice softened and he said her name like it meant something—

Her anger splintered into something else. Something she

didn't know how to name without breaking.

Maybe he was right. Maybe she *wasn't* ready. Maybe she never would be.

The thought made her chest tighten, her breath catch. She hated how much she cared about what he thought—how the memory of his gaze lingered, heavy and unreadable, long after he left the room.

"He says it's important to learn," she repeated more quietly, mostly to herself this time. "But what's the point of learning to control something if the Imperium plans to use it to destroy me anyway?"

They grabbed their food, each tray heaped with steaming saffron rice, roasted lamb rubbed in deep spice, and golden rounds of kofta, still warm from the griddle. The flatbread crackled at the edges but remained soft at the center, perfect for scooping up the tangy eggplant stew ladled beside spiced lentils. Bowls of pickled vegetables—crisp, sharp, and sour—lined the end of the buffet, along with dates glazed in honey and sprinkled with sesame.

Talah moved automatically, the familiar scents stirring an ache low in her chest. Jawahra's food had tasted similar, but never quite the same. It lacked the weight of ceremony, of joy. Here, everything—even the meals—felt like strategy.

As they made their way toward Adine's table, a few heads turned in their direction—whispers rising just enough to reach her ears before vanishing back into the hum of conversation.

"She's the one they had to vote on, right?"

"No training, no experience. Just a name."

"She thinks her daddy's title makes her special."

"More like easy prey."

Talah kept her head high, jaw tight. She didn't look at them. She didn't have to.

Rayen's voice, loud and clear, cut through the room like a drawn blade.

"Careful," he drawled from his place among the Signborns, lazy amusement curling around every word. "You wouldn't want to scare her off before the Trials even begin." Those around him snickered, and those less bold froze to listen in.

Talah halted in her tracks, fingers tightening around the tray in her hands. Her gaze found his across the wooden table.

Rayen continued. "Unless that glare is your strategy for winning, by all means—carry on."

"Ignore him," Mazin muttered, shifting beside her. "It's not worth it."

Except it was. Not just because of Rayen. Not really. It was *everything else* that mattered. The weight of every eye waiting to see if she would fold or raise the stakes. To see if she would prove the whispers right—that she was too weak to be here. Too pampered. Too protected.

Talah let her tray fall to the table, the food scattering, forgotten for the moment.

Rayen straightened ever so slightly in his seat, amused interest sharpening into something closer to a challenge.

"If you underestimate me this much, you'll have a rude awakening when it truly matters," Talah replied evenly.

His chair screeched back, legs scraping against the stone floor as he stepped around the table, sizing her up. "Is that a threat?"

"That's a promise."

The tension thickened around them. Rayen stood there, frozen for a moment, assessing.

His lips slowly slid into a smirk. "If all your father taught you were clever comebacks... I don't think I'll have anything to worry about."

Her fist caught him off guard, a clean strike to the ribs that knocked the breath from his smug laugh. He recovered quickly, retaliating with the speed of someone who'd been taught how to fight before he could walk. Those at the tables around them scattered as competitors jumped to their feet. From the far end of the room, the mentors rose. A few watched with interest. Others exchanged glances but made no move to stop it.

Rayen lunged, but Talah dodged, grabbing his arm and using

his momentum to shove him sideways into the edge of the table. Trays clattered. A few gasps echoed through the hall. He caught himself, eyes lit with something hotter than amusement now. Pure hatred radiated from him in waves.

As an Aries, he had strength. But not speed. Not control. He fought like a hammer—loud, relentless, and unyielding. He swung again, wide and aggressive.

She ducked low, pivoted on her heel, and swept his legs—not to knock him down, but to shift his balance just enough. As he stumbled, she rose and pressed forward, not with brute force, but precision. A feint with her left. A sharp elbow to the ribs. She wasn't trying to overpower him—she was dismantling him, piece by piece. He growled under his breath and lunged again, this time faster, more reckless.

Which was exactly what she was waiting for.

She baited him—stepping back just enough, drawing him into overextending again—and when he did, she hooked his wrist and twisted, forcing him off balance a second time. His foot slipped, skidding across the polished floor, and he crashed into a bench, cursing under his breath.

Talah didn't press the advantage. She straightened, breath steady, watching him with that same unreadable expression she'd worn when she walked in. Rayen rose slowly, a furious smile curving his lips. He wasn't used to being outmaneuvered. And definitely not by someone who never needed to throw a single drop of power to do it.

"*Enough.*"

The command sliced through the hall like an arrow.

Talah hadn't seen Iras come into the mess hall, but she was fully aware of him now. He stepped forward, every movement deliberate. The crowd parted for him instinctively, the buzz of whispers shrinking to a breathless hush.

Rayen straightened slowly, rolling his shoulders with deliberate nonchalance, like he was shaking off an inconvenience rather than the humiliation of being outmatched. Talah noted the tightness of his jaw and curled fists, however.

Iras came to a stop between them, his gaze passing over Rayen first. Silent. Stony.

"Save it for the Trials," he sneered, voice cold as ice. "You're going to need it."

Rayen let out a short, humorless breath, then ran a hand through his hair, forcing a grin. "Just warming up," he muttered. With one last heated glare at Talah, he stalked back to his table without another word.

Her mentor's gaze landed on her, cool and unreadable—until the faintest flicker of derision cut through, as if her little display had confirmed exactly what he'd expected: reckless, emotional, untrained. For a moment, he said nothing—just studied her, gaze flicking from the tension still in her shoulders to the faint tremor in her fingers she tried to hide. His expression didn't change, but something passed through his eyes: not approval, not quite concern. Something murkier. More careful.

"What exactly did that prove?" Iras asked, his voice low.

Talah lifted her chin, gaze steady. "Exactly what I needed it to."

She expected him to argue, to mock her for her defiance, but instead his lips pressed into a thin, unreadable line. His silence scraped against her nerves like sand against glass. "I misjudged you earlier, Aasifati."

She hesitated. "What?"

"I'll see you at the arena in two hours. We need to work on your form if you're going to fight anyone." His eyes cut briefly to where Rayen sat, nursing his pride. "And next time, try winning without the dramatics."

Talah watched him head back to the mentor table, slipping into a seat beside Kamaria.

Zayd let out a low whistle as she slid into the seat beside Adine. "Well," he said, grinning as he speared a chunk of kofta with his fork, "that was subtle."

"Not everything has to be subtle," Talah muttered, trying to ignore the sting in her knuckles.

"It does when you're trying not to paint a giant target on

your back," Zayd replied, chewing thoughtfully. He gestured vaguely with his fork. "First your dad… now this."

Mazin leaned forward, tone sharper. "You're lucky he didn't hurt you," he said. "You can't afford any injuries with the Trials starting in just a few days."

Talah dropped her gaze to her tray. The sting in her knuckles pulsed in time with her heart. "If I'm lucky," she muttered, "then this will show the others they can't mess with me during the Trials."

Zayd made a noncommittal noise and leaned sideways to peer around her. "I don't know about that," he said, casting a sidelong glance at Rayen's table. "That guy's face is screaming 'I'm plotting something petty.' Like, I-wouldn't-be-surprised-if-your-pillow-catches-fire-tonight petty."

"He could try," Talah said, a bit more forcefully than she meant to. "But he'd regret it."

Adine, who had been silently pushing the pickled vegetables around her tray, finally stilled. Her fingers released the spoon, and she glanced up. Her face was neutral, unreadable as ever, but something sharp flickered in her gaze.

"You could've picked a better time to show off," she said simply.

Talah stiffened. "You think I was wrong?"

"I think," Adine said calmly, "you gave them a show. One they'll be dissecting for the rest of the day. But they aren't the ones you need to be memorable for. You should save it for the spectators during training. You might need their bids."

Her tone wasn't cruel—just honest.

"Still," she added, "that last move? That was impressive for someone who hadn't specifically been training for the Trials their entire life."

Talah blinked, surprised by the shift in tone. "Thanks."

Adine gave a small shrug, eyes already returning to her tray. "Don't get used to it."

Zayd leaned toward Mazin and mock-whispered, "That was, like, a full compliment. Should we celebrate or…?"

Adine didn't look up, but the faintest twitch at the corner of her mouth betrayed her amusement.

"Well, one thing's for sure," Mazin said, rubbing the back of his neck. "If they weren't watching you before... they are now."

Zayd raised his cup in a dramatic toast. "To terrifying first impressions."

Talah let out a soft laugh—small, real, and unexpected. The knots in her chest loosened just a little.

"To surviving them."

TALAH
XIII

By the second day of training, every muscle in Talah's body screamed in protest.

Exhaustion hung over them like a second skin, but no one dared be the first to admit it—not when the others were still pushing forward. Mazin groaned beside her as they sat in the sand of the arena, their backs against the stone wall.

"If I don't survive the Trials, it'll be because my body just gives up out of spite," he mumbled, head tilted back as the afternoon sun beat down.

Zayd snorted, his dark hair plastered to his forehead with sweat. "You'd actually have to move fast enough to be in danger of that happening."

Mazin scowled, lifting a hand. A shimmering ripple of illusion coiled in the air between them, briefly taking the shape of Zayd tripping over his own feet. The image collapsed almost as soon as it formed, too weak to hold.

"Maybe you should conserve whatever energy you have left," Adine said, giving a short, sharp-edged laugh.

"Mock me all you want," Mazin muttered, rubbing his temples, "but when the time comes, you'll all be eating your words."

Despite herself, Talah smiled. The ache in her arms, the burn in her lungs—it all felt lighter with their voices circling her, teasing each other as if they weren't all being broken down piece by piece. Sure, she'd just met them the day before, but it didn't feel that way. Their small group had fallen into an easy alliance, something that felt all too natural despite their predicament.

Still, when the mentors barked for them to line up again, the laughter died quick enough. Talah hesitated before taking Mazin's hand as they stood, struggling to their feet. Her eyes darted over the stands, skipping over those who had come from the city to watch them train and landing on the councilors. Only three showed up today, standing above everyone else in their private box. Saahira, Musa, and Asad, the Aries councilor.

Talah was about to join the others when she caught sight of a fourth person. He was dressed in black, his dark hair falling in waves to brush his shoulders. There was something about him... something in the way he moved, in the way he held himself, that seemed familiar.

"Who is that?" Talah asked quietly, leaning against Mazin.

He followed her line of sight before answering. "That's Kamal Soulinus."

"The Kaed." It wasn't a question. She'd heard of him, though she'd never actually met him before.

His title preceded him. General of the entire military, the Kaed was known to be ruthless. Born into one of the oldest Signborn lines, he had inherited command as though it were his birthright, the position passed down like a crown. Yet his cruelty was not dulled by privilege—only sharpened. To the Imperium, he was unshakable order. To those beneath him, he was a wolf in gilded robes.

The Kaed whispered something in Saahira's ear. Talah watched as the Libra Councilor straightened before turning on her heel. The other two followed close behind her, leaving the

Kaed alone in their box. He hesitated, his face turned toward the arena, watching the competitors. Talah felt a chill roll down her spine, though she knew he wasn't looking directly at her.

Was he going to stay and watch?

Why would the Kaed care about the Trials?

"Tal." Mazin's voice broke through her thoughts, pulling her back to the arena.

The other competitors had already lined up, facing the mentors. Talah shook off the strange feeling as she took her place beside Mazin and Zayd. All of their mentors stood before them...except one.

Hers was missing.

Talah frowned, wondering when Iras had slipped out.

And why.

"Next drill," one of the mentors barked, clapping his hands. His voice cut through the scattered chatter like steel. "You'll work in groups."

"Why?" Nadir's voice rang out despite keeping an even tone, commanding attention.

He stood at the center of his group, like a sun the others orbited. Even drenched in sweat, he looked composed—posture perfect, smile polished, his words drawing chuckles from those around him. His gaze flicked across the yard, catching hers for a moment.

The mentor leveled a look at him before he realized who had spoken. "These Trials aren't just a competition. They're a test of loyalty. Of your resolve. To see who will fight to the death to better this nation and strengthen the Imperium."

They were herded toward a brutal course of wood, rope, and stone, sprawling across the packed-dirt yard like something built for punishment rather than training. A hush fell over the competitors as they took it in. It wasn't the sort of drill you shrugged through.

It sprawled across the training yard—a monstrosity of wood, rope, and stone meant to punish, not teach. The air itself felt heavier, tense with the knowledge that this wasn't playacting anymore. Someone was going to bleed. Someone might not walk away.

The first wall loomed over them, jagged planks slick with sweat and streaked dark where blood had already dried. Splinters bristled from its face like barbs, catching skin the second you touched it. Beyond, narrow beams stretched across a yawning pit of rock, the kind of drop that would snap a spine on impact. And at the end came the ropes, strung high and fraying, already stained rusty brown with old blood.

Talah's throat tightened. Her body already ached from the morning drills, every muscle trembling with fatigue. But this... this wasn't about sore arms or bruised knees. This was about survival.

The mentor's voice carried like a whip-crack across the yard. "Work as a unit. No one left behind. If one of you falls, the rest finish without them. And if you can't finish..." His gaze swept the course, lingering on the pit. "The course will take care of you."

A ripple of unease moved through the competitors.

Zayd muttered under his breath, "Well. That's not terrifying at all."

Mazin gave him a sharp look. "Try not to fall, then."

Adine rolled her shoulders, her braid sticking to the sweat on her back. "We don't have a choice. We get through this. Together."

Talah didn't respond. Her eyes darted over the mentors again, still searching for one in particular.

Why wasn't he here? Where the hell did he go?

The first group was called forward—four Signborns who sauntered up with mocking grins. Rayen vaulted the wall like a panther, hauling the others up after him. They sprinted across the beams, their steps light and sure, their balance unshakable even as the planks swayed dangerously. No one faltered. They skimmed across the ropes as if born to them. Their laughter echoed behind them, sharp as blades.

Talah's stomach twisted. Signborns like them didn't need

to prove themselves. They already carried the weight of family names that opened doors. For them, the Trials were nothing but a proving ground. For the rest… it meant so much more.

For a fleeting second, she wished Firas were there. Not because he'd say anything comforting—he never did—but because he had a way of cutting through her panic without even trying. He'd bring logic to soothe her wild thoughts, pointing out the truth. He'd make some dry remark, something infuriatingly calm, and she'd remember to breathe.

Why isn't he here today of all days? The space beside her felt too empty without his quiet certainty anchoring it. She scowled, shoving the thought away. She didn't *need* him.

They watched in silence as the second group moved toward the obstacle course. It was a mix of Crossborns and Signborns—those who had trained their whole lives for this and those only hoping for a chance at a better life. Talah watched them move forward, nails digging into her palms.

The group struggled over the wall, the hesitancy in helping each other clear enough. Every lift came a second too late, every grip too slippery with sweat. By the time they reached the beams, their rhythm was already broken.

One of the Crossborn girls wobbled halfway across, her thin arms flailing wildly as the plank bowed and swayed beneath her boots. Her face drained of color, eyes wide and terrified, searching for something—anything—to steady her. The laughter from the sidelines cut off as the wood gave a violent lurch.

The girl slipped.

The crack of the girl's body hitting the rocks silenced the yard. It wasn't just a fall—it was the kind of sound that went through bone and stayed there, echoing in the chest. Too high, too hard. Her scream cut off before it finished, choked off by the impact.

She didn't move.

For a heartbeat, no one breathed. Then the blood came, soaking through her tunic, running down the stones in bright, startling streaks. It spread fast, pooling beneath her like the earth itself was swallowing her life.

Someone screamed her name—a raw, broken sound that carried over the training yard. Another competitor tried to lunge forward, only to be yanked back by a mentor's hand clamped on their shoulder.

The air stank of copper, sharp and heavy, coating Talah's tongue. Her stomach turned violently, bile rising. She pressed her lips together until they ached, forcing it down.

The mentor didn't flinch. He didn't even look twice. "Next group," he barked, as if a girl hadn't just died in front of them.

Two guards jumped down into the pit, their boots splashing through blood as they dragged the girl's limp body out by her arms. Her head lolled, braid streaked red, eyes open and glassy. She left a dark trail in the dirt as they hauled her away like discarded meat.

Around Talah, the competitors stood rigid. Some stared wide-eyed, pale as parchment. Others looked away, jaws clenched, pretending indifference they didn't feel. A few Signborns smirked, as though this was proof of what they already believed—that the weak weren't meant to survive.

Talah's nails bit harder into her palms until she felt the sting of blood. Her throat was tight, breath ragged. That could have been her. That could be *any* of them.

And no one here would care.

Yet, when their names were called, Talah stepped forward with the rest of them, trailing behind Adine.

The wall loomed larger with each step. Talah tilted her head back, trying to see over the boards stained with blood and sweat.

They hadn't even bothered to clean this off since the last time it was used, she thought.

Talah flexed her hands, grit grinding into her raw palms. No one left behind. Her gaze flicked to Mazin, to Adine, to Zayd. They looked as worn down as she felt—sweat dripping, breathing heavily, clothes clinging to their skin. But there was a steadiness in their eyes, too. The thought of dragging them down, of being the weak link, tightened her chest more than the obstacles ahead.

This wasn't just a test of endurance. It was a test of loyalty. And she couldn't afford to fail them.

Zayd glanced around, his usual bravado muted. "Well," he said, "good thing we're all very coordinated."

Mazin grinned. "Which is why you'll be the first to fall on your face."

"Shut up," Zayd muttered, though a flicker of amusement softened his scowl.

Adine barely hesitated. She vaulted upward with a strength that seemed to belong to someone twice her size, her boots finding narrow holds, fingers gripping the edge. With the ease of someone who had climbed cliffs all her life, she pulled herself over and landed lightly on the other side. Talah watched her go, half in awe, half in envy. Adine made it look effortless—like she belonged here. Talah's chest tightened. She'd never had that kind of certainty. Every step she took felt like a test she wasn't meant to pass.

Talah studied the wall's surface, scanning for cracks or hand-holds, anything that would make it possible. The wall loomed higher up close—hot under the sun, dust clinging to her palms. Her throat felt dry. It wasn't just the climb that made her stomach knot; it was the eyes. The mentors. The Signborns. The unspoken expectation that someone like her would fail.

She pressed a hand to the wall again, feeling its heat bite her skin. Her pulse thudded in her ears. She could almost hear Firas's voice—calm, infuriatingly sure—telling her to think, not panic. To move, not hesitate. The memory stung. He wasn't here. No one was going to pull her up.

She set her jaw. The only way forward was up.

Her arms trembled even before she leapt. The wood scraped her palms raw, dirt biting into the shallow cuts left by training weapons. She hauled herself upward, every muscle screaming. For one terrible breath she dangled, legs kicking uselessly against the wall.

I can't. I'll fall. They'll all see me fail.

A hand closed around her wrist—Mazin's, steady and strong. His grip burned with warmth, anchoring her. "Got you," he said through clenched teeth. With a heave, he pulled her up beside him. Talah stumbled over the edge, gasping, but his grin steadied her more than his hand had.

The balance beam was just three narrow planks stretched across uneven blocks, swaying under the faintest weight. From the ground, they had looked manageable. Standing before them now, the thin strips of wood seemed no wider than a hand-span. She had always hated heights. Even this—just a few feet up—was enough to make her palms slick with sweat.

One wrong step, and you'll hit the dirt hard. And everyone will see it.

Adine took her first step on the closest beam as if it were solid ground, her arms extending for balance. Each movement was measured, her boots finding the exact center of the plank, her golden braid swinging like a pendulum behind her. She crossed with a poise that made it look easy, springing to the other side without a single glance down.

"Show-off," someone muttered from the sidelines. A ripple of laughter followed, but it was grudging, admiring.

Zayd grinned as if this were some sort of game before sprinting across, his body fluid and quick, leaping the last gap with careless ease. He landed in a crouch, arms raised in mock victory. Turning, he shot Mazin and Talah a quick smirk. "See? Easy."

"Try that when the beams aren't nailed down," a voice jeered. "Bet you eat dirt first."

Zayd only smirked, brushing off the jab with a theatrical bow.

Mazin grimaced, ignoring him. He climbed onto the first beam, his face already pale, jaw locked tight. The wood shifted beneath his weight, groaning softly. He froze for a heartbeat, then forced his foot forward. Arms flailing wildly, he tottered across, every step a near disaster.

Talah wanted to look away but couldn't. Mazin was stubborn to a fault—always was—but this was different. This was fear, real and raw, written across his face for everyone to see.

"Careful!" someone called, mock-sweet. "We don't need more bodies to scrape out of the pit."

"Bet he doesn't make it halfway," another competitor snorted.

The laughter that followed was sharp as glass. It prickled under Talah's skin, a reminder of every time she'd been someone's entertainment. She could almost feel that same heat crawling up her neck—the mix of humiliation and defiance that always came with being underestimated.

Zayd made a strangled sound, trying to cover it up with a cough.

"Don't laugh," Mazin hissed, voice strangled with concentration. His eyes were fixed on the plank, unblinking, as though looking anywhere else might doom him.

Zayd cupped his hands around his mouth. "I'm not laughing—I'm marveling."

Mazin shot him a murderous glare, nearly overbalancing in the process. The beam swayed violently, and a gasp rippled through the groups watching. Talah's heart lurched into her throat.

He's going to fall.

But somehow, by sheer will or stubbornness, Mazin staggered across, dropping to his knees the instant his boots touched the block on the far side. His shoulders slumped in relief.

The plank seemed to stretch longer when Talah stepped onto it, narrow and unstable beneath her boots. Her breath came shallow, too loud in her ears. The world tilted as the wood bowed slightly under her weight.

Steady. Just steady. One foot. Then the next.

"Careful, little girl!" someone shouted. "Wouldn't want to break a nail."

A chorus of snickers followed, buzzing in her ears like wasps.

Her legs shook as she moved, arms spread to keep balance.

Below, the churned dirt and jagged stone yawned up at her. The more she tried not to look, the more her gaze dragged downward, dizziness tugging her off center.

"Eyes up, Talah," Adine's voice cut sharp across the gap. "Don't give the ground the satisfaction."

Talah clenched her jaw and forced her focus forward—on Adine, on the far side, on the goal just beyond reach. She took another step, then another, her heart pounding so hard it drowned out the noise around her.

Halfway across, the plank gave a sudden wobble. Her breath caught, balance tipping. A strangled noise escaped her throat as she windmilled her arms. The plank creaked dangerously.

No. Not here. Not in front of them.

"Breathe," Mazin called, his voice soft.

She did. She forced the air back into her lungs, pressed down the panic clawing at her chest, and pushed forward. Step by step, she crossed until her boots found solid stone again. Relief flooded her chest—then vanished when she looked ahead.

The ropes.

They dangled over the rocks, high enough that a fall could crack ribs. Two fraying lines stretched between posts, sagging low in the middle. The fibers were dark with old blood, frayed so thin in places that they looked ready to snap. Competitors were meant to hook onto them, drag themselves across with nothing but their arms and balance, dangling over the churned ground like prey in a trap.

Zayd whistled low. "Well. That looks inviting. Can't we just say we tried and skip this one?"

Adine shook her head, braid sticking to her damp neck. "We get across, or we fail. No shortcuts." Her gaze flicked over each of them.

Talah swallowed hard. The beams had felt like walking a knife's edge—this was worse. The ropes looked ready to dump anyone who dared touch them face-first into the jagged stones. Already, the groups watching had shifted closer, waiting to see who would die next.

"Let me go first," Zayd said, his grin sharp and careless, though his eyes darted to the sagging ropes. "I'll test it."

Before anyone could argue, he leapt onto the lines, hooking his legs and arms with fluid precision. His body seemed to flow over the rope like water, shoulders rolling with each pull. He crossed with infuriating ease, twisting into a mocking bow when he dropped down on the far side. "See? Perfectly safe."

"Show-off," Mazin muttered.

Adine climbed up next. Her movements were slower, deliberate, her arms flexing with each drag forward. She didn't look down, didn't waste a breath. She set the rhythm—pull, hook, pull—that the rest of them could follow.

Mazin, however, was another story. He got halfway across before his foot slipped free. The rope jerked violently beneath him, swinging him sideways. His shout cracked the air, drawing immediate laughter from the sidelines.

"Hold your weight closer!" Adine called from ahead, urgency sharpening her tone. "Wrap your legs tighter, Mazin. Lock them—like this!" She demonstrated, squeezing her thighs around the rope until it steadied beneath her.

"I'm trying!" he spat, clinging like a cat over water.

Talah's stomach knotted as she stepped forward. She forced her trembling arms onto the rope, the coarse fibers biting instantly through her thin shirt. Her chest pressed into it, ribs grinding against the taut line as she hooked her legs and pulled forward.

Her arms burned almost immediately, muscles shrieking in protest. She gritted her teeth, dragging herself inch by inch. The world tilted beneath her, the dirt yawning up like a threat. By the time she was a third of the way across, her shoulders already felt like they were tearing apart.

I can't do this. I'm not strong enough. I don't belong here.

Ahead of her, Mazin was still cursing, every word she knew and a few she didn't. Zayd's unhelpful laughter drifted across the pit, though she could hear the tight edge beneath it.

"Keep moving," Adine's voice cut across the ropes, calm but

firm. "It's worse if you stop. One pull at a time. You've got this."

The words sank into Talah's chest, a fragile thread keeping her from letting go. She forced her arms to move again, and again. Pain seared through her shoulders, rope fibers biting into her skin. Inch by inch, she dragged herself forward, sweat stinging her eyes, her breath breaking into short, ragged gasps.

By the time her boots scraped against the far post and she dropped to solid ground, her arms were jelly. Her body threatened to crumple beneath its weight. But she was still upright. Still standing. Barely.

She turned just in time to see Mazin still clinging like a half-drowned cat, his legs loose and slipping, the rope swaying with every frantic movement. His face was chalk white, teeth bared in a grimace.

"I can't—" he wheezed, his grip faltering.

"Yes, you can," Adine snapped, her voice sharp as a whip. She'd already crossed and now crouched low at the edge, one hand stretched toward him. "Come on, Mazin. Reach!"

"I'll fall—"

"No, you won't." Zayd dropped beside her, arm braced on the post for leverage. He extended his other hand, fingers straining. "We've got you. Just let go with one hand."

Talah swallowed her exhaustion and knelt too, forcing her shaking arms forward. "Mazin, look at me," she said, her voice low but steady. His wide, panicked eyes flicked up. "We're not leaving you. Reach for us."

Mazin groaned, his fingers twitching against the rope. Then, with a hoarse curse, he let go with one hand and flung it toward them.

Zayd's grip caught first, Adine's second, their arms locking around his wrist. Talah grabbed his sleeve, adding what little strength she had left. Together they hauled him up, muscles straining, until he rolled onto the platform with a graceless thud.

He lay there on his back, gasping, sweat slicking his face. "I hate this place," he muttered, staring up at the sky.

The mentor's sharp voice cut through the arena. "Sloppy.

Barely passable. But you didn't leave anyone behind." He was already checking his board for the next names to call, dismissing them.

Talah's chest still heaved, her arms like lead, but when she glanced at her friends—Zayd grinning, Adine brushing strands of hair from her flushed face, Mazin sprawled like a corpse—something loosened inside her.

We did it. Together.

But the sound of laughter still lingered, cutting through her fragile calm. The Signborns were watching, their smirks polished, their words sharp enough to draw blood. And when her gaze swept the sidelines, she found one pair of eyes fixed not on the group—but on her.

Nadir Khatri.

He stood with the other elites, posture straight, expression composed. But there was something in his gaze that made her chest tighten. He didn't jeer like the others.

Nadir only smiled faintly, as though he already knew how the Trials would end.

FIRAS
XIV

Dawn spilled over the training yard in strokes of gold and ash, painting shadows long across the dirt as the competitors dragged themselves from their beds. The air was cool with morning, sharp with the scent of trampled grass and dust, and Firas stood still amid it all, watching, measuring, waiting.

Firas had underestimated Talah, and that mistake gnawed at him more than he cared to admit. He had seen competitors break in a hundred different ways before—seen them crumble under fear, fold beneath pain, or shatter when hope was ripped away.

He'd wanted to stay, to watch her fight her way through the obstacle, but the moment the Kaed strode into the private box, Firas's chest went tight. Without a sound, he melted into the shadows and slipped out before those cold eyes could sweep the crowd and find him.

If anyone would recognize him… it would be the Kaed.

Firas's gaze found Talah in the arena now, her dark hair tied back, sweat already beading at her temple. She looked smaller among the mass of bodies, but there was a tightness to her shoulders, a readiness in the way her fingers curled around the blade she carried. Her eyes lifted, finding his across the yard. For an instant, the air seemed to shift, sharp and inevitable.

Talah moved toward him without hesitation, sweat already dampening the collar of her tunic, a wooden practice blade gripped in her hand. She looked small against the rising sun, but there was nothing small in the way she met his gaze.

Firas gave her a single curt nod. "Ready?"

Her chin tipped upward, the faintest flare of defiance in her dark eyes as she sheathed the blade at her hip. "Where did you go yesterday?"

His jaw tightened. For a moment it looked like he might answer, but then he only exhaled through his nose, gaze shifting past her. "Doesn't matter."

"It does to me."

A muscle ticked in his cheek. "Not enough for you to hear it."

"Is that so." Talah's arms crossed over her chest.

"Yes." His eyes caught hers, daring her to argue. "Drop it, Aasifati."

He shifted into stance, planting his feet in the dirt, rolling his shoulders loose. The practice blade felt too light in his grip—mock steel compared to the weight of what he was used to carrying. Still, it would serve. He lifted it in a smooth arc, angling his body so his shadow stretched long across her feet. Then, with a flick of his wrist, he gestured for her to attack.

For a heartbeat, she hesitated. He saw the twitch of her throat as she swallowed, the tightening of her grip on the hilt. She wanted to needle the answers out of him—he could practically see her debating whether to press for more information or not.

It shouldn't have bothered him when she called him out earlier, but it did. Not because she was wrong—but because she *saw* him. Too clearly. Her words had struck deeper than any blade could, brushing against truths he'd buried under discipline and duty. He didn't like that feeling—being exposed, even for a breath.

He caught her gaze again. There was defiance there, sharp and unyielding. It burned hotter than the sun overhead. And despite himself, something in him tightened—some pulse of respect, irritation, and something darker that he refused to name. He steadied his breath, the faintest smirk ghosting his mouth.

"Go on, then," he said quietly. "Show me if you mean it."

He could see the final decision in her eyes before she moved. Talah came at him fast, faster than he'd expected—but speed without precision was nothing. Her blade cut a wide arc, too wild, too easy. He blocked with a flick, twisting his wrist just so. The wood connected with a sharp crack, and he turned her momentum against her. She stumbled sideways, breath catching as her boot slid through the dust.

Firas's lip curled faintly, though not in amusement. *Too much strength, not enough control.*

But before he could press the advantage, she righted herself. No pause, no surrender. She came back at him, swinging hard again, shoulders tense, her braid snapping across her back like a whip.

The strike was just as clumsy, but her eyes were sharper this time—focused, fixed on him as though sheer will might carry her blade where skill could not. Firas blocked again, his arm hardly moving. His muscles coiled and released in practiced rhythm, as natural as breathing. He shifted his stance to absorb the blow, then rolled his wrist, sliding her strike off course.

The blades met with a hollow clap. Her blade jarred, but her grip didn't falter. He watched the strain ripple up her arm, saw the sweat already gathering at her temple. She was breathing too fast.

Firas tilted his head, studying her through the veil of dust rising between them. *Stubborn. Reckless. She doesn't know when to stop. That kind of fire keeps you alive in the desert—and gets you killed in the Trials.*

"Again," he said, his voice low, almost a growl.

She came at him quickly, swinging hard, but her strike was clumsy—too wide, too obvious. Firas shifted his weight with barely a thought, catching her blow in a sharp crack of metal against metal. The vibration thrummed up his arm. He twisted his wrist, redirecting the force, and she stumbled a step, boots skidding in the dust.

The scent of sun-baked earth rose as her heel dragged across the ground, a faint cloud kicking up around them. She coughed once, low in her throat, then came back at him without pause.

Again, he blocked. Again, he parried. His movements were spare, efficient, a predator conserving energy. He shifted only when necessary, letting her waste herself against his guard. Each strike rattled like drumbeats in the hollow morning air, sharp cracks echoing across the training yard.

Her rhythm faltered, then picked up again, faster, angrier. Her blade smacked against his, jarring her arms with every failed attempt, but still she pressed on. Her breath grew ragged, each exhale a harsh rasp. Sweat slid down her temple, beading along the curve of her jaw. The braid trailing down her back slapped against her shoulders in time with her movements.

Something within her shifted. Instead of another wild swing for his chest, she angled low, quick and sharp. The strike rattled through his bones, the crack of impact louder this time, the jolt biting up through his wrist.

A flicker of surprise cut through him. *She's learning.*

For the briefest instant, the corner of his mouth curved—almost a smile, almost amusement. He smothered it before it could surface, but it was too late.

She caught the look.

Her eyes narrowed, dark and blazing, her lips tightening as if daring him to underestimate her again. With a low grunt, she surged forward, her blade cutting sharper lines through the air, movements cleaner, more controlled. She was still unpolished, but she was adjusting. Adapting.

Dust clung to her skin, streaking her sweat-slicked cheek.

Her tunic, damp at the collar, clung to the lines of her body. He shouldn't have noticed. He told himself he didn't. Yet his gaze lingered too long on the stubborn fire in her expression, the way her determination burned hotter than the sun pressing down on the yard.

She drove him back a step, then another. Not because she had forced him there, but because he let her, curious to see how far she'd go. Around them, the din of other sparring pairs swelled and broke like a tide, but the clash of their blades cut its own rhythm. Wood on wood, the grit of boots sliding across dirt, the rasp of breath between each strike.

He pivoted, decisive and fluid, sliding his blade across hers, wrenching her weapon wide. In the same breath, he caught her wrist, strong fingers wrapping around hot, damp skin, and pressed the flat of his blade against her shoulder.

She froze.

"Too slow," he murmured, his voice low enough that only she could hear.

Her jaw clenched. "Or maybe you're just faster because you cheat."

A corner of his mouth twitched. "I don't need to cheat to take you to the ground."

Her chest heaved, the sharp tang of sweat and dust hanging between them. They were close enough for him to see the flecks of grit caught in her lashes, the tremor of her pulse beneath his thumb. Close enough that her unsteady breath fanned against his jaw, quick and uneven.

"Then do it," she shot back, breathless, eyes flashing up to meet his.

For a heartbeat, he forgot to breathe. Her pulse fluttered beneath his thumb—fast, reckless, alive. They were close enough for him to see the flecks of grit caught in her lashes, close enough that her unsteady breath fanned against his jaw. The noise of the yard dulled, swallowed by the rush of blood in his ears, the thrum of her heartbeat reverberating through his hand.

He released her first. Slowly, deliberately, though his fingers lingered half a second longer than they should have.

"Next time," he said, voice rougher than he intended, "don't hold back."

"I wasn't," she breathed. Talah took a sharp breath and stepped back, rolling her wrist as if testing the joint. Her lips curved into a faint, breathless smile. "You could at least pretend to break a sweat."

Firas's blade lowered, but he didn't step away. The corner of his mouth twitched—almost a smile, almost not. His voice came out rougher than he intended, low enough that only she could hear. "If you want to survive, you'll need to fight like someone with nothing left to lose."

Her expression shifted. The smile faltered, the humor in her eyes flickering into something more uncertain, more searching. For the space of a heartbeat, neither of them looked away. The heat of the morning pressed heavy between them, thick with dust and sweat, and Firas felt the dangerous pull of it—of her.

Firas forced himself to step back, forcing the heat of her gaze out of reach, then gave a curt nod meant to end the spar. Talah wiped her brow with the back of her hand, her blade dropping to her side, but he could still feel the weight of her attention brushing against him like a touch he hadn't invited.

"Break!" one of the mentors barked, clapping his hands sharply. The clamor of sparring died down, the yard buzzing with the chatter of competitors as they lowered their weapons and sought water or shade.

Firas stayed where he was, his blade balanced loosely in his hand, his breathing already steady again. Years of practice had trained his body to fall into rhythm, to mask any sign of strain. Yet when his gaze drifted back to Talah, he caught the faint tremor in her arm as she re-wrapped her grip on the weapon, the flush across her cheeks, the stubborn set of her jaw.

And then someone else noticed her, too.

Saahira's golden heir moved through the crowd like a polished blade, every line of him smooth and assured. Even winded from drills, Nadir looked immaculate, his tunic barely rumpled, his dark hair falling perfectly into place. Firas felt a faint twist of disgust curl in his chest.

Nadir's smile was practiced, his tone smooth as silk when he stopped before Talah. "You fight with spirit. It suits you." His words dripped with a courtesy that was too careful, too exact—bait dressed as compliment.

Talah stiffened, suspicion flashing across her face. "I don't need your approval."

"Approval?" Nadir's laugh was light, but his eyes flickered, weighing her reaction. "No. Not approval. A recognition of potential. You could do better than… this." His gaze flicked briefly toward Mazin and Zayd, where they lounged on the edge of the yard, before returning to her. "There are alliances forming, whether you see them or not. Why waste your strength propping up deadweight when you could—"

"I'm not interested," Talah cut in, voice sharp as steel.

The smile on Nadir's face faltered, then recovered in a flash, polished back into place. But Firas had seen the crack—brief and telling. Nadir wasn't used to being refused.

Before the boy could press further, Firas stepped forward, blade still loose in his grip. "Careful," he said, his voice low, even. "Some alliances will bleed you dry before the Trials even begin."

Nadir's eyes slid to him, narrowing, the smile still fixed but colder now. "And others," he said smoothly, "offer survival."

Firas didn't look away. Neither did Nadir. The silence stretched taut until Nadir inclined his head, a mockery of respect, and withdrew into the waiting knot of Signborns, who welcomed him back with easy laughter.

Talah exhaled, her grip tightening on her blade. She glanced at Firas, her brow furrowing. "You think I can't see through him?"

Firas studied her—the hard line of her mouth, the fire in her eyes. He almost said yes—that she was still too green, too stubborn, too trusting—but the memory of her standing on that swaying beam, refusing to fall, stilled the words on his tongue.

Instead, he said quietly, "See through him. And the others.

Trust no one too easily."

Her gaze lingered on his a moment longer, the weight of it heavier than he wanted to admit. Then she turned away, striding back toward her group, leaving him in the dust and morning sunlight, the echo of her pulse still beating against his fingers.

Firas watched Talah rejoin her little cluster—Zayd smirking at something, Adine shaking her head, Mazin still looking half-dead from drills. They were laughing, shoulders brushing, their voices carrying faintly across the yard. For the first time since Aphelion, she looked like she belonged.

The sight lodged in his chest like a splinter.

"You're getting sloppy."

Firas didn't need to turn to know who it was. Kam's voice cut through the hum of training, low and sharp. She moved beside him without ceremony, tall and wiry, her braids catching the morning light as she crossed her arms.

"I'm training her," Firas said flatly, his gaze still fixed on the group across the yard.

"You're *protecting* her," Kam countered, her tone edged with warning. "And people are noticing."

He shifted his grip on the practice blade, rolling it once in his palm before lowering it to his side. "She would've let that viper Nadir sink his teeth in if I hadn't stepped in."

Kam snorted. "She cut him off before you even opened your mouth. You think she's helpless, but she isn't. And if you keep stepping in, you risk putting the spotlight on yourself. Especially with *you know who* making an appearance." Her gaze flicked over the yard, to the other mentors watching. But he knew who she really meant.

The Kaed.

The faintest breeze tugged at the dust between them, carrying the sweat and iron tang of the training yard. Firas forced his shoulders to stay loose, his face unreadable, but his chest tightened.

"I can't let her fail," he said at last, the words slipping out quieter than he meant. "You're the one who told me I had to at least give her a fighting chance."

Kam's sharp eyes caught the slip, narrowing. "No. You can't let her fail because if she does, all of this collapses on *us*. But I don't remember saying you should coddle her either."

He clenched his jaw, heat crawling up the back of his neck. He hated her words because they were true.

Kam shifted closer, her voice dropping lower, softer but no less cutting. "You've spent your whole life surviving by hiding what you feel. Don't forget that now. Not for her."

With that, she turned and left him standing in the yard, the clamor of sparring rising up again around him.

Firas tightened his grip on the blade until the wood creaked. He told himself Kam was right. That distance kept him alive, kept them all alive.

And yet, when his eyes drifted back across the yard, they found Talah anyway.

FIRAS
XV

The sound of leaves cracking beneath Talah's feet sounded sharper to him than the clash of blades. Each brittle snap carried too far in the stillness, splintering against his ears until he sighed, arms folded tight across his chest as he waited for her to come into range.

"A herd of elephants would be more stealthy than you," he said at last, not bothering to turn.

There was a pause, followed by the quick huff of her breath, before she pushed free of the trees. The mentors had taken the competitors beyond Aphelion's stone walls and into the sparse woods that fringed the city. Pale bark peeled from pines that had clawed their way through dry soil, and the air carried the resinous tang of sap mixed with the faint bitterness of dust. The shade here was thin—slats of gold sunlight spilled unhindered between the branches, warming the back of his neck even as the breeze rasped dryly through the undergrowth.

The others were still fumbling through their survival tasks: coaxing sparks into flame, cupping brackish water into skins if they lacked a Water Sign's gift. Firas had drilled Talah through all of that in the past few afternoons; compared to her peers, she was ahead there at least.

Staying quiet, on the other hand…

"I'm not loud," Talah shot back. "You just have the hearing of some cursed bat."

He exhaled through his nose, more amused than he wanted to admit. "Again." He gestured toward the trees, fingers brushing against the rough ridges of a pine trunk.

She shot him an irritated look—dark eyes flashing in the sun—before obeying, slipping back into the brush. Sunlight tangled through her hair as she moved, and for an instant his focus faltered. He told himself it was instinct—the need to track her form through the shadows, to assess her mistakes—but the truth pressed tighter, heavier. He noticed too much. Always had.

He shouldn't.

Firas forced the thought away, forcing himself into stillness. The forest magnified everything: the dry rattle of her sleeve against a branch, the faint scuff of her heel against gravel, the restless whisper of leaves stirred by her passing. He let her go a while before following, veering wide to her right. The coarse needles prickled beneath his boots, but he moved without stirring the silence. That was how it should be—quiet, detached, disciplined. She was a student. A liability, if he let himself forget why he was here.

When she finally stilled, he caught sight of her tucked between a thicket of ferns at the base of a pine. She crouched low, hair catching in the dappled light, the sharp green of the ferns brushing against her shoulders. For all her effort, she looked more cornered animal than shadow.

Firas let the quiet stretch, watching her try to blend into the shadows. Her shoulders hunched, every muscle strung too tight. She thought stillness was enough, but the way her weight sat heavy on her heels betrayed her. If a hunter had been nearby, she'd have been gone before she drew her next breath.

He moved without a sound, the ground giving nothing

beneath him. The faint resin of pine clung to the air, mingling with the musk of sun-warmed earth. When he crouched beside her, her head snapped toward him—eyes wide, lips parted in the smallest hitch of surprise.

"Not like that. You're holding everything too tight," he said quietly, his voice more breath than sound. "Tension makes noise. Noise gets you killed."

He reached for her wrist, guiding her hand away from bracing against the ground. His palm brushed hers, cool skin meeting warmth for a fraction of a heartbeat too long before he set it against her thigh instead. His touch lingered as he shifted her knee, narrowing the space between them until the ferns whispered against both their shoulders.

He shouldn't have been aware of the way her breath hitched. He shouldn't have cared. But the sound lodged somewhere inside him, sharp and electric.

"Your weight," he murmured, angling closer until his chest hovered just behind her back. "Distribute it here—" His hand skimmed down, settling lightly at her ankle before tracing the air up her calf, showing her the balance she lacked. "And here."

Talah stiffened at the proximity, but she didn't pull away. Her breath caught, shallow, and he noticed—because he was too close not too. He could feel the heat rising off her skin, hear the sound of his own pulse filled the silence, steady but too loud.

He told himself this was only training. Only instruction. But every line of her body contradicted him—alive, fierce, impossibly near. The edge between discipline and desire blurred until he couldn't tell which side he stood on.

"Roll your feet. Don't stamp." He demonstrated, his fingers ghosting over her instep before he drew away. "Pause between steps. Let the ground tell you if it's safe."

When she moved again, it was jerky, uncertain. Firas leaned forward, closing the small space left between them, close enough that his lips brushed the shell of her ear as he spoke. Her scent—something faintly sweet beneath dust and pine—made it harder to keep his tone even.

"Every step you take is a choice," he whispered, letting the words sink in. "Step wrong, and you'll never take another."

Her breath stuttered, louder than the wind rustling the canopy. He saw the way her throat worked as she swallowed, the smallest shift of her jaw as if biting back a retort. But she didn't move away. She stayed exactly where he'd placed her, surrounded by shadow and sunlight, his nearness pressing in until he was certain she could feel the heat rolling off him the same way he felt hers.

Firas forced himself to ease back, to put air between them before he did something reckless. The distance was only a small mercy. His hands still remembered her warmth, and his chest felt uncomfortably hollow because of it. She was his competitor. His responsibility. And every second he lingered close enough to taste the warmth of her breath, he risked forgetting that.

A low voice cut through the stillness.

"She doesn't need your help."

Firas stilled, every muscle locking as he straightened from his crouch. The cool shade gave way to the sharp weight of the sun filtering between branches, outlining Mazin's figure where he stood at the tree line. His hands were clenched at his sides, shoulders squared, the faint rise and fall of his chest betraying how quickly he'd crossed the woods to get here.

Talah's head whipped toward him, surprise flickering across her features before it hardened into something unreadable. The silence that followed was thick, disturbed only by the restless hiss of wind through the sparse canopy and the soft creak of Mazin's boots grinding into gravel.

Firas met his stare, eyes hardening, voice flat. "She'll die if she keeps stepping like a soldier on parade."

The space between them thrummed, alive with a tension that pressed like a storm against the skin. Firas didn't move, didn't blink. For a moment, he swore Mazin might swing—the tilt of his jaw, the flare in his nostrils, the way his fists curled tighter as though he needed the weight of them just to hold himself back.

The sight almost made Firas laugh. Amusing, really, how

Mazin tried to bare his teeth like a guard dog when the boy had no idea what it meant to be dangerous. If this was meant to intimidate, it failed—Firas felt nothing of the threat, only a flicker of wry satisfaction at how easily the boy's composure cracked where Talah was concerned.

Talah shifted uneasily, the ferns brushing against her thighs as she rose to stand. Dust clung to her boots, sunlight sparking against the damp at her temples. She looked between them as if caught between fire and flint, about to spark herself.

"Mazin," she said carefully, but her voice seemed to vanish into the pressure hanging in the air.

He didn't take his eyes off Firas. "The others are gathering. Another group exercise." His tone was clipped, protective, his body angled subtly toward her as though to shield her from something—or someone.

Firas's jaw tightened. He could smell the faint brine of sweat, sharp under the resin-rich air, could hear the restless pulse in his own ears matching the rhythm of Mazin's measured breaths. If Mazin wanted to make this into a challenge, it would take only a step, a glance, for everything to shatter into violence.

But Firas had survived too long to be baited. Slowly, deliberately, he straightened to his full height, letting the shadows slide off his shoulders. His eyes remained cold, unreadable, but the weight of them pressed into Mazin until the boy shifted his stance, feet grinding into the earth as though bracing for a blow that never came.

The woods seemed to hold its breath. Even the wind quieted, and for a moment there was nothing but the thrum of tension between them, sharp enough to cut.

Finally, Firas flicked his gaze away, turning toward the path that led back to Aphelion. His voice was even, but laced with steel. "Then take her."

The dismissal hit its mark, and Mazin stiffened, pride bristling, but he moved to Talah's side anyway. His shoulder brushed hers as if to mark a claim, his presence hot and unyielding compared to the cool shadow Firas left behind.

Firas followed at a distance, his footsteps near-silent, his expression stony. But inside, every step was its own choice: to walk away, to let the heat of jealousy burn unspoken, to pretend her silence between them didn't weigh more than all the noise she ever made in the woods.

The trail sloped gently back toward the clearing where the mentors had assembled the rest of the competitors. Smoke from half-built fires curled lazily into the afternoon air, carrying the tang of charred bark and sap. Voices rose in uneven patches—water gurgling as someone siphoned it into a skin, a laugh too sharp, the clipped bark of a mentor correcting poor form. The woods themselves seemed to hum with it all—the rustle of dry branches overhead, the faint crunch of boots scattering pine needles.

Mazin walked at Talah's side, close enough that his shoulder brushed hers whenever the path narrowed. Protective. Possessive. As though he thought she needed guarding from everything—even him. It might have been laughable if not for the way she let it happen, her gaze flicking toward Mazin at intervals that Firas noticed too easily. Every small gesture between them was a reminder of the danger tightening around him: not Mazin, never Mazin—but her.

She was already too dangerous. Not because of her lack of stealth, not because of her stubbornness—but because of what stirred in him whenever she looked his way, whenever she let silence fill the space between them like a thread pulling taut. He'd seen enough to know where such threads led. And he couldn't afford it.

But it wasn't just attraction alone that pulled at him. That would have been easier to dismiss, something he could set aside like hunger or thirst. What unsettled him was the way respect had begun to take root, unbidden. Despite her background, despite the blood in her veins that should have marked her as untouchable, Talah was proving herself each day—or at least trying to. She failed often enough, tripped where others glided, but she never stayed down. That stubborn fire in her... he knew what it cost to keep striking flint against stone when the world expected you to break instead.

By the time they reached the clearing, the air was thick with wood-smoke and heat, shafts of light breaking across the circle of gathered students. Sparks hissed where kindling still smoldered, carrying the sharp tang of resin and ash.

One of the mentors stepped forward, voice cutting through the murmurs with the weight of command.

"Survival isn't only about fire or water," he said, his tone clipped, measured. "It's about silence. About moving where others cannot find you. Today, your task is simple: get past us. If you're seen, if you're heard, you fail. The ones who learn to disappear are the ones who live."

A ripple went through the group—half excitement, half dread. Some competitors straightened eagerly, eyes bright at the challenge. Others shifted uneasily, adjusting straps on their packs, fingers fidgeting at their sides. A boy with broad shoulders muttered a curse under his breath, drawing a sharp glance from the mentor.

Firas scanned the faces—sweat shining at brows, throats bobbing with nervous swallows, the restless shuffling of boots grinding into pine needles. Tension hung heavy, pooling like still water that waited for a stone to disturb its surface.

His eyes slid to Talah again despite himself. Her posture was rigid, but not with fear. He caught the way her chin lifted at the words, defiance sparking in her eyes. She wanted to prove herself here too. To him, it was reckless—but it was also exactly what made her dangerous. That relentless drive to be something else, something more.

Mazin leaned subtly toward her, whispering something too low for Firas to catch. She laughed once—soft, fleeting—and it scraped through him worse than any blade. He exhaled slowly, steadying himself. The Trials, the Imperium, had already taken enough from him. He wouldn't let this girl—this reckless, impossible girl—become another weakness carved out of his bones.

Another mentor continued with the directions. "We'll go first, standing between you and Aphelion—you will need to slip past us all. Only then do you return home."

A murmur rippled through the competitors—low, uneasy, quickly silenced by the stern look he leveled across the circle.

"When the horn sounds, you move. Fail, and you'll try again until you don't. There are no excuses."

With that, the mentors broke away. They moved with quiet efficiency, vanishing one by one into the sparse woods. Their boots barely disturbed the earth, their silhouettes swallowed by dust and pine. The forest seemed to darken with their departure, silence rushing back in to fill the space where their presence had been.

The competitors shifted restlessly, the tension ratcheting higher with every heartbeat. Some leaned forward as if they could track the mentors' movements by sound alone; others glanced nervously at their partners, sweat beading at brows despite the shade. Dust hung in the shafts of light, stirred only by the scrape of boots and the ragged rhythm of breathing.

Firas's gaze slid to Talah one last time before he moved. Her chin was lifted, eyes fixed on the tree line where the mentors had disappeared. Not afraid. Not resigned. Determined. Mazin shifted beside her, close enough that his arm brushed hers as if to anchor her, to tether her down before she leapt headlong into risk. Firas's mouth hardened. Without a word, he turned and melted into the shadows with the other mentors, his footsteps vanishing into the crackle of pine needles and the dry rasp of leaves overhead.

But he didn't go far.

The clearing stilled. Dust hung in the shafts of afternoon light, motes drifting in the silence. Then, across the circle, a hollow call split the air. Deep, resonant, drawn from bone and brass. It rolled through the trees like a war cry, scattering birds from their perches, echoing off stone and bark until it felt as though the earth itself vibrated with its command.

He watched as the competitors surged forward in pairs,

shadows swallowing them as they crossed into the woods. Breathing grew ragged, hurried. Gravel shifted, branches snapped—sounds that betrayed even the most careful step. One by one, they vanished into the hunt.

Talah slipped among them, low and measured, her movements sharper now, more deliberate. She threaded through the underbrush, pausing, rolling her weight as he'd shown her. For a moment, she almost disappeared into the rhythm of the forest.

Almost.

Firas tracked her with ease, his steps swallowed by the forest, silent as the resin-scented breeze that slipped through the branches overhead. Talah moved well enough now—lower to the ground, pausing between steps, rolling her weight the way he'd shown her—but still, he could hear the faint catch of breath, the scrape of fabric against bark. She thought she was invisible. She thought she was free.

He let her get close—too close. Her path curved back toward Aphelion's walls, sunlight glinting faintly off stone far in the distance. He heard her breathing quicken, her stride lengthen as if she could already taste victory on her tongue. That was when he moved.

One step from the shadows, his hand shot out, iron-fast around her wrist. She gasped, the sound strangled in her throat, eyes flashing wide before she could school them. The shock of his touch stilled her instantly. Beneath his grip, her pulse thudded hot and fast, hammering against his palm.

He drew her in a fraction, close enough that her shoulder brushed the rough bark of a pine, close enough that his body shadowed hers. Her breath faltered, loud in the hush of the woods. She tilted her chin up, defiant despite the fact that he held her caught, rooted, unable to slip away.

He leaned in, lowering his head until his lips hovered near her ear, so close that the warmth of his breath stirred the strands of hair that clung damply to her temple. "Better," he murmured, voice pitched low for her alone. "But you still breathe too loud when you're afraid."

For a heartbeat, the forest seemed to hush. The resin-thick air, the rasp of leaves above, even the distant calls of other competitors faded until there was only the heat of her skin beneath his fingers, the wild thrum of her heartbeat, the closeness of his voice in her ear.

Her chest rose against him with each shallow breath, her defiance warring with something quieter, something far more dangerous. He felt the tension straining through her body—the urge to wrench free, the temptation not to.

Then, before the moment could fracture, he released her. Slowly. Deliberately. His hand fell away, leaving behind the ghost of heat where his fingers had pressed into her pulse.

His features remained composed, carved into calm, betraying nothing.

"Again, Aasifati," he said, before fading back into the shadows.

TALAH XVI

The scent of dew-damp earth and blooming jasmine carried on the morning breeze, pulling Talah forward through the hush of dawn.

It struck her then how quickly the days had blurred together. Five days of drills and tests, of bruises layered over older bruises, of nights spent too restless to truly sleep. And now, only one more day of training remained—one more chance to sharpen herself before the final trial—before everything began. The thought settled heavy in her chest, not fear exactly, but something tauter, sharper, the weight of knowing time was running out.

The gardens spread ahead, sprawling terraces of pale stone and cypress, where sunlight pooled like gold across the fountains. A few early risers crossed the paths—students gathering herbs for the infirmary, a mentor speaking softly to a pair of novices—but Talah slowed as a figure stepped from the shade of an olive tree to intercept her.

Nadir moved with the same practiced ease he always did,

robes brushed immaculate despite the dust of training, a faint smile playing at his lips as though they were old friends meeting by chance. His dark eyes caught hers, steady and unhurried, and he spread his hands as if to welcome her.

"Talah," he said smoothly, his voice pitched low so it didn't carry down the hallway. "Last day of training, and still you walk alone." His gaze flicked toward the cluster of students at the far fountain, then back, sharpening. "You should reconsider my offer. You don't have to go into the Trials without allies."

She folded her arms, the cool morning air at her back seeping through the fabric of her tunic. "I've already told you, Nadir. I don't need your alliance."

He chuckled softly, but there was no warmth in it. He stepped closer, and she caught the faint scent of oud oil clinging to him, sharp and heady, a reminder of Aphelion's wealth. "It isn't just about surviving the Trials," he murmured. "It's about what comes after. My grandmother's voice carries further than most in the Council chamber. With her favor, doors would open for you—doors you could never touch on your own. If you truly mean to follow your father's path, if you want to become a councilor one day, this is your chance."

Talah's jaw tightened. Saahira's name wasn't spoken, but it hung heavy between them nonetheless. Everyone knew the iron behind her words, the way her gaze could cut through a person like a blade. Dangerous, merciless, always watching. And here was Nadir, carrying her ideals like a torch, wielding them as though they were an inheritance.

"No," Talah said, firmer this time. "I don't need your grandmother. I don't need anyone to clear a path for me. I'll prove my own worth."

Something flickered across his expression then—gone too quickly to pin down. He leaned just slightly closer, enough that she felt the heat of him press into the cool breath of morning air.

"This part you're playing? The girl who refuses alliances, who wants to stand on her own?" His smile thinned, eyes too sharp for comfort. "It's a dangerous role. People admire it… until they don't. And when the Trials begin, admiration won't keep you alive."

The words slid under her skin like the edge of a blade. Her breath hitched before she could stop it, a shallow pull of air that caught somewhere between her ribs. The instinct to step back flared—and she crushed it, forcing her boots to stay planted against the stones. He wanted her to flinch, to yield. She wouldn't give him that satisfaction.

The silence stretched, heavy with the hum of bees in the lavender beds and the trickle of water from the nearby fountain. The sweetness of the flowers suddenly felt cloying, thick in her throat.

Talah held his gaze, unblinking, though her pulse beat hard enough to make her fingertips tremble. Her hands curled into fists at her sides, nails biting crescents into her palms—pain to ground herself, to keep the fear from showing. When he finally stepped back, the space he left behind felt colder, her skin still prickling where his presence had pressed too close.

Nadir inclined his head, robes whispering as he stepped aside. "Think on it, at least," he said, his tone light again, though the weight behind it lingered like a shadow. "Time is running short."

Talah brushed past him, following the stone path deeper into the garden. The sunlight filtering through the olive leaves should have been calming, but it only made her stomach knot tighter. The echo of Nadir's warning clung to her like the scent of smoke. She tried to ignore the feeling, heading toward the mess hall, though she was anything but hungry after that.

"You alright?" Mazin asked, making room for her at the table.

Talah set down her food, pushing it away slightly. "I'm fine."

The word sounded hollow even to her own ears, but Mazin didn't press. He just leaned forward, elbows braced against the scarred wood of the table, his shoulder a steady presence at her side.

Across from them, Zayd lounged with his tray half-finished, one long leg kicked out under the bench. He flicked a crumb toward her with a grin that didn't quite reach his eyes. "You don't look fine. You look like you're ready to set the whole mess hall on fire. Which, honestly, would make dinner more interesting."

Adine rolled her eyes, the movement sharp, but her mouth softened. She nudged Zayd's tray away with the edge of her hand. "Don't encourage her. We're supposed to be resting, not giving the mentors another reason to breathe down our necks."

The scrape of utensils and hushed voices around them seemed to fade as the four of them settled into their small circle. For the first time all day, Talah felt the tightness in her chest ease, just a little.

Mazin leaned closer, lowering his voice. "I heard some of the guards talking earlier. The spectators are already making bets. Who wins. Who dies. Who lasts the longest." His jaw flexed, eyes hardening. "We're not just entertainment—we're wagers."

He hesitated, his gaze flicking toward Talah before dropping back to his plate. "They mentioned us. Said we weren't high on the lists. Not favorites to make it through."

The words settled like a stone in her stomach. She could almost hear the faceless crowd outside Aphelion's walls, laughing, trading coin over names, weighing her life against odds scrawled on parchment. To them, she wasn't a person—just a number, a risk, a game.

Zayd let out a sharp laugh, though his fingers tapped restlessly against the table. "Good. Let them count us out now. Nothing's sweeter than proving gamblers wrong." He raised his cup in a half-salute, though his eyes darted toward Talah, gauging her reaction.

Adine frowned, her mouth tightening. "It's not a game. They'll want to see blood. The lower they rank us, the more they'll cheer when we fall."

Talah's chest tightened. She could feel the weight of their stares—their faith, their doubt, their fear—pressing in on her like the heat of the braziers lining the hall. Her father had walked these same corridors once, had been cheered and cursed in equal measure. She wondered if he'd felt this too: the gnawing awareness that his life was nothing more than a spectacle for others.

She set her hands flat against the rough wood of the table, grounding herself. "Then we give them nothing easy to bet on," she said. "We make them wrong. All of them."

Mazin's mouth curved faintly, but it wasn't quite a smile. Zayd tipped his cup higher. Adine gave the smallest nod.

Around them, the hall remained heavy with silence, but between the four of them, something firmer had taken root—defiance, sharper than fear, stronger than doubt.

Talah's boots crunched softly on the gravel path that led behind the dorms. The night air was crisp, cooler than it had been all week. Above her, the stars shimmered in unfamiliar constellations, reminding her of just how far from home she really was.

Stone steps wrapped around the side of the building, narrow and worn with age. Talah took them slowly, her fingers trailing along the rough outer wall of the dorms. The stone was cool beneath her touch, flaking in places, catching on her skin like it wanted to remember everyone who'd climbed this way before her.

The rooftop was flat and bare, surrounded by a low ledge just high enough to lean against. The wind greeted her first—sharp and clean, threading through her hair, pulling at the heat still clinging to her skin. She crossed to the edge and looked out.

The courtyard stretched below, empty and still. Beyond it,

the ziggurat cut sharp lines into the night, and farther still, just visible through the haze, the lights of Astrome flickered. Waiting.

Talah let out a slow breath and sat down on the cold stone, drawing her knees to her chest. The stars above seemed closer from here. Silent. Expectant.

She should have felt relief—it was over for the night, another test survived. But all she could think of was the way Iras had looked at her when they'd trained together: that steady, unreadable calm masking something heavier beneath. He'd pushed her harder than anyone else had, forcing her to confront the edge of her fear until it splintered. She'd hated him for it. For making her feel small and seen all at once.

When he'd told her she was stronger than she realized, she'd wanted to believe him. But now, alone beneath the stars, she wasn't so sure. The memory of his voice—low, even, almost gentle—echoed in her head, blurring with the whisper of wind across the rooftop. She tilted her face to the sky, watching the constellations shimmer faintly in the distance. Somewhere, he was probably still awake, preparing, calculating. And for a reason she couldn't quite name, that thought steadied her as much as it unsettled her.

The stars didn't answer, but they felt like they were listening.

Tomorrow would be the start and end of everything she'd ever known. All she had to do was get through the maze, beat the others, and survive everything that would be trying to kill her. To kill all of them. She hadn't let herself think of it before, but now it hit her like a blow to the chest. Mazin, Zayd, Adine... they'd all be facing the exact same thing she would.

Would they survive? Would she feel it if they didn't?

Mazin had been her best—and only—friend since they were young. He'd been with her through the years she'd been locked away behind those villa walls. Her partner in crime the few times they'd dared to sneak out. Her confidant, her...everything.

She'd already given it all up—her family, her home. What would happen if he didn't make it? If she lost him too?

"Can't sleep just yet?" Mazin pulled himself over the ledge

by the stairs, making himself comfortable beside her. The world around them had fallen into darkness. Moonlight flickered across his face, casting long shadows.

"I don't know if I'll be able to sleep at all tonight," she admitted.

"Scared?"

She considered it for a moment. "Scared. Excited. Nervous. Probably every emotion you could possibly name."

He nodded in understanding. "Honestly, if you weren't here...I don't know how I would feel."

Something in his voice—quiet, unguarded—stirred a warmth and a weight in her chest all at once.

"Have your parents reached out to you?" she asked.

"Just once." He grimaced. "They... weren't too excited about it. But I think they understood why I'm doing it."

She could almost taste the bitterness beneath his calm. His parents had a choice. The luxury of disapproval. Hers had never given her that much.

"Their letter sounded as if they were worried," Mazin went on, his voice quieter now. "I'm sure my mother cried. But in the end, they said it was ultimately up to me."

She glanced sideways at him. The tension working into his jaw said more than his words did. He carried guilt like a bruise—hidden, but tender to the touch.

"They know what you mean to me," he said. "They saw it a long time ago. And they know I couldn't let you do this alone..." He trailed off, fingers picking absently at an invisible thread along his sleeve.

Her throat tightened. She wanted to say something—to tell him that she hadn't asked him to follow her into this, that she didn't deserve his loyalty—but the words wouldn't come.

Footsteps broke the stillness.

"We heard you guys talking from below. This the spot then?" Zayd crept from the shadows, Adine following close behind him.

Zayd flopped down across from them, stretching out against the cold stone.

"Apparently," Talah replied.

Zayd reached into his pockets, pulling out a roll of flatbread wrapped in cloth. "Kitchen door was open," he said, not quite a confession. "I noticed hardly any of us actually ate. Figured if we're going to die tomorrow, we might as well enjoy some good bread before that."

Adine joined them, tentatively taking a seat. "Breaking the law I see."

"Honor among thieves," Zayd replied, tearing the bread into quarters and passing it around.

They ate quietly at first, the stars their only witnesses. The silence wasn't empty—it was heavy, alive, full of things they didn't know how to say. The air smelled faintly of dust and smoke, and Talah found herself tracing constellations across the dark, wondering which ones would still be shining after tomorrow.

For most of her life, it had been her and Mazin against the world. But now, looking at them—Zayd's restless grin, Adine's careful composure—she realized how much that world had changed. They weren't just competitors anymore. They were all standing on the same edge.

"I keep trying to picture it," Adine said after a while, still picking at her bread. "The arena. The maze. But all I get is a blur of lava and drowning and falling from the sky."

"That's probably accurate," Zayd muttered.

"I mean—floating platforms in the air? That's not a test; that's a death sentence." Adine tossed the rest of her bread into the darkness. Zayd looked as if he were about to protest before thinking better of it.

"I don't know how anyone is supposed to survive this." Mazin shuddered beside her. "One biome? Sure. But four? And finding these tokens while fighting for our lives? It's madness."

"It's the Trials," Talah reminded him.

"It's not about surviving everything," Zayd cut in. "It's about surviving just enough."

"Comforting," Mazin replied dryly.

Adine hugged her knees to her chest. "I'm scared."

And there it was—the truth none of them wanted to voice aloud.

"I think we all are," Talah said quietly.

"Nah," Zayd said casually. "I'm just here for the complimentary near-death experience. Heard the screaming is top tier."

Adine choked out a laugh before falling silent again.

"You ever think that maybe this whole thing's just some twisted joke?" Mazin asked, leaning back against the wall. "As if fighting to the death proves anything."

"I mean," Zayd said, voice dry, "if this is their idea of character development, I'd like to formally file a complaint."

Talah smiled faintly, but it felt forced. "I keep wondering who I'll be after... if I'll still be me."

Adine rested her chin on her knees. "Assuming we make it."

The words hung between them, fragile as glass. And though none of them said it aloud, Talah knew they were all thinking the same thing—*if* they made it, nothing would ever be the same again.

They fell quiet again, the silence hanging heavily between them.

"Then we just remind each other of who we are," Mazin said finally. "No matter what these Trials throw at us. No matter what it tries to take."

It wasn't a formal agreement. There was no blood oath. But something passed between them in the silence that followed—an understanding, solid and unspoken. If they couldn't guarantee survival, they could at least promise each other this; they wouldn't go through it alone. The silence stretched, heavy but not unwelcome, each of them retreating into their own thoughts.

Zayd broke it, though his voice was quieter than usual. "Why are we even doing this? Really. We could've walked away. Nobody forced us to climb those stairs and sign our names."

Adine shifted, arms tightening around her knees. "Because if I didn't, I'd never leave my family's shadow. My brother's death would just... hang there forever, and I'd always be the girl who was too afraid to step where he fell."

Mazin stared down at the stone between them, his jaw tight. "I wanted more than the life my parents carved out for me. And Talah—" he glanced at her, voice softening, "—I couldn't let her do this alone."

Zayd gave a half-smile that didn't quite reach his eyes. "Me? I just wanted to prove I'm not the useless son they think I am. That maybe I can make it somewhere they don't get to write the script."

They all looked to Talah then, the night air sharp with expectation. She hesitated, the words catching in her throat, but finally she let them fall.

"Because I don't know who I am outside of this. Outside of proving that I can be more than the daughter they tried to silence. If I survive... maybe I'll finally know."

The wind stirred around them, tugging at their sleeves.

Adine stood first, looking uncomfortable as she brushed her hands off on her pants. "I should go. Try to sleep before I talk myself out of this."

"Same," Zayd said, stretching as he stood. "I'd like to be fully rested before being emotionally and physically obliterated."

Mazin glanced at Talah, a question in his eyes.

"I might stay a little bit longer," Talah said softly. He offered her a small nod, lingering a second longer before following them down the stairs.

Then finally she was alone.

Talah crossed to the edge of the rooftop and rested her arms on the low stone wall. The wind curled around her, tugging at her sleeves, carrying with it the scent of distant storms and scorched earth.

She stared out across the night toward the shadowy outline of the arena. Tomorrow, that place would open its mouth and try to swallow her whole. Fire, flood, stone, sky—it would tear at her until there was nothing left but the pieces that refused to break.

And she didn't know if that would be enough.

But up here, above the whispers of doubt and fear, beneath the stars that had watched a thousand Trials come and go, Talah let herself feel it all. The fear. The weight. The impossible pull of the unknown.

Then, without a word, she turned and climbed back down into the dark.

FIRAS
XVII

Firas stalked through the quiet paths of Aphelion's courtyard, the moonlight pooling over the stone like spilled milk. He should've been poring over the texts they'd found in the archives, but had forced himself to take a break. The more they read, the less sense it made. Fragments, mostly. Half-burned pages and mistranslated glyphs. A journal written in a dialect no one had used for centuries. Symbols that didn't match any of the twelve Signs.

At first, they thought it was a mistake. A scribe's flair. But the pattern kept emerging—always in the margins, always erased or crossed out. Mentions of an unnamed group, one that 'did not belong' yet was bound to it all the same.

The Ambigua.

One passage had stuck with him more than the others.

'Where the twelve converge, the forgotten one waits in silence. Not a sign, not a servant. A weapon born of balance broken.'

They still didn't know what it meant. None of it made sense, and yet, somehow, it felt familiar.

Like a memory he'd never lived.

He ran a hand through his hair, frustration curling tight in his chest. The Council clearly hadn't wanted anyone to find those records. Which made him wonder—how much of the Zodiac's history had been rewritten? How many truths had been buried beneath layers of doctrine and fear?

And what was this weapon they kept mentioning? *A weapon born of balance broken.*

His boots scuffed against the gravel path as he passed the dorms, the slightest movement in the shadows catching his eye. A silhouette slipped from around the corner, silent as the night. Instinctively, he took a step back, heart kicking once before he recognized her.

Talah stopped short when she noticed him. He stared back, surprise and a slow, clawing suspicion making his voice colder than he'd intended.

"What the hell were you doing up there?"

She crossed her arms defensively. "Not that it's any of your business, but I just wanted to be alone for a minute. Is that a crime?" Talah's eyes narrowed in a challenge.

"On a roof?" He raised an eyebrow, wanting to question it further. There was just something about her that made him want to press her, to dig into the why. But then he *really* looked at her.

Her breath was uneven, chest rising and falling a little too quickly. Her eyes nervously flicked between him and the dormitory door as if she were calculating the escape routes. There was something almost brittle in the way she held herself, like one more word might shatter her entirely despite the hardened facade. And yet...she didn't run. She stood there, spine stiff with that same stubbornness she wore like armor.

Only now that armor was cracking.

There was a tension in her—something fragile, drawn taut under the weight of her silence. He hadn't noticed it before. He hadn't *let* himself notice. There was more than just the sharp edges and the defiance. But the *fear*. The weight she carried like it had been welded to her very bones.

And maybe it was the moonlight, or the way she carried herself now, but for a moment, she didn't seem untouchable. She seemed human.

And beautiful.

Not the polished, practiced beauty of someone trying to be seen, but the kind that crept in unnoticed. That revealed itself in soft shadows and vulnerable pauses. The kind that caught him off guard. Her silent strength called to him.

He swallowed, throat suddenly dry. Whatever words he'd meant to say slipped away, lost to the look in her eyes.

The edge in his tone melted. Sighing, he rubbed the back of his neck. "I get it," he said quietly.

She said nothing, only waited.

"I thought I was going to die in the second round of my Trials." The words slipped out before he could stop them—too quiet to be casual, too honest to take back. "My father drilled it into me from the moment I could stand: our family doesn't fail. Failure wasn't just shameful—it was dangerous. It meant exile. Silence. Being forgotten."

He exhaled sharply, as if the memory still lived somewhere in his ribs.

"Every second I was in there, I kept thinking about how I'd disappoint them. And what kind of funeral they'd give a failure."

"But you didn't fail." He was almost surprised to hear her reply.

He gave a short, bitter laugh. "No. Not quite," he said. "But not because of him. The moment I stopped caring about what he wanted, what he expected... that's when I started surviving."

Talah's voice wavered slightly. "I wish I could do that. Stop caring."

"But it's different for you," he said quietly.

She nodded once. "I've been hidden away like a secret my entire life. And I don't even know why." She sighed. "Maybe they were just being overprotective. But now... it feels like the Trials are the only place I'm allowed to exist... and, even then, only if I beat them."

Firas studied her closely. There was something raw in her tone—something that cracked through the stubborn confidence she usually wore. Before he could think better of it, he found himself leaning closer, the air between them charged and thin.

The firelight caught along the curve of her cheek, the faint line of a bruise near her jaw from training. Stray wisps of hair clung to her skin. She looked breakable and fierce all at once, and that contradiction tugged at something in him he didn't want to name.

Her eyes flicked to his, questioning. Not scared, but cautious, like she wasn't used to being seen without the armor she wore.

He swallowed, unsure if the ache in his chest was empathy or something more dangerous. Every instinct told him to look away, to pull back before she saw too much—but he didn't. Couldn't.

"You don't have to beat them," he said at last, voice low. "You just have to survive them."

Firas hesitated, then reached up, fingers brushing a loose strand of hair from her face. The movement was slow, uncertain, as if he wasn't sure what he was doing until he was already doing it. His fingers lingered for a heartbeat too long against her cheek—warm, real.

Talah didn't pull away.

Her eyes locked on his, and for a moment, neither of them moved. It wasn't dramatic. No sweeping music, no sudden pull of gravity. Just a quiet stillness. A shared breath. A fragile, unexpected understanding blooming in the dark.

"I always fought against what they wanted me to be," she whispered. "But I don't even know who I am outside of that. Outside of those walls."

A councilor's daughter. Raised in the heart of the Zodiac elite but never able to really be a part of that world. He'd spent years resenting everything she represented—everything *he* used to represent. Power. Privilege. Control.

But now, in this quiet corner of the night, she seemed as trapped as he had been. As they all were. She was willingly risking her life for a chance at what she believed to be freedom. Just as he was.

Just as he had done before.

He let the silence stretch before answering. "And here I thought people like you had it easier."

"People like me?" Her head tilted to the side, voice humorless.

Firas silently berated himself for the slip-up. "You know," he said, eyes flicking away. "Born into privilege. Into status. All those doors that were already open." Doors that had once been open to him before it had all been stripped away. Doors he'd taken for granted.

Talah shook her head. "The doors open, but they only lead where they want you to go. And even then, not every door is open to you. If you step off that path—just once—it all slams shut."

He studied her, the way her jaw tensed like she was used to biting back her thoughts. He saw it now—the same pressure that haunted his own steps. When he looked at her, he could almost see himself.

"Guess we've both been trained to play roles we didn't ask for, Aasifati," he murmured.

Talah's eyes softened. "Guess we're not so different then."

And that—more than anything—unnerved him. Because he'd spent so long defining himself by who he wasn't. Who he wouldn't become. But now she stood there, not as the councilor's daughter, not as a rival or an enemy. Just a girl trying to breathe.

And he wasn't sure what scared him more: how much she reminded him of himself... or how badly he wanted to reach for her again.

Talah shifted her weight, glancing down, then back up. Her voice, when it came, was barely above a whisper. "You ever think about walking away from it all? Just... disappearing?"

"All the time," he admitted before he could stop himself. "But then I remember—I don't know who I'd be without it."

Her lips twitched—not quite a smile, but something like

understanding. "Ana kaman." *Same.*

Another beat passed. The air between them changed, charged with heat and silence.

Firas stepped closer. Not out of impulse, but instinct. As if his body had already decided he needed to be closer, before his mind could talk him out of it.

His hand brushed hers—light, uncertain.

Talah looked up at him, her eyes wide but steady.

And suddenly, the space between them felt unbearably small.

Their gazes locked, held.

He leaned in, just enough to feel the whisper of her breath against his. Just enough for her eyelashes to flutter.

They didn't speak. There was nothing left to say. His hand came up again, fingertips grazing her cheek, tucking another strand of hair behind her ear with quiet reverence. Her breath hitched. She didn't move.

Their faces tilted. Closer. Closer still.

He froze.

Some part of him—sharper, colder—snapped back into place. He blinked once, as if waking from a dream, and jerked back. Because that's what this was. A dream. Reality was much more brutal. Her people were out to erase his, and yet she had no notion of the invisible war they fought. She still had the privilege of living just because she wasn't different. Because she wasn't like him.

And he couldn't afford to want this.

Not now.

Not with her.

Not when he didn't even know who she really was.

He stepped away, heart pounding for all the wrong reasons, guilt knotting in his chest like a blade twisted sideways. He couldn't look at her—not at the confusion in her eyes, not at the hurt he knew he'd just caused.

"This was a mistake," he muttered, voice low and tight. "I shouldn't have…"

He didn't finish.

Didn't wait for her to speak.

Firas turned, forcing himself to leave her behind as if it had never happened at all. The night air bit at his face as he moved, each step pounding against the stone like punishment. The campus was hushed at this hour, the winding paths between buildings wrapped in shadows, but he barely saw any of it. His mind raced faster than his feet—flashes of her eyes, her voice, the way her breath had hitched when he'd touched her. He kept moving until the familiar silhouette of the mentor dorms finally came into view. His chest ached—not from the brisk walk back, but from everything he hadn't said. Everything he'd let himself feel for one reckless moment too long.

The door to his dorm creaked open under his hand, and he stepped inside with the weight of too many thoughts pressing against his skull.

Only to find Kamaria waiting for him.

She sat cross-legged on his bed, her fingers twisting a copper bead around and around the length of her braid, the only sign of her impatience. Her eyes flicked up as soon as he entered.

"There you are. Where the hell have you been?"

Firas sighed, shutting the door behind him. "Didn't realize we had a schedule to keep."

"We do when we're risking our necks for this." She slid off the bed and stood, arms crossed. "I've been keeping an eye on those we identified this morning."

"And?"

"If they're Ambigua, they're hiding it well. Probably have no idea what they are—or they do, and they're terrified of being found out."

Firas leaned against the desk, brow furrowing. "So we help them. Get them out before the next Trial begins."

"That's the plan." She paused. "Or it was. Assuming you've actually come up with a strategy."

"I'll think of something," he said, voice low. "Give me tonight."

Kamaria raised an eyebrow. "We reconvene tomorrow, then.

Before the first trial. I don't want to improvise mid-round."

He nodded, distracted. She didn't move. Silence stretched.

"You okay?" she asked finally. He didn't answer. Her eyes narrowed. "This have something to do with Talah?"

His jaw tightened.

"Firas," she said, voice edged with warning now. "Tell me you didn't—"

"I didn't," he cut in, too fast. Too defensive.

Kam gave him a long look, the kind that said she didn't need him to say it out loud. She already knew.

"I know she's not who we thought," she said carefully. "But don't forget who she is either. Councilor's daughter. Dangerous bloodline. You let your guard down with her, it won't be a clean fall."

He looked away, jaw clenched, throat thick with things he couldn't explain.

"Samira, Rafiq, all the others—they're counting on us. We have a mission, and we cannot stray from it," Kam reminded him.

"I know that," he replied, voice tight with irritation.

Kam sighed. "Just—stay focused. We've got too much riding on this."

She turned to leave, pausing in the doorway. "Get some sleep. You look like hell."

When the door clicked shut behind her, Firas finally let himself exhale.

But the quiet of the room did nothing to silence his thoughts. And no amount of planning would make him forget the way Talah had looked at him in the dark—like she'd seen something in him worth trusting.

And that was the most dangerous thing of all.

TALAH
XVIII

The stairs to the underground chamber were slick with condensation, the air growing heavier with every step. Talah descended in silence, each footfall echoing faintly against the ancient stone. The hallway twisted deeper into the earth, where the scent of damp earth and flickering torchlight signaled their arrival beneath the arena.

The room they entered was vast and circular, carved straight into the bedrock beneath Aphelion. Pillars lined the edges like silent sentinels, and in the center, a glowing emblem pulsed faintly with the Zodiac crest—its twelve symbols circling a void that almost seemed to hum. Around her, the other competitors filed in, their footsteps quiet, their faces taut with anticipation.

Talah's stomach twisted.

The first trial would begin in less than an hour.

Zayd sidled up beside her, eyes scanning the ceiling like he expected it to collapse at any moment. "If I die in the first round, tell my mother I went out bravely," he muttered.

Adine snorted. "You screamed just the other day in training

when your mentor used his ability against you."

"Bravely screamed," Zayd corrected. "There's a difference. Besides, he'd explicitly said not to use my power, and yet he did it anyway. That was just unfair."

Talah smirked despite herself, tension easing slightly. "You're not going to die," she said firmly. "None of us are."

Mazin appeared on her other side, arms folded, calm and unreadable. His eyes softened as he glanced down at her. "We've trained. We'll survive. Together."

Their presence steadied her. Which was strange considering they'd been complete strangers just a few days ago. Now, their presence was the only thing keeping her sane.

But the steadiness was only surface deep.

Beneath it, her thoughts clawed at her. Relentless. Circling. She couldn't stop thinking about him. About how close they'd come to something she couldn't name. The way his eyes had lingered. The way he'd left without a word.

She clenched her fists at her sides.

You don't have time for this.

A loud clang echoed from the center of the chamber, reverberating through the stone like a warning bell. The glowing Zodiac crest split cleanly down the middle and began to lower with a deep mechanical groan, revealing a circular pit pulsing with radiant energy. For a heartbeat, there was silence—then a surge of power as a smooth obsidian platform rose in its place.

Footsteps echoed in the chamber.

All eyes turned as a figure emerged from the shadowed archway opposite the competitors. Tall, robed in deep indigo lined with gold thread, Director Khalias stepped into the torchlight. His face was hard angles and ice, his eyes glittering with cool precision. His presence alone seemed to quiet the room further. It was the first time he's made an official appearance, though Talah had seen him among the spectators placing their bets throughout the week.

He stopped just short of the emblem, folding his hands behind his back. "Competitors," he said, voice crisp and amplified by the acoustics of the coliseum, "you now stand on the threshold of the Elemental Crucible—the first of this year's Trials. As tradition dictates, you will enter alone, separated and tested by the maze itself."

A murmur rippled through the gathered competitors.

"The platform you see before you," Khalias continued, nodding toward the emblem, "will lift you into the maze above. Once there, you will have access to only one sector at a time. The maze is alive—constantly shifting. No two paths will be alike."

Talah's fingers curled into fists.

Khalias stepped closer to the edge of the crest. "Your assigned entry points are as follows. Competitor Rafi Noorani, Air sector. Competitor Rayen Al-Dahhak, Earth. Adine Morad—Water sector. Zayd Amir, Earth." Khalias continued to list off names, designating them to their first section of the maze.

Talah waited, holding her breath until she heard her own.

"Talah bint Khalid... Fire sector."

A sharp pang twisted in her chest, but she gave no outward reaction.

Khalias turned back to the group. "The maze will test not only your elemental adaptability, but your endurance, your strategy, and your ability to withstand the unknown. Trust no one. Expect betrayal. Survive."

A hiss rose from the earth, and the platform began to hum beneath their feet. Above them, the circular ceiling aperture unsealed with a grinding moan, and through it came the first roar of the crowd. Thousands of voices came crashing down like thunder. A cacophony of voices, shouting, chanting, stamping in anticipation as the Trials began. It all washed over them like a wave, distant but thunderous. A voice boomed across the space, amplified to reach both competitors and spectators alike.

"Welcome to the first trial. Each of you will face his or her section of the labyrinth alone. Succeed, and you advance. Fail—"

Talah blocked that last part out. She couldn't—wouldn't—fail. No matter what.

Khalias stepped back, lifting a single hand.

"Step forward when your name is called to your assigned Sign. The maze awaits."

Mazin whipped around, his hand reaching for hers. "*Fire?*"

Adine's brow furrowed, her eyes darting between Talah and Mazin. "They're splitting us up."

"Which isn't surprising," Talah reminded them. "They knew we were all forming alliances. It would make sense they'd throw this at us now."

"We're going into Water," Mazin said, his voice laced with disbelief. "And they throw you into Fire? Alone?"

Talah tried to hold their gaze, to look composed. "It's fine. I can handle it."

Mazin shook his head. "You shouldn't have to handle it alone."

"None of us should," Adine added quietly.

Talah forced a smile she didn't feel. "You'll be together. That's something."

Before anyone could reply, Zayd appeared beside them with a lopsided grin that didn't quite reach his eyes. "Ah yes, classic Trial strategy—split the emotionally fragile kids like firewood and see which ones burn first."

Adine rolled her eyes. "Not helping, Zayd."

"I'm always helping," he said, though he tugged at the cuff of his sleeve with fingers that wouldn't stay still. "It's just…you know. In a psychologically questionable way."

Talah studied him for a beat longer than usual. His smile was intact, but his jaw was tight, his eyes flicking too quickly between exits and shadows. He was cracking jokes the way someone clings to a ledge. Because falling was worse than pretending they weren't hanging on at all.

"You're Earth, right?" she asked softly.

He nodded. "Yeah. Grounded. Stable. Emotionally rock solid. Definitely not about to throw up."

"Zayd…" Mazin started.

"I'm fine," he said too quickly. "We're all fine. This is fine." He motioned vaguely at the glowing crest. "Sure, we're about to get thrown into a sadistic magical labyrinth in front of half the city while being evaluated on how quickly we die, but it's poetic, right?"

Adine huffed, but there was a flicker of fondness in her expression. "Poetic."

Mazin stepped closer, his voice low but fierce. "We trained for this together. We figured things out together. They're counting on us being split up. You know that, right?"

"I do." Her voice barely wavered, but something in her chest twisted. "But that's the game."

Adine looked at her for a long moment. "Just don't do anything reckless, Tala. If it gets bad—get out. No one's keeping score for dying bravely."

Talah let out a breath, her throat tight. "You too. All of you."

The hum of the platform intensified, pulsing like a heartbeat beneath their feet. A line of white light swept across the obsidian, marking the start.

"I hate this," Zayd muttered.

Adine glanced sideways at him. "Better not cry. If you cry, I swear—"

"I don't cry."

"You cried when the soup was too spicy."

"I wasn't *prepared*, Adine!"

Talah bit back a small smile, her nerves calming slightly. The platform trembled beneath them, and the first wave of competitors began stepping onto their marked positions.

Mazin hesitated, then looked back at Talah. "We'll see you on the other side, yeah?"

Talah nodded, even though she wasn't sure she believed it.

Adine held her gaze one last time. "Don't lose yourself in there."

Zayd gave a lazy two-finger salute. "Try not to get incinerated. I'm pretty sure ash-gray isn't your color."

The platform jerked upwards, nearly sending them flying. Talah staggered, catching her balance just in time as a column of light enveloped them. The obsidian beneath their feet pulsed like a heartbeat, rising faster now—higher, higher—toward the blinding ring of light above.

The roar of the crowd swelled, thundering down from the open arena like a living thing. It crashed against her ears, a tidal wave of noise and bloodlust, as if the very sky were shouting in anticipation.

Wind whipped around them as the platform breached the edge of the underground chamber and emerged into the crucible above—a sprawling nightmare of shifting biomes stitched together like a patchwork of chaos. Flames roared in the distance, geysers hissed in the mist, and islands of jagged stone floated in midair, tethered by nothing.

They rose up to meet the maze.

The air tasted of metal and ash, sharp in her lungs. Talah's sector pulsed to life at her feet, brilliant, red-hot light flaring in a ring around her rune. The others around her began to vanish, one by one, teleported by Libras hidden from view. The air cracked with each disappearance, a chorus of dissonant thunderclaps.

She clenched her jaw, heart pounding like war drums in her chest. The noise, the heat, the smell of smoke—it pressed in from every side.

For a heartbeat, she closed her eyes. And in that split second of stillness, she saw him—his hand closing over hers, the quiet steadiness in his voice when everything else had been chaos. Her pulse steadied just enough.

And then, everything vanished.

Light consumed her vision, searing, soundless, all-encompassing. For a heartbeat, she wasn't sure if she was falling or floating. There was no ground beneath her, no air around her, just the raw pull tearing her from one place to the next.

When sensation returned, it did so with violence.

She hit the ground hard, heat slamming into her like a wall. The air was thick with smoke and the sharp tang of sulfur, scorching her lungs on the first breath. Cracked earth stretched beneath her hands. She pushed herself up, wincing. The heat instantly slicked her skin with sweat.

The Fire sector.

She was still in the arena. She knew that. The rumble of the crowd hadn't vanished entirely. It echoed faintly from above, dulled by the towering hedge walls that boxed her into the Fire sector. The hedges were impossibly tall and dense, but not perfect. Through a thin gap above, she caught a glimpse of the stands: blurred faces, flashes of banners, and movement like a restless tide.

The arena hadn't disappeared. It had just transformed.

Her section was its own pocket of chaos—of suffocating heat, broken terrain, and flame-drenched obstacles that stretched into the horizon. Jagged obsidian cliffs pierced the haze like black teeth. Lava coursed in molten rivers between them, bubbling and hissing as the ground shifted beneath her. Above, the sky wasn't real, but the illusion held well—blood-red clouds churned overhead, laced with flickers of ember light.

Somewhere in the maze, the others were already moving. Fighting.

Surviving.

Talah clenched her fists, breath shallow. The way back was closed off—swallowed by the hedge wall. Ahead, a narrow ridge stretched forward, flanked by flames and bridges that looked anything but stable. Each step forward sent tremors through the cracked stone beneath her boots, and the heat curled around her like a living thing, greedy and sharp.

Above, through the break in the towering hedges, she caught a glimpse of the arena stands again. They were safe from the Trial's dangers and given the perfect view. She reminded herself that she wasn't alone. That every movement, every mistake, every *weakness* was being carefully watched.

A flicker of movement behind her snapped her attention back to the arena.

Footsteps—fast and steady. Too deliberate to be panic.

She spun around just as a figure emerged from the shimmering heat. He moved like smoke, fluid and graceful.

Stopping a few paces away, his hands at his sides, posture calm. Too calm. Talah recognized him from their training sessions the day before. A Scorpio.

"You don't have to keep running," he said, voice low and smooth, like oil sliding over water. "You've done enough."

Talah took a step back. "Get out of my way."

The boy tilted his head, eyes sharp and unreadable. "Why? What are you trying to prove?"

Something in his tone caught her off guard. It wasn't a threat. It was almost... gentle. Persuasive.

"You shouldn't even be here," he continued. "Thrown into fire for what? To impress your parents? To chase a lie about worth? You're not even sure why you're doing this anymore."

The words slipped under her skin, deeper than they should have.

She narrowed her eyes. "Khallas."

But even as she said it, her thoughts began to blur. Her heartbeat slowed. The maze felt farther away now—less like a battlefield, more like a stage. Her limbs felt heavier. The heat warped around her, and the Scorpio competitor's voice seemed to fill the air.

"You're a pawn, Talah. Just another name to sacrifice. Why not make it easier? Sit down. Rest. Let go."

Her body relaxed, knees bending to the scorched earth. She realized too late she'd been staring at him. Straight into his eyes.

The world twisted.

The flames around her bent into strange, mirrored shapes. The ground rippled like disturbed water, the heat pressing into her head, muddling her focus. A tremor rolled through her as her knees buckled slightly.

This isn't real.

But the voice in her mind whispered otherwise.

You're not enough. You never were. They're all better off without you.

Her grip on the moment began to slip—until a single memory cracked through the fog:

Adine's fierce glare. "Don't lose yourself in there."

Mazin's determined voice. "We'll see you on the other side, yeah?"

Her fingers found the edge of a jagged stone beside her. She clutched it, letting the pain cut through her palm like truth. Real. Grounded.

Talah's eyes shut.

She couldn't listen. Not anymore.

The moment I stopped caring about what he wanted, what he expected...that's when I started surviving.

Something inside her shifted.

She didn't know how. Didn't think. She just reached out with something deeper than muscle or instinct, something rooted in the marrow of her bones.

And the air answered.

The heat around her warped, shimmered. Threads of moisture—scarce, nearly nonexistent—gathered at her command, drawn from the smoke, from the sweat clinging to her skin, from the very breath in the space between them.

With a strangled cry, she slammed the invisible force downward.

A burst of steam exploded from a glowing lava fissure near the Scorpio—violent, sudden, and massive. The blast swallowed the path in an instant, thick enough to blind, loud enough to stun. The pressure in her skull snapped like a rope gone taut. The fog lifted; the voice was gone. Her mind was her own again.

The Scorpio stumbled back, coughing, caught off guard as her shoulder slammed into his chest. She didn't try to finish him—just unbalanced him enough to send him skidding toward the cliff's edge.

And then she ran.

The path ahead twisted into a blackened tunnel, the floor breaking apart beneath her as she bolted across it. Behind her, the ground collapsed with a roar, sealing the Scorpio competitor on the other side.

Only when the heat faded did she slow.

She stumbled into a cavern lit by flickering firelight, not chaotic like before, but eerily still. A wide chamber stretched before her, carved from obsidian and ash. Flames curled around the edges like watchful eyes.

Talah slid to the ground, her back pressed against the heated stone. For now, she was safe.

One opponent down. Many more to go.

She didn't know how many of them would make it past the first sector, but she knew one thing for certain.

She needed to find that token before someone else tried to kill her.

TALAH
XIX

Talah's lips cracked as she tried again to draw water from the air, but the heat devoured it faster than she could shape it. Her stomach gnawed at itself, a hollow echo of failure, as the Fire sector offered nothing but stone and ash.

Sleep had been impossible, tucked away inside the heated cavern, jumping at every sound. Every breath reminded her that survival was not given, but clawed for. It was the first time she had felt truly alone. By morning, her body moved sluggishly, her tongue heavy against her teeth. The cavern she had huddled in all night reeked of sulfur and smoke, its jagged walls pressing in like clenched fists. She had searched every crevice in the gray stone before leaving, fingers scraping raw against the sharp edges, hoping against hope to glimpse the glint of a token. There had been nothing—only dust, only heat, only the hollow echo of her own heartbeat hammering in her ears.

The silence was worse than the dark. It magnified everything—the shuffle of loose rock when she shifted, the rasp of her own shallow breaths, the faint crackle of embers still smoldering outside. Sleep had never come. Every time she closed her eyes, she'd snapped awake at the imagined tread of feet, the hiss of fire, the thought of another competitor slipping a blade across her throat.

Now, as the sun rose higher, the cavern felt more like a furnace. Heat poured in through the narrow opening, searing her skin before she had even stepped outside. The air itself seemed to shimmer, thick and suffocating, as though she were breathing through a veil of ash.

Her legs ached as she climbed out, pausing at the threshold to scan the ridge beyond. The Fire sector stretched endlessly before her—black ridges splitting the horizon like jagged teeth, ground cracked and brittle beneath the weight of ages. Not a blade of grass, not a single tree. Nothing but stone, ash, and heat. The kind of place where hope came to die.

She set out anyway. Each step jarred her bones, sending sharp pangs through the blisters forming on her heels. Her lips split when she licked them. Thirst gnawed at her worse than hunger, though her belly twisted painfully with every movement. She tried again—pulling at the air, willing the faintest trace of water to gather—but the heat swallowed it, leaving her palms dry and empty.

The sun blazed mercilessly overhead, and the ridges seemed to ripple in its glare, warping into false shapes that vanished the moment she neared them. Once, she thought she saw movement at the corner of her vision—a flicker of color against the black stone—but when she turned, there was only emptiness, the silence too deep to trust.

Her mind began to fray at the edges, the heat working its way into her thoughts as much as her skin. *This is what they want*, she realized bitterly. *To see how long it takes before we break.*

Above the arena, she could just make out a few pieces of the stands between the cavernous ravines. They were empty right now, but she knew they wouldn't remain empty for long. The citizens of Astrome would arrive, ready for another day of bloodshed and bets.

Her knees buckled slightly before she caught herself. *Get up*, a voice echoed in her mind—not her own, but his.

She forced herself forward, driven by the knowledge that she couldn't afford to waste more time searching the same stretch of wasteland. Somewhere in this cursed sector, the tokens waited, and she would never find them if she curled back into a hole to wither away.

With her head bent, her vision swimming, she nearly didn't notice the figure ahead until she was nearly on top of him.

Talah froze, reaching for a weapon at her hip that didn't exist.

Nadir sat with his back against the stone, forehead beaded in sweat. Despite the oppressive heat, he looked as if he were on holiday, tanning himself beneath the morning rays. His dark hair clung damp to his temples, yet somehow it only made him appear deliberate, composed—like even the sweat was just another accessory he wore with ease. His bronze skin caught the sunlight, gleaming as though the fire sector itself bent to illuminate him.

His tunic, though dust-stained from the maze, still looked finer than most—embroidered cuffs fraying only slightly, the fabric clinging to the lean strength of his frame. His features bore the unmistakable cut of privilege: sharp cheekbones, a straight nose, and a mouth that curved in a perpetual smirk that never reached his eyes. Those eyes—cool, calculating amber—watched her with the lazy patience of a predator that already knew its prey would tire before escape.

He lounged with one knee bent, one hand lazily turning the linen-wrapped loaf in his palm as though it were nothing of consequence, though Talah knew he'd calculated the moment with precision. Every movement, every gesture, was practiced nonchalance, a show of ease meant to mask the sharp edge beneath.

There was always something disarming about him—how charm and threat sat so comfortably in the same breath. Even when he smiled, her pulse never quite settled. It was as if standing near him meant walking a line she couldn't see until it cut her.

She folded her arms, forcing her expression into something neutral, but her body betrayed her in small ways—the slight tension in her shoulders, the instinctive urge to take a step back that she refused to give in to.

Nadir's gaze flicked up, and for an instant she felt the weight of it—cool, assessing, searching for a crack. The air seemed to thicken around her, the lazy turn of his hand over the bread somehow louder than the wind rustling through the garden leaves.

He wanted her off balance. And the worst part was, it was working.

"You look like you could use this," he said smoothly, as if they were standing at a banquet table instead of in a wasteland built to kill them. He broke off a piece, the soft white crumb jarring in its tenderness against the blackened world around them.

Talah's throat tightened. She hated the way her body leaned toward it, the way her stomach clenched at the smell. "I don't need your help."

They weren't supposed to bring anything into the maze, though she knew those rules wouldn't apply to all of them.

"You do," he said easily, stepping closer. "But you don't want to admit it. That's fine." He offered the piece of bread anyway, holding it just far enough to make her reach. "All I ask is that you listen while you eat."

Her eyes narrowed. "And what plans are worth a crust of bread?"

"The kind that keeps people like us alive," he replied, his voice dipping lower, conspiratorial. "You and I—we aren't like them. We have councilor's blood running through our veins. We were never meant to crawl in the dirt with Crossborns. Together, we could make sure we don't."

The words curled like smoke in the air between them. Talah's hunger screamed, but her pride and suspicion screamed louder.

"I'll survive without you," she said at last, steel cutting through her hoarse voice.

Nadir's smile only deepened, though his eyes flickered with something sharper. He placed the bread on a rock between them, dust clinging to its edges. "Take it, then. Consider it a gesture. One day, you'll see the sense in what I'm offering."

"Why?" Talah challenged. "Why me? It can't just be because my father is a councilor."

Nadir tilted his head, studying her. "Libras can speak to others with their minds… but they're also extremely good at reading people. Our diplomatic nature and desire to understand motivations make us adept at sensing what others are feeling and understanding motivations. There's something about you…" He didn't elaborate further.

His words lingered like smoke in the heated air. Talah kept her face still, schooling her expression into something close to consideration. The bread sat on the rock between them, the scent drifting upward, maddening in its simplicity. Her stomach growled so loudly she was sure he could hear it.

She crouched and picked up the piece, turning it over in her fingers as if weighing his offer. She forced herself to bite; the dry crumb sticking to her tongue, soaking up the last of her spit. The shame of it curdled in her gut, but she kept her eyes on him, nodding faintly as if she were listening.

Nadir leaned back against the stone, satisfied. Talah chewed slowly, forcing her face to remain neutral. The bread was dry, clinging to her throat, but she swallowed it down as if considering his words.

Leaning forward, he lowered his voice as if they were conspirators. "You've seen the others. They fight for scraps, for a chance they'll never earn. Even if they survive, they'll never stand equal to us. But you and I—together—we could be untouchable."

Talah let the silence stretch, watching him through lowered lashes. He wanted her to ask, wanted her to lean closer. So she did neither.

"You don't have to answer now," he went on, gesturing broadly to the wasteland. "But think of what we could build. When the dust settles, Aphelion will still be ours. We'll stand above the rubble while the others burn themselves out trying to climb higher than they're allowed."

Her jaw tightened. "And what happens to those who get in your way?"

His smile sharpened. "They stop being a problem."

The words hung between them, heavy as stone. Talah forced another bite, nodding faintly as if she were weighing the offer, though her pulse hammered against her throat. He was testing her—not just her hunger, but her loyalty. The bread sat heavy in her stomach, every crumb a reminder of her own desperation. She made herself hum low in her throat, feigning thoughtfulness.

Nadir's gaze lingered on her for too long. Those amber eyes narrowed, cutting past the mask she wore. The lazy smirk faded.

"You're pretending," he said softly, almost amused. "You think you can fool me into feeding you like some stray dog." He leaned closer, voice dropping into a hiss.

Her fingers tightened on the crust. She made herself meet his stare, steel against steel. "I told you already—I'll survive without you."

For the first time, his composure cracked. The bread slipped from his hand, forgotten, as his blade flashed free of its sheath.

Talah barely had time to duck. Steel sang as it cut through the air where her head had been, sparks biting from stone. She stumbled back, heart slamming into her ribs, yanking her knife from her belt.

"You should've said yes," Nadir breathed, his smirk snapping back into place, sharper now, dangerous.

The next blow came fast—faster than she expected—and the impact jarred her whole arm when her small blade caught the edge of his. Pain rattled up to her shoulder, but she forced her feet to hold. Another strike came, and another, each blow measured, practiced. He wasn't fighting to test her anymore. He was fighting to end her.

Talah twisted sideways, the blade grazing her collarbone, burning a shallow line across her skin. She lashed out with her boot, catching his shin. He snarled but barely staggered, already recovering, already swinging again.

Her chest seized with panic. She couldn't match him, not like this, not when her arms trembled with fatigue and her stomach felt like a hollow pit. Hunger dulled her reflexes, thirst blurred her vision. He was faster, stronger, better fed. If she kept fighting, she'd be dead.

So she didn't.

On the next strike, she twisted with the blow instead of against it, letting the momentum drive her sideways. Pain flared through her shoulder, but it gave her the angle she needed. She shoved hard against his chest with all her weight, catching him off guard. The force sent her stumbling backward, sand and grit sliding under her boots. His blade sliced through the air inches from her face as she let the recoil fling her away.

She didn't wait to see his recovery. She turned and ran.

Heat pressed against her like a living thing, searing her lungs until each gasp came ragged and shallow. Sweat stung her eyes, blurring the black ridges into a smear of shadow and light. Her hands clawed at the rocks for balance, fingers splitting open when the sharp edges cut through her skin.

Behind her came the sound of boots striking stone—steady, unhurried, like he was savoring the chase. And then, his voice: laughter, low and cruel, curling up the slope after her.

Her heart stuttered. She pushed harder, scrambling on hands and knees where the incline steepened, grit grinding into her cuts. The ridge loomed above her like the back of a beast, sharp and endless. She threw herself over it at last, tumbling hard into the hollow beyond.

Stone tore at her palms as she caught herself, chest heaving, hair sticking to her damp skin. She didn't dare stop. She forced herself upright and plunged deeper into the maze of rock spires and ravines, weaving between their jagged shadows until the sound of his footsteps dulled behind her.

Behind her, laughter rang out—low and cruel, chasing her into the wasteland.

Her lungs burned as she staggered forward, weaving through the maze of jagged spires. Every turn looked the same—black stone, fractured ground, shadows stretching like claws. Her ears strained, desperate, and then she heard it: the steady crunch of boots on gravel behind her.

He was following.

Her chest tightened, panic clawing up her throat. Left or right? The ridge split into two paths, both narrow, both twisting into darkness. If she chose wrong, she'd corner herself.

"Talah."

The voice was soft, urgent, almost a whisper threaded through the heat. For a heartbeat, she thought she imagined it—heat-sick, half delirious.

"Left," it said again, firmer now. "Now."

Her breath caught. She didn't question, didn't think. She turned left and shoved herself into the narrow cleft of rock, scraping her shoulders as she forced through. Jagged stone tore at her skin, snagged her clothes, but she squeezed until the light dimmed behind her and the sound of pursuit dulled to an echo.

Inside, the air shifted—still hot, but different, thick with the sharp tang of soot and something older, something that prickled along her skin like static. She stumbled forward, the passage widening just enough to allow her through.

Then she saw it.

A small cavern opened at the heart of the stone, its walls blackened with fire long spent. In the center stood a pedestal of charred rock, ringed by a faint glow of embers that pulsed like dying coals.

And a token resting atop it.

Roughly palm-sized, forged of obsidian, its surface etched with symbols that seemed to pulse faintly in time with her heartbeat. She took a step closer, chest heaving, her eyes locked on it. It looked ancient, carved by hands long dead, yet defiant against every flame that had tried to consume it. The glow lit her face in flickering gold, casting her shadow huge against the cavern walls.

Talah stepped forward, chest still heaving. Her fingers trembled as she reached out, closing around the token. The heat around her flared—then extinguished, as if bowing in recognition.

Silence fell.

And then she was gone.

TALAH
XX

The air around her shifted, the heat fading before being replaced by cool, sharp winds. Beneath her hands was solid rock—not the blackened expanse of the Fire sector, but a frigid, dry hardness that scratched her palms. Glancing up, she sucked in a breath.

The world around her looked surreal. Massive floating stones were suspended in the open air above the arena, connected only by thin bridges. Wind surrounded her as if it were a live entity whose main goal was to send her plummeting to her death. She could see the people below, just a swatch of dark colors as the faint roar of their cheering reached her ears. The gusts tore at her clothes, threatening to knock her from the stone she had been teleported to.

Shaky, she slowly stood. The rock dipped beneath her feet. It was about ten feet wide, twelve long. She held her hands out, trying to maintain her balance on a floating rock with nothing to stabilize it but the grace of the stars. Movement to her right caught her eye, and she ducked back down, clinging to the rock.

A girl Talah recognized from their group had just landed on another rocky outcropping. Her dark hair whipped around her face, nearly blinding her as she tried to get her bearings. Talah faintly remembered hearing her name—Lira. A Crossborn. No name, no title. Nothing to give her any sort of advantage in the Trials.

She *was* a Leo, however.

Talah blinked, and she was gone. In the girl's stead was a falcon, taking flight from the unstable stone. She watched the girl take off through the air effortlessly.

But the Trials would never allow it to be that easy.

Arrows whistled through the air, shot from the clouds around them. Talah tried to scream a warning, but the wind snatched it away just as quickly.

Lira dodged one, then two, her lithe body twisting, wings tucked.

The third buried itself in her chest.

Talah watched, frozen to her rock, as the girl's body plummeted, a bird no longer.

Her nails gripped the stone, heart thrashing in her chest as Lira disappeared into the maze below. The crowd cried out, but Talah barely heard it. Her eyes darted from wisp to wisp, trying to see where the arrows had come from. She could see nothing.

But she couldn't just stay there.

Hesitantly, she stood again. The rock tilted, bobbing in the air as if it were floating on water.

"Do *not* look down," Talah muttered, blatantly ignoring the jagged edges around her. "Do not look down."

Inching her way toward the stone bridge, she kept her eyes on the rock just ahead of her. She had no idea where to look for the tokens—the first had just been pure luck. She could spend ages darting across these rocks searching for it. How long did she have before another competitor found her? Before the maze itself tried to take her out?

Focus.

Her hands gripped the sides of the stone bridge as she took

one small step forward. It wasn't long, just a few feet across, but it swayed in the wind, each stone rocking against the currents. Her muscles strained to keep her upright, to keep her from toppling over the side to her death.

Just a few more feet.

"There you are."

Talah's head whipped around. Behind her, a girl had teleported to the same stone she'd been dropped on. She recognized her—Halima. One of Rayen's little Signborn followers. Her hair was the color of the richest earth, braided down her back. Dark eyes narrowed as she smiled.

"We had a bet, you know," Halima said, taking a step closer. She moved confidently. Evidently not so worried about falling.

But of course not. Talah knew what she was.

She ignored the girl. If she could just get across this bridge...

"Whoever took you out first," Halima continued. "Rayen promised a pretty big reward for you."

Talah gritted her teeth. Just a few more steps. The bridge was too narrow and too unstable to take Halima on face-to-face. The girl appeared before her, waiting at the end of the bridge. There was blood flecked along her cheek, her dark eyes wild.

"A blood favor," Halima called out. "A blood oath to return the favor—whatever, whenever. And with his family being who they are—that could be an awful lot indeed."

The words struck like a spark against dry tinder, igniting a dozen questions she didn't have the breath to ask. *His family. Return the favor.* What had she stumbled into? And why did Halima sound almost gleeful about it?

She didn't answer. She couldn't. Her silence was answer enough, though her pulse pounded hard enough to drown out thought.

"Still not much of a talker, huh?" Halima grinned, then—vanished.

Talah jerked back just as a weight landed in front of her with a crack of air. Halima's boot swiped at her knee, fast as lightning.

Talah jumped, arms windmilling for balance. Her knees cracked against stone, palms scratching against the rough surface as she caught herself.

Another rush of wind behind her.

She spun too late—Halima was already gone.

The Sagittarius was everywhere. A flash to the left, a strike from the right. She moved too fast to track, here and then not, a flicker of grinning teeth, a braid snapping like a whip. Talah's breath came shallow and fast. The bridge trembled underfoot, heat rising through the stone. She wasn't just fighting an opponent—she was fighting panic, the creeping realization that even after all those months of training, she might not be fast enough.

Talah ducked, barely avoiding the next attack, barely avoiding being tossed over the edge.

"I thought you'd be more fun," Halima taunted, appearing at the far edge of the next platform. "But you're just scared, aren't you?"

Talah said nothing. Her lungs burned. Her mind raced.
You can't win like this.

She backed toward the edge. Her heart pounded in her ears, loud as thunder. The platform creaked under her weight. It would collapse soon. And still—Halima kept disappearing.

Breathe.

Her fear split open into something sharper. Threads of silver sprung from her fingertips, an illusion that crackled like static before sliding up her arms. At the edge of the crumbling platform, a version of her stepped forward.

It shimmered, refracted—like heat rising off hot stone. A perfect mirage of her form, standing still and tense. Talah ducked as she felt the wind shift.

Halima reappeared. Snarling.

And lunged.

The illusion flickered—and Halima's fist passed clean through.

"What the—?" she gasped.

Talah's real self was already moving, ducking around the side, scrambling up a narrow ledge behind a broken pillar. Her pulse still danced with whatever had just happened.

Before she could think, Halima screamed in fury. The Sagittarius zipped across the platforms again, her movements even more erratic now—less composed. The ground cracked as she teleported just above Talah's ledge, arm raised, ready to strike.

No way out. No cover. No time.

"Get down!"

The shout cut through the wind like a blade. A flash of movement to her left—a body slamming into Halima's mid-air. Talah stumbled back as Halima let out a shocked cry, her form twisting in the air. Talah barely registered them before she saw it—Halima plummeting. No teleporting this time. Nothing to save her.

Why isn't she teleporting?

Her screams echoed into the chasm below.

Talah flinched as she heard Halima's body hit the platforms below. Talah scrambled to the edge of the rock, forcing herself to peek over the side. Halima's body was twisted at an odd angle. Blood pooled around her head; her lifeless eyes stared out across the Air sector, seeing nothing. Talah closed her eyes, forcing back the bile. When her eyes opened again, she turned, staring at the person who had saved her.

Her mentor stood where Halima had been but a second ago. Beside him stood a girl in black, eyes sharp and her expression unreadable. Her silver hair whipped out in the wind like a flag of surrender.

She turned, words caught in her throat. But he was gone, along with the girl. As if he'd never been there in the first place. It had only been seconds, though it had felt longer. They hadn't been there long enough for anyone in the stands to see them.

Talah stood frozen, the last echoes of Halima's fall still ringing in her ears. Her body trembled with aftershocks—adrenaline crashing in waves, nerves frayed and burned out. The bridge swayed behind her, but the air around her was still again, almost reverent. The illusion—the shimmer—the way Halima had fallen for it without hesitation; it had felt like a reflex, a breath pulled from somewhere deeper than muscle or memory.

And this was only the beginning.

FIRAS
XXI

Halima's scream still echoed through the chasm when Raven's hand closed like iron around his arm, yanking him back beneath her shroud. The wind tore the sound away, swallowed it into the abyss, but Firas could still feel the vibration in his bones, the sickening certainty of what he'd done.

They shouldn't have been there at all. The plan had been simple: slip into the maze's hidden corridors, reach the Air sector first, and get Naima Bashir out before the Imperium buried her alive. Then Kareem Fayez. Quiet and clean. No witnesses. No trace left behind.
But the maze had other designs.

And yet, the moment he'd seen Talah stumble on the cliff's edge, the blade at her throat, his body had moved before his mind could stop it. A single breath of air, a push too sharp, too precise, and Halima was gone.

Her eyes had found him—if only for a heartbeat, if only through the veil of storm and shadow. He told himself she couldn't have seen clearly, that Raven's invisibility would hold, but deep down he knew better. The way her gaze had snapped toward him, the shock written plain on her face—he had been caught.

He could still see her, even now, hair whipping in the gale, blade flashing as Halima drove her back inch by inch. He hadn't thought—hadn't planned. He had only moved, shoving his will into the air itself, sending Halima plunging into the void.

Raven's fingers dug into him, sharp with warning. *You risked everything for her*, her silence seemed to say.

Firas clenched his jaw, forcing his breathing steady. He couldn't afford to think about Talah, not here, not now. His mission was the Ambigua. It had always been the Ambigua. And yet, as the storm howled around him, the image of her face—stunned, searching—burned hotter than any vow.

Raven gave him no time to dwell. She pulled him deeper into the shroud, forcing him down a sloping passage that cut away from the cliffs. The roar of the wind faded into a damp hush as stone closed in around them once more.

"Naima first," Raven whispered, her voice no louder than the scrape of breath. "Focus. For the lost, for the hunted..."

Firas swallowed hard, pushing Talah from his mind. "For those who refuse to fall."

He couldn't afford distraction, not when every step in this cursed maze could turn into a grave. The Imperium had sent Naima here as a death sentence. That meant she wouldn't be alone—someone would be hunting her, just as Halima had been hunting Talah.

The tunnels widened into a cavern carved by centuries of wind, the air sharp and metallic. Somewhere within, a faint sound pricked his ear—ragged breathing. Firas stilled, straining to hear.

There, tucked into a shadowed corner beneath a jag of stone, a figure crouched low. At first, she looked like part of the rock itself—hollowed, brittle, almost broken. Her skin was chalky beneath the grime, stretched tight over sharp bones, her lips split and bleeding where the wind had scoured them raw. Dark hair hung in tangled ropes around her face, stiff with dust, whipping whenever a gust curled through the cavern mouth. Her limbs shook with a faint, uneven tremor of someone who had gone too long without food or warmth—shaking not with fear, but with the body's last reserves of strength.

Naima Bashir.

The name clanged in Firas's skull like a struck bell. Once proud, once fierce—he remembered her in Aphelion's training yards, her stance sure, her strikes clean. But here in the maze, stripped by hunger and the endless punishment of the Air sector, she looked more like a wraith than a competitor.

Her eyes flicked toward the faint sound of their approach, fever-bright in the half-light. Wide and wild, darting as though every shadow might lunge at her. She pressed herself tighter against the stone, chest heaving with shallow, rasping breaths, her body coiled to flee though she had nowhere to run. The feral set of her jaw made her look less like the Naima he remembered and more like a cornered animal, waiting for the killing blow.

She had heard them, though she couldn't see through Raven's veil.

Firas's stomach twisted. Rage seared hot under his ribs—not at Naima, but at the Imperium. They hadn't even needed weapons; the maze itself was their executioner. Hunger and wind, thirst and stone—crueler than a blade, slower than fire. They had thrown her into this sector to break her, both body and mind, and it was working. If they'd come any later, she might not have lasted another day.

The thought clawed at him, cold and sharp: what if she snapped before they could get her out? What if the hunger hollowed her too far to come back from?

For the first time since stepping into the maze, fear dug deeper than his anger.

"She won't last long," Raven murmured, her voice flat, unyielding. Her eyes swept over Naima with the precision of someone assessing a blade's fracture point, not a girl's body. "We have to move—now—before she collapses for good."

Her words struck with the finality of judgment, cutting

through his spiraling thoughts. Raven saw a liability where he saw a life. And that difference burned in his chest almost as much as the sight of Naima herself. Harsh, yes—but necessary. Firas hated that she was right.

Naima's lips parted, her breath rattling like dry leaves. She blinked hard, her gaze flicking between them, suspicion warring with the faint spark of recognition.

"Mentor...?" she whispered, voice rasping, more ghost than girl.

Relief punched through his chest. "Yes. We're here to take you out."

Raven shifted closer, her hand tightening on Naima's arm—not cruel, but firm. Urgent. Firas didn't need her to speak. He already knew what came next.

A disappearance would raise alarms. The Imperium needed to see death, to mark another competitor lost to the maze. If Naima simply vanished, suspicion would bloom like fire, and the entire rescue would be compromised.

Firas hated it. Hated the cold necessity of it. But he couldn't deny the logic.

His gaze swept the chasm yawning just beyond them, the wind howling through its depths like the hungry mouth of the maze itself. There was no better stage.

He met Naima's eyes, saw the fear and understanding dawning there. "It has to look real," he said quietly. "But you'll walk out alive. That, I promise you."

She gave the faintest nod, her body trembling as Raven pulled the veil tighter around her, until her presence dissolved into the shimmer of air.

Firas crouched, scooping up a jagged stone and bundling it in the ragged length of Naima's cloak as quickly as he could. The cloth was stiff with dust, stained with her blood and sweat. But the cloak alone wouldn't be enough. Not for the Imperium. Not for the crowd.

So he reached.

Drawing in a sharp breath, Firas pushed his power

outward—past the veil, past the cliffs, past the roar of the storm. His mind unfurled like a net, straining against the hundreds of watching thoughts, each one buzzing at the edges of his consciousness. The effort burned, a searing weight pressing behind his eyes, but he shoved deeper, twisting the threads of perception.

You saw her fall.
You saw her body tumble.
You saw Naima Bashir die.

The whispers tore through their minds, subtle but insistent, until they believed. He felt it take root—the ripple of acceptance, the crowd's sharp intake of breath, the Imperium's satisfaction. They saw what he needed them to see.

With a ragged exhale, Firas hurled the cloaked stone into the gorge. The cloth flared wide, catching the wind, then vanished into the abyss. A perfect echo of the lie he had already sewn into their minds.

When it was done, he staggered back, chest heaving, sweat slicking his palms despite the cold bite of air. His head pounded with the weight of too many voices, the drain of bending so many at once.

To the Imperium, Naima Bashir was dead.

But beneath Raven's shroud, she stood alive and shaking, hidden in plain sight.

Firas clenched his jaw, swallowing down the ache lancing through his skull.

One safe. One more to go.

TALAH
XXII

She forced herself to move.
    One foot, then the other. Her legs felt unsteady, like her bones had forgotten how to be solid. Emotion itched under her skin. There was too much to hold on to—fear, confusion. Guilt. But she couldn't stop. Not here. Not when she didn't know what was waiting next.

    And yet, her pulse still spiked. Anger rose before she could name it. *Why couldn't he just stay away? Why couldn't he let me prove I could do this on my own?*

    Why was her mentor interfering in the Trials?

    She crossed a narrow stone path to a rope bridge, so thin and frayed it barely seemed real. It swung lazily with every breath of wind, groaning under its own tension. Her hand clenched around the hilt of nothing—no weapon, no rope, no ally. Just herself now. Talah hesitated at the next intersection of floating rock paths. Left would take her toward the distant glint of firelight—more competitors, she guessed. Right led to another island, isolated and nearly hidden in the curling fog.

A feeling in her gut drew her to the right. She didn't know why she trusted it. But she did.

The bridge creaked beneath her steps as she followed the tug toward the one floating island. The air felt different here—thinner, colder. Sharper. The kind of wind that whispered secrets if you listened long enough.

The island she reached was small. No cover. No shade. Just a single flat plane of gray stone, barely wide enough to pace across without risking a fall.

And in the middle of it, floating above the ground, was a pedestal.

It hovered, untethered by rope or pole, suspended several feet in the air as if it had been plucked from the ground and hung in place by the wind itself. Perched atop it was another token.

It was the same size as the last token, about palm-sized. It looked as if it had been forged of pale, pearlescent stone. Silver symbols traced delicate paths across its feather-shaped surface, pulsing gently with light that felt less like fire and more like breath. Faint etchings along the shaft of the feather glowed with a quiet rhythm—not burning, but moving—as though it inhaled the wind around it and exhaled starlight.

It looked old. Not broken, not pristine. Weathered.

Worn like cliff stone carved by centuries of wind, yet unshaken. A relic of every storm that had ever tried to tear it apart—and failed.

Talah's eyes searched for a way up.

There were no handholds. No ropes. No stepping stones. Just the howling wind swirling around the pedestal in unpredictable gusts, sending her curls whipping across her face. The air pushed upward, unstable and chaotic, like the breath of a storm trying to build itself.

Her stomach dropped.

She realized what she had to do.

Not climb. Not fight.

Jump.

The idea sent ice down her spine. But the pull in her chest grew stronger, more insistent. As if something inside her already knew what would happen. As if that strange new instinct—whatever had bloomed during the fight—was leading her here. Testing her.

Not with logic. Not with strength. With trust.

She took a breath, backed up to the edge of the platform, and exhaled slowly. The wind seemed to wait with her, watching. Listening.

She ran, forcing her legs to take her over the edge. With one last breath, she leapt. The air caught her. For one singular moment, she didn't fall—she floated. Suspended like a leaf on a breeze. The wind curved around her body in a silent spiral, lifting her just high enough—just long enough.

She reached.

Fingers brushed stone.

The instant her skin met the token, it pulsed—soft, warm. A breath. The air around her stilled, as if holding itself in surprise.

Then gravity returned.

She hit the stone hard, a grunt torn from her lungs. Pain flared in her hip and elbow, but she was alive. The token lay in her palm, glowing gently.

Something inside her shifted. Not just the sense of victory—a change so deep it ran through her bones. She didn't know what she was becoming. But she was sure of one thing.

She was not the same girl who had first stepped into this maze.

Not anymore.

The light around her fractured.

Her body jerked, tugged through space as the token's glow swelled and consumed her.

She hit the ground, the breath knocked from her lungs. Talah choked, trying to draw air as she rolled onto her back, eyes searching the maze to see where she'd ended up this time.

Massive stone walls stretched to the sky, their skeletal fingers seeming to brush the clouds. Roots crawling like veins covered the rough rock beneath. Photoluminescence moss covered the walls, glowing faintly in the dim lighting of the maze floor. The air around her was thick, damp, and buzzing with unseen life.

Various pathways cut through the stone, leading off in different directions. Some were darker than others, some so covered in vines it seemed nearly impossible to get through. Each one different, each one leading to a death of some kind or another. Talah tried to study them through the pain, still trying to take in air.

The earth beneath her began to rumble, the tremors running through her bones. She could feel the movement in the walls beside her. As if the maze were alive. Earth sector. It had to be.

Talah was still studying her surroundings when she heard movement behind her.

"Tal?" A cough dragged her gaze away from the towering walls.

Mazin knelt a few feet away, hands on his knees. He gasped for breath, shoulders shaking. Dirt and blood were smudged across his face, making the blue in his eyes pop even more.

"Mazin." She scrambled to her feet, her legs screaming as she went. Falling beside him, she reached out, needing to feel if he was real. If he was actually alive.

"You okay?" His eyes dragged along her body, checking for injuries.

"As okay as I can be," she admitted.

"Talah? Mazin?" Adine rounded the corner of the narrow ravine they'd been dropped in, Zayd hanging from her shoulder. He groaned, his head falling forward slightly. Despite the fact they looked on the edge of death, Talah's heart lightened at the sight of them.

Mazin swore, hoisting himself up to help her. "Is he…?"

"Still breathing, at least." Adine glanced down at Zayd. "They weren't particularly gentle when they dropped us in here."

Talah stepped up beside them as they laid Zayd against one of the walls. He groaned again, lashes fluttering open.

"Are we all dead?" he asked. "Because if so, I did not think you all would be in my afterlife. We just met, after all."

"Stars and skies," Adine muttered, eyes rolling upwards.

"Can you get up?" Mazin asked, ignoring him.

Zayd glared up at him. "I just got dropped out of the sky. Will you give a man a minute?" When Mazin didn't reply, he sighed, using the wall to climb to his feet. He was shaky, but standing. "This work for you?"

Mazin glanced around. "It doesn't seem like anyone else was teleported near us. Which is good. We can stick together for this part, at least."

"We have to find the tokens," Adine reminded him. "They don't just group all of those together, you know."

"Right," Mazin muttered, looking around. "Right."

"We can at least work together to find some of them," Talah cut in. "Just for a little."

Adine glanced up at the sky. "Lights fading. It'll be dark soon. We should try to find shelter. Or at least attempt a fire. Maybe find some food."

No one protested.

All four of them looked the worse for wear. Adine's tunic was ripped across her stomach, dirt smeared over her arms. Her hair was tangled, hanging down to her waist. Zayd blinked a few times, shaking his head as if to dry off imaginary droplets of water.

They picked their way toward a small overhang of rock, just enough space to huddle beneath. Adine crouched nearby, pressing her palm against the ground, her eyes narrowing in concentration. A few minutes later she rose, triumphant, holding out a small cluster of red berries.

"Not much, but edible," she said, brushing dirt from her palms. "Better than nothing."

Zayd grinned and plucked one from her hand. "I'll take better-than-nothing over starving."

Adine slapped his wrist before he could pop it in his mouth. "Not until we've made sure. Eat one, wait. If you don't keel over, then we can split them."

Zayd sighed theatrically but obeyed.

Meanwhile, Talah knelt beside him, dragging sticks and dried moss into a pile. Zayd struck flint together clumsily, sparks catching and dying as quickly as they came. "Why isn't this working?" he muttered.

"Because you're trying to fight it," Talah said. She pressed her hands to the wood, willing her water to flow into the brittle moss. Steam hissed; the air dampened just enough. "Try now."

Zayd's eyes flicked to hers, and this time when he struck, the spark caught. A thin flame licked upward, fragile but alive. Talah shielded it with her hands until it grew steady.

"There we go," she said softly, relief washing through her chest.

For an instant, the crackle of flame carried her back to that first day of training—kneeling in the dust while Iras barked at her to try again, to stop thinking like a fighter and start thinking like someone who wanted to live. *Fire first*, he'd told her, shoving kindling into her hands. *Without it, you'll freeze before you ever swing a blade.* She hadn't understood then, too proud, too impatient. But now, crouched in the shifting maze with nothing but exhaustion and hunger, she finally did.

Mazin dropped down beside her, opening his palm. A sphere of water shimmered into being, rippling like glass. With a flick of his wrist, it split into smaller globes, floating toward each of them.

"Drink," he said simply. His voice was tired but steady, and when Talah met his gaze, there was a flicker of the boy she remembered beneath the exhaustion.

Adine finally allowed the others to eat the berries after Zayd survived his dramatic countdown to death.

"Still breathing," he said, shrugging. "Guess we're good." Adine rolled her eyes but smiled faintly as she handed out the berries.

For a few minutes, they ate in silence, the fire snapping softly, shadows dancing across their faces. It wasn't enough food. It wasn't enough water. But it was something. And for the first time since entering the maze, Talah felt the faintest thread of comfort, bound together with the others against the night.

Zayd broke the quiet first, leaning back against the stone and letting out a long groan. "Never thought I'd be happy to eat half-squished berries for dinner." He held up the last one between two fingers before popping it into his mouth. "Guess near-death really lowers your standards."

Adine snorted, pulling her knees up to her chest. "You'd complain if it were a feast laid out in front of you."

"I wouldn't," he said around the berry, voice muffled. "I'd just… criticize the seasoning."

Mazin rolled his eyes, but a faint smile tugged at his mouth. "Some things never change."

The sight of his smile—small, tired, but real—loosened something tight in Talah's chest. She shifted closer to the fire, letting its warmth sink into her skin. "What happened to you three in the water sector?" she asked quietly.

The question sobered them. Adine glanced at Mazin, who stared into the fire as though replaying the memory in its glow. His hands curled loosely over his knees, knuckles pale.

"It wasn't good," he admitted. "The current pulled me under almost the second we landed. I couldn't… I couldn't get my bearings. It felt like being swallowed whole." His voice rasped, and for a moment he seemed far away, caught in the water again.

Adine's jaw tightened. "He would've drowned if I hadn't dragged him up. Even then, the water wouldn't let go. It kept shifting, like it wanted him more than the rest of us."

Mazin gave a humorless laugh, shaking his head. "I panicked at first. Tried to fight it. But water doesn't listen when you thrash—it drowns you faster. I had to… stop fighting. I let it take me deeper, just enough to gather it in." His fingers lifted, a small sphere of liquid rising into his palm, trembling faintly with the memory of strain. "I pulled it back around me, shaped it into air long enough to breathe."

Talah's stomach knotted as she watched the sphere shiver, reflecting the firelight. "You almost died."

"Almost," he agreed, lowering the water until it hissed into the flames. He looked at Adine then, his voice soft. "She's the one who kept me alive long enough to think straight. She fought off two others who tried to finish me when I was under."

Adine shrugged like it was nothing, though her cheeks flushed faintly. "You'd have done the same."

Zayd, sprawled on the ground beside them, stretched his arms overhead and grinned faintly. "I did help, you know. Pulled them both back to the surface after Adine nearly broke their ribs."

Adine shot him a glare. "You nearly got yourself drowned trying to show off."

"Worth it," Zayd said, smirk widening. "At least we're all here now, right?"

Talah felt the truth of that settle deep in her bones. For all the hunger, for all the fear, they were still here—together. She wanted to tell them about what she'd seen: Iras in the maze, speaking with the strange girl whose presence had unsettled her to her core. The words hovered at the back of her throat, begging release. But something stopped her. A weight, heavy and sharp. She wasn't ready—not when she didn't even understand it herself. Not when she wasn't sure she could trust what she'd seen.

Instead, she swallowed hard and said, "We've all been through worse than we should've survived." Her gaze drifted around the circle—Adine's steady eyes, Zayd's restless grin, Mazin's quiet strength. "Maybe that means something."

Mazin tilted his head, studying her. "Maybe it means we're stronger together than we are apart."

Adine leaned forward, resting her chin on her knees. "Then we'd better hold on to that. Because the maze isn't done with us yet."

The fire popped, casting sparks into the night. They sat a little closer after that, shoulders brushing as the darkness deepened around them, the faint hum of the shifting maze somewhere beyond the walls. For the first time, Talah let herself believe they might actually stand a chance—so long as they didn't let go of each other.

She didn't know how long she'd last on her own. Which almost made her laugh, bitter and low, considering her entire goal of entering the Trials in the first place. She had wanted to prove herself—to her father, to the Council, to the world. To show she didn't need anyone's protection, that she wasn't fragile, that her survival would be earned by her hands alone.

But the maze didn't care about pride. It stripped it away, piece by piece, until all that was left was bone-deep truth. And the truth was this: she wasn't standing here because of her strength alone. She was standing because Adine had dragged her out of the line of fire more than once, because Zayd's reckless humor cut through the weight when despair pressed too heavily, because Mazin had split water from air when her throat had been too parched to speak.

The thought twisted in her chest. She'd built walls so carefully, so stubbornly, to keep from needing anyone. And yet, when the world was burning and crumbling around her, it wasn't the walls she leaned on. It was them.

Maybe she'd been too stubborn before. Maybe survival wasn't about standing alone at the end, but about finding people worth enduring for—people worth bleeding for.

The thought lingered as silence settled again. The fire burned low, its glow a fragile circle in the heavy dark. Around it, their breathing slowed, the edges of exhaustion pulling them down.

Adine stretched out on her side, one arm tucked beneath her head, her braids spilling over her shoulder. Zayd sprawled against the rock as if he had no bones left to hold him up, muttering something about "keeping first watch" before promptly snoring. Mazin remained seated a little longer, staring into the embers until his shoulders finally sagged and he lowered himself to the ground beside Talah.

"You should try to sleep," he murmured, his voice barely above the whisper of the fire.

Talah nodded, though she doubted rest would come easily.

Still, she lay back against the cool stone, the faint crackle of the flames and the quiet presence of the others a fragile kind of comfort. For the first time in days, she allowed her eyes to close without fear swallowing her whole.

The maze was not merciful. But for now, she had them.

Sleep pulled at her, heavy and slow. She wasn't sure how long she drifted before the ground shuddered beneath her.

The fire snapped, scattering sparks as a deep groan reverberated through the earth. Talah jerked upright.

The wall behind Zayd shook violently, moss and leafy vines tumbling in a rain of green. Talah's heart lurched. The fleeting calm she'd allowed herself evaporated, replaced by a rush of cold adrenaline.

"Is it just me, or is that wall getting closer?" Zayd asked, scrambling to his feet, sleep still heavy in his eyes.

As if answering his question, the ground rumbled again, the air growing thicker, heavier, as though it pressed against their lungs. The moss fluttered, the stone shifting with a deep, grinding sound. The wall creeped closer—inch by inch, deliberate and unstoppable.

"We need to move," Adine said, eyes wide as she seized Zayd's arm. "The maze is changing."

TALAH
XXIII

Talah glanced around, her heart dropping. The walls of the labyrinth that had once seemed fixed in place now shifted, sliding like puzzle pieces into new configurations.

"I don't think we're going to get out if we stay here," Zayd muttered, staring at the shifting maze.

A loud thud echoed, and Talah flinched as a section of the maze to their left collapsed in on itself, sending a cloud of dust into the air. The wall behind them groaned again, now only a few millimeters away. The air thickened, as if the entire structure were alive, pressing in on them.

"Go!" Talah shouted, dragging him into a new corridor that had opened to their right. But even as they ran, the stone walls of the maze seemed to close in around them, shifting with an almost malevolent intent.

She was not going to die like this.

Talah darted down the passageway, with Mazin and Adine close behind her. She could hear their labored breaths, feel the heat from their bodies as they struggled between the walls, still closing in. Talah could see the end, just a narrow opening now some feet away. If they could just get there...

She tripped through the opening, nearly colliding with Zayd. Righting herself, she glanced around. They were in some sort of pocket within the maze—a hexagonal space that was covered with vines and moss glowing faintly in the limited light. Vines hung overheard, from one wall to another, creating a sort of natural ceiling. Six passageways led in different directions.

"Well, we've got six choices here," Zayd said slowly, turning in a circle. "Pick one, and if it leads to trouble, I'll pretend I told you to go left."

Adine snorted. "You first, then."

"Wait," Mazin held up a hand, stilling. "Listen."

The group fell silent, straining to hear over the settling groans of the maze. Talah could barely make out anything over the straining rock, whisper of the vines, and shifting earth.

"Wha—?"

There.

Footsteps.

There were at least two or three of them, their footfalls echoing between the stone walls. One set of sounds came from the right; the other to their left. Talah instinctively stepped back, her shoulder brushing Mazin's.

"Stay close," he muttered, fingers flexing at his sides.

Talah tensed, waiting for whoever else was in the Earth sector to reveal themselves.

A sudden scream tore through the silence.

Talah spun just as vines exploded from two alcoves behind them. A flash of movement—then the gleam of a blade as a figure lunged from the shadows. She ducked instinctively, feeling the blade cut through the air where her throat had been. It seems like she and her friends were the only ones who had naively listened to the 'no weapons' rule.

"Ambush!" Adine shouted.

Mazin was already moving, staggering toward Zayd just as a second attacker—a tall, silent Capricorn—slipped from the vines like a ghost. His hand shimmered for a moment before his body flickered out of sight entirely. Talah didn't remember their names. But she remembered their powers.

"Invisibility," Mazin growled.

Talah's breath caught in her throat, her fingers twitching. There was a third figure—lean and fast—rushing from the left corridor. Aries. She saw the glint of heat ripple across his skin before he barreled into Mazin, tackling him to the ground.

The fight erupted into chaos.

Adine moved first. Her palm slammed against the ground, sending a violent shudder through the stone. The maze trembled, and with a groaning crack, a section of the tunnel roof collapsed in a spray of dust and debris, sealing off the corridor the Aries had come from.

"Nice aim," Zayd wheezed, ducking as a vine lashed past his head. His eyes darted across the battlefield—serious, for once. He swept his arms up, the air around him thickening with force. Debris from Adine's collapse twisted into a shield, swirling before them in a chaotic dance of shattered stone and dust. "Covering us!"

Talah narrowed her eyes, heart hammering. She couldn't feel him but she could sense him. She didn't know how; she just knew. There was a slight pull from the right, a feeling in her gut that was screaming for her to listen.

As the invisible figure moved in, her body snapped upright—and with a hiss of breath, an illusion shimmered to life behind her, a second version of herself conjured in the blink of an eye.

The Capricorn struck the illusion. His moment of confusion was all she needed.

Talah twisted low, sweeping her leg under his feet. The illusion vanished in a flash as he slammed into the stone floor, groaning.

There was a shout behind her. Talah whipped around, hands raised and ready.

Mazin, blood dripping from his brow, surged upward from where the Aries had pinned him. His movements were sluggish—but precise. He feinted right, then drove his shoulder into the Aries' chest. The boy staggered back just long enough for Mazin to punch him hard in the ribs.

"We need to move," he gasped.

Another low groan rumbled through the ground—the maze was shifting again. Almost as if it had heard him.

The hexagonal room split open.

The ground beneath them jerked and shifted. One wall cracked, sliding inward. Pathways spun and reformed; the exit they had come through now completely sealed behind rubble. The stone beneath their feet tilted, separating, forcing the group to scatter.

"Stick together!" Talah shouted—but the words were lost in the chaos.

Mazin and Adine were swept one way, a wall rising between them.

Zayd grabbed for Talah, but the floor cracked down the middle—and with a shuddering lurch, she fell back alone into a new corridor, the maze snapping shut behind her.

For a second, there was nothing but silence. The maze groaned above her.

Darkness swallowed her whole.

The pain returned first, sharp enough to steal her breath. Gritting her teeth, she forced herself onto her stomach and lifted her head to take in her new surroundings. Vines hung like snakes from the criss-crossing hedges above her. Silence hung heavy amongst the scent of moss and earth as she caught her breath. A glimmer down the pathway caught her eye.

Several tokens were suspended in the air, wrapped in vines.

Wary, she stood, brushing the dirt from her hands. There was no one else around, none that she could hear anyway. Talah took a hesitant step forward, trying to figure out just how she'd reach the tokens. They were a good five feet above her head, swinging slightly in the breeze.

Climbing the walls seemed like the only option.

Which is exactly what the maze wanted her to do, most likely. And that meant...

She needed to figure out another way. Climbing the walls made her too vulnerable.

Talah made her way across the dirt, eyes latched onto the tokens. She was so close. Just one more sector and she would be free. At least free from this nightmare of a maze. As she stretched her fingers toward the token, the air shifted—cool and sharp, like breath before a storm.

A shadow unfurled in her periphery.

The body tumbled through the maze's tangled walls. His tunic clung to his large frame in tatters, scorched at the sleeves and slashed across his wide chest, revealing a latticework of bruises and fresh gashes. Blood was smeared along his jaw, trailing from a cut just beneath his eye.

But she didn't think the rest of the blood staining his clothes were his.

Rayen righted himself, his smile stopping her cold.

Silence pulsed between them, thick with the smell of ozone and scorched leaves. She could see it then—beneath the smirk, the mask was cracking. His stance was looser than usual, his balance not quite centered. But he hid it well, pretending he didn't need to lean ever so slightly on the wall for support. Pretending the blood in his mouth didn't taste like failure.

"I'll give you this," he murmured, circling slightly, forcing her to pivot with him. "I didn't think you'd make it this far."

She didn't rise to the bait. Her eyes flicked to the token, barely two feet behind her. Close enough to reach—if she were willing to pay the price. Yet, she still hadn't figured out a plan to get it down—not without making herself a target.

Rayen saw the glance. His smile deepened. Confident. Cruel.

"I could end this now," he said. "I should." His fingers flexed once at his side, crackling with the residual hum of fire.

"But," he added, stepping forward, "where's the fun in that?"

"If you think this is fun, you need better hobbies," Talah replied before she could stop herself.

"Big talk for such a little girl," Rayen sneered.

Talah turned halfway, keeping him in her line of sight. "I don't have time for this."

"Of course you don't," he said, stepping closer. "Because you know you don't belong here."

She paused, spine straightening.

"Killing the others was nothing," Rayen said, tone casual. As if this was just a game. "They were nothing. But you? I'll enjoy killing you. I want everyone to know just how unworthy you were of this glory. Of Aphelion and everything it gives to those who are."

Chills crept along her spine, raising the hair at the back of her neck. He was *enjoying* this.

He stepped closer, smile gone, voice low and venomous.

"And you?" His breath curled like smoke between them. "You're a mistake. A liability. Like those other Crossborns, you thought you could just waltz in here and claim power that wasn't yours. That you didn't even fight for. You should've stayed hidden, where you could at least keep pretending you matter."

The first strike caught her off guard—a brutal blow to her side that knocked the wind from her lungs. Pain splintered through her ribs. She stumbled, barely blocking the second hit as he swung a flame-forged knife toward her throat. The heat seared the air, slicing just past her cheek, and she twisted away, flinging her hand toward the stream.

Water answered.

Two ribbons surged forward, one striking out like a whip, the other swirling into a shield between them. She snapped her wrist, sending the first at his legs, trying to unbalance him, and launched the second straight for his chest.

Rayen sliced clean through both without flinching. The water hissed against his blade, evaporating on contact. His eyes glinted, wild with something between thrill and fury.

"That all you've got?"

He charged again—no flourish, no taunt. Just force.

She dodged, barely rolling to the side as his knife buried itself in the dirt where she'd just stood. Her back hit the hedge wall with a painful thud. She reached for more water—anything—but he was already on her again.

She needed an opening. A breath.

An illusion cracked from her fingertips like light through water, something she'd done a thousand times with Mazin back home. Pisces' illusions could mimic real life, tricking those around them into believing the lie. Copies of her rippled into existence across the path, blinking into being—eyes wild, bodies bruised, all of them panting like her.

Rayen slowed, gaze flicking between them.

For a moment, she thought she had him.

Then his lip curled.

"I've seen better tricks from children," he sneered, and turned.

Right toward her.

A breath later, he was in motion—blade sweeping through the false copies, dissolving them like mist until only she remained.

She backed away, nearly tripping on the vines behind her. The token swayed above her head, just out of reach. Her powers couldn't pull it down—not yet. Not without exposing her.

"You're not worthy," Rayen said, stalking closer. "*You* don't even believe you belong here."

Talah gritted her teeth. She could hear Halima's voice again—screaming. The white-haired girl, standing above her. Iras, not stopping it. The blood seeping through Rayen's clothes—none of it his.

She could still feel the weight of that moment, heavy in her chest.

Talah had always known she would have to take lives to win the Trials. She thought she'd been prepared. But nothing could have prepared her for this. Not really.

Rayen wasn't going to stop.

And she was running out of time.

He stalked forward, the fire along his blade burning white-hot now, licking up his arm like it wanted to consume her next. Either she fought back… or she died. There were no other options.

"At least you tried," Rayen spat. And lunged.

Time slowed. Something within her, already cracked and broken, finally snapped as she stood rooted in place. Something deeper.

Something older.

It rose up inside her like a scream buried for far too long. Talah's hands snapped up, toward Rayen as he soared through the air.

There was a deafening crack, the earth buckling with a deep, wrenching groan. Roots tore from the soil—thick, knotted things, *angrier* than the flame Rayen wielded. Vines whipped around his ankles, dragging him back to the earth. Water was ripped from the leaves, the air, swirling around him until even Talah had a hard time keeping track of him. His eyes widened, his reaction too slow.

"How—?" he started.

He never got to finish.

The vines turned to wood, impaling him mid-sentence. Wood split flesh with a wet crunch, jerking his body backwards. Rayen's mouth opened once, then closed, but no sound could escape. His flames vanished, fire dying along his fingertips.

Water continued to swirl around him, hiding the truth of what she'd done.

Talah stared, her breath caught in her throat.

Between the swirls of water, she could see wooden stakes

holding him in place, the vines around his body twitching as if alive. As if they knew what they'd done. Blood trailed from his mouth, mixing with the moss and earth beneath him. His eyes never left hers, the fear forever frozen within them.

The vines withdrew on their own as the water receded. Rayen's body dropped limply to the earth with a heavy thud. The wall behind him was streaked with red, the kind that didn't wash away.

Her hands shook. Her knees buckled.

Time slowed for a second time.

And then came the shaking. It spread up her arms, through her chest. A tremor deep within her soul. She knew—*knew*—she would have to kill. She'd told herself that she was ready. That she was prepared.

All she'd wanted was to survive—just survive—and now...

The roots. The vines. The ground answered her call as if it had been waiting for her command. She stared down at her trembling hands, expecting to see something—anything—that would give her answers. But they were just hands.

Earth was not her power. It wasn't who she was.

It couldn't be.

A strangled breath clawed its way from her chest. She stumbled up and backwards until her back hit the opposite hedge wall. Away from him. Away from what she'd done. The vines felt cold against her spine. She wanted to disappear into it.

It wasn't me. It couldn't have been me.

But the truth was pressing in, thick and heavy and impossible.

She had felt it.

That surge. That *pull*.

Like something inside her had cracked open, and the world had responded.

And something else, something stranger—an energy that had rippled through her like a storm breaking surface. A wind not summoned, but born.

She curled forward, hands against her mouth, fighting the

rise of nausea.

What if someone had seen me?

Her head snapped up, but she couldn't see the stands or the crowd from where she stood. She could still hear them, faintly. Maybe no one saw what she'd just done. Maybe they hadn't been paying attention. Besides, the water had been too tumultuous, hiding what she'd done. It had been hard enough even for her to see through the wall of liquid.

She wanted to scream. To sob. To tear it all from the earth and take it back.

But instead, she sat there in silence.

She wanted to move, to do something, but her limbs were slow, heavy. Then she heard it—too soon. The soft shuffle of feet against dirt. Controlled. Stalking. Her head snapped toward the sound, and time slammed back into motion.

Another competitor.

A boy—not much older than her, but built heavier, broader. His robes were scorched at the sleeves, and soot streaked across his jaw and forehead. One of his eyes was swollen half-shut, the other wide and wild. His hands were empty, but there was murder in his gaze.

She tried to lift her hands, to conjure something—anything—but there was nothing left. She felt hollow. Spent. Her body too slow.

The boy charged with a growl, launching himself toward her. Talah staggered back, arms raised more by instinct than defense.

She never stood a chance.

A blur of green and brown hit him from the side with a brutal crunch. The two of them tumbled to the dirt, rolling in a chaotic tangle of limbs and breathless grunts. Talah saw the glint of a blade flash, but it didn't connect—yet.

"Mazin," she breathed, stunned.

He slammed the boy down with a growl, but it was clear he was already faltering. His tunic was soaked through with blood on one side, dark and spreading fast. His steps were uneven, his knees buckling under his weight. His left arm hung uselessly at his side, blood dripping from his knuckles.

He barely looked at her. He didn't have to.

"Talah," he choked, his voice a mix of pain and urgency. His eyes locked onto hers. "*Look.*"

With his good arm, he pointed over her shoulder. She turned as if in a dream, her eyes catching the glint of something silver. A singular token spun above their heads, entangled in the vines.

The attacker roared—feral and enraged. He darted toward the wall, hands and feet scrambling in the foliage. Mazin darted forward, dragging him backwards.

"Tal—*go.*"

Talah started forward automatically, her movements jerky. She scaled the wall, hauling her exhausted body up higher and higher until the token was at eye-level. Hesitating, she glanced down.

Mazin and the boy were fighting now, locked in hand-to-hand combat as they dodged each other's elements. Wind whipped around the two of them, snatching at their clothes, trying to knock Mazin off his feet.

He was fighting… for her.

So she would have a chance.

"Maz!" She didn't know what made her call out to him.

His head turned toward her, giving his opponent the seconds he needed to take advantage.

"No!" Talah jerked forward but it was too late.

The boy collided with Mazin like a freight train, driving him to the ground. Mazin barely had time to brace before fists and elbows slammed into him, fast and merciless.

"Maz!" Talah clung to the wall.

"*JUST GO,*" Mazin roared.

Talah hesitated before taking a deep breath. She needed to go. Now. Maybe then the boy would leave Mazin to go search for another token.

Gathering the last bit of strength, Talah launched off the wall, her hand closing around the token. Vines snapped as gravity dragged her down. Light exploded around her.

She gasped, the air sucked from her lungs as the world folded.

Mazin's last shout was cut off. The forest vanished. The blood. The attacker. The vines.

Gone.

FIRAS
XXIV

The lie still pulsed in his skull.
    Firas could feel it—the faint echo of a hundred minds carrying his whisper as truth. Naima Bashir had fallen. They had seen it. They believed it. And if he faltered now, if the thread of that illusion snapped, the Imperium would know.

    Raven walked ahead, silent, her silver hair catching stray glints of torchlight beneath the maze. Her stride was sharp, unwavering, but she kept glancing back at him—measuring the drag in his steps, the pallor in his face. She didn't ask whether he was fine. She didn't have to. They both knew he wasn't.

    They had one left. Kareem Fayez. But first—they had to get Naima out.

    Her weight leaned heavily against his side as they picked their way through the tunnels, her breaths shallow, her body trembling with hunger and exhaustion. Raven led the way with the ease of someone who had memorized every passage, every crack in the stone. Down, down into the bowels of the maze, until the roar of the wind above was replaced by damp silence and the smell of earth.

The tunnels here were older, carved before Aphelion had ever been raised—narrow arteries of rock that twisted beneath the Trials' stage like the veins of a beast. No competitor would ever stumble this far; no Imperium eyes could reach them here.

At last, faint torchlight glimmered ahead. Two figures waited at the junction—Kam's tall silhouette unmistakable, Rami slighter but no less sharp. Relief loosened something in Firas's chest.

"You got her," Kam said, already moving forward to catch Naima as she sagged. The clink of water flasks and the rustle of cloth followed as she and Rami steadied her, pressing food into her hands, wrapping a cloak around her thin shoulders.

Naima's gaze flicked between them all, confusion mingled with dawning realization. For the first time since finding her, she whispered without suspicion: "I'm not dead."

Rami smiled faintly, though his eyes were shadowed. "No. You're not. And we'll keep it that way."

Firas let himself look at her for one heartbeat longer—frail, but alive. Naima's face was half-shadowed by the hood Kam had pulled over her, her lips still cracked, her eyes hollowed by hunger. But there was breath in her chest. Color would return to her cheeks. Strength could be rebuilt. For the first time since they had entered the maze, he allowed himself a thread of relief.

It was gone as quickly as it had come. There was no time to hold on to it.

He turned back to Kam. "Kareem?"

Her nod was curt; her voice edged with iron. "Earth sector. Last I checked."

The word alone was enough to harden his gut. Earth. A place meant to grind competitors into dust, to crush them beneath their own weight or bury them alive in shifting stone. If the Imperium had chosen it for Kareem's death, then they intended it to be slow, suffocating, inescapable.

They didn't linger. Couldn't. Every moment here risked the illusion unraveling in the minds above—the delicate lie Firas had planted that Naima was gone, that the chasm had claimed her. He could feel the threads of it tugging faintly at the edges of his mind, a reminder that one slip, one fracture in his concentration, would expose everything.

Raven tugged the shroud back over them, her hand brushing briefly against his arm—a warning, not comfort. *Stay sharp.*

Moments later, they were swallowed once more by the twisting veins of the maze. The air grew heavier the deeper they climbed, damp with soil and thick with dust. The sound of the wind from the Air sector faded behind them, replaced by the groan of shifting stone—deep, guttural, like the belly of the world itself was moving.

The tunnels narrowed, roots jutting like ribs from the walls, sharp and splintered. Every tremor underfoot rattled pebbles loose, sending them clattering into unseen depths. The Earth sector loomed ahead, alive and restless, and somewhere within it waited Kareem Fayez.

And Firas knew—before they left it—he would have to weave another death.

The air grew heavier the higher they climbed, dust clogging their throats, the press of rock closing in from all sides. Unlike the Air sector's open cliffs, this place was a labyrinth of jagged passages, sharp roots punching through the walls like claws. The ground trembled beneath their boots with the sector's living pulse—sometimes steady, sometimes violent enough to knock stone from the ceiling.

And somewhere in this death trap was Kareem Fayez.

The deeper they pressed into the Earth sector, the more the air thickened—dust hanging in the passages like smoke, the tremors of shifting stone rattling beneath their boots. Every turn threatened collapse, every hollow could have been a tomb. It felt like the maze itself was hunting them, burying its prey alive.

The search dragged longer than Firas liked. The Earth sector was a labyrinth within a labyrinth—corridors narrowing into knife-thin slits, chambers collapsing into dead ends, roots coiled like serpents waiting to snare ankles. Dust hung thick in the air, clinging to his skin, clogging his lungs until every breath felt like swallowing grit.

They pressed deeper, listening for anything—movement, a breath, the scrape of stone. More than once they stopped, holding still as tremors rippled through the walls, a low groan like the sector itself was warning them back. Once, Raven caught his arm and jerked him aside just before the ceiling gave way, stone crashing down in a violent cascade where they had stood a heartbeat before.

Kareem *had* to be here. He had to be. And yet, with every hollow they entered, every echo that led to nothing but dust and silence, Firas felt the knot in his chest tighten. The Imperium might have buried him already.

Then—faint, almost lost beneath the groan of shifting stone—a sound. A scrape, like wood grinding against rock. They followed it down a sloping passage, the air growing hotter, heavier, the walls closing in until they could barely move side by side.

At last, the passage widened into a hollow where the walls had partially collapsed, a jagged wound in the earth. The air was thick with dust, so heavy it stung Firas's eyes and scraped his lungs raw with every breath. Rubble was scattered like broken bones across the floor, and amid the ruin lay Kareem Fayez.

He was half-buried beneath a slab of stone, his body twisted awkwardly against the rock. Dust and blood streaked his dark skin, his tunic torn and smeared with dark red the color of rust where jagged edges had scraped him raw. His once-steady hands shook as he tried to wedge a broken length of root beneath the stone, prying at it with desperate futility. His lips were split and dry, his breath rattling shallow in his chest. And yet—his eyes burned. Defiance, sharp and unyielding, glared out from the ruin.

Raven let the shroud slip, enough for Firas's face to catch the dim glow of fractured stone-veins. The moment he spotted them, Kareem flinched, his jaw tightening. Suspicion flared, hard and bright, even through the haze of exhaustion. "What is this?" he rasped, voice sand-scraped and ragged. "Another test?"

Firas took a step forward. "No test. We're getting you out."

For a brittle moment, Kareem only stared. Then a short, harsh laugh cracked from his throat. "There is no getting out. Not unless it's in a death shroud."

"Under normal circumstances, yes," Firas said evenly, crouching beside the stone. "But this time, it's different. *You* are different."

Kareem's face twisted in confusion. "What are you talking about?"

Raven and Firas exchanged a quick look.

Firas drew in a steady breath. "You're Ambigua. That's why they sent you here, why they wanted the maze to bury you. They don't want you to live, Kareem. They want you erased."

For a heartbeat, silence pressed down heavier than the stone itself. Then Kareem barked a laugh, bitter and broken, his expression curdling with fury. "Ambigua?" He spat the word like poison, forcing himself upright even as his wounded leg buckled. "Don't you dare put that curse on me. I'd rather be crushed under this rubble than branded a monster like you."

"Kareem—listen to me—"

"No!" His voice cracked like a whip, jagged with denial. "I am not one of you. I'll never be one of you!" His wild eyes darted toward the shattered wall, his hands clutching the broken root. He swung it against the stone with a roar.

The impact splintered the wood—and the sector answered.

A deep, bone-shaking groan thundered through the hollow. Cracks spidered overhead. Then the ceiling gave way.

The collapse came all at once: a roar of shattering rock, roots tearing free, a choking storm of dust.

"Move!" Raven's hand clamped on Firas's arm, dragging him sideways as a boulder crashed where they had stood a heartbeat before.

Kareem wasn't so lucky. The first slab struck his shoulder, spinning him sideways with a sickening crunch. He screamed, the sound ripped raw from his lungs, and tried to crawl free—but more stone poured down, pinning his leg, his hip, his chest.

Firas lunged, heart hammering, dropping to his knees in the storm of debris. He seized Kareem's arm, straining to pull him out, but Kareem's blood-slick grip kept sliding, dust turning everything into ash and grit.

"Hold on!" Firas bellowed, though his throat burned with dust.

"I said let me die!" Kareem spat blood, eyes wild with fury even as more stone pressed down. "Better this than your curse!"

"Shut up and fight!" Firas snarled, yanking harder, muscles tearing with the effort. Raven was there too, bracing against the shifting rubble, teeth bared as she shoved at the slabs crushing him.

But the sector wasn't finished.

A final shudder ripped through the hollow, and the largest slab gave way. It came down with brutal finality, burying Kareem beneath a wave of stone. His scream cut off in an instant.

The silence that followed was suffocating. Only the settling rattle of dust remained, choking the air, clinging to their skin.

Firas stared at the mound of rock where Kareem had been, his chest heaving, every muscle in his body trembling with strain and failure. His hand was still outstretched, smeared with Kareem's blood.

Raven's voice was flat, cold with necessity. "He's gone."

But Firas couldn't let it be that simple. The Imperium was watching. If they saw Kareem fight them, refuse them, die defiant, the truth would unravel everything.

So he reached. He reached into the minds above, tearing himself open, forcing them to see what he needed them to see—*crushed beneath rubble. Nothing more.*

And as the lie wove itself into their thoughts, Firas sagged, sweat and blood mixing on his skin. Each deception cut deeper. Each lie buried him closer to breaking.

TALAH
XXIV

The world washed over Talah in a rush of sound and salt. She stumbled as her feet landed on slick stone, the air around her changing in an instant—thick, humid, alive. The scent of brine hit her like a wave, sharp and overwhelming. Moisture clung to her skin, soaking into every thread of her robes within seconds, until the fabric felt heavy, suffocating. Salt stung the cut on her lip, the tang of it bitter on her tongue. Her breath came hard, ragged, as if the air itself pressed against her lungs.

She was in the Water sector.

She had thought it would feel familiar. Comforting, even. A place that would steady her, that might remind her of long afternoons by the shore, of the salt spray and the ebb of waves against her ankles. Instead, it was heavier. Stranger. The air was saturated, oppressive, more weight than breath. Shadows clung to the dripping walls, the sound of rushing water echoing from unseen depths, hollow and distorted. Every drop that fell from the cavern ceiling struck like a warning, like the sector itself was watching.

It didn't feel like home. It felt like a test—like the sea had turned its back on her.

Dripping echoed around her like a heartbeat, slow and constant, falling from unseen crevices above. A single droplet struck her shoulder, cold as ice. She looked up—and the light fractured into a thousand shards across the cavern ceiling. Everything shimmered. Bent. Twisted.

Stone walkways unfurled before her, ancient and worn smooth by centuries of tides. Some rose like ribs from tide-pools, slick with algae and riddled with cracks. Others dipped into the dark water that surged and receded with rhythmic force. One path was submerged entirely. Another shook beneath her step, already beginning to sink.

The walls of the sea-cave maze curved at impossible angles—some covered in carvings half-eroded by time, others draped in translucent sheets of seaweed that fluttered like ghostly curtains in the currents.

This place felt old. Older than the Trials. Older than the university. Like it had always been here.

A sudden cheer broke through the stillness—distant but unmistakable. She froze, head whipping toward the sound. High above, just past a jagged gap in the cavern ceiling, she caught a glimpse of them. The stands. The crowd was still there—watching.

Talah could just make out silhouettes against the glow of hovering lights. Their faces were obscured, blurred by distance and mist, but the sound reached her: gasps, murmurs, applause. Someone had just landed in a different sector. Another battle won. Or lost.

She pressed her hand to her chest, her fingers brushing the damp cloth where Mazin's token had vanished in the teleportation surge. It felt warm. Or maybe that was just her.

Talah didn't know how long she had until another competitor came crashing through the same shimmer of space she had—driven by panic or strategy or desperation.

Still, she didn't move. She was standing in her element. Surrounded by the thing that was supposed to make her feel strong. But all she felt now was cold.

And yet she couldn't give up now.

The water lapped at the stone beneath her feet, cold fingers tugging at her ankles as if it wanted her to step in, to let it pull her down. The sound filled every hollow of the cavern—dripping, rushing, whispering currents that shifted without warning. She wrapped her arms around herself, but it did nothing to stop the chill sinking deeper with every breath.

She tried to move. One step, then another, across a walkway slick with algae. Her toes slipped, her balance wavering, and for an instant she felt the void yawning below—black water swallowing the path whole. She clutched at the wall, breath ragged. The stone was clammy beneath her palm, slick with condensation.

Talah closed her eyes, trying to summon something—anything—that might feel familiar. Memories of tides breaking against the shore. The quiet peace of swimming beneath the waves, hair weightless, limbs strong. But when she opened her eyes, all she saw was black water stretching into caverns without end. Shadows shifted in its depths, too deep to be light, too restless to be still.

It wasn't home. It was hungry.

Her stomach growled, low and angry, echoing in the vast silence. She pressed a hand against it, feeling the hollow ache. She had lost track of time—hours since she'd eaten, maybe more. The taste of salt clung to her tongue, thick and metallic. She tried not to think of Mazin's face as he'd thrown the token to her, tried not to imagine what had become of him in the Earth sector. Every time she blinked, she saw him bleeding, surrounded, falling beneath blows she couldn't stop.

The cavern floor trembled faintly underfoot as a distant surge rolled through. She staggered again, catching herself on the wall. A pulse of water washed over the walkway, soaking the hem of her torn robes, dragging them heavier against her legs.

"Keep moving," she whispered, though the sound barely carried above the drip-drip-drip.

She forced herself onward, deeper into the maze. The passages narrowed, opening into chambers strung with seaweed like translucent curtains. They brushed against her skin as she passed, damp and slimy, clinging like hands that didn't want to let go. She pushed through, shivering, and the path widened into a tidepool chamber. The air was heavy with the stench of rot and brine. Small crabs scattered at her approach, skittering into cracks. Fish bones littered the edges of the pool, pale as ghosts.

Exhaustion pressed on her shoulders, dragging her down. Her knees wobbled as she lowered herself against the stone, tucking into the curve of the wall. Cold seeped in instantly, her wet robes sucking away what little warmth remained. She pulled them tighter around herself, though it made no difference.

Above, the crowd's roar rose again, muffled but unmistakable. Another death. Another victory. Another step closer to the end of this nightmare.

She wanted to close her eyes. Just for a moment. But she knew better. In the Water sector, sleep could mean drowning. Even on dry stone, the tide was unpredictable. Pools filled without warning; currents surged from nowhere.

Her fingers brushed the token she still held, its glow faint against her palm. It should have made her feel stronger. Instead, it felt like a weight, a reminder of everything she'd already lost to hold it.

What if I don't make it out? The thought was sharp, treacherous. She shoved it down, curling tighter against the wall.

No, she would not give the maze that satisfaction.

Salt stung her lips as she whispered into the darkness, her voice shaking but still alive:

"I'm not done yet."

The water answered with a low surge, as if mocking her.

There was a gurgle somewhere deeper in the cavern, a constant rush that reminded her she wasn't alone. The sector was alive—always moving, always shifting—and it wanted her broken.

She tucked her knees to her chest, trying to preserve heat, but her body wouldn't stop trembling. Her skin burned where salt rubbed into open cuts, a thousand tiny stings that wouldn't fade. Each breath scraped her lungs raw, thick with brine and moisture. Her stomach cramped with hunger, sharp enough to make her double over.

She tried to count the seconds with each drip that fell from the ceiling. One. Two. Three. But the rhythm slipped away too easily, time unraveling in the endless dark. The roar of the crowd above became part of it too—distant shouts rising and falling like tides, marking battles she couldn't see but could imagine all too well.

Mazin. Adine. Zayd. Were they still fighting? Still alive?

Her nails dug crescents into her palms. She couldn't afford to think about it. Not now. Not when the maze demanded every shred of focus.

Her head dipped forward, eyelids dragging shut, but a sudden surge crashed through a nearby tunnel, sending icy spray across her face. She startled awake, heart racing, the token slipping from her hand. Its faint glow bobbed once on the water's surface before she snatched it back, clutching it to her chest.

"No," she whispered hoarsely. "You're not taking me."

Her voice was swallowed whole by the water's echo.

The darkness pressed closer with every heartbeat. Time seemed to cave in on itself until she didn't know just how long she'd been there. The darkness overhead swallowed everything whole. The dripping became rhythmic, steady as a drumbeat. One. Two. Three. She closed her eyes, and for a moment it sounded like footsteps.

She jerked her head up. No one was there. Only the seaweed swayed in invisible currents, whispering against the stone.

Her breath quickened. The air seemed thicker, wetter. The walls rippled as though water moved through the rock itself. Shadows wavered, taking on familiar shapes. She blinked—and Mazin stood at the far edge of the pool, blood staining his tunic, eyes hollow.

"Talah," he rasped, voice warped by the chamber's echo. *"Why did you leave me?"*

She scrambled back, heart hammering, chest tight. *"You're not real."*

The shadow wavered, stretched—and became her father. His stern gaze locked on her, his voice cutting as the waves behind him swelled higher and higher. *"You've dishonored us. You were supposed to be stronger."*

Salt filled her mouth, choking her. She clamped her eyes shut, pressed her palms over her ears, but the voices were inside, not out. When she opened them again, the figures were gone. Only black water lapped at the edge of the stone, calm and indifferent, as though nothing had happened.

Her body trembled harder. Maybe it was exhaustion. Maybe it was madness. The maze didn't care which.

She clutched the token in her fist, squeezing until its edges dug into her skin. *"I will not die here,"* she whispered, her voice shaking but defiant.

Talah jerked awake, heart pounding. She curled tighter against the wall, shivering, the token pressed hard against her chest. Her thoughts frayed at the edges, memories bleeding into the present until she wasn't sure if she was awake or already dreaming. The seaweed fluttered like phantom hands in the corners of her vision, and every shadow seemed to shift when she wasn't looking.

Time unraveled. Seconds, minutes—hours?—slipped away into the black. Hunger gnawed at her gut, sharper now, like teeth. She had fought sleep. She swore she had. But at some point, exhaustion had won.

Her body ached from the cold, her limbs stiff, her mouth dry as bone now. Droplets pattered down from the ceiling, splashing against her face, and she flinched as though it were more than water.

She dragged herself upright, legs trembling beneath her, robes heavy with damp. Her breath fogged in the humid air as she stared into the cavern's endless dark.

Another night survived. Barely.

She pressed her palm flat against the wall, forcing her body forward, forcing herself to move. The maze was still shifting around her. Competitors were still fighting, dying, clawing for survival. She couldn't let herself drown in the silence.

She took one unsteady step, then another. The Water sector waited.

And so did whatever came next.

TALAH

Talah moved cautiously through the winding corridors of coral-covered stone, each step careful on the slick surfaces. Water dripped steadily from above, echoing down the passages like distant footsteps. Her entire body ached—shoulders bruised, ribs sore, knees stiff. But worse was the ache behind her eyes, the ringing weight of Rayen's death still humming through her bones.

Mazin.

He'd saved her. Given up his chance at taking that token so she could escape. And she had been teleported away while he bled on the ground. She didn't even know if he was still alive.

The walls closed tighter around her, and she forced herself forward through a low corridor where coral curled like knotted fingers. Murmurs echoed ahead—too soft to make out, but close enough to know she wasn't alone.

She crept toward the sound, barefoot steps muffled on damp stone. Water lapped at her ankles as the tunnel sloped downward into a half-flooded passage. The sound grew clearer: whispering, the shift of movement, the soft clink of something being set down.

She rounded the corner—and stopped.

A vast chamber stretched before her—sunken and submerged in parts, lit by pale shafts of light that pierced the cracked ceiling above. It shimmered across the rippling surface of a central pool, illuminating strands of kelp that swayed gently like ghostly fingers reaching from the deep.

The silence was thick here. Reverent. Sacred.

At the far end, a platform of jagged stone jutted up from the swirling water. Coral bloomed along its base in sharp, bright clusters. At its peak, spinning slowly above a vortex of water, hovered a token—black stone, spiraled like a seashell, veined with silver that pulsed in rhythm with the maze itself.

Talah wasn't alone.

A figure stood waist-deep in the water, hauling himself up onto the pillar.

Broad shoulders. Dark, slicked hair. Armor glinting with droplets.

Talah inhaled sharply. She remembered him from training—another Signborn, a traditionalist. A Taurus of weather and warfare, born into legacy, trained for domination. Salim. Another one of Rayen's lackeys.

He turned at the sound of her breath, water sluicing from his arms as he rose to his full height on the stone. His dark eyes locked onto hers.

"Too slow, princess," Salim sneered. His voice echoed against the stone, cold and confident.

Talah stepped to the edge of the water, her legs unsteady beneath her. They still trembled from the fight with Rayen—from the heat of his blades, from the sight of his body pinned and broken, from the raw, terrible surge of power that had torn through her to make it happen. Her hands wouldn't stop shaking, the aftershocks of it rippling through her bones, through her breath. The images clung behind her eyes, refusing to be blinked away: the roots, the blood, the look on his face as the life left him.

The shock pressed heavy on her chest, a weight that felt too large for her ribs to contain. The weight of everything she couldn't unsee. Couldn't undo.

And yet—when she opened her mouth, her voice held. Steadier than her limbs, sharper than her heartbeat, it cut through the cavern air like a blade.

"I'm not here to be fast," she replied evenly.

The world around her felt... disconnected. As if none of it was real anymore. As if the moment she'd killed Rayen had torn something open and she was still falling through it. She could hear the water surging in low, deep pulses beneath the whirlpool, a breath she couldn't quite sync with.

She could smell it too—brine and rust, like old blood on metal. The air clung to her skin, thick and heavy, tasting of salt. And beneath all of that, she could feel her body fraying at the edges. Her ribs ached with every inhale. Her knuckles throbbed, her power thrumming just below her skin, raw and unsteady. She wasn't ready for another fight.

But there were no breaks in the Trials. No mercy in this maze.

She forced her bare feet into the water. The first touch made her flinch—the liquid colder than she expected, shocking against her overheated skin. It crept over her toes, seeping between them, rising until it lapped at her ankles with a weight that felt almost alive. The chill sank deeper, biting through skin into marrow, as though the water meant to claim her from the inside out.

Her robes darkened instantly, the fabric dragging heavy against her legs, tugged by the gentle pull of the current. Each movement stirred ripples that spread out into the stillness, silver light flickering across the cavern walls as if the sector itself was watching. The scent of brine rose thicker, coating her tongue, filling her lungs with the sharp taste of salt and something older—something that didn't welcome her.

She let it chill her bones. She let it anchor her, even as it tried to pull her down.

Salim moved with the force of a crashing tide, charging straight into the water with a roar that sent droplets flying like glass in moonlight. The chamber came alive around them—wind picking up from nowhere, slipping across the surface in erratic gusts. Mist rose from the pool, thick and blinding, coating the air in cold, shifting fog.

Talah barely had time to duck. His first swing passed over her head, close enough for her to feel the air split—wind-laced and sharp enough to slice skin.

She dropped under the water.

Salt rushed into her nose and eyes, burning. Her ears filled with the low, ever-present hum of the whirlpool above. The chill seeped deep, sinking past skin and sinew until it settled in her bones. The stone beneath her feet was treacherous, etched with the grooves of ancient currents and coral skeletons.

She twisted underwater, summoning a pulse of current from her palm, using it to add force to her sweeping kick. Her foot connected with Salim's shin—but he barely moved. He stood like a reef-rooted stone, unshaken.

His hand found her wrist.

He yanked her up with a violent twist, fingers like iron digging into her skin. Panic spiked hot in her chest. She thrashed, twisting hard, nails raking against his arm until his grip slipped just enough. With a desperate wrench, she tore herself free.

She broke the surface with a choked gasp, coughing saltwater. Cold air slapped her soaked face. Her lungs burned as she dragged in another breath—but she barely had time to catch it before she saw him, already gathering a cyclone in his hand.

Tiny. Focused. Deadly.

He flung it at her chest. She didn't think. She only moved—flinging her arm up, twisting her fingers through the air, casting.

Illusion sparked. A shimmer of herself darted left as she rolled hard to the right. The cyclone passed clean through the fake—striking the cavern wall with a splintering crack. Coral shattered. Bits of stone rained into the pool.

Salim snarled. She saw his boots slip on moss as he pivoted to find her again, but Talah was already moving.

She summoned a narrow wall of water—thin but fast—like a crashing tide turned upright. It smacked into him, unbalancing him enough for her to dive for cover behind a spire of jagged rock.

She could barely breathe.

Every part of her screamed. Bruises spread across her ribs with every breath, lips split and stinging with the taste of salt and blood. Power wavered inside like a candle guttering in the wind, each flicker a warning that the fight was burning through the last of her strength.

But she couldn't give up.

Not now. Not after Mazin. Not after Rayen. Not after everything.

A sudden crack sounded behind her—stone splintering—and she turned just in time to see Salim hurl a blast of wind like a battering ram. It struck the spire and shattered it, sending coral shrapnel flying.

One shard cut across her cheek. She cried out, fell, rolled into the water. The taste of blood filled her mouth. Her limbs felt like anchors.

Salim advanced, slow and merciless. He was panting too, now—bloodied but relentless, the edge of his mouth curled in a cruel, confident smile.

"You really thought you could take me?" he growled. "You don't even belong here."

Talah's hand closed around something underwater. A loose chunk of coral. Jagged. Sharp. The water around her rippled—not by accident. She summoned it again.

Illusions. Two of them this time—darting out to either side, creating a flickering echo of herself circling him. Salim cursed, turning to strike one down.

She rose.

The real Talah surged up from the water, teeth clenched, and drove the coral into his side with all the strength her shaking arm had left, finding the opening between his armor. His scream was raw, full of rage and pain. He spun, catching her with a wild elbow to the ribs. Something gave way.

She couldn't breathe. Her vision exploded with stars. But she didn't let go.

Her world shrank to instinct—raw, desperate. She slammed into him again, using water to strengthen her attack, driving him back toward the cavern wall. They hit it with a brutal crunch, and the jagged coral embedded there finished what she'd started.

Blood bloomed in the water around them like dark smoke.

Talah stumbled back, nearly collapsing. Her breath rasped in her throat like sand. Her arms shook. Her knees wanted to give out.

The token still spun above the whirlpool. Calling to her.

She turned toward it, every nerve in her body screaming as she waded forward. The pillar was slick with algae and blood—hers, his, the maze's. She dragged herself up inch by inch, nails catching on stone worn smooth by centuries.

Her knees slammed against the rock, skin peeling open as they ground against the rough surface. Each shift left a smear of blood, warm trails mingling with the cold damp clinging to the stone. Fabric tangled around her legs, the weight of her soaked robes dragging her back. The coarse weave snagged on jagged edges, ripping with sharp, tearing sounds until shreds clung to her like seaweed.

Still she climbed, the stone biting into flesh, every inch a battle between body and will.

The current pulled at her—vicious, sentient, punishing. Her shoulder struck coral. Pain flared. Her shin caught on an outcrop. She bled freely now, red mixing with salt. She couldn't see clearly. Couldn't think.

But she climbed.

And at the top, with the wind howling through the cracks in the cavern ceiling, she leapt. The whirlpool caught her in midair, spinning her violently. She lost all sense of direction—up was down, down was sideways, air and water blending into a blur.

Her heartbeat pounded in her ears.

Her fingers stretched and closed around the token. It was ice cold in her palm. Smooth. Spiral-shaped. Veined with silver that pulsed softly, almost like breath. The moment she touched it, the current vanished.

Stillness fell like a curtain. The chamber quieted. The mist thinned. Even the distant sound of dripping water hushed. Talah collapsed to her knees on the pillar, soaked, bloodied, and shaking.

But she had the final token. And that meant one thing.

She'd survived.

The seashell-shaped stone pulsed again, brighter now.

And the world dissolved around her.

TALAH
XXVII

There was a deafening crack as her knees met cold, hard stone. She gasped, her hands scrabbling as she struggled to take in air. Her clothes clung to her body, soaked and heavy. Blood and salt started to dry in patches along her skin. Her lungs seized as she tried to breathe—too fast, too shallow. The roar of the whirlpool still echoed in her ears despite the cloying silence of wherever she ended up.

She wasn't in the maze anymore. Instead, she was right back where they started, in that dim, circular chamber beneath the arena.

And she wasn't alone.

There were only a few figures that lay slumped around her, either curled up or sprawled across the polished floor. Some groaned, holding on to themselves as if to keep their own bodies from falling apart. Others didn't move at all.

Talah blinked rapidly, trying to focus. Her fingers clenched and unclenched, revealing empty palms. The token was gone, just like the others. Her vision swam, ribs throbbing as she tried to suck in air through her teeth. The teleportation had ripped through her body, unmaking her and remaking her. She felt as though she might throw up.

But none of that mattered.

She forced herself upright, bracing one arm against the wall. Panic edged her vision in black as her gaze darted from competitor to competitor. Counting heads. Searching faces.

Not Zayd.

Not Adine.

Not Mazin.

They could still be in the maze. Or they could have gotten through the maze before she had. There was no way for her to tell just yet.

"Stars," she whispered. "Where are—"

There was a flash before another body came hurtling into the chamber. Talah flinched, her heart stuttering as she caught sight of dark hair.

Zayd landed hard, the crack of his body hitting the ground sharp enough to echo off the stone. The thud vibrated through her bones, and for an instant the world tilted sideways. But it wasn't him she saw—it was Halima. The memory slammed into her unbidden.

Halima's scream tearing through the chasm, the hollow snap of her body striking the platform below. The way the sound had carried—too loud, too final, as if the maze itself had swallowed it whole.

Talah's stomach lurched with the remembered weight of it, that sick certainty that she had crossed a line she could never uncross. She blinked hard, forcing herself back into the present. Zayd was on his elbows, shoulder wrapped in blood-soaked fabric, face pale and dazed—but alive. That was all that mattered. She drew a shaky breath and pushed forward, weaving through the bodies. Ignoring those who had made it. Ignoring those who had not. She refused to look at their faces, refused to count the dead, refused to hear how each lifeless fall echoed Halima's in her mind. Not yet.

"Well, look who's still alive," Zayd gasped, struggling to his knees. "Didn't get roasty-toasty princess after all."

"You look like hell," Talah replied, reaching for him. "Can you stand?"

"That's insulting," Zayd scoffed. He allowed her to help him up, taking a few seconds to regain his balance before looking around. "The others?"

Talah shook her head. "Mazin... helped me in the maze. But I didn't see what happened to him." Fear coiled in her stomach, low and writhing.

"He'll be fine, Talah," Zayd said quietly. "They both will. Maybe they're already out, who knows."

But he didn't know that for sure, as much as Talah wanted to believe him.

"Are you okay?" Zayd studied her now, eyes searching for any injuries.

Talah opened her mouth to tell him she was fine, but was she? Her body ached, screaming at her to lay down and rest. Her skin burned, bones weary. She had no clue whether the blood drying along her skin was hers... or someone else's.

"I'll live," she said finally.

"At least until the next trial," Zayd joked, but it fell flat.

There was another flash of light, another hard crack against stone. Talah flinched as they both whipped around, hopeful. Adine coughed violently as she crawled onto hands and knees, hair half unbound, a deep gash above her brow. She blinked up at them, disoriented.

Talah's breath caught.

Two were safe.

She moved without thinking, steadying Adine as she staggered upright. Her skin was clammy, hands trembling where they clutched at Talah's arms. Her gaze flicked around the chamber as if she didn't quite yet believe she was still alive.

"Is this real?" she gasped.

Talah gave a hollow nod. "It's real."

Adine let out a sound mixed between a laugh and a sob. "I thought... stars, I thought I was going to drown." Her voice cracked. "The vines wouldn't let go, and then, I think I passed out at some point. It's all a blur."

Talah tried to ignore the echoes of the maze that clawed their way back into her mind. But they came anyway—unbidden, merciless.

Rayen's eyes widening in shock, disbelieving, as the roots she hadn't meant to summon drove through him, pinning him to the wall. His lips parting, no sound but blood bubbling up in his throat. The way his token had clinked against the ground, soft and damning.

Each memory struck like a blow, cutting through her chest, forcing the air from her lungs. She saw their faces too clearly—saw them in the flicker of torchlight, in the shadows that clung to the corners of her vision. She could still feel the tremor in her hands, the rush of power that had come too easily, too hungrily, when she'd fought them.

Her stomach turned. She dug her nails into her palms, hard enough to break the skin, grounding herself in the sting. She couldn't afford to collapse here, not now. Not when others were watching. Not when she had to keep moving.

She guided Adine to the wall, Zayd trailing behind them. Adine slid down to sit, hands still shaking.

"You're alive," Talah said softly. "That's all that matters."

"I lost my token," Adine murmured, blinking hard. "Had to take someone else's." Her eyes met Talah's, something haunted flickering in their depths. "He didn't make it."

Talah didn't ask who. She didn't want to know.

"You did what you had to do," Zayd told her quietly. "We all did."

Adine's hands curled into her lap. "How many?"

"We don't know."

The silence dragged. Around them, the chamber was slowly filling with the bruised and broken. Those who hadn't stirred when they'd been dropped, began showing signs of life. One-by-one, more bodies arrived in stuttering bursts of light—some limping, some crawling. But not him.

Talah's hands curled against her knees. Her breath

came faster now, edged with a panic she couldn't hide. She scanned every face, every flicker of movement, desperate for something—anything—that would tell her he was alive.

Nothing.

She knew he hadn't made it out before her. If he had, she would have felt it. She would have known.

"Come on, Maz… you promised," she whispered. Adine's hand covered hers, squeezing gently. Zayd's shoulder brushed hers as he scanned the room.

The silence of the chamber pressed harder, more suffocating than any whirlpool current, until a violent burst of light flared across the center of the chamber. A body crashed to the ground.

Talah surged forward, her knees nearly giving out beneath her. "Maz!"

He groaned, one arm bent awkwardly beneath him, blood streaking his temple. His shirt was torn and scorched, but his eyes met hers immediately.

"Talah," he rasped, his voice rough but real.

"Took you long enough," Zayd muttered, a relieved grin slowly sliding across his face.

Relief broke over her like a wave as she dropped to her knees beside Mazin, breath catching, a sob escaping. "You absolute idiot," she choked, brushing his blood-matted curls from his brow. "What took you so long?"

He grinned weakly. "Wanted to make an entrance."

She pressed her forehead to his for a moment, trembling. He was here. He was alive. They all were.

"Twenty-four," Zayd said quietly.

Talah and Mazin turned toward him, Adine standing at his side.

"What?" Mazin asked, struggling to sit up.

"Twenty-four," Zayd repeated, looking around the chamber. "Out of thirty-six."

They fell silent. The number hung heavy in the air.

Not just numbers, Talah reminded herself. Names. Faces. *People.* Talah felt it like a weight against her chest—a count of survivors, but also the record of the lost. A loss she contributed to.

Before they could speak again, the doors opened with a sharp bang behind them.

"Stand." The voice echoed, low, resonant, commanding.

The remaining competitors turned as one. At the doors, Khalias stepped forward, his face lined with the kind of stillness that only came with the experience of something terrible.

"Congratulations," Khalias said simply. "You have passed the first trial."

The chamber went still, his words settling like lead upon their shoulders.

"Those who are injured may report to the infirmary. The rest of you may return to your dormitories. You will be summoned tomorrow for training. Tonight, you will meet in the hall for dinner to celebrate your win."

A murmur swept through the small crowd—a mix of relief and exhaustion.

"However—" Khalias' gaze searched the group. "Rana Dawoud. Rafiq Noorani. You will stay behind."

Heads turned. The two named—both Crossborns—flinched. Confusion flickered across their faces, but neither spoke.

Talah's eyes darted between the two competitors, to Khalias watching them with unreadable eyes. She didn't know how she knew… but this wasn't random. Whatever had happened in the maze, whatever they'd done, something told her she wouldn't see them again.

Mazin nudged her forward, forcing her back to reality. "Come on," he said quietly, "we need to get you to the infirmary."

The others were already leaving, filtering through the door as fast as they could despite their injuries. Talah hesitated, glancing back as Mazin led her from the chamber. The two Crossborns were left alone, standing in the center, fear in their eyes.

She watched until the double doors shut between them.

The dinner was nothing like the opulence of the Convocation. There was no music. No laughter. No vibrant colors or Signborns to entertain. A long table had been set beneath the low-burning lanterns in the academy's hall, lined with survivors.

No seats were left empty, but the absence of the others stretched like shadows between them all.

Talah sat between Mazin and Adine, her bandaged leg stretched stiffly beneath the table. Mazin had forced her to the infirmary, refusing to let her out of his sight until she saw a healer. The Virgos had worked tirelessly, stitching and fixing the survivors for hours before finally releasing them.

Now, they all sat at the table, the scent of roasted lamb and rice clinging to the air. Most of the food went untouched. Those who did eat did so mechanically, quietly. Talah's own plate sat in front of her, still steaming.

"Should've called this a memorial, not a dinner," Zayd muttered across the table. His voice broke the silence like a crack in glass.

Talah's gaze swept the table. Bruises mottled skin in ugly purples and greens. Burns streaked arms and shoulders, raw and angry. Dark hollows sat beneath every pair of eyes, carved deep by exhaustion. These weren't the same competitors who had entered the maze only hours ago—they looked like survivors dragged from a battlefield.

No one mentioned Rana and Rafiq—the two who had been asked to stay behind. The two who hadn't been given a chair tonight. No one had asked, but she could see it in the glances exchanged across the flickering candlelight. Everyone noticed. They knew.

"We should toast," said an Aries girl down the row. Her arm was in a sling, a healing cast wrapped tight around her ribs. "To the maze," she said, raising a cup of water. "For not killing us."

"Yet," Zayd added grimly.

A hollow chuckle rippled through the room.

A voice carried from further down the table, smooth and deliberate, too measured to belong to anyone exhausted.

"Better to drink to survival than to dwell on ghosts," Nadir said casually.

Even after hours in the maze, he looked put together in a way that felt unnatural. His robes were smudged with dirt, yes, and a shallow cut marked his temple, but his posture was straight, his dark hair tied neatly at the nape of his neck. He didn't look like a survivor; he looked like a man already rehearsing for a speech.

He raised his own cup, his smile thin but polished. "To those of us who had the foresight to endure. To those who will be remembered, not forgotten." His eyes slid across the table and found Talah's. The corners of his mouth ticked upward. "Some of us more than others."

Heat crawled into her chest, the bruises on her ribs throbbing in time with her heartbeat. She remembered the way he'd cornered her before—the subtle pressure of his words, the promise of power wrapped in a velvet snare. Twice now he had extended his hand, cloaked in charm and calculation. Twice she had refused.

Her stomach felt hollow. The food on her plate was nothing but ash on her tongue. She could barely stand to be here, sitting and eating as if none of it had happened—like the maze hadn't torn strips from their bodies and left its mark on their minds.

A sharp *crunch* shattered the silence—bread torn, teeth grinding down. Talah flinched. For a split second, it wasn't food she heard—it was the wet crack of Halima's body slamming into the platform. The sound rattled through her bones all over again, the echo of finality that no cheering crowd could drown out.

The steam rising from a bowl across the table turned her

stomach too—suddenly it was smoke, thick and acrid, clinging to her lungs the way it had after Rayen's knives burned the air. Even the smell of roasted meat carried the tang of blood, hot and metallic, the way it had soaked into her hands no matter how hard she tried to wash it away.

Her chest tightened. The walls of the hall pressed in, voices muffled like the echoing tunnels of the maze. She dug her nails into her palms, grounding herself with the sting, but the memories clawed higher, faster, until she thought she might choke on them.

Her chair screeched across the stone floor, loud and jarring in the quiet room. The legs scraped against the uneven tile and nearly tipped as she shoved herself upright, catching it just in time before it clattered backward.

Every pair of eyes turned toward her.

She didn't care.

She couldn't stay here—not another second. The walls were closing in. The candlelight flickered too low, too soft, like dying stars. The scent of roasted meat and stale wine was suddenly cloying, sticking to the back of her throat. Her pulse beat against her ears, hot and frantic.

"Tal?" Mazin's voice reached her like it was underwater. Distant. Careful.

She didn't meet his eyes. "I'm going to bed," she said too quickly.

She turned, her footsteps echoing too loudly in the hall as she passed through the arched exit. The cold air of the corridor hit her like a slap—damp, sharp, clean. She sucked in a breath, then another, but it wasn't enough. The walls were too tall. The ceiling too high. The shadows moved too much.

Behind her, she heard the soft scrape of another chair, then footsteps. She didn't have to look to know who it was.

Talah let him follow, trailing her down the long hall lit by flickering wall sconces. She moved automatically, her boots tapping too loudly against the stone.

The corridor stretched endlessly before her, like another

maze. The walls weren't made of coral this time—but of silence, of dread, of memories she couldn't outrun.

The maze was gone. She *knew* that. She wasn't in the vine-covered labyrinth, wasn't atop the floating stones. She wasn't in the half-flooded cave with broken coral slicing her skin, wasn't breathing in blood and salt. But her body didn't believe her mind.

Her fingers trembled. Her stomach lurched. Her heartbeat wouldn't slow.

Mazin caught up to her just as she passed a window overlooking the darkened training yard. Moonlight spilled across the tiles, silver and still—but all she saw was water, endless and black, rising in her mind.

"Talah." Mazin's voice was gentler this time, right behind her.

She stopped but didn't turn.

"I'm fine," she said, voice raw and frayed at the edges.

"You're not," he replied quietly. "None of us are."

Silence stretched between them.

Her shoulders shook. "I keep hearing it," she whispered, voice cracking. "The dripping. The crashing. His voice. The scream when I—when I—" Her throat clenched. "I can't shut it off."

Mazin stepped closer. Slowly. Carefully. "I know."

"What we did—"

Mazin's expression didn't shift. "When I fought that guy so you could get to the token, I thought that was it. That I'd die right there."

Talah's breath caught. The hallway blurred.

"I still don't know how you made it out," she murmured.

"Luck," Mazin said with a shrug, but his voice was heavy. "And maybe spite."

She almost laughed. Almost. But something inside of her cracked instead.

"Spare me," Talah snapped, the sudden sharpness in her voice echoing off the stone walls.

Mazin blinked. "What—?"

"You don't get to joke about that," she cut in, turning on him fully now. "You *threw away* your chance at that token, Mazin. You just handed it to me and just—stood there bleeding like it didn't matter. Like *you* didn't matter."

He opened his mouth, but she didn't let him speak.

"You were supposed to make it out, to fight your way through like the rest of us, not throw your life away like some kind of tragic hero."

"I wasn't—" he started.

"Yes, you were." Her voice cracked. "You were trying to protect me. Again."

"And I'd do it again," he snapped, stepping closer.

She backed away. "And that's the problem, Mazin. You always try to protect me. Like I'm fragile. Like I can't survive this on my own."

"That's not what I think—"

"Isn't it?" she spat. "Because that's sure as hell how it feels. You don't trust me to fight my own battles. To make my own choices. You think sacrificing yourself for me is noble, but it's not. It's selfish. You could have *died* because of me."

Mazin's expression twisted—hurt, confused. But she couldn't stop now. The storm had already broken, and it was all spilling out.

"You didn't even ask. You didn't give me a chance to refuse. You just decided I was worth saving more than you. And maybe I wasn't. Maybe I wasn't worthy. Maybe you should've kept it for yourself."

She was shaking now, chest heaving, hands curled into fists at her sides.

"I don't need you to throw yourself in front of every blade for me. I don't need you to be the hero. I need you to trust that I can be the one who survives. Even when it's ugly. Even when it's hard."

A long silence stretched between them. The hallway felt colder now, the light dimmer.

"Talah—" he said, quieter now.

She turned away.

"I'm done," she muttered, already walking.

"Talah, wait—"

"No," she said, not looking back. "I'm done being the one who has to be saved."

She left him standing in the flickering light, alone.

XXVIII FIRAS

The knock came, sharp and sudden.
Firas froze, fingers tightening around the worn leather spine of the tome in his lap. Candlelight flickered across the cramped room, casting long shadows that shifted across the stone walls like ghosts. The diagram on the page was half-finished—an old schematic, circular and strange, with notations in three dialects and a faded sigil that made his pulse race. He was close. Closer than he'd ever been.

The knock came again, louder this time.

"Firas!" Talah's voice was low and furious, shot straight through the door. "Open the damn door."

He sighed, rubbing the side of his brow where a headache had begun to pulse. He slid the tome shut, tucking it beneath the mattress in one fluid motion, careful not to crease the fragile binding. He grabbed the stray quill from the table, wiped the ink from his fingers, and crossed the small space to the door. The latch gave with a soft click.

She stormed in, fury in motion, eyes sharp enough to cut

steel. She looked like a wild thing, untameable.

He raised an eyebrow, unbothered. "Good evening to you too, Aasifati."

"Don't," she snapped. "Don't start with me."

He let the door swing shut behind her. "Alright then. We can skip the pleasantries."

"The maze, Iras. I want to know what you were really doing in there," she demanded, already crossing the room as if it belonged to her.

"I—"

"No," she cut him off, voice rising. "I don't want the lies. I want the truth, Iras. What were you really doing? My father couldn't have set you up to this, not after how you two butted heads at the Convocation. So why were you helping me?"

Firas scoffed, but didn't answer.

Her eyes narrowed. "You were interfering. And I want to know if you're planning on doing it again."

He leaned against the wall, arms crossed. "You think I'm some kind of puppet master?"

Her voice cracked. "You interfered for a reason. You could have gotten me disqualified if anyone had seen you."

A beat passed.

"Is that all you care about?" he asked slowly.

"If I didn't care about this, why would I be here? I watched people die in that maze. I *killed* people. If this is all for nothing then—"

"I'm trying to stop this," he said, his voice low, controlled. "All of this."

"And how are you doing that?" she snapped. "By playing god?"

"You would've died without us."

"Then I die!" she shouted.

He fell into stunned silence.

Talah's hands were shaking now, clenched at her sides. "I need to do this on my own. I've been protected my entire life. Told I couldn't do things on my own. But I *need* this. I need to prove that I can do this without help. Without anyone protecting me."

"You can," he said quietly.

She laughed—cold and bitter. "If you believed that, then you wouldn't have interfered."

Firas didn't move.

"I didn't need a shadow in the maze," she said. "I needed to know I won because I fought for it. Not because someone cleared my path while I wasn't looking."

She turned toward the door, the tension radiating off her like heat. Firas stepped forward, not enough to stop her, but enough to catch the space between them.

"You really think I don't respect you?" he asked, voice softer now, but low and direct. "After what you did in there? After what you've survived so far?"

Talah froze.

"You think I interfered because I don't believe in you?" His voice was calm, but there was something sharper beneath it. "I interfered because I do. Because I'd misjudged you before and made the same mistake as everyone else."

She turned back toward him slowly, her expression still set in stone, but her eyes flickered with something else entirely. Uncertainty. Fire. Something much more.

"Then let me do this," she said, voice quieter now. "Don't wrap it up in good intentions. You can believe in me without doing things *for* me."

"I know." And he meant it. But stars, it would've been easier if he didn't.

Because now, standing here with her eyes locked on his, the air between them too close and too charged, he wanted to say more. He wanted to tell her everything. About the real reason the Imperium continued the Trials. About those he'd been so desperate to save in the maze. The war that was only rumors to people like her.

But he couldn't.

She took a step forward—they were closer now. Closer than

either of them had intended. Her breath hitched. His didn't come at all. He looked down at her—lips parted, jaw set, hair falling in damp curls that clung to her neck. Her fury still clung to her, but underneath it was something else, humming through the air like a storm not yet struck.

"Why are you looking at me like that?" she asked.

"Because I don't know how else to look at you right now."

Her lashes fluttered slightly.

"You're not who I thought you were," he said, voice lower now.

She flinched at his words, glancing away.

"I don't trust you," she said, and this time, the pain was laced into every syllable. "Even now. Especially now."

"I know."

The space between them felt like it was shrinking by the second, tension thick enough to cut. He stepped back, forcing space between them. Not because he wanted to.

Because he had to.

"I meant what I said," she told him. "Don't try to protect me again."

And with that, she turned and opened the door. This time, she didn't hesitate, disappearing into the corridor without another word.

Firas stood alone in the quiet hum of candlelight, his hands clenched at his sides. The mattress shifted slightly behind him, the hidden tome beneath it glowing faintly in the dark.

He could've told her. He wanted to tell her. But if he did... it would only make her hate him more. And he wasn't quite ready for that.

The silence in his room lingered after the door shut. Candle wax dripped onto the edge of the table. Firas exhaled, low and tired, and crossed the room. He slid the book out from beneath the mattress, careful not to disturb the other hidden scrolls beneath it. The symbol on the cover still shimmered faintly—a spiral sigil he'd never seen before. One he still couldn't figure out.

Firas snapped the book shut, tucking it beneath the mattress once again. Grabbing his cloak, he stepped out, shutting his door firmly behind him. He found himself alone in the corridor, the quiet nearly suffocating. Ignoring it, he started down the hall.

The meeting room was carved deep into the hollow of the wall. Kam was already there, pacing, her boots scuffing faint trails in the dust. Her arms were crossed, jaw tight, braids coiled tight behind her shoulders like whips.

Rami leaned against the far wall, flipping a copper coin across his knuckles. Raven was crouched near the wall, uncoiling the hood from her cloak, eyes sharp and alert.

"You're late," Kam said without turning.

"I had an unexpected guest," Firas replied.

Kam shot him a look, but said nothing—yet.

Raven stood. "You missed a lovely dinner," she said, sarcasm dripping from each word.

Firas didn't answer.

Rami's coin caught the candlelight. "How is your little competitor?"

Firas met his gaze coolly. "That's not what we're here to discuss."

Raven stepped forward, shrugging her cloak off. "There might be a few more Ambigua among the competitors."

Firas raised an eyebrow. "Might be?"

"I know, I know," she said. "We have to be sure."

"Yes," Firas replied evenly. "We do. If we make even one mistake—reveal ourselves to the wrong person—us and the entire rebellion could be put at risk."

Kam nodded slowly, then looked at Raven. "We need to check out the ones you noticed. And if they are actually Ambigua, we need to get them out before the next trial."

Rami pushed off the wall, eyes darker now. "There's been news, by the way. There was an attack yesterday in the Fire Province—government barracks burned to the ground. The Imperium's blaming the Ambigua. Again."

Raven's face twisted. "But it wasn't us."

"No," Rami said. "It wasn't. But that doesn't matter now, does it? They're stoking this fire on purpose."

Firas exhaled, his stomach sinking.

Kam's eyes were on him again. This time, she didn't look away.

"We stay focused," Firas told them firmly. "It doesn't matter what's going on outside these walls right now—we have a job to do. Let Rafiq and Samira deal with that. Keep an eye out for any more Ambigua. Get them out. Keep studying the old tomes for any more information about us. That is our mission."

"Aye, aye, captain," Rami replied, giving him a mock salute.

When Raven and Rami slipped out, Kam stayed behind.

The room fell quiet, but not peacefully. The kind of quiet that warned a storm hadn't passed—it had just changed shape. Kam didn't speak right away. She watched him for a long, heavy moment, eyes narrowed. She waited until the last of the footsteps faded into nothing.

"Talah caught you helping her, didn't she?" Kam asked quietly.

Firas didn't deny it. There was no point.

She stepped closer, boots crunching faint grit against stone. Her arms were crossed, posture controlled but rigid, like a blade she hadn't drawn yet.

"You stepped in for *her*."

"I needed her to survive," Firas reminded her. "If she goes, I go. And all of this will have been for nothing."

Kam's jaw ticked. "That's not why you did it."

He said nothing.

"She caught you. Do you understand what would happen if she reports that?" Kam asked, furious. "You could be taken. Killed."

Firas's chin jerked up. "Then so be it."

"Don't you dare," Kam snorted. "We need you alive, and you know it. We can't risk you being caught. If you're caught we all could be. You're getting distracted."

"I'm not," he said flatly.

"She's not one of us, Firas. Rafiq and Samira would say the same. We can't risk exposure for someone we aren't sure is Ambigua."

"She might be one of us."

"And if she's not," Kam repeated, stepping closer now, her voice like ice, "then everything we've worked for is at risk. The Imperium is tightening the leash. You felt it today—what they did to those two kids. Gone without a word."

Firas clenched his fists at his sides.

Kam didn't stop. "They're not trying to hide it anymore. Rami said it—the fire in the province, the public accusation. This is it. They're making it real now. Open. They've already been working on turning the people against us. It won't stop."

Firas felt the weight of it settle in his chest.

"The whispers used to be manageable," Kam continued. "Rumors. Speculation. We could move around it. Deny it. We used to be nothing but conspiracy theories. But this?" She shook her head. "This is a declaration. Intentional. The people already feared us when we were nothing but bedtime warnings to children. But it's changing now, Fi."

He looked at her. "Which means we're running out of time."

"Yes," she said. "And we need every Ambigua still breathing. We need to find them before the Imperium does. Before the *Kaed* does."

"We're working on it, Kam," Firas muttered.

Kam's voice cracked—just slightly—with urgency. "Then don't make this harder than it already is. We don't have the luxury of being loyal to anyone who isn't us."

Firas looked away.

"You think I don't see what's happening?" she said more softly now. "You've been circling her since the banquet. You hesitate when she's involved. And that hesitation—Firas, it's dangerous."

Firas stared at the wall. *She's right*, he thought. *I know she is but...*

"She's connected to this somehow," he said out loud. "I feel it. I don't know how, but I do."

How do I even begin to explain this?

Kam's voice was quiet but hard. "That's not enough."

"She's not like the others."

Kam shook her head. "You don't know what she is yet. That's the point. Her father is the *councilor*, Fi. He knows everything. You think he would have allowed his daughter to live this long if he had known she was one of us? Even if he didn't know…these people are willing to sacrifice their own children to the Trials just to kill us. They could be using her for all we know. And until we're sure she isn't either a trap or a spy, she can't be the reason you break rank."

"I'm not breaking—"

"You will if this keeps up."

Firas swallowed the knot rising in his throat. "I'm trying to lead them."

"Then act like it," Kam said, stepping back. "You're our anchor. If you drift, the whole mission will scatter with you."

He didn't answer, the guilt weighing heavily on his shoulders. Kam stared at him a second longer, then moved toward the hidden passage.

"Don't make me choose between you and the cause," she said over her shoulder.

Firas watched as she disappeared. He didn't move. Didn't breathe.

He didn't want to choose either.

But soon… he might not have a choice.

FIRAS
XXIX

The arena seemed smaller the next day after the maze. The illusions of Pisces that once bent light and reshaped the landscape had disappeared, leaving only flat training platforms, chalk-lined sparring rings, and racks of dulled practice weapons glinting under the rising sun. The absence of illusions made the arena feel more dangerous, not less.

He stood at the edge of the overlook, arms folded as he watched the survivors file in below. Twenty-two left. All of them battered, some still bandaged. But alive. And each one carrying ghosts the maze hadn't been able to bury.

His gaze swept the yard, calculating—not just who limped, but who moved like they didn't trust the ground beneath their feet anymore. Who looked too eager to prove themselves. Who didn't meet anyone's eyes.

Talah entered late, her stride taut with something unspoken. Her eyes were fixed forward, jaw clenched, power coiled tight beneath her skin like it was waiting for something to push it too far. Firas tracked her without meaning to, noting every detail—

how she ignored Zayd's wave, how she positioned herself apart from the others, how her hand flexed at her side.

Kam's warning still echoed in his mind like a second heartbeat.

Don't make me choose...

Watching Talah now, he wasn't sure what choice he'd make.

He descended from the overlook and crossed the sparring ground, weaving through the low murmur of conversation and the rhythmic crack of training staffs. When he reached her, Talah was rolling out her shoulders with slow, deliberate focus, her hair tied back, her sleeves pushed to her elbows, a training blade already strapped to her side.

She didn't look at him.

"Ready?" he asked.

"I'm here, aren't I?" she replied, still not meeting his eyes.

"The next trial is nothing like the maze," he said, ignoring her. "It's not a test of cleverness or cooperation."

That made her glance up, just briefly.

He continued. "No teams, no mercy. It's you against another competitor—random matchups. You fight until someone's unconscious... or dead."

Talah's eyes narrowed slightly, but she didn't interrupt.

"They want to see your raw combat ability. Strategy. Endurance. No one can yield. If you hesitate, you're disqualified. If you hold back, they'll make sure you don't get another chance."

She was listening now, muscles tense.

"It takes place in the Coliseum," Firas added. "And it won't be just a flat ring like today. The arena shifts during the fight. Firestorms. Floods. Sandstorms. The environment turns against you without warning."

"If I survived the maze, then I can survive this," Talah replied evenly.

Firas gestured toward the empty ring closest to the far wall—away from the others. "Then let's see what you remember."

She followed without a word.

He took his place across from her, keeping his stance neutral. "Start with what you'd do if I came at you with speed first—no ability. Just instinct."

Talah flexed her fingers, trying to ignore the way her pulse thudded in her throat. "So you're really going to make me fight you again?"

A ghost of a smile touched his mouth. "Unless you'd rather stand there and think about it."

Her lips pressed into a thin line. "Fine."

That was all the warning she got before Firas lunged.

She reacted fast—faster than she had during orientation a few days ago. She ducked, sidestepped, struck low. But her form was still raw. Fluid, yes—but unrefined. Muscle memory hadn't caught up with her instincts yet, and her grip was too tight, too rigid.

"Overextended," he muttered after disarming her in a single pivot. Her blade skittered across the ring.

Talah glared and snatched it back. She struck first this time, shoulder lowered, footwork cleaner. He let her land a hit on his shoulder, barely wincing.

"Better," he admitted, his breath light. "But your stance—"

"—works for me," she cut in.

Firas paused. The heat in her voice didn't match the cold calculation in her eyes. She wasn't just angry. She was testing him. Holding back just enough to see what he'd do.

"You don't trust me," he said quietly. It wasn't a question—merely an echo of what she'd declared the night before.

She raised her blade again. "Smart of me, isn't it?"

Firas lowered his stance slightly. "You're not wrong, Aasifati."

That gave her pause. But before either of them could say more, a voice rang out across the yard.

"Come on, princess. You survived the maze—surely you can handle a practice round."

Firas's attention snapped toward the commotion.

Nadir was already walking toward them, twirling a practice

spear between his fingers with the kind of swagger that had no place here. Talah turned to face him, her jaw tight.

Nadir strode into the ring without waiting for permission, his boots kicking up dust with each dramatic step. A semicircle of onlookers began forming around them—eager for a spectacle. Nadir didn't look at Firas, only at Talah.

He forced himself to stay still, jaw flexing. Talah didn't need him stepping in, didn't need saving—but every instinct screamed to put himself between them anyway.

"The girl who cheated death in the maze."

Talah said nothing, her eyes locked on him like flint on stone. He'd promised himself he wouldn't interfere. But if Nadir pushed too far, that promise would break easily.

Nadir smiled coldly. "People are whispering that you're the one who killed Rayen. That true?"

A few heads turned. The air in the arena shifted.

Talah's jaw tightened. "He left me no choice."

Nadir *tsk*ed, wagging a finger. "That's not how I heard it. Rumor says he was already half-dead when you finished him off."

"And how would anyone know that?" Talah challenged, not bothering to correct him. "We were alone."

Nadir chuckled, stepping closer. "Come now. We all know how you made it through."

Talah's eyes darted toward Firas, but only for a second.

Nadir circled her now, slowly, deliberately. "I'm surprised you even made it through at all. When you turned down my offer, I didn't think you'd make it. But I guess we all have lucky days."

Talah turned, never taking her eyes off him. "Say that again."

He grinned. "Gladly."

Firas stayed still. This time, he didn't intervene. He couldn't.

She has to do this on her own.

Talah didn't look at either of them. She stepped forward and lifted her blade in response.

The other competitors had stopped training now, eyes turning toward the ring. There was something in the air—anticipation, tension, maybe even hunger. They wanted a show.

Nadir was ready to give them one.

The spear cut the air with a whistle, the wide arc slicing toward her ribs with brutal speed. Talah barely got her blade up in time. Metal clanged against wood, and Firas flinched. Her grip faltered for half a heartbeat. Nadir noticed.

He pressed forward like a flame whipped by wind—aggressive, relentless, his form loose but lethal. The next strike came low, sweeping toward her knee. She leapt back, twisting to avoid the brunt of it, only for his follow-up jab to slam toward her shoulder. She blocked—just barely—but it forced her off-balance.

Nadir advanced, eyes glinting with confidence, aiming the shaft at her ankles. She jumped again, but it was too close. His weapon grazed her boot, nearly toppling her. She skidded backward, sand spraying around her heels as she dropped into a defensive crouch.

"You forget I'm a Libra," Nadir called out, twirling his spear again. "I can read your mind. Know what move you're going to make before you make it."

The crowd murmured.

Firas moved a few paces closer to the edge of the ring. With his arms folded tightly across his chest, every muscle tensed as he tracked her with his eyes. He could see it in her stance. Controlled. Measured. She was trying to fight clean. Trying to beat him the way she'd been taught—strike, guard, breathe, repeat. But Nadir wasn't fighting by those rules. He was out to humiliate her.

And her pride was in the way.

"Talah," Firas muttered under his breath. "Let it go."

Another strike. Harder this time.

Nadir spun the spear with a showy, almost arrogant flourish, and landed a punishing blow to her ribs. The sharp crack of impact echoed through the arena. Talah grunted, staggering sideways. Her breath hitched. Her blade dropped slightly in her grip.

Nadir stepped in, looming over her like a lion closing in

on the wounded. "Still think you're a threat?" he mocked, loud enough for the onlookers to hear.

Talah looked up—face twisted, jaw clenched. Something passed through her eyes, fast and unreadable. She straightened as if something inside her had flipped a switch. Her eyes narrowed. Her breathing slowed.

Firas saw it before he felt it. A subtle shift in pressure. Like the world was holding its breath.

Talah's stance relaxed, not with surrender, but with intent. Her blade dropped slightly, angled loosely in her fingers. Nadir lunged again, spear flashing forward—

But she was already moving.

She twisted under the strike so fast it looked like she vanished for half a heartbeat. Her shoulder ducked low, spine arching smoothly. Her foot slid across the sand like water, and in one swift pivot, she was behind him. Her blade came up in a blur. She drove the hilt into his gut, knocking the wind from him with a guttural gasp.

He wheezed, stunned—but she wasn't finished.

She spun again, her elbow cracking into his side to destabilize him, and in the same fluid motion, she caught the shaft of his spear under her arm, twisted it free, and sent it flying across the ring.

Two heartbeats.

That's all it took.

Gasps rippled through the crowd like wind catching dry leaves.

Nadir stumbled back, off-balance and breathless, blinking at her like he'd just witnessed something impossible. His hands were empty. His footing—gone as he tumbled into the sand.

Talah stood over him. Her chest barely rose and fell. She wasn't panting. Wasn't trembling. Her blade remained raised, steady in her hand, gleaming under the pale sun as if it had never been dropped.

The crowd around them buzzed, half in awe, half in suspicion. Some looked at her as if they'd never seen her before.

And from the edge of the ring, Firas watched in silence.

He knew that power. Strength. Speed. None of it belonged to a Pisces.

Could she be...?

Nadir slowly pushed himself up, blinking in confusion. "What the hell was that?"

Talah didn't answer. The spectators were murmuring now, some impressed, others clearly unsettled. But Firas couldn't stop staring at her back as she walked past him.

It hadn't just been adrenaline. He'd seen enough Ambigua break under pressure to recognize the moment it cracked open. And she had cracked open. Not completely. But enough.

He didn't know if she'd even realized what she'd done. And that terrified him more than anything else. Because if she was Ambigua, she had no control over it. And if she didn't understand it soon...someone else would.

Firas exhaled long and slow as murmurs rippled through the gathered trainees. A few stepped away from her as she exited the ring, as if they might be next. But he saw the confusion on her face as she walked past them. The way her brow furrowed. She didn't know what she'd done or how she'd done it.

And that, more than anything, almost confirmed what he feared.

She was Ambigua. She had to be.

But without control? She was a fuse waiting for the wrong flame.

He tore his gaze away from her and turned toward the edge of the arena. The sun had shifted, casting long golden shadows across the yard. The scent of dust and sweat lingered in the air. Behind the ring, two students resumed sparring half-heartedly, their movements jerky, unfocused.

Firas walked toward the archway that led out of the arena, each step heavy with thought. He didn't acknowledge the curious stares that followed him. He barely felt the heat beating down from the high stone walls. All he could feel was the pull of two thoughts circling each other like blades in his chest.

Talah is Ambigua.

If it were anyone else, she would have been destroyed a long time ago. But her father was a councilor. The very faction that sat at the heart of the Imperium. She'd grown up inside the beast's walls, fed on politics and protocol. They could be using her. She could have been planted here to find others like her.

He stepped out from beneath the marble arch and onto the observation promenade that curved above the arena. Wind caught the edge of his clothes, tugging at the folds. His fingers tightened around the railing as his eyes lifted and found Saahira.

The Libra Councilor sat high in their private box, elegant and composed in her silver-threaded robes. She didn't smile. Didn't frown. Saahira simply watched. Not the other competitors nor the field but *Talah*. Her gaze didn't waver. And next to her, leaning forward with his chin resting lightly on one gloved hand, was the Scorpio Councilor. Musa's expression was guarded, refusing to reveal his thoughts.

It wasn't surprising to find Saahira watching the competitors, not when her own nephew was among them. But something told Firas it wasn't Nadir she'd come to watch.

Firas felt cold settle at the base of his spine. He forced himself to step back into the shadows cast by the colonnade, obscuring his face just enough. He couldn't afford to be seen watching them. Not like this.

A breath slipped through his teeth, slow and quiet.

He needed to be sure. Of her.

Of everything.

FIRAS
XXX

While the city slept that night, Firas sat across from the two people the Imperium most wanted dead.

The cellar was damp and close, the stone walls sweating with condensation, the air heavy with oil smoke from the lanterns set along the table. The scent of dust, sweat, and old parchment clung to the space, pressing in from every side. But it wasn't the air that made Firas's chest tighten. It was them.

The Imperium might have ruled the city above, but here in the underground gloom, it was Samira and Rafiq who reigned. Their presence filled every shadow, as suffocating as iron chains and as volatile as fire.

Samira sat with her spine straight, her tarha catching the lantern light, her sharp hazel eyes sweeping the room like storm winds. She didn't need to raise her voice or even shift in her chair—authority clung to her like a second skin. Each silence she let stretch was sharper than a blade, and it cut deeper, too.

Beside her loomed Rafiq, all coiled muscle and restless energy, his broad frame forcing the low rafters to feel smaller, more fragile. He stood instead of sitting, blades strapped across his back, the smell of dust and iron clinging to him like he'd just stepped out of a battlefield. His amber gaze burned hot, flaring over each rebel in turn, daring them to falter under its weight.

The true leaders of the Ambigua rebellion were fearsome in their own right—two figures shaped by different tempers, one cold steel, the other smoldering fire. And together, they were enough to make even Firas's breath catch, his heartbeat a steady drum against his ribs.

Samira didn't need to raise her voice or even lift her gaze to command the room. Her eyes cut over them once as she sat at the lone chair at the head of the table, her spine straight, her hands folding neatly, but the scar beneath her cheekbone caught the lantern light and reminded everyone that her control had been forged in fire.

Rafiq didn't sit. He never did, not if he could help it. He stood at her side, broad shoulders crowding the low ceiling, his twin blades glinting across his back. He rolled one shoulder, impatient, his amber eyes catching on each of them in turn. Firas felt the weight of that stare settle, hot and heavy, before it passed on.

"For the lost, for the hunted," Rafiq's deep baritone echoed around the chamber.

"For those who refuse to fall," Firas answered along with the others.

"I hope you have something to report," Samira said at last, her voice calm, precise, cutting through the cellar like a knife through butter. "The Imperium grows bolder, and every day these Trials continue, more blood is spilled for their spectacle. We cannot afford any losses."

Firas kept his expression neutral, though the words coiled sharp inside him. His thoughts slid unbidden to Talah. The councilor's daughter. The girl who might be Ambigua.

The girl he hadn't told Samira about.

Kam, Raven, and Rami stood behind him, their presence just as heavy as the leaders before him. Kam was like a wall at his back, tall and unyielding, her wiry frame radiating the kind of strength that didn't need weapons to be felt. Raven lingered like a shadow, silent and unreadable, her white hair catching the lamplight in a way that made her look more specter than woman. And Rami—slighter, quieter—still carried an intensity that pressed on Firas's shoulders, the sharpness of his watchful eyes betraying a mind that rarely rested. Together, they formed a wall of expectation, their silence heavy enough to crush.

Samira's gaze swept the table again, steady and unyielding. "Each of you has seen what the Imperium is willing to sacrifice. Tell me what you've learned."

Rami cleared his throat, surprising all of them. "We found records," he said hesitantly.

Samira nodded for him to continue, her long nails tapping the wooden table between them.

"It's... hard to decipher. But we think these records discuss our origins. How we came to be, what we are exactly," Rami shifted behind Firas slightly. "I need more time to go through them, though."

Samira's lips pursed. "We don't have much time," she reminded him.

"We do have some other news," Kam said quietly. "We were able to rescue one girl from the maze."

"Just one?" Rafiq asked, one eyebrow arching.

Firas could feel Kam tense behind him. "There was another one. But he refused to come with us."

"What do you mean?" Samira asked. There was no malice in her words, only curiosity.

"He was a Signborn," Raven cut in. "He didn't like what we had to say."

"That's putting it mildly," Kam muttered.

Samira and Rafiq exchanged quick, dark looks. "Unsurprising," she said at last. "They've been taught to fear us since they were children. This propaganda is one of the Imperium's strengths... as we all know." She paused, letting her words settle. And then Samira's storm-colored eyes landed on him, sharp and unwavering. She tilted her head the slightest fraction, silence deepening around them until it seemed to demand his voice. "And you? Do you not have anything to report?"

Firas kept his jaw tight, forcing his breath even. "Nothing the others haven't already said."

The lie sat heavy on his tongue, but he didn't flinch.

Samira's gaze lingered a moment longer, sharp enough to cut. Her silence pressed against him like a weight, as though she could see the truth buried under his skin. But finally, she leaned back, the faint scrape of her iron ring against the table breaking the tension.

"Very well."

Rafiq shifted where he stood, rolling his shoulders, the fire in his eyes sparking hotter. "Then you know your orders. We need more than fragments. Keep digging through those scrolls, Rami—pull every truth from them the Imperium has tried to bury. History is our weapon, and the Imperium has sharpened theirs for centuries."

Samira nodded once. "And rescue more of our people. As many as you can before the Trials consume them. Every Ambigua saved is one less life for the Council to burn for their spectacle." Her voice grew quieter, but the weight of it filling the cellar. "We believe the Imperium has something special planned for the last trial. Something meant to break more than just the competitors."

"We haven't figured out what that is just yet… but we will," Rafiq promised gruffly. Firas could tell that bothered him—the not knowing. Not knowing the Imperium's next move meant he couldn't plan his own.

"We heard there was an attack in the Fire Province?" Kam dared to speak up.

Rafiq and Samira exchanged dark looks. "It wasn't us, if that's what you're wondering about," Rafiq replied roughly.

"The Imperium is upping the stakes. Fanning the flames, so to speak," Samira added. "Flames you shouldn't be worrying about right now." Her eyes swept over them one final time, stormy and unyielding. "You have your orders. Do not fail us."

No one dared to answer.

Samira rose without another word, the faint scrape of her chair against stone loud in the silence. Rafiq was already in motion, rolling his shoulders as though the cellar was too small to contain him. Together they moved to the narrow stairwell, their steps unhurried, certain, the air seeming to follow in their wake.

Then the door shut, and the cellar was left hollow, their presence lingering like smoke in the lungs, sharp and impossible to shake.

For a long moment, none of them moved. Firas sat with his palms flat against his knees, listening to the distant hush of night pressing down on the city above. Raven leaned against the wall, arms folded, eyes shadowed. Kam's braids caught the lamplight as she shifted, restless, while Rami busied himself gathering the scattered scrolls into a neat stack.

Only after the weight of silence became unbearable did Firas finally stand. They would wait a few minutes, give their leaders a head start, and then disappear into the alleys before dawn betrayed them.

When he deemed it safe enough, Firas motioned for them to follow. He moved through the doorway and into the shadows, grateful for the cool night air on his face.

"Why didn't you say anything?" Kam's voice was low, sharp, dragging him up short. She stepped out into the darkness beside him, the gold in her braids glinting in the lamplight.

Firas motioned for Raven and Rami to go ahead. Rami looked as if he were about to protest when Raven grabbed his arm and they disappeared from sight, teleporting back to their hideout in Aphelion.

When he was sure they'd gone, he turned to Kam. "About what?" he asked.

Her arms crossed, the gold beads in her braids clicking together softly. "Don't play dumb with me. Why didn't you warn them about Talah?"

He clenched his jaw, keeping his voice flat. "Because I'm not sure about her just yet."

Kam's lip curled, somewhere between a snarl and a bitter laugh. "You don't need to be sure. You just need to warn them. If she's Ambigua—"

"And if she's not?" His voice came out harder than he had intended, cutting across hers. He dragged a hand through his hair, forcing himself to look her in the eye. "She's the daughter of a councilor, Kam. If I speak without proof, if I bring her into this and we're wrong, Samira will make her move—and the fallout will burn every one of us. You know it."

Kam stared at him, breathing fast, her shoulders taut with frustration.

Firas dropped his voice, low and strained. "I'll keep a closer eye on her in the next trial. I'll know for certain then."

For a moment she said nothing, her storm-dark gaze raking over him as if she could pry open his chest and drag the truth out herself. Finally, she shook her head, sharp and curt.

"You'd better," she muttered, stepping back into the shadows. "Because if you're wrong—or if you're protecting her—it won't just be you who pays for it."

TALAH
XXXI

The arena was alive once again.

Stone tiers stretched high into the open sky, packed with spectators draped in jewel-toned silks and shaded overhangs. The banners of the Zodiac fluttered above them, each Sign rendered in their colors. Councilors sat in their private balconies above the crowd—watching, whispering, judging.

Talah stood at the edge of the sand-floored ring, heat radiating off the ground beneath her boots. The air was thick with incense and sun and tension, all of it mixing into something that scraped the back of her throat. She swallowed, hands clenched at her sides.

Everything felt louder here. Brighter. Sharper. Like the moment before a blade strikes flesh.

One ring. Two competitors. One survivor.

The scent of iron and incense hung thick in the air, heavy and sweet and wrong. Above her, the stands buzzed with anticipation—nobles in silk robes and glittering pins craning for a better view, their laughter muffled beneath the hum of enchantments and the rustle of fans. The rising sun flashed against a thousand reflective surfaces: gems, crests, ceremonial blades.

She forced her breathing slow. *You're fine. You're in control.* But the lie trembled in her head. She wasn't in control—not of this, not of the storm coiled beneath her ribs since the Trials. Every crowd, every spotlight, seemed to wake it like a sleeping animal.

A shadow passed in front of her. Talah turned, half expecting to find her mentor. Instead, Mazin stood a few feet away, already armored in layered leather and cloth. His shoulders were taut, his expression hesitant. For a moment, neither of them spoke.

"Hey," he said at last, voice careful.

She didn't answer immediately. Her throat felt tight, her palms still prickling with the aftershocks of that flicker of power. She hadn't spoken to him since the night she left him in the corridor—raw, angry, and shaking. She didn't know what she'd expected if they ever had this conversation again. Maybe distance. Indifference.

Not... this. Not the ache of familiarity or the reminder that despite everything, he still looked at her like she hadn't changed into something dangerous.

"You don't have to talk," Mazin added quickly. "I just wanted to wish you luck out there."

"What?" she asked, throat suddenly dry.

He gave a faint, bitter smile. "Even if we're fighting, I'm still on your side, Tal. We've been friends too long for anything less than that."

The silence between them stretched, tense and uneven, filled with all the things they hadn't said since their fight.

"Good luck to you, too," she said finally.

Before he could answer, heavy footsteps echoed through the competitor's tunnel behind them. The group of remaining competitors turned as Khalias emerged from the shadowed corridor. He was dressed in his deep violet robes, the silver crest of Aphelion glinting at his chest. His expression, as always, was stoic.

He looked at them not like a man addressing students, but like soldiers walking to the edge of a battlefield. The wind stirred the hem of his robes. The arena quieted above them as the spectators waited with bated breath.

"This trial is not about heart. It is not about hope. It is about whether you can survive when the rules shift and the ground burns beneath you," Khalias said firmly. He stepped forward, gaze sweeping over each of them. "Each of you will face one opponent. You do not know who. You do not know when. You will fight until one of you cannot continue. If you hesitate, if you falter, if you reach for mercy—understand that the arena will not offer it."

A few students flinched. Talah refused.

"You may use your Sign abilities and any approved weapon," Khalias continued. "But remember—this arena shifts. The field will test your limits, not your strengths." He paused, his eyes briefly settling on Talah. Then the others. "And the Imperium is watching."

His words sank into her bones like ice.

Khalias turned toward the gate, raising his hand toward the arch. "When your name is called, you enter. Alone." Then he vanished through the gate as it creaked open with a deep, ancient groan.

The crowd above thundered to life.

A horn blared, its sound echoing through the coliseum like a summoning spell from a forgotten age. Talah's pulse pounded as the first name rang out.

"Mazin al-Sahri of Pisces."

Her breath hitched.

Mazin turned back to her, a half-smile breaking through the tension. "I'll be fine," he said. "I can't let you beat me, now can I?" He walked through the gate, golden light cutting across his shoulders as the arena swallowed him whole.

She stepped out into the shadow of the coliseum's inner wall, joining the cluster of competitors gathered along the sidelines— far enough to stay out of the way, but close enough to feel the heat radiating off the stone.

"Talah." Zayd's voice broke through the din. "You alright?"

She turned, finding Zayd and Adine weaving their way through the crowd, both wearing matching expressions of concern and curiosity.

Adine gave her a sidelong glance. "We saw Mazin talking to you. You two make up or...?"

Zayd grinned. "Was that a reunion or the dramatic third act of a lovers' quarrel?"

Talah shot him a glare sharp enough to slice stone. "Zayd."

He threw up his hands. "Too soon. Got it."

Adine nudged him, then looked back at Talah. "What's going on?"

Talah's gaze stayed locked on the arena below. The field had already begun to shift. Stone peeled back like rippling skin, revealing a new battlefield—charred rock, blackened soil, ash still falling in the far corners like dying snow. No water. No cover. Just heat and open space.

No advantages.

"Mazin al-Sahri of Pisces," the herald called. "Versus Galen Rafeq of Aries."

Talah knew Galen by reputation more than interaction, though she'd watched him train with the rest of them in the arena every single day. He was a Signborn Aries, deadly in sparring, coldly tactical beneath a deceptively easy grin. He was the kind of opponent who didn't just fight to win.

The arena shimmered, and the illusion shifted. The stone floor cracked, reshaping itself into a wide, sun-scorched crater. Jagged rock spines jutted upward along the perimeter, and the sand glittered beneath the noonday sun, dry and treacherous. Heat waves blurred the far end of the field.

Mazin stepped out of the gate's shadow slowly. Across the ring, Galen strode out with the confidence of someone who expected to win. He rolled his shoulders, twirled his zulfiqar once in one hand, and smirked like this was already done. A hush fell over the arena as a horn blared low and deep.

Galen covered the distance between them in sharp, efficient steps. His zulfiqar came down in a punishing arc, fast and heavy. Mazin ducked narrowly avoiding the blow and countered with a slash toward Galen's ribs.

Sparks flew.

Galen turned with the blow, deflecting the dagger and responding with a vicious hook of his elbow into Mazin's ribs. The sound of the impact cracked across the arena, audible even above the cheers.

Talah flinched. The noise echoed somewhere deep inside her chest—a hollow ache that had nothing to do with pain.

Mazin stumbled back, boots skidding across hot sand. He didn't fall—but it was close.

"He's fast," Zayd muttered.

"Galen's testing him," Adine added, arms crossed tightly. "Figuring out his rhythm."

Talah said nothing. Her fists were clenched so tightly her nails bit crescents into her palms. Mazin's stance, the way he rolled his shoulder and shifted his weight—it was too familiar. Iras had taught her the same thing. The same movement, the same precision. And now, watching Mazin use it here—against someone who could kill him—felt like watching the ghosts of both of them fight at once.

Mazin pivoted, adjusting. He circled wide, using the rock formations to his advantage. When Galen advanced again, Mazin went low—too low to track above the stones—and came up behind him in a sudden flash of movement. His dagger caught Galen across the thigh, a shallow but strategic slice.

The Aries snarled, spinning to retaliate.

Mazin was gone again.

"Why in the stars did he not go for the tendon?" Adine muttered.

Talah's throat felt tight. "Because he's not trying to defeat him," she murmured, almost to herself. "Not yet."

Before Adine could respond, the arena shifted.

A windstorm roared to life, blasting across the field and filling the air with searing grit. Sand flew in whirls, blinding and hot. Visibility dropped to near zero. Talah struggled to make out the two fighters, narrowing her eyes against the raging sand. In the chaos, Galen's fire lit the dust like an amber flare, illuminating the battlefield in flashes.

Talah squinted into the haze. Her heart thudded against her ribs. She caught brief glimpses—steel against flame, a figure ducking low, another recoiling from a hit. She could barely make out a thing, her anxiety rising as she waited with the others.

She felt a shift in the air as Air users along the high walls of the arena let the wind die down. The dust settled, scattering across the arena floor. Talah leaned forward, fingers gripping the stone wall before her.

Galen stood with one arm hanging useless at his side, a deep cut running from shoulder to elbow, blood dripping onto the cracked earth. Mazin stood behind him, one dagger pressed lightly to Galen's throat.

Galen let his zulfiwar fall.

The crowd erupted.

Talah let out a sharp breath, her body sagging slightly, but her eyes never left Mazin. He didn't smile, didn't raise his arms in triumph. Instead, he scanned the crowd—slowly, warily.

And then, he found her. Their eyes locked across the expanse of the arena. The sand had barely cooled from Mazin's final blow when the next horn blared.

"Adine Amari of Taurus… Aarif El-Najjar of Leo."

"Well, that's me," Adine said, rolling out her shoulders.

She stepped out into the arena, passing Mazin as he made his way back. He gave her a short nod, muttering something to her as they passed. Adine barely glanced at him, keeping her eyes on her opponent as she unsheathed her kilij, its curved blade glinting in the sunlight.

Aarif was already in the center, twirling his golden-tipped glaive like it was an extension of his ego. He wore his arrogance like a crown. The crowd went wild as she stepped closer.

Aarif struck first—always first. Always with flair. His weapon spun in a blinding arc of light and motion, sweeping toward Adine's ribs. She blocked it just in time, barely absorbing the force of the blow as it knocked her two steps back.

But she didn't fall.

She reset her stance, feet digging into the cracked earth, and slammed her palm to the ground. Stone answered. A jagged ridge of rock erupted upward toward Aarif's legs, forcing him to leap back to avoid the sudden spike. Dust billowed around her as Adine rose, sweat streaking her brow, her arms braced as if she could will the entire arena to stop spinning.

Aarif laughed, teeth bared like a predator. "Come on, little girl," he taunted. "Try harder. Or do Taurus signs only know how to distract and run?"

He struck again.

And again.

His glaive flashed through the air, slicing and sweeping, a storm of speed and precision. Every strike came with a flourish, a performance—a Leo through and through. But Adine didn't match his flair. She didn't dance. She dug in.

Each blow drove her back—but not down.

Every time she staggered, she caught her footing. Every time he came close to breaking her guard, she met him with brute resistance. She stopped trying to land clean hits and started forcing him into mistakes, slamming shards of earth into his footing, luring him toward uneven ground she'd raised seconds earlier.

But it still wasn't enough.

Aarif spun low and drove a boot straight into her chest. The sound of impact cracked like thunder. Adine flew backward, slamming into the sand hard enough to leave a crater. Her head bounced against the ground. She didn't move.

Talah leaned over the railing, heart hammering. The arena blurred.

"Get up," she whispered, barely breathing. "Adine, get up."

Below, Aarif stalked toward her, weapon spinning lazily in one hand. "You're finished," he called. "They won't remember your name after this."

He raised his glaive—gleaming, curved, fatal.

Adine's eyes snapped open. She let out a raw, wordless cry and shoved both palms into the sand. A burst of stone exploded beneath Aarif's feet, unbalancing him just enough. She was already moving, launching forward in a staggering rush, grabbing the edge of his armored leg and pulling.

He collapsed onto one knee with a curse. She didn't stop. Her fist, stone-coated and shaking, cracked across his jaw. He reeled. But he wasn't out.

Aarif caught her arm mid-swing, twisted, and drove a knee into her side. She grunted in pain, staggering, and they fell into a brutal grapple—limbs tangled, bloodied and raw, their weapons lost somewhere in the dust. Aarif's hand dropped to his belt.

Talah's breath hitched.

There was a flash of metal. Adine's eyes widened, unable to stop his next move. So she did the only thing she could.

She drove her elbow into his throat before seizing the blade from his hand and turning it upward between them. His own dagger punched beneath his ribs with a sickening, final sound.

He gasped once. The arena fell deathly still as Aarif crumpled, blood spilling from his mouth when he collapsed into the sand. Adine stood over him, her body heaving. Her hand still clutched the blade. She didn't move.

The horn blared twice.

The crowd's reaction broke like a wave—some cheering, others recoiling. Shock, awe, horror. It didn't matter. Talah's eyes stung with the heat. It was either her… or him. And the Trials didn't make space for mercy.

Adine stepped out of the arena in silence. She didn't speak as she passed the competitors, didn't meet anyone's gaze—not even Talah's. She simply walked through the arches, disappearing into the shadowed corridors.

Talah felt cold settle into her chest. It coiled there, heavy and quiet. She knew the look on her friend's face. She knew how it felt.

They had all known killing would be part of the Trials. Most of them had to do it in the maze. But knowing and doing were not the same, and Talah doubted many could stomach taking lives again and again.

Talah was pulled from her thoughts when she felt someone settle beside her. She didn't have to see who it was. She could feel Iras's warmth against her arm, both reassuring and electric at the same time.

"I can help," he said quietly.

"You already did," she replied. "Back in the maze. Without asking."

He didn't flinch. "You're still angry."

"I don't have the luxury of not being angry," she snapped, turning to face him. "Why are you even here, Iras? You made it clear you don't approve of all this."

His gaze didn't waver. "Because I was you. Once. I don't want you to go through this alone... like I had to."

She said nothing.

"I walked into that ring thinking strength would save me," he continued. "That if I pushed hard enough, survived long enough, it would mean something."

"And it didn't?" she asked softly.

"It did," Iras replied, turning to face her. "But not in the way I thought. Not when I realized who was watching. Who got to decide what survival was worth."

Talah shook her head. "It's still worth it. For the power. For the place it gets you. For the name."

Iras took a step closer. "Is it though? Really?"

Her breath caught. Because for the first time since this all began... she didn't know.

Before she could answer, the horn blared again.

"Talah bint Khalid of Pisces. Nadir Khatri of Libra."

The heat around her thickened. Not only was she going up against a competitor who had trained his entire life for these moments... she was being forced to face the Libra Councilor's own nephew. If she won, she could face the wrath of one of the most powerful families in the nation. If she lost, her father, and everyone who agreed with him, would be proven right. And her chance of proving herself would vanish. All of this would be for nothing.

She didn't look at Iras again as she turned toward the gate, wiping the sweat from her palms along her sarwal. But as the door creaked open, and the crowd began to stir, one thought rang louder than the roar of the stands.

It has to be worth it.

TALAH

The heat hit her first—dry and biting, like a breath from an ancient furnace. Then came the noise. A wall of sound slammed into her; the shouting, cheering, murmurs, like drums beating in time to her pounding heart. She stepped out onto the sand.

The arena was vast under the blinding midday sun, every grain of golden grit burning beneath her boots. The stone beneath was cracked and bloodstained, worn from decades of combat and death. Her shadow stretched long before her, cast sharply across the arena floor. Above her, the councilors watched like gods on their marble thrones. Talah didn't look up at them. She couldn't. She didn't want to know whether or not her father had deigned to watch her survive... or die.

The scent of sweat, ash, and blood was thick in the air. It clung to her throat, metallic and bitter. Her heart thundered in her ears as Nadir stepped into the arena. Tall, lean, dressed in close-fitting armor the color of burnished steel. No excess, no flourishes. Even his steps were silent, as if the sand parted just to let him pass. The curved blade on his back gleamed only when it caught the sun at the perfect angle. His expression didn't change when he saw her.

Talah felt it—the weight of him. Cold and distant. It was as if she were staring into a mirror made of frost and shadows. He was a Signborn, like her. A Libra.

Saahira Khatri's nephew.

Talah stepped forward, heart hammering so hard it shook her ribs as the horn blared across the sand. The world narrowed. The arena's roar dimmed to a dull throb in her ears. The heat pressed against her skin like a second weight, baking into her armor, soaking through her boots. Sweat trickled down her spine, caught in the crook of her collarbone. Her scimitar felt too loose in her hand.

Across from her, Nadir didn't move. He didn't draw the blades hanging at his hips. He watched her like a viper coiled beneath cool stone—*waiting*. Just waiting for her to make the first mistake.

Her pulse raced in her throat.

I fought him before and won, she reminded herself. *This is just like what we did before.*

Except it very much was not.

Nadir moved instantly, flicking his wrist too fast to track. A throwing knife sliced through the air, forcing her to make her move. Talah jolted to the side, nearly tripping over her own feet. Her pulse spiked, heart thudding so loud that it echoed in her ears as she rolled behind a dune of sand, swept together from the last fight. A whisper curled beneath her focus, low and quiet.

I won't make it out of this.

"Don't forget, princess. I can read your mind," Nadir called out, tapping one finger to his skull. "Every idea, every thought. You *won't* make it out of this."

Cold fear coiled through her chest. Illusions wouldn't be enough.

Not for him.

Talah swallowed hard, forcing her mind to go still, watching him with narrowed eyes. She surged from behind the low mound of scorched sand, sliding on one knee. The knife flicked from his hand with a sharp hiss through the air. Talah twisted sideways, feeling the sting of air slice across her cheek as Nadir bent the wind around the blade, making it curve unnaturally close to her throat. She dropped low, rolling over rough stone, and the crowd roared.

She thrust her palm out. A wave of water surged from the mist, snapping into a whip that lashed toward his legs. But Nadir was quicker—air gathered beneath his feet in a sudden burst, lifting him just high enough that the whip cracked harmlessly against stone. He landed lightly, another knife already in hand.

Nadir smiled.

He wasn't just fast—he was reading her, pulling her movements from her mind before she even acted. The knives weren't his true weapon. His mind was.

She needed to throw him off.

The ground beneath their feet rumbled, towering stone jutting from the ground. Talah ducked and rolled behind one as it shot up, taking cover. Illusions shimmered at her fingertips. A second Talah broke free of her body, darting to the side, sprinting across the rocks. Nadir's eyes flicked, just for a heartbeat, and he threw. A blade buried itself in her double's chest. The illusion dissolved into spray.

Real Talah surged forward, blinding him with water before her scimitar slashed through the air. He twisted just enough to avoid the full arc of the blow—but she felt it connect. His armor took most of the hit, but blood bloomed from beneath the seams. She moved again, faster this time, casting a second illusion—this one more exact, more grounded. It lunged low, blade aimed at his stomach. Nadir drew his curved knife in a single, fluid motion—cutting across the illusion's path—and pivoted toward her actual position without hesitation.

But she wasn't there.

Talah vaulted over the rocks at his flank, water coiling around her legs to propel her higher. She crashed down on him, shoulder first, driving him to the ground. His knives skittered across stone. The breath went out of him in a harsh grunt.

The air snapped. A gust slammed into her, staggering her

sideways so hard her shoulder cracked against stone. Pain jolted through her, white-hot. A swift downward kick caught her shin as she tried to move back. Pain exploded through her leg. Her balance slipped. She fell.

"Why are you even still trying?" Nadir hissed, one foot coming down against her stomach, holding her in place. "Go home to your baba, princess. Give in."

Sand scraped her skin. Talah gritted her teeth, forcing water up from the cracked earth where underground channels leaked into the arena. It burst upward, a sudden spray that blinded him for half a breath.

She didn't have too much time, however. Knives flew in rapid succession, flashing silver as they tore through phantoms. Air exploded outward. It ripped her off him like a rag doll, hurling her across the arena. She hit the ground hard, the impact punching the air from her lungs. Dust filled her mouth, bitter and choking.

Her shoulder slammed into the ground. Her blade went spinning. She rolled just in time as his daggers came down where her neck had been a heartbeat before. A crack sounded beside her. Stone split under the weight of the strike. She scrambled to her feet. Nadir was already on her.

Mechanical. Relentless.

He struck again, a backhand slash that cut low. Every movement was laced with lethal intent. There was no emotion on his face. No pride. No anger. Just purpose.

Talah reeled as another blow ripped across her thigh. She gasped, stumbling, blood soaking her sarwal. Her blade dragged through the sand as she fought to raise it. Her own thoughts were slipping. Too fast. Too sharp. Talah couldn't breathe. Her chest burned. Her limbs trembled. Her body screamed with every parry and deflection.

This was nothing like their sparring during training.

He'd been holding back.

She barely deflected a strike to her hip, his blade grazing her side, tearing fabric. Blood welled and trailed down her thigh as she hissed through her teeth. He struck again, and she ducked. He aimed for her shoulder, and she blocked, but the force jolted her entire arm numb. Her heel struck the edge of the arena wall.

Trapped.

Talah, think.

Her head throbbed with the force of her thoughts, like invisible nails digging into her mind. She bit down on the scream, forcing herself upright. Her vision blurred, but the water still answered. It swirled around her, condensing at her sides, forcing Nadir back.

His knives lifted from the ground, caught in his wind, spinning like a storm of steel between them. Water and air collided, droplets flung skyward, blades whistling past her face. The crowd was on its feet, the arena itself trembling with the force of their clash. He raced forward, slashing toward her ribs. She twisted, the blade grazing her side. Pain bloomed sharp and wet.

Talah gasped. "No— "

You're just going to kill again.

Her hands trembled. Her blade drooped.

This is it.

He's going to kill me.

Let him.

"No!"

She forced herself to move, shoving off the wall and throwing a trio of illusions into the space around him. They darted in different directions, circling him like phantoms as Talah mixed in with them. He paused. Just for a second.

It was all she needed.

Talah rolled left, came up low, and slammed her fist into the back of his knee. He buckled. She lunged forward, going for his throat. But his hand snapped up and caught her wrist mid-swing. They locked, bodies straining. Arms shaking. Blades trembling. Sand clung to her bloodied arms. Sweat poured down her back. They pressed against each other, faces inches apart, breath hot and shallow. Talah's hand shook. Her blade hovered at the hollow of his throat.

Faintly, distantly, she noticed the look in his eyes.

He was going to kill her. Not out of hatred. Out of necessity.

A lance of pressure slammed into her mind. Rayen. His scream. His blood. Mazin. Dying. Her father. Turning away. A flood. A fracture.

You're not meant for this. You were never enough.

Their foreheads nearly touched. Sweat rolled between them. Her heart pounded against her sternum like it wanted out. Their breathing, ragged, hot, tangled. And in her chest, something cracked. Halima's scream echoed in her head. The sound of Rayen's body hitting the ground. The blood in the water. The moment she crossed a line she couldn't uncross.

I don't want to do this again.

She shook—not from fear—but from the weight of knowing what came next.

Not again.

Please not again.

She couldn't stop because he wouldn't stop. Because no one was coming to save her.

Survive.

Her knee came up with a desperate, furious snap into his gut. Nadir gasped and reeled. She reversed the grip on her blade as she drove it into his side, into the place no armor could protect.

Nadir went rigid as his blade fell from his grip. The breath left his body in one slow exhale, his eyes going wide. Not in fear, but with acceptance. Talah nearly fell forward as his body went limp, the full weight of him nearly taking her down.

The crowd froze, as did she. Her hand still clutched the hilt of her weapon, blood trailing down her fingers. She couldn't feel her legs. She couldn't hear her breath, only the pounding in her ears. Only the truth settled in her bones.

She killed Nadir Khatri.

She'd killed the Libra Councilor's nephew.

The horn blared two sharp blasts. The crowd erupted into chaos, cheering and shouting. But none of it touched her.

Talah stood over his body, blade trembling in her grip, blood soaking the hem of her robes. Her stomach turned. Bile rose in her throat. She didn't feel strong. She didn't feel victorious. She felt hollow.

The blade slipped from her fingers. It hit the sand with a dull thud, barely audible over the chaos surrounding her. Talah's vision blurred at the edges. Her knees buckled and for a heartbeat, she thought the world tilted. The sun was too bright. The cheers too loud.

His eyes were too blank.

Then suddenly everything hit her at once—sound, heat, light, the sting of sweat in open wounds. She staggered back a step, then another. Then the screams started all over again.

Not from the crowd, but from her memory. Halima, her body falling through the sky. Rayen, his body ripped at the center. The taste of salt and guilt. And now she had one more memory to add to the others: Nadir's empty eyes.

Her breath hitched. Her chest cinched as if a fist had closed around her lungs. She couldn't get enough air. She couldn't get any air.

No. No, not now—

The edges of the arena spun. Stone and sky twisted in sickening spirals. Her legs gave way, and she collapsed onto her knees in the sand. Too loud. Too bright. Too much. Her heart slammed against her ribs like it wanted to break free. Her throat closed. Her arms trembled uncontrollably.

She couldn't stop shaking.

I killed him.

"Talah."

Talah hadn't heard Iras approach until he was right beside her, kneeling, one hand hovering over her shoulder, not yet touching. His eyes searched her face, his brows drawn—not angry. Concerned.

"Look at me, Aasifati," he said. "You're safe."

Her fingers curled into the sand.

Get up. Get up.

She couldn't. Her lungs refused. Her vision tunneled.

"I can't—I can't—" Her voice cracked, barely audible over the screaming in her mind.

"You're safe, Talah," Iras said, more gently this time. "You're here. With me. You won. You're not alone."

He moved carefully, shielding her from the view of the crowd, from the others watching—from Mazin, who had started toward her from across the waiting platform.

"I'm going to get you out of here," he said quietly. "Can I touch you?"

Talah nodded, barely breathing. He slipped an arm around her shoulders, anchoring her as he helped her to her feet. He supported most of her weight as she limped against him, unsteady, her muscles refusing to cooperate. The heat of him felt steady. Grounding.

Real.

They moved as quickly as Talah could—out of the arena's reach and into the shadowed corridor beneath the stands. Each step was jagged, a struggle. Her breath came in ragged gasps, shallow and panicked. She didn't see where they were going. She didn't care. Until suddenly the noise faded away.

Iras pushed open the door to an unused room. It was a quiet space lined with empty racks and cracked stone benches. She barely heard the door shutting behind them. Talah sank down against the wall before her legs gave out again. Her hands clenched in her lap, nails digging into her palms. Her chest was tight, face burning.

She still couldn't breathe.

"I shouldn't be here," she whispered. "I shouldn't have—"

"You did what you had to," Iras said, crouching in front of her. "He would have killed you."

"That doesn't make it better."

"No," he agreed, meeting her eyes. "But it's the truth."

Her responding laugh was full of bitterness. She scoffed, looking away. "I thought I was prepared to kill. I told myself I was before coming here. But saying you can do it is different than actually doing it."

"Unfortunately, it's not something one gets used to," Iras muttered.

"And you would know that how?" she asked warily.

"I was you once," Iras reminded her, voice lower now, more honest than she'd ever heard it. "I thought I could kill, too. We all thought that. But, like you said, thinking it and actually being able to do it are different. If you don't take care of yourself here," he tapped his temple lightly, "it will consume you."

"And if it does?" she rasped.

His gaze darkened. "It won't. You're stronger than you think. Isn't that why you came here? To prove that to yourself? To your family?"

Her breathing slowed then, still ragged but more manageable. Suddenly, she became all too aware of his presence, still and steady. She hadn't realized she'd been crying until his thumb brushed against her cheek, stealing away what pain he could. His fingers left behind a trail of fire against her cheek, blazing straight through her. She looked up at him, mouth opening to say something—anything.

The door creaked open. Iras jerked away from Talah like he'd been caught mid-crime, the brief softness in his expression vanishing in an instant. He moved swiftly and deliberately, planting himself between her and the figure that stepped across the threshold with quiet authority.

"Councilor Khatri," he said, voice like drawn steel.

Saahira stood in the doorway, draped in deep violet and silver—colors that shimmered like law and menace. Her hands were folded neatly in front of her, her every movement precise, deliberate, as if even her stillness was part of some long-calculated plan.

Talah felt frozen, fear slicing through her.

Saahira didn't acknowledge Iras beyond a glance. Her gaze settled on Talah.

"Impressive," she said, her voice like a blade wrapped in silk. "My nephew was a formidable opponent. And you defeated him."

Talah struggled to rise, her legs threatening to give out. She couldn't tell if Saahira was furious at her for killing her own heir or not. Iras caught her gently, his arm a solid brace around her back. Her body leaned into him without meaning to, breath ragged, hands still shaking.

Saahira watched the gesture, but her expression didn't change. "I assume you think I'm angry with you. That I'll exact some sort of revenge." The councilor sneered then. "Do not worry. If you could defeat Nadir, then he was too weak to carry on our name. The Trials demand sacrifice to obtain power. To keep it. He disgraced his family today...and you," her head tilted slightly, "you have honored yours."

"He—he was your nephew," Talah forced out. "How could you say that?"

Saahira's eyes narrowed. "Power is everything, dear. Isn't that why you're here? Why you killed him?"

Talah's pulse pounded in her ears. Iras said nothing, but Talah could feel the tension radiating off him, coiled and ready. His hand didn't move toward a weapon, but it was close. Ready.

Would he dare attack a councilor? At Aphelion of all places?

Saahira stepped farther into the room, forcing Talah's attention back onto her. Not threatening. Just present. Like a shadow lengthening.

"I imagine you're beginning to see the Trials for what they truly are," she said. "The way they peel back the lies we tell ourselves—about strength, about sacrifice. About what we're willing to destroy in order to remain strong."

Talah said nothing, but her silence was enough of an answer.

Saahira smiled slowly. "There's clarity in blood, you'll find. The kind of clarity your father never had the stomach for." Her voice dropped to something softer—almost intimate. "But you? Clearly, we have all misjudged you."

She let the words hang in the silence. Her smile thinned. "I do hope you survive the next round. But if you don't..." She glanced toward Iras, just briefly. "Well, we will see."

Talah and Iras watched as she swept from the room, the scent of jasmine trailing behind her.

XXXIII FIRAS

The corridor was deathly silent.
　No breeze reached this deep into the bones of the academy. No moonlight. Just the flicker of a single lantern, burning low against the wall, its flame anemic and blue. It smelled of dust and oil. Down here, behind the main training arena and beneath the dormitories, no one came unless they meant to disappear.

　Firas paced once then leaned against the wall, head tipped back, eyes closed. The silence was heavy. Every breath scraped like flint across his ribs. Every heartbeat ticked like a countdown. It had only been two days since the tournament, but it felt like an eternity. They'd been given a day of rest before the next trial, though rest was the last thing he'd found.

　His mind kept circling back to the same image—Talah on the ground, shaking, her eyes gone glassy and distant while the arena around her burned. He'd seen panic before. He'd lived it. But this—this had been something else. The kind of fear that eats its way inside you until it becomes part of the bones.

Firas ran a hand over his face, exhaling slowly. He could still feel the way her pulse had fluttered under his fingers when he'd touched her arm, the way her breath had hitched when he spoke her name. He'd meant to pull her back—to steady her—but part of him hadn't wanted to let go.

You're safe, he'd told her then. The words had felt wrong on his tongue, like a lie. Because he couldn't promise that. Not here. Not in this place that demanded they fight and bleed for spectacle. But it was all he'd had to give her in that moment.

And when her eyes had focused again—when she'd looked at him and actually *seen* him—it had undone him more than any wound could.

He hated how easily she could shake him. How her fear cracked something open in him he'd spent years trying to bury. Protecting her wasn't part of the plan. He was supposed to stay detached, to keep his distance, to remember why he was really here. But somewhere between the fights and the lies and the long nights, she'd become something he couldn't look away from.

He pushed off the wall, jaw tight. The lantern flame stuttered with the movement, shadows clawing across the stone. Maybe she'd forgotten that moment already. Maybe she'd buried it the way she buried everything that scared her. But he hadn't. He couldn't. Because when she broke in his arms that night, it had felt like the first honest thing in a world built on deceit.

And that terrified him most of all.

He heard Kam before he saw her. Her boots made no sound, but the weight of her presence always arrived a second before she did. Kam stepped into the light without a word, braids tucked tight beneath her hood, hand already on the knife at her hip.

Raven and Rami followed, one in silence, the other fidgeting with a trigger ring that sparked every few seconds between his fingers. The scent of copper and old oil drifted in behind them. They didn't speak. Not until the door behind them sealed with a soft, final thud.

"You said it was urgent," Kam said, eyes sharp. "How bad is

it?"

Firas opened his eyes. He looked at each of them—his most trusted. The ones who'd bled and lied and stolen for the rebellion. For him. The ones who had burned pieces of themselves to keep the spark of rebellion alive.

"Word from Rafiq. One of the competitors was taken after the last trial," Firas reported.

Kam's jaw tightened. "They just...took him?"

Firas nodded. "He didn't report back to his dorm the next day. I sent word to Rafiq to see if there had been any transports coming in and out of the capital."

Rami stopped twirling the ring. "Who?"

"His name is Tamar."

A beat passed.

"The Gemini?" Kam asked, brows lifting, clearly remembering him from training.

"The Gemini who clearly controlled earth in the arena the other day," Firas added. "I was going to try to find him after. They got to him first."

A long silence followed. Even the lantern seemed to dim slightly, as if the weight of it all choked the flame.

Firas looked at each of them in turn. "They'll probably try to say he took his own life. Maybe even fabricate a letter."

"And everyone will believe it," Raven added, voice hard. "Because they always do."

"No body," Rami murmured. "No questions."

"That's the idea," Firas said. Behind him, the lantern flickered. "The last two they'd taken were too public after the first trial. The Imperium must have miscalculated how loyal the competitors are. Some questioned it. This time, they'll want to keep it under wraps."

Raven leaned against the wall, the blade at her wrist half-drawn. "Where is he now?"

"The cells beneath Qasr al-Nujūm," Firas replied.

Kam hissed under her breath. "That place is locked down. You know this."

"I know," Firas said. "But we've broken in before."

"Barely," Kam shot back. "Hence why it's *locked down*."

"Then we'll do it better this time." He stepped forward, shadows slashing across his face as he pulled a map from his pocket, unfolding it quickly. Kneeling, he flattened it against the ground, smoothing out the edges. "Kam, you're on the outer stairwell. North quadrant. Watch for shift changes and perimeter relays. We'll need your signal before the second handoff. If they spot us too early—"

"They won't," she said.

Firas gave a tight nod.

"Rami—you take the forge access under the reservoir hall. There's a dead vent shaft they never resealed years ago. That's our breach point."

"Noise or stealth?" Rami asked.

"Stealth until you're spotted. Then noise. Draw them wide. Raven, you're extraction. I'll need you with me. I won't be able to check the cells if they're locked. You'll need to teleport in. He'll be cuffed, maybe sedated."

Raven adjusted the leather strap on her shoulder, her expression hard to read in the flickering torchlight. "I can get us in, but getting back out… with Tamar, with all of us? I won't have enough energy to do that."

"Then we get out without teleportation," Firas replied firmly.

"And you?" Kam asked.

Firas hesitated.

Just a moment.

"I'm going in through the archive passage. I've done it before."

"You'll be exposed," Kam said. "It runs past the west tower entrance. They'll have soldiers posted there."

"I'll handle it."

The others didn't argue. They knew him too well. But something in Kam's gaze lingered. Not just concern. The look on her face was foreign enough for him that it took Firas a second to decipher it.

It was doubt.

"Watch out for yourself," she said quietly, not accusing.

Firas didn't respond. His thoughts had been scattered since the arena. Since he held Talah as she shattered in silence. Since the look on her face when Saahira stepped through that door. Instead of answering, he just turned toward the shadows.

"We need to move. Now."

The ground beneath Firas's feet shifted with a sickening lurch. For half a breath, his body felt suspended between worlds—weightless and disoriented, Raven's power clawing down his spine like ice. He couldn't breathe, couldn't think…until he was slammed back into his body.

The courtyard around them stretched wide and silent, encased by pale marble walls and laced with creeping silver vines carved into the stone. Qasr al-Nujūm, Astrome's palace and the Imperium's seat of power, loomed above like a sleeping beast—spires curled like blades, banners motionless in the still night air. Somewhere beyond the walls, a fountain murmured.

Firas adjusted, crouching low in the brush beside the inner cloister, eyes sweeping the perimeter. To his right, Raven appeared beside him, crouched and already watching the eastern guard post. Rami was just behind her, barely steadying himself against the edge of a crumbling statue. Kam, silent as a breath, was already moving toward cover.

No alarm was raised.

Not yet, anyway.

They'd landed inside the western garden, one of the blind spots they'd mapped from their previous mission. The guards here rotated on twenty-minute shifts and only seemed to patrol the outer path—not the garden's core.

Firas let his hand brush the ground to stabilize himself. The air here felt different; cooler, damp, rich with the scent of crushed lavender and spices. Moonlight filtered thinly through a trellis of dark ivy and marble beams, fractured by the creeping mist that hugged the earth.

Low hedges shaped into spirals framed narrow paths of dark, glittering gravel that barely crunched under their feet. The trees were too tall for this part of the city—imported from the north, with bark that shimmered faintly in the dark and leaves like coiled silver. Everything was cultivated to simply *look* wild, but not a single leaf was out of place.

At the garden's center loomed a stone sculpture of a winged woman with her hands outstretched and her mouth slightly open. Her eyes were carved from obsidian, glossy and unblinking. Cracks ran down one cheek like dried blood. Firas still didn't know who—or what—the woman was supposed to represent. He just remembered her haunting look from the last time they'd been here.

Beyond the statue, the palace rose in tiers of pale limestone and black-veined marble, shaped like a temple and a fortress in one. Towers pierced the sky, curving outward like blades meant to catch starlight. Golden domes dotted the sky, glinting almost silver in the moonlight. Windows were sparse. Most were set high and narrow, more like slits than anything ornamental. This wasn't a place made for hospitality. It was designed to be impenetrable.

Firas exhaled slowly, every sense on edge.

No wonder they hide their monsters here, he thought.

It didn't feel like a palace.

"Rami—forge access under the reservoir hall," Firas reminded him. "Raven, with me."

Raven nodded once, already shifting her weight, eyes scanning the sloping garden path that would lead them along the palace's west edge. Her expression didn't change, but her shoulders rolled back slightly, tension bleeding into readiness. She checked the compact blade at her thigh and the concealed lock pick rig under her cuff.

Rami was already pulling out a coiled length of insulated wire from the satchel strapped across his chest. Next came a small pouch of iron shavings, a sparker ring, and what looked like a folded pocket-sized trap box.

"No explosives," Firas warned.

"I know," Rami muttered, rolling his eyes. "Just noise. Gear-rattling, echo-baiting noise. I'll trip the boiler alarm—make it sound like pressure's about to blow a valve. Let's hope their maintenance logs are as sloppy as their patrols."

"You have ten minutes to breach, fifteen to extract. Then light it up," Firas said. "No more."

"Please," Rami grinned. "I'm insulted you think I'd need fifteen."

Firas arched an eyebrow. "Just don't get cocky."

Rami clapped Firas's shoulder once and slipped off into the hedge. His lithe form vanished onto the mist-slick path, silent as a wraith. Kam peeled off next, vanishing along the opposite side of the garden, her outline swallowed by the curvature of the perimeter wall. Raven shimmered out of existence, going ahead of Firas to track the soldier's routes.

And then Firas was alone.

The scent of damp moss and cold stone pressed in around him. The statue of the winged woman loomed ahead, still watching with those glossy obsidian eyes. He exhaled slowly and turned toward the rear vestibule.

The old archive passage lay buried beneath a neglected shrine alcove—half-covered in vines and age, its stone frame cracked and softened by time. No one had used it for years.

He crouched beside the door, dug out a stiff strip of flattened wire, and inserted it into the locking plate. The click came quickly—rusted from disuse. He doubted anyone had used this route since the last time they'd been here, sneaking it to try to gain intel about the Imperium's attacks on the rebels. He lifted the bar and eased the door open with both hands, careful not to let the hinges groan too loud. It opened onto a narrow, spiraling stairwell that dropped steeply into shadow.

You don't leave anything behind this time.

He moved fast, quietly weaving past the shelves until he reached the last descent. Below, a metal door stood partially ajar—its latch hanging loose. Voices echoed from somewhere beyond. Boots scuffed over stone. Someone muttered an order.

Firas's breath hallowed as he counted in his head.

Seven, eight, nine…

Before he reached ten, there was a sudden rumble, the sound of an explosion rocking the underground corridors. He heard voices raised in alarm, boots thudding away from where he waited behind the door. Firas tightened the grip on his blade, slipped through the half-open door, and descended into the sublevel like a shadow.

The corridor narrowed as Firas reached the end. He crouched beside the final archway, chest rising and falling too fast. The air felt old and stale, tinged with the bitter bite of rust. Torches sputtered weakly along the walls, casting long, broken shadows across the cracked tile floor. Every footstep sounded like thunder.

He caught movement ahead—Raven, eyes already sweeping the hall, one hand resting lightly on the handle of a blade she hadn't drawn yet. She gave a tight nod toward him. Rami followed close behind, breath shallow but silent, the spark ring missing from his fingers. Kam appeared moments later from the opposite wing, slipping into the shadows beside a collapsed archway.

Firas nodded toward Raven, giving her the order. She disappeared, the sound of her landing in the first cell muffled beyond the steel doors. They stood waiting as she moved on to the next cell… and the next. Finally, after what seemed like forever, Raven reappeared.

"Fourth cell down. Right side."

"Why didn't you grab him?" Firas asked.

"He's not chained up… just sitting there," Raven replied hesitantly.

"So?" Kam hissed. "Get him and let's get out of here. Who cares if he's chained or not? That just makes it easier for us."

"Wait—" Rami shifted, head tilting. "This seems almost *too* easy. We barely made it out of here alive last time. And this time… you're sure he wasn't chained? Nothing barring him from escaping except the door?"

Raven shook her head. "No. Nothing. I mean, he's in pretty bad shape, but otherwise… he's just there."

Rami and Firas exchanged a look. "It's a trap," Firas said, grimacing.

Footsteps echoed from the corridor ahead, heavy and deliberate. Firas ducked back behind the wall. Raven pressed herself into a recess in the stone. Kam vanished into the dark like smoke. Rami hesitated before tucking himself behind a pile of crates stacked near the hall's edge.

Three figures rounded the corner; three soldiers in high-collared black coats, their faces sharp and humorless, curved swords at their sides. They stopped ten feet from Tamar's cell. The first reached for his ring of keys, the sound echoing through the corridor.

Firas could feel every heartbeat in his skull.

Too soon. We're not ready.

One guard drew a curved sword. The other stepped forward, eyes narrowing into the dark as the door creaked open in protest. The first ducked his head in, only to step back almost immediately.

"Nothing. They haven't been here… yet," the royal guard growled. He slammed the door shut, not bothering to lock the door. "Make the rounds. Check every crevice, every corridor. We know they're here."

The guards hesitated. But only for a second. Boots scraped against stone, fading as the guards jogged down the side hall, swords ready.

Firas had moved before they cleared the corner. He darted to the door, pulling it open. Inside, the room was dim and reeked of damp cloth and sweat. Tamar sat against the wall—wrists and ankles unbound, head lolled forward. His skin was pale, and one eye was swollen nearly shut, but he lifted his head the second Firas entered.

"Who... who are you?" he rasped, voice raw but alive.

"On your feet," Firas said, moving fast. "Now."

Raven moved to help Tamar up, while Kam held the door. Rami was already moving to cover the hallway. They had maybe thirty seconds before the royal guards came back.

Tamar stumbled forward—barely steady. "I don't understand," he muttered. "I don't understand. Why did they take me? I haven't done anything wrong. I didn't—" his voice cracked, "I didn't *do* anything."

Firas's chest tightened. "No, you didn't do anything wrong," he replied softly. "They took you because of what you are."

"What?" Tamar struggled to focus on Firas with his one good eye.

"You're an Ambigua," Raven said, trying to help. "Like us."

Firas braced for Tamar's reaction, his mind going back to Kareem in the maze, how *he'd* reacted.

Don't you dare put that curse on me.

I'd rather be crushed under this rubble than branded a monster like you.

"Stars," Tamar breathed. "That explains... so much."

"We're going to get you out of here," Firas said, relief washing over him. It didn't surprise him, however. Tamar wasn't a Signborn. From what Firas had gathered, he didn't even have a family. He'd entered the Trials to fight for a better life for himself.

"*Waghl!*"

The shout cracked down the hall like a whip. The guards reappeared, weapons raised.

"Intruders!"

One of the palace guards surged forward with a grunt, spear angled low. Kam was already moving. Fire shot from her hands, the flash of light temporarily blinding him. She slipped beneath the strike, driving a sharp elbow into the man's ribs and twisting. The crack of bone echoed in the narrow corridor. He staggered, only for her to slam a knee into his face. Blood splattered the stone, and he crumpled in a heap.

Another guard lunged from the left, curved khanjar raised, but Rami met him in a blur. His blade slid in a shallow arc, slashing across the inside of his thigh. The guard buckled with a cry, clutching at the wound. Rami didn't hesitate, spinning him into the wall where his head cracked against stone.

But the fight was far from over.

Boots pounded the tile. More guards rounded the far corridor—dark cloaks sweeping the ground, faces half-shadowed beneath iron helms etched with the Imperium's seal. The sharp hiss of drawn blades cut through the air.

There was no time.

Firas twisted around. "Tamar—go!" he barked, voice sharp as steel.

Raven was still holding the boy upright, one of Tamar's arms looped over her shoulder. The younger Ambigua struggled to right himself. His breath was short and shallow, feet dragging across the floor.

"Raven, get him out of here," Firas ordered.

Raven glanced between him and Tamar. "I'm not leaving you behind," she snapped. "And you know I can't take four people!"

"Raven—" A flash of movement caught Firas's attention. One of the guards lunged for something attached to the stone wall. A lever.

No.

He knew what came next. The gate would seal. The corridor would lock down. And Raven wasn't strong enough to teleport them all. Kam tried to intercept the guard, but was blocked by another.

"Raven, now!" Firas shouted again. "Get him out of here!"

But Tamar wavered. He looked up, eyes dazed, then narrowed. He saw the guards, the weapon glinting in one's hand. The one Raven hadn't noticed in time. The guard slammed into them—knocking Raven sideways, tearing Tamar from her grip.

"No!" Raven shouted, scrambling forward.

Tamar hit the stone hard, rolling onto his side. He coughed, blood flecking his chin, and tried to rise. A soldier stepped over him, dagger in hand. Firas roared, the sound tearing from his throat. He lunged forward.

Too slow.

The dagger drove down—clean, brutal—between Tamar's ribs. The boy arched, a strangled sound escaping his lips, then went still. Raven screamed, voice raw and guttural as she launched herself at the soldier. Kam swore violently as she dodged another hit, setting the corridor alight with more fire. Firas reached Tamar's side as Raven drove her blade through the man's gut and ripped it free. Blood sprayed across the wall. Heat scorched their backs.

Firas dropped to his knees. The boy's eyes were open, staring at the ceiling with a heavy emptiness. The torchlight flickered across his face, catching on the faint scar above his brow, the bruise along his jaw. Firas grabbed his hand, but it was already too late. None of them could heal and even if they could, he was too far gone.

A horn sounded from above—distant but unmistakable. The gate at the far end began to grind downward, heavy iron plates descending like the jaws of a beast.

"Firas!" Kam shouted. "We have to move!"

Rami was pulling Raven back, her face pale, eyes wide with horror. Firas knelt beside the boy for a breath longer. He closed Tamar's eyes with shaking fingers.

Then he turned and reached for Raven.

XXXIV TALAH

The cold night air scraped against her throat as Talah slipped through the outer gate of Aphelion, the academy walls disappearing behind her in the dark.

Above her, the stars seemed to have nearly vanished, smothered behind a curtain of drifting mist. She didn't need the light, however. There was only one road in and out of Aphelion, heading out toward the city. And she wouldn't even be heading that far into the city, either.

Astrome was built in rings, with Qasr al-Nujūm, the Palace of the Stars, at its center. The farther one traveled from the palace, the grander the villas became—and the purer the bloodlines that owned them. Though Talah had never been, she knew her father owned one such villa on the outskirts of the city. It hadn't been hard to ask around to find out which one belonged to her family.

He was the Pisces Councilor after all.

She didn't know what had compelled her—what voice in her head had whispered that she needed to see her father, as if the weight of this pain would be lighter with his voice to anchor her. It was stupid, especially after their little talk at the Convocation. He had warned her, and then he had abandoned her. Or at least that's what it felt like.

Talah's shoulders tensed as the city of Astrome drew nearer, its lights burning against the dark horizon. From afar, it looked almost like a mirage—lanterns and firelight shimmering through the mist, rising and bending. The clustered flames of its countless homes flickered like a forest fire, casting a soft glow that reached for the stars. Beneath the haze, the silhouette of Astrome took shape: domed rooftops glinting faintly in the night, spires like dark spears piercing the sky, and the faint outline of the palace rising above it all, its marble walls catching the moonlight like bone. The air carried with it the faint tang of smoke and spice, a whisper of life within the walls. Even at this distance, the city pulsed—alive, restless, waiting.

She stopped just as she reached the outer ring, villas as big as the dorm building back at Aphelion dotting the road. Walls towered over her on either side, hiding the vast lawns and gardens. Talah checked the numbers on the walls closest to her, continuing down the path in the dark.

Her family's villa rose like a mirage from the mist-soaked slope of the upper quarter—its outer walls tall and sun-bleached, trimmed with green tile and crowned in latticed stonework. Twin brass lanterns hung from iron hooks above the arched entryway, their glow faint behind filigreed glass. The scent of orange blossom drifted on the wind from the garden beyond, mingling with the sharper note of cedar and oiled stone. High above, narrow mashrabiya windows jutted from the second story—carved wooden screens allowing air to pass but keeping prying eyes out.

At the door, Talah hesitated, her fist raised to the wooden gates. Her father had never once come to any training session. She hadn't seen him among the councilors during the Trials. Neither he nor her mother had shown up in the past two weeks. They weren't expecting her now, and it was late—not too late to where they would be deep asleep, but late enough. Even then, she wasn't even sure if they *wanted* to see her.

Without thinking it through, Talah scaled the stone walls, dropping onto the other side into the grass. The central courtyard, hidden behind the heavy wooden doors, wrapped around a sunken fountain of black marble where water whispered day and night. Pomegranate and olive trees cast long shadows along the colonnade. She moved along the marble path, heart hammering in her chest, until she saw warm light flickering in the upper room.

So at least one of them is awake.

Talah crept along the side of the villa, finally finding a window that was unlatched and slightly ajar. She checked the hall, making sure there were no servants about before slipping inside. The sneaking around was nothing new—she'd been forced to do that back in Jawahra countless times when she was younger. Now, however, it felt... off. Like she was committing a crime.

Don't be stupid, Talah thought. *This is your home. Or at least one of your family's homes.*

Remembering which room had been alight, Talah stepped into the cool hush of her family's villa. The main entrance opened into a wide hall floored with polished stone, its surface veined like flowing water, warmed by rugs woven in deep crimson and gold. A carved cedar screen stood to one side, its latticework catching the glow of the oil lamps, throwing patterned shadows across the walls.

The air smelled faintly of rosewater and cardamom, the lingering traces of the evening meal. Brass lanterns hung from the arched ceiling, their colored glass casting shards of emerald and amber light onto mosaics that traced constellations across the plaster. At the far end of the hall, the stairs curved upward in a graceful sweep, their balustrade inlaid with mother-of-pearl. The silence of the villa pressed in, broken only by the soft rustle of palm fronds in the inner courtyard beyond, where water trickled steadily from a small fountain.

Talah moved toward the staircase, each footfall muffled by

the thick rugs, hoping most of the servants had already retired—either to their small rooms tucked along the outer wing or gone home to their families in the city.

The second-floor hallway stretched ahead, long and shadowed, its walls lined with niches holding brass lamps that had long since burned low. The faint glow from one door stood out against the darkness—the soft spill of lamplight filtering through a narrow crack.

Talah's steps slowed. Her pulse quickened as she drew nearer, her gaze lingering on the thin band of light striping the carpet beneath the threshold. The study. It had to be her father's study. He was the only one who kept such late hours, the only one who would have reason to be awake now with pen and parchment, surrounded by shelves of scrolls and ledgers.

She lifted a hand, meaning to knock, to announce herself. But just as her knuckles hovered close to the wood, a sound caught her—low, clipped voices from within. Talah froze, breath caught in her throat, straining to listen.

"... they were both already on our watchlist," said a deep, unfamiliar voice. "Their powers were escalating. It was only a matter of time."

"You still should've let me handle it more discreetly," came her father's voice. "Making it so public—"

"The only competitors who would question it are those who show the least loyalty to the Imperium," the other voice cut in, rougher this time. "Besides, we handled the others more discreetly, if that's what you're worried about." There was a heavy silence before the voice spoke again. "The Ambigua are not children. They're dangerous. The longer we wait, the harder it is to eliminate them."

"They weren't dangerous. They didn't even know what they were," her father said quietly.

"Neither was my son," the stranger snapped. "But now? Now he's their greatest weapon."

Her father's voice—steady, measured, almost pleading—rattled through her bones. The other man's words clawed at her chest, raw and merciless. The Ambigua. Dangerous. Her mind spun, piecing fragments together faster than she could stop herself. The missing competitors from the first trial... had there been more that they didn't know about?

Neither was my son... but now he's their greatest weapon.

Talah had no idea who this person or their son were.

"This is why we created the Trials, Khalid. To draw them out. You would do well to remember that," the voice warned.

Time seemed to slow. The words hollowed her. The Trials—the thing she had bled for, broken herself for—were never about proving worth. Never about power or honor. It was a trap. A hunt. And she, like every competitor, was nothing more than bait.

How many people know?

The councilors surely knew if this was their plan. Which meant... Talah covered her mouth, trying to muffle the sound of her gasp. Saahira's nephew had died in the Trials. Saahira had to have known about this. Which meant she had willingly sacrificed her nephew—not for power and strength—but to keep the ruse going. Did the other Signborn nobles know? Had they offered up their younger children as sacrifices so the Imperium could root out and destroy the Ambigua?

Her knees weakened. She pressed a hand to the wall, nails digging into the plaster as if she could steady the ground beneath her. The pride she had carried, the desperate need to prove herself worthy, splintered inside her chest. Every bruise, every scar, every sleepless night—meaningless.

And her father... he'd known all along. He's allowed it to continue—allowed the Imperium to keep murdering innocents who didn't even know what they were. Talah felt something inside her snap, like a line pulled too tight.

Anger came first—sharp and blinding, cutting through the haze. It burned up her throat, hot and choking. But beneath it, something colder coiled tighter—a kind of grief that felt too heavy to hold. It pressed against her ribs until she could barely breathe.

She'd built her entire life on his approval, on the belief that everything she endured meant something. Now, that belief lay in ruins at her feet.

"I understand," her father replied, his voice calm though anger simmered beneath. "How is your mission going, by the way? Is your son still managing to slip through your fingers, Kaed?"

The Kaed's son. That's who they were talking about.

Talah had heard the rumors. He'd been a prodigy, sharper and stronger than most, trained from childhood to bring honor to his bloodline. He had entered the Trials and dazzled the crowds, only to vanish after the second. Some swore the Ambigua had claimed him. Others swore he had *always* been one of them, hiding in plain sight until the Imperium's games forced him into the open. Whatever the truth, his name had become a shadow spoken with unease—a traitor's son turned rebel, a weapon the Imperium could not control.

And the Kaed had been dishonored, forced to prove his loyalty. Which was probably why he had focused all of his attention on eradicating the Ambigua rebels.

"I'm close," the Kaed hissed. "Don't you worry about that, *Councilor*. You have bigger problems... especially with your only daughter risking her life in the Trials."

"Get out."

The finality in her father's voice made Talah flinch as if the word had been struck against her. A chair scraped across the floor inside, heavy footsteps shifting toward the door. Her heart lurched. If the Kaed stepped into the hall now, he would find her standing there, the truth written all over her face.

She spun, her boots whispering against the carpet as she fled down the corridor. Her pulse hammered in her ears, drowning out the rise of voices behind her, the soft creak of the door beginning to open. She didn't stop until she reached the stairs, half-stumbling down them, desperate to put distance between herself and that room, that conversation.

The villa's silence seemed to press tighter around her as she crossed the entrance hall, every flickering lamp suddenly too bright, every shadow too deep. She shoved the heavy door open, slipping into the night air before anyone inside could call her name.

Talah ran all the way back to Aphelion. Her lungs burned by the time she scaled the outer slope of the Aphelion wall, slipping back onto campus under the cloak of shadow. The stone beneath her fingers felt cold and slick. Her limbs trembled. Her breathing wouldn't settle. She didn't know if it was rage.

Or grief.

Or guilt.

What if this was all for nothing?

The thought hit harder than any blade. Not just because the Trials were a lie—but because she had believed them. Needed to believe them. That if she just worked harder, fought harder, proved herself in every arena, she could make her place undeniable. Earned what no one could take from her.

But now? Now she didn't know if she was proving herself... or playing directly into their hands.

She wasn't so sure she could live with that.

The hush of the academy grounds swallowed her whole; the walk back to the dorms felt longer than it should have. The campus was deathly quiet, the kind of silence that pressed against your ears like pressure beneath water. No wind. No voices. Just the soft slap of her boots against the stone.

She cut through the western courtyard, where the path forked beneath the ancient olive trees—twisting things with silver leaves and thick, gnarled roots that cracked the stone. Their shadows stretched long across the ground, thrown into strange shapes by the low lanterns flickering in the alcoves.

The air smelled of dust, warm stone, and the faintest trace of lingering incense from the dusk prayers—spicy, cloying, with a bitter undertone that reminded her of home. She passed the edge of the astronomy hall, its arched windows dark and watching. Beyond it, the courtyard opened onto a colonnade ringed with lion statues, each one carved from pale stone and draped in ivy.

That's where she saw him.

Iras was slouched in the shadow of the largest lion statue—the one at the center, its mouth open in a silent roar. His back rested against the pedestal, legs stretched in front of him, one hand loosely cradling a metal cup. A half-empty flask glinted beside him in the moonlight, its silver seal stamped with a mark she recognized from the inner markets of Astrome.

Araq—clear, strong, and unforgiving. The scent hit her long before she approached him—sharp, like crushed fennel and bruised anise, undercut by the harsh bite of alcohol.

He didn't look surprised to see her. Didn't even flinch. He lifted the cup slightly, the movement lazy and practiced. "Bit late for a walk," he muttered, voice low and rough. "Or early. Hard to tell anymore."

Talah stepped into the courtyard light, arms crossed tightly over her chest, shadows clinging to her shoulders like wet cloth. Her pulse hadn't settled from the run, and the ache behind her ribs hadn't let go since her father's words at the villa. Iras took another slow sip from the cup. The scent of araq was stronger now.

His gaze drifted across the darkened arches, unfocused but not unaware.

"I didn't think you were the type to drink alone," she said finally.

"I'm not." His voice was hoarse, raw from too many swallowed words. "But most people aren't worth drinking with."

The silence between them stretched.

He cut it with a bitter laugh. "Let me guess. You couldn't sleep. Decided to take a stroll. Maybe count the stars and pretend none of this is real."

She flinched.

"I get it," he added, tilting the flask toward her. "Tried it myself, once. Doesn't work."

She eyed the bottle. "You shouldn't be drinking that."

He looked up, finally meeting her eyes. "I shouldn't be doing a lot of things, Aasifati."

Talah lowered herself onto the stone beside him. The lion statue loomed behind them both, half in shadow, its marble jaws frozen in a silent roar. "Why do you call me that?"

"Call you what?"

"Aasifati. My Storm." Talah's eyes narrowed slightly.

His head tilted back, his gaze never leaving hers. "You were the tsunami I never saw coming."

Talah said nothing for a moment. "I thought the Trials were meant to test us," she said quietly. "To prove we were worthy."

Iras scoffed, shaking the cup in his hand. "They are. Just not in the way you think."

Does he know something?

She glanced at him. "Then what are they really for?"

He swirled the drink once. It caught the light like a polished mirror.

"To divide," he said. "To distract."

Talah didn't speak. Her throat had gone dry.

He has to know… right?

Iras turned his face to the stars above, blinking as if they might hold some answers. "It's a game. It's all a game."

Her stomach turned, her mind replaying the conversation at her father's house—his careful silences, the way he'd looked at her without really seeing her. A cold understanding had begun to take shape since then, one she hadn't wanted to face.

Her nails bit into her palms. "That's not what they told us."

"They tell you what you want to hear. And they tell you early—so it sinks deep."

Talah swallowed hard. The ache behind her ribs deepened. *He knows something,* she thought. He always did. He spoke like someone who'd already made peace with truths she hadn't yet found the courage to name.

"And what about the Ambigua?" she asked.

Iras froze—just for a breath. Most probably wouldn't have noticed, but she did. The flicker of hesitation, the way his hand tightened on the cup before he tipped it back again, buying time.

"I've heard the rumors," he said, shrugging. "Same as everyone else."

She wanted to believe that. She wanted to, but the small shift in his tone told her otherwise.

"And?" she asked, voice softer now. "Do you think they're dangerous?"

Iras exhaled slowly. The flame from the nearest lamp fluttered as if stirred by his breath. "I think anything the Imperium calls dangerous is usually something they can't control." He looked over at her, gaze steady but dark. "That doesn't make it evil."

The words settled between them like smoke. Talah stared at him, her pulse uneven. He wasn't just guessing—she could *feel* it. He was speaking from somewhere deeper, somewhere lived. And for the first time, she wondered what else he'd seen, what he'd done, and why a part of her wasn't sure she wanted the answers.

"So you don't think they deserve to be hunted?"

His jaw tensed. The bottle tapped softly against the stone. "I don't think anyone deserves to be hunted just for existing."

The silence wrapped around them again, thick as smoke. In the distance, the wind shifted through the courtyard trees—rattling their silvered leaves like teeth in a bowl. Somewhere deeper, a bell chimed the third hour before dawn.

Talah pressed a little further. "What about the Kaed's son?"

At that, Iras's head tilted slightly. His brow furrowed, but he kept his voice even. "What about him?"

She shrugged, trying to seem casual. "You're older than I am. I thought maybe you knew him. He was in the Trials, wasn't he?"

Iras didn't answer right away. Instead, he leaned forward, resting his elbows on his knees, the cup dangling from one hand. The glow of the lantern beside them carved his face into angles—jaw shadowed, cheekbones hollowed. The scent of araq hung thick between them.

"You hear that name from your father?" he asked, too casually.

Talah tensed, just slightly. "Why would you think that?"

"Because most people wouldn't dare bring him up."

Her silence was enough of a response.

Iras leaned back against the lion statue, letting his head rest against the cool marble. His eyes closed for a long breath. When he opened them again, they were fixed on the stars once again.

"I remember him," he said quietly.

Talah turned toward him, heart hitching. "Really?"

"He was too cocky for his own good. Too... privileged," Iras said, voice heavy.

Talah's brow furrowed. "What happened to him?"

Iras's hand tightened around the cup, knuckles whitening. "He disappeared," he said, the word flat and final. "That's what said anyway. Convenient, isn't it?"

"And no one questioned it?" she asked, voice sharpened by disbelief.

"Oh, they did. For about a week." He let out a dry, humorless breath. "Then another Trial started. Another ceremony. Another reason to forget. The Imperium's good at moving forward before anyone asks why the ground is stained."

Talah looked down, her fingers curled into her robe. "Do you think he was... Ambigua?"

Iras rolled the cup between his fingers, watching the way the liquid shimmered in the moonlight.

"I think," he said slowly, his words slurring slightly, "that anyone who doesn't fall into line gets labeled something eventually. Ambigua. Rebel. Terrorist. It doesn't matter what you are—it just matters that they can't control you." He turned to her then, his gaze hard and knowing. "And I think you should be careful asking about people who vanish," he said, his voice quiet and edged. "Some of them disappear for good reason."

She met his eyes. There was something raw there—feral and familiar. Like he was daring her to keep going. Like he needed her to. And for a breath, Talah felt the thread between them stretch tighter than it ever had.

He knows something.

Her chest heaved, the weight of everything she had

overheard pressing down until she could hardly breathe. The Trials—nothing more than a trap. A ruse to root out the Ambigua, to slaughter them under the guise of honor. The councilors, her father, the Signborn nobles—they might all know about it. They had all sent their children into the fire as willing sacrifices so the Imperium's blade could keep swinging. And she, foolish and desperate to prove herself, had bled for it. Had believed in it.

The betrayal hollowed her. Rage and grief tangled until her throat burned. Her own father's voice still echoed in her head, calm and complicit, while the Kaed's venom lingered like ash. How many had already died for this lie? How many more would there be?

She wanted answers—needed them—but Iras's silence was a wall she couldn't break through.

Iras set his cup down with a quiet clink of finality. His voice was low when he spoke, rough and tired. "Go, Talah."

She shook her head, a soundless plea clawing at her throat. "You know something. You—"

His voice cut like a blade. Sharper, firmer. "Don't waste it sitting in the dark with someone who's already lost too much to give you answers."

The words knocked the breath from her lungs, leaving only the hollow ache of betrayal in their place. She pushed away from the wall, from Iras, from the suffocating silence that refused to give her answers.

The dormitory halls felt narrower than before, pressing in on her as she walked. Every carved star in the plaster, every flickering lantern seemed to mock her, whispering of a world built on lies. The Trials weren't a path to honor. They were a cage. A hunt. And her father—her *father*—had helped build it.

By the time she stepped into her room, the air was sharp with cold, but her blood burned hotter than fire. She no longer trembled with fear or grief. Only fury. Fury at the Imperium, at the councilors, at the nobles who smiled as they sent their children to die. Fury at herself for ever believing in them.

And as the fury burned through her, Talah knew she would never play their game the same way again.

TALAH
XXXV

The door slammed open with a crack like splintering bone. Talah bolted upright, heart thundering. A torch flared, too bright, searing across her eyes. Shadows writhed against the dormitory walls, twisted by motion—boots, cloaks, weapons. Her sleep-fogged mind scrambled to catch up as a voice barked a command.

"Up. Now. You've been summoned."

Adine was already sitting up in the cot beside hers, blinking hard, hair sticking to her cheek. Talah tried to rub the sleep from her eyes. It had been late when she'd finally gotten back in after her conversation with Iras. To Talah, it felt like she hadn't gotten any sleep at all.

"What—what is it?" she asked, voice hoarse.

No one bothered to answer. The soldiers moved with machine precision—pulling open trunks, yanking cloaks from hooks. Their uniforms bore the crest of the Imperium, pressed deep into the black. One of them dropped a bundle at Talah's feet: thick wool, a sash, her boots. Talah's fingers trembled as she dressed while the soldiers waited outside.

At least they gave us some privacy, Talah thought, annoyed.

The dormitory floor was cold against her bare feet. The air stank of sleep and damp stone, of torches burning oil too old. Somewhere behind the walls, other doors slammed open—distant shouts, footsteps pounding through the halls. And beneath it all, Talah felt her thoughts buckling—too many threads, pulled too tight. Everything from last night came rushing back.

The Trials are a lie, a sacrifice.

My father knew. Tried to warn me.

How many others have died for this farce? How many Ambigua have they killed?

Her chest ached, her anger burning away the biting cold.

Adine bumped her shoulder gently. "You ready?"

No, she wasn't sure she'd ever be ready again, but she nodded anyway.

The march through Aphelion's outer halls was done in silence. The soldiers flanked them on all sides, grim and faceless beneath dark hoods. Outside, the city was cloaked in mist. The moon hung low, sharp-edged and veiled, ready to depart and allow the sun to rise. Their boots scraped over mosaic stone slick with dew, the chill biting through the soles like needles.

Other competitors joined them as they were herded in: Zayd, jaw clenched. Mazin, pale and watchful. Two from Virgo. A bruised Capricorn girl rubbing blood from her eye. No one spoke. No one needed to ask why they'd been dragged from their beds.

Ahead, the silhouette of the coliseum rose like a crown of fangs, its jagged upper ring catching the torchlight in glints of gold and stone. The torches that lined the outer gates burned brighter than they should have, casting their shadows long and monstrous across the stone. Talah stared at the gates as they neared. Her stomach twisted.

The third trial.

She'd heard whispers. Nothing certain. Nothing kind. A trial of the mind. Of the self. The kind that didn't leave wounds on the outside. Only inside. She didn't know how much more she had left to lose.

They were marched into the coliseum through the northern gate. Talah squinted against the brightness of the arena torches. Unlike the previous trials, the coliseum was empty of spectators. No cheers. No roaring crowd. Just wind slipping through the high arches and banners.

It's all a lie.

Khalias stood at the center of the ring, robed in black with silver scales stitched across the chest. His eyes roved over them, cold and cruel. Behind him, on a raised dais, loomed an enormous stone.

It was taller than any man or woman here, its obsidian surface shimmering in the early morning starlight. Veins of silver pulsed beneath its surface, the rhythm slow and ominous.

The Mirror.

It was aptly named, though no one knew where or what it had come from. According to the rumors, it was a gift from the stars when this world first began, able to show the truth in one's heart and mind. Some claimed it was created by two Zodiacs forging their powers together, long before such an act was outlawed by the Imperium.

They'll know everything, Talah thought wildly. Her pulse jumped in her throat, hands starting to sweat despite the chill in the morning air.

She tore her gaze from the stone to the outer edge of the arena where the mentors had gathered in a narrow row of shadows just beyond the torchlight. She scanned their faces looking for one in particular.

He looked like hell.

Not in the bruised, bloodied way most of the competitors did after a fight. But hollow. Like something had been torn out, and only the shape of it remained. His shoulders were tight. His eyes sunken, ringed with sleeplessness. His clothes seemed to hang looser, his cloak pulled too tight over his chest like he was bracing himself against the cold.

She remembered the flask in his hand last night. The bitterness in his voice. His gaze flicked to hers now, briefly, across the space. And she saw it there, even if no one else did. A fracture in his mask. A tension behind his eyes that hadn't been there before. He knew something. And whatever it was, it was eating him from the inside. Talah looked away, pulse spiking.

The soldiers arranged them in a line, competitors on each side, standing shoulder to shoulder in the cold morning mist. Khalias spoke without ceremony.

"This is the third trial." His voice carried across the space like a blade drawn from its sheath. "The Mirror was a gift from the stars when this world began. A gift that allows us to see inside the hearts and minds of those who would pledge loyalty to the Imperium."

"You will step up one-by-one to place your hand on the surface. The Mirror is not a test of strength, but of the self. It will show you what you truly are." A ripple moved through the line. Someone swallowed too loudly. Another shifted their weight. "The Libra mentors and mentalists will watch," Khalias added. "They will see what you see. But they will not feel what you feel."

Talah's mouth went dry as she forced herself to stare straight ahead at the stone. Everything she'd heard last night, everything she'd talked to Iras about—*they might see it all.*

"The Mirror draws on your thoughts, your fears, your truth," Khalias continued. "You cannot lie to it. You cannot hide from it. You may emerge changed... or destroyed." He turned to the soldiers. "Begin."

The line began to move, the first competitor making their way up the dais. His hand shook as he reached for the stone, pressing his palm against its smooth surface. The Mirror shimmered, its silver light flickering like breath on black glass. The competitor stilled. His eyes glazed, his body frozen in place, as if time had halted around him.

And then he began to scream.

It pierced the air, full of torment and fear. His arm shook, but his hand remained against the stone. His body convulsed, curving in on itself as he continued to wail. The sound sliced through Talah like a blade, chilling her to her core. The flames of her anger were replaced with icy fear.

Finally, after what seemed like hours, his body finally collapsed. He curled into a ball, arms wrapped around his legs as he mumbled wildly to himself. Talah couldn't make out what he said…but she knew it probably wasn't good. His eyes were wide open and wild-looking, twitching from side to side. Two soldiers stepped up beside him, hoisting him up. He was still muttering as they dragged him away, back through the arena gates.

Khalias didn't even flinch. "Next."

One-by-one they went, each one more horrific than the last. Each scream, each breathless wail, raked across Talah's ears. She wanted to look away, wanted to flinch at each sound, but the soldiers were watching everything—every flinch, every hesitation.

The air felt tighter now, thinner with each name called. Her own breath scraped her throat. Her heart wouldn't slow. Her gaze finally drifted to her friends. Zayd stood three places ahead, arms crossed, jaw set. But even he looked shaken. No swagger now. Just a taut thread of defiance barely holding. She noticed the tremor in his hands when his name was called.

"Zayd Al-Mansur."

He smirked, but it didn't reach his eyes. "Let's get it over with," he muttered.

He pressed his hand to the Mirror and stilled. At first, Talah thought nothing had happened. But then his shoulders seized, his body jerking once, violently, as if struck by lightning. And then—nothing. Stillness so complete it was wrong, unnatural.

The silence stretched. A minute, maybe more. Long enough for the hairs at the back of Talah's neck to rise, long enough for her chest to tighten with a fear she didn't understand. His breath rattled out of him in shallow bursts, fogging the glass. His fingers dug into the surface, tendons straining white against his skin.

Then came the sound. A low murmur that scraped like stone dragged across stone. Words tangled on his tongue, too garbled to make sense at first—then sharpening into fragments. Names. Pleas. Begging that broke apart into sudden, startled laughter. Not the kind of laughter she knew from him—the easy, careless sort—but jagged and hollow, a sound that scraped bone.

When he finally tore his hand free, the sound cut off at once. He staggered back as if the Mirror had ripped something vital out of him. His hand hung stiff at his side, knuckles bone-white, as if he still felt its pull. He didn't look at her. Didn't look at anyone. He simply returned to the line, silent, shoulders rigid, a tremor still running down his arms.

Talah's heart slammed against her ribs. Her palms were slick with sweat.

They're going to see. Everything. What she'd heard. What she now knew. What if the Mirror revealed it all?

What if it saw something else?

"Talah bint Khalid."

Her name rang out, echoing across the sand. Talah stepped forward. The Mirror loomed over her, pulsing faintly with silver veins that shifted just beneath the obsidian surface, like breath trapped under glass. The closer she drew, the more it felt alive—watching her, waiting. Her fingers trembled as she raised her hand.

Don't think. Don't feel. Just— She touched the surface.

The air vanished. The arena, the line of competitors, the stone beneath her feet—gone. Darkness swallowed everything. Then... there was light. Too much of it. It blinded her, forcing her eyes to close. When it finally dissipated, she slowly re-opened them, expecting the worst.

Instead, she found herself standing before a version of herself.

The world around the real Talah was warped and endless, like she'd been dropped into the middle of a black sea made of mirrors. No sky. No ground. Just endless shimmering glass beneath her boots, around her, reflecting a thousand fractured versions of herself from every impossible angle.

One version of her stepped forward. She seemed older. Sharper. Her movements were precise. Fluid. Regal. Crowned in water and fire and wind. Eyes lined in silver, cold and clear. Her cloak bore no insignia of any Zodiac.

"I've been waiting," the reflection said.

Talah swallowed. "You're not real."

"I'm what you hide," the reflection said. "The part you're too afraid to become."

Talah clenched her fists.

The reflection smiled, tilting its head. "Tell me, did you really believe them?"

The world around them seemed to fall away, the tightness in Talah's chest constricting around her lungs.

"You made a choice, Talah. The moment you plunged a blade into Nadir. The moments you killed in the maze. You chose this path."

"I didn't know," Talah hissed.

"And you believe that," her double murmured. "You could have found out sooner. Could have looked deeper."

"I—" The words locked in her throat. The reflection—*her* reflection—was right. She could have looked into it more, could have done *something* while her parents kept her from society all these years. She'd had the time.

But she had been too naïve.

"Now you'll pay the price, little one. Just like all the others. Just like the ones *you* killed." The reflection lunged forward, hissing.

Talah barely dodged, her mind still whirling. A blade of pure illusion came slicing toward her, impossibly fast, scattering light in its wake. She ducked, rolling to the side, her fists coming up to protect herself.

The reflection smiled wider. "See? Your reaction is to fight back, but only for your own survival."

They clashed. Illusion against instinct. Water against light. With every strike Talah made, the reflection countered. With every illusion she cast, it unraveled. The reflection didn't tire. Didn't bleed. Didn't hesitate. It knew her too well.

Because it *was* her.

"Why can't I beat you?" she gasped, stumbling backward after a parried strike.

"Because I know your fear," the reflection whispered, stepping closer. "You don't think you belong here. You're terrified they're right about you—that you're nothing more than privilege and borrowed power."

Talah flinched.

"You want to prove them wrong so badly," the reflection hissed, "you'll kill to earn their approval. Even if the system is a lie."

"Stop," she breathed. "That's not—"

"True?" the reflection said. "Then look at what's left of you."

It held up a hand, and the mirrors around them cracked open.

Images spilled across the space. Halima's scream as she fell into the abyss during the first trial before the darkness swallowed her. Rayen's face twisted in pain, blood streaming from his mouth as the earth pierced his body. Mazin, eyes wide with panic, his blood pooling beneath him, his voice fading into nothing as she ran from him. Nadir, unflinching, certain, even when she drove her knife between his ribs. Each memory hit like a wave. No time to breathe. No space to brace. Talah staggered.

Her reflection watched with cool detachment. "This is who you are," it said. "A survivor. A weapon forged with other people's blood."

Talah pressed her hands to her ears. "Stop."

"Why?" the reflection whispered. "You've already stopped being afraid of killing. You're more afraid of what that means than whose life you take."

"I didn't want any of this," Talah whispered, voice hoarse.

"No," the reflection said, lowering its weapon. "But you kept going. And that makes it worse."

The ground began to tremble. Talah closed her eyes, waiting

for the moment her own reflection buried a dagger in her chest. There was a sound of something shattering, filling the space around her like thunder.

Something within her finally cracked—her pain, her fear—ripping from within, as if every nerve in her body had snapped at once. Light exploded behind her eyes, her knees buckling as she slammed back into her body. Her mouth opened, but no sound came. When she finally opened her eyes, she was back in the coliseum, gasping, soaked in sweat, hands trembling.

The sky above her was spinning. The world around her roared—torches hissed, mentors shouted, soldiers converged with wide eyes and drawn weapons. But no one touched her. No one dared. Not when the obsidian surface behind her had gone dull, the stone cracked, its veins extinguished.

Her limbs wouldn't work. Her lungs burned as if she'd been drowning. Everything she'd seen, everything she'd done, burned in her memory. Halima's fall, Rayen's blood, Mazin's sacrifice, and Nadir's last breath still ricocheted inside her skull, too fast to follow, too sharp to ignore. She collapsed to her side, vision tunneling at the edges.

Look at what's left of you.

Arms wrapped around her shoulders, strong and familiar.

"Easy," said a voice—rough, frayed, but low enough that no one else could hear. "I've got you, Aasifati."

Iras had stepped down from the arena edge, past the line of soldiers, past the mentors who didn't stop him. His grip was firm but careful as he helped her up on shaking legs, pulling her out of the sand. He draped a cloak over her shoulders before anyone else could see the way she was trembling.

Talah blinked hard, eyes stinging. "You're not supposed to be here."

Iras gave a humorless smile. "Don't worry. I'm not trying to help you. This is purely for selfish reasons."

His hand lingered on her shoulder. She could feel the tension in him—his muscles taut beneath the fabric, jaw locked, gaze scanning the ring like a predator waiting for a threat.

"They saw inside," she whispered, throat raw. "All of it. Everything I've done."

"No," Iras said, too fast. "They saw what the Mirror let them see."

She looked up at him, brow furrowed. "What does that mean?"

He hesitated before speaking, his voice dropping. "Talah… you *broke* the Mirror."

Talah's heart stuttered. "What? What does that even mean?"

Iras met her gaze—steady, unflinching. "I don't know," he said. But his voice was too quiet. Too careful. "But it's not normal."

She wanted to ask more. Press harder. But the world was tilting again. She clutched the cloak tighter, the weight of the moment catching up to her in waves. Iras urged her forward silently. At first, she resisted.

"You can fall apart later," he said gently. "Right now, you need to walk out of this arena."

Talah gave a weak nod, allowing him to help her. She didn't know what the Libra mentors had seen from her time in the Mirror, nor did she understand what Iras had meant when he said she'd 'broken it'. All she knew was that, whatever had happened in there, had changed her forever.

XXXVI FIRAS

She shattered the Mirror.

Firas shut the door behind them, leaning into it for a breath. His pulse still pounded, his palm still burned faintly from where he'd gripped Talah's arm to pull her off the coliseum floor. She hadn't resisted, but she had trembled the whole way here. Now she stood in the middle of his private quarters—still wrapped in the cloak he'd thrown over her, her face pale, her eyes glassy, staring into nothing.

She looked so broken, and yet, he couldn't look away from her.

She shattered *the Mirror.*

He'd watched it happen with his own eyes. The Mirror of the Zodiac—the Imperium's most invasive weapon—had cracked and failed at the feet of someone it was meant to expose. Someone who, by all logic, been broken by it instead. But she hadn't been, and that terrified him more than anything else.

The room around them was dim, lit only by a single lantern. The air smelled of old parchment and myrrh, the dust of desert spices embedded in the stone. It was still plain, with no personal belongings there. The tomes they'd stolen had been moved to the storage room where Rami could continue to study them. Nothing here would incriminate him in any way.

He took a step toward her. She didn't move away. Talah's body trembled, shaking harder now as she struggled to remain standing. He reached for her, hesitating, before gently resting a hand on her arm.

"Talah," he said quietly. "You're safe. For now."

She blinked once. Then again. But her eyes were too wide, too far away.

"It's not real," she whispered. "It's not here."

Firas frowned. "What isn't?"

Then he saw it. The wall behind her shifted. Not physically—but in light. Just a flicker. They looked like illusions and yet... weren't. The shadows behind her rippled. Brief flashes of memory—Rayen falling, Nadir gasping, Mazin bleeding—flickered through the space like oil-slick ghosts, faint and broken. Distorted by fear. Talah's uncontrolled power was bleeding into the room.

She doesn't even know she's doing it.

Firas stepped in fast, close enough now to see how her fists were clenched, white-knuckled at her sides, her breathing shallow, uneven.

"Talah," he said again, firmer now. "You're not in the Mirror anymore. Look at me."

She didn't. The visions behind her surged—Rayen's scream ringing through the space, bouncing off the stone walls. Her chest was rising and falling too fast now. Her feet shifted as if she didn't know where she was standing. He grabbed her shoulders—firm, anchoring, solid. She flinched like he'd struck her. Not a twitch. A full-body recoil.

Her breath hitched. Her eyes lost focus, flaring with something wild. Not panic exactly, but the echo of it, like her mind had been dragged somewhere she couldn't claw her way out of. He didn't let go.

"Hey," he said, keeping his voice low and steady. "Breathe. Look at me. You're here. You're real."

Her lips parted. Nothing came out for a second.

"I—" Her voice cracked open, hoarse and small. "I didn't mean to. I didn't want to kill him. Them. Any of them."

Firas's grip gentled, but he didn't release her. "You didn't have a choice," he said quietly. "You had to survive."

Her head jerked. Not in denial, just... rejection. Like the words couldn't land. Like nothing could. "I saw everything," she whispered. "Everything I've done. I can't stop seeing it."

The air around her shifted again. Firas's breath caught as the shadows behind her trembled, rippling like disturbed water.

Firas swore under his breath. "Talah—stop. You're bleeding it out. You're projecting—"

But she couldn't hear him now. She was shaking, shoulders rigid under his hands, her body somewhere between holding still and falling apart. Her eyes were wide and vacant. And what terrified him most was the silence. The way she didn't scream. Didn't cry. The way she just unraveled, quietly, like a paper burning too fast to leave ash.

Firas moved before he could think.

He wrapped his arms around her and pulled her against him, hard enough to make her stumble into his chest. Her breath caught at the impact—sharp, shallow. She resisted for half a second, hands curling against his chest like she didn't know what to do with them. Her fists gripped his shirt and held on. Her head dropped to his shoulder. Her breathing was ragged and stuttering, like her body was still trying to fight even now, but there was nothing left to fight with.

Firas tightened his hold, one hand braced between her shoulder blades, the other sliding to cradle the back of her head.

"You're safe, Aasifati," he murmured, again and again. "You're safe." But even as he said it, he knew it wasn't true.

Not really.

Talah's breathing slowed, but only barely. She still trembled in his arms, like her body wasn't fully convinced she was safe.

Like she hadn't quite come back from wherever the Mirror had taken her. Firas didn't loosen his grip. He kept his hand pressed between her shoulder blades, the other resting gently at the nape of her neck, grounding her. The illusions had faded—but the memory of them clung to the air like smoke.

"You're not in the Mirror anymore," he said softly. "You're here. With me. Here, name five things you can see. Just five."

That got her to stir. Just slightly. She shifted in his hold, enough to look up at him—her face pale and streaked with dried sweat, her eyes raw but steady.

"What?"

"Name five things you can see. Anything you can see."

Talah's eyes flicked around the room slowly. "I see a chair."

"Keep going," he murmured.

"And the desk. The walls... the ceiling. The door?" She glanced up at him, confusion in her eyes now instead of that empty blankness.

"Name four things you can smell."

"Iras."

"Please," he said quietly. "Just humor me."

Talah let out a soft sigh. "I can smell the smoke from the lantern. It smells like... old parchment in here."

"Anything else?" he pressed.

"I—I can smell the gardens outside. The jasmine. The food cooking from the kitchens across the courtyard. Why are you asking me to do this?"

"Because it helps me sometimes," he replied. "It helps ground me."

The silence between them stretched thick with everything unsaid. Firas could feel the heat of her skin where their bodies touched, the shudder of her breath against his chest. He didn't want to let go. Not yet. But he forced himself to. Slowly, he stepped back, just enough to see her without the haze of memory clouding her expression.

"I've seen a lot of people lose control in the Mirror," he said, voice low. "But I've never seen anyone break it."

Talah winced. "I didn't mean to."

"I don't think you did," he replied. "That's what makes it worse."

She didn't answer. Instead, her eyes drifted toward the far wall, as if afraid of what else she might conjure just by thinking. Her hands were still balled at her sides. Firas tilted his head slightly, studying her.

"Have your illusions... always been like that?" he asked.

Talah frowned, pulling the cloak around her shoulders tighter. "What do you mean?"

"Piscean illusions—they're good. So good that most people will think they're real if they don't know any better. But they're just that—illusions. There's no sound. No feeling. No smell. They're simply projected images," Firas said. "But that... what you did just now. I could hear them. I could feel them."

Talah said nothing.

"Has that happened before?"

"No," she said quickly. "I don't know. Maybe?"

He watched her closely. She seemed to be telling the truth. Or else she was an extremely good liar, even when shaken.

"You said in the coliseum," she went on slowly, "that whatever's in me... it's not normal."

Firas exhaled through his nose. "No. It's not."

She looked up again. And this time, there was something sharp in her gaze. Not fear. Curiosity. Or maybe hope. "You've seen it before?" she asked. "Something like it?"

Firas hesitated. It would be so easy to lie. To redirect. To tell her it didn't matter. But the truth was, he hadn't seen anything like what she'd done. Ambigua bent the rules of their Signs, yes, but their powers still stayed within familiar lines—an Aries's strength was still strength, a Leo's shapeshifting was still just the changing of flesh. A Pisces's illusions, though? They were tricks of the eye, shadow and light with no weight. You couldn't touch them, couldn't hear their breath or feel the press of their hand. Yet with her... he had. Her illusions had substance, presence, as if she weren't only weaving lies from water and mind, but pulling something real through with them.

"No," he said finally. "I haven't seen that exactly. But I've seen… other things."

Her throat worked. "Ambigua."

He didn't confirm it. Didn't deny it. He simply held her gaze and let the word hang between them like a blade on a thread.

Talah folded her arms over her chest. "You think I'm one of them?"

"I think," Firas said slowly, "that the Imperium would like an excuse to say you are. That's all they ever need."

She swallowed hard. "Would you?"

He arched a brow.

"Would you believe I am?" she asked again, voice quieter now. "Would you trust me if I were?"

Firas studied her face. Every inch of him wanted to say yes. But the stakes were too high. The war too close. His people were still in danger. And she was still the daughter of a councilor— one who knew what was really going on. One who had always known. Talah was still tied to the Imperium, whether she wanted to be or not.

"I don't know," he said honestly. "But I want to."

Her lips parted. She didn't move away. Didn't recoil. And neither did he. Their silence folded in on itself, tighter and tighter, until there was nothing left between them but breath and the shared awareness of it. He watched her eyes flick to his mouth. Just once. Barely a shift. But it was enough.

Firas's voice dropped, rough at the edges. "You should sleep."

"I'm not tired."

"Doesn't matter. You need it."

She didn't argue. But she didn't leave either. And neither of them moved—just stood there, a hand's breadth apart, tethered by something neither of them had words for yet.

Firas cleared his throat, breaking the tension before it snapped. "You can stay. Just for tonight."

Talah gave a small nod, then looked away. "Thank you."

Firas said nothing as he turned toward the door, closing it behind him with a soft click, the weight of it sinking into the stone. The corridor outside was quiet. Empty. But the air still felt heavy—saturated with the echoes of what had just passed between them. Firas ran a hand down his face.

You can't afford to feel this way.

Not when he still didn't know what she was. Not when the cost of guessing wrong could get people killed.

He turned down the hall, his footsteps muted against the old runner stretched along the floor. Every shadow along the way felt sharper tonight. Every creak in the beams more intrusive.

Kamaria's quarters were tucked away in the southeast wing, where most mentors never bothered to tread. Close enough to respond fast. Far enough that she could vanish without drawing attention. He didn't knock, instead choosing to slip through the door and found her exactly where he expected—sitting cross-legged on her bed waiting for him as she sharpened one of her blades. She didn't bother to look up.

"You always enter rooms like a ghost," Kam said. "One day I'm going to throw a dagger before asking who it is."

Firas leaned against the doorframe. "If you missed, I'd be disappointed."

Kam snorted. "You sound like hell."

"I feel worse."

That made her glance up. Her expression shifted, something close to concern, if Kam ever allowed herself such things. "Did something happen? After?"

He didn't answer right away, closing the door behind him, and dropping into the chair across from her.

Kam studied him, shifting on the bed. "Did you take her to your room?"

Firas nodded once. "She's sleeping now. Or trying to."

Silence settled between them for a beat.

"I think she might be one of us."

Kam's brow lifted slightly.

"But I'm not sure."

She leaned back against the wall, the lamplight flickering across the lines of her collarbone and the long scar down her shoulder. "We all saw what she did to the Mirror. But that doesn't make her Ambigua, Fi."

"Then what would that make her?" Firas snapped. "She's not just a Signborn, Kam. She's... something else."

Kam's fingers resumed drumming lightly on her knee, the tempo steady and sharp. "So, what—you think she's a different kind of Ambigua?"

"I—I don't know," he admitted. Firas rubbed the side of his jaw, exhaustion threading through his words. "Her father is one of the highest-ranking men in the Imperium. Maybe he was hiding her away for a reason. Maybe he knew and was protecting her."

Kam scoffed. "You don't know that for sure. This is all just speculation."

Firas arched a brow. "You think she would turn on us if we told her the truth."

"She could be watching you, us, anyone they think is Ambigua," Kam said carefully. "The Imperium's not stupid. Maybe they decided to start using spies now instead of just outright killing us off."

"Perhaps," Firas admitted. "Or she could not know. Same as I did once."

Kam's voice sharpened. "Except you weren't the child of the man who signs execution orders for Ambigua."

"No... I was just the prodigal son of one who carries those orders out," Firas snapped. Kam looked away, jaw clenching. She was quiet for a moment, fingers drumming against her wrist.

"I'm not blind," he said, quieter now. "But she's not the same girl who entered the Trials. Something's changed in her. And we don't know yet what she's going to become." Firas looked down at his hands. He could still feel the way her body had shaken in his arms. The way she'd looked at him—like she wanted to believe she wasn't alone. Like she wanted someone to see her and not turn away.

"You need to be sure before you tell her the whole truth," Kam warned. "Or else you'll put all of us at risk."

"She's not ready," he said. "She's not ready for the truth just yet."

"None of us were."

TALAH
XXXVII

The morning air was brittle, like the night had seeped into her skin and refused to leave.

The halls of the dormitory were quiet. Too quiet. There was no usual buzz of morning drills or competitors dragging themselves to breakfast with bruised egos and half-buttoned tunics. No idle chatter. Just silence. Heavy. Expectant. Her steps felt louder than they should have. Every scuffed sole on the tiled floor, every exhale. The soft ache in her ribs pulsed with the rhythm of her footsteps. The sound pressed against her ears until it became something close to guilt. She hadn't slept. Not really. Just closed her eyes and drifted somewhere too shallow to find rest.

Every time she closed her eyes, the image came back—the Mirror shattering around her, the sound of it breaking like the crack of bone. The way the air had shifted afterward, humming low in her chest as though something inside her had answered.

She didn't know what she was anymore.

Mazin's room was at the far end of the east wing, tucked

between old pillars and beneath a drafty window that always smelled of dust and sun-warmed stone. She paused outside the door. Her hand hovered just above the wood, fingers curling once.

What if he sees it? The thought lodged deep, sharp and cold. What if he looks at her and knows she's not like them anymore? Talah drew in an unsteady breath and knocked.

For a moment, there was no answer. Then the door creaked open. Mazin stood there barefoot, hair a tousled mess, dark circles bruised under his eyes. He wore the same shirt from yesterday, the collar wrinkled, sleeves rolled haphazardly to his elbows. He looked like he hadn't slept—or hadn't bothered trying.

She wanted to say something, anything, but her throat felt tight. The silence between them carried too much—fear, guilt, and something dangerously close to relief that he was still here, still human, when she wasn't sure she was anymore.

He said nothing as he stepped aside, leaving the door open. Talah looked around as she entered. The dorm was dim, the shutters still drawn. One bed, the one closest to the door, was slept in and unmade, sheets tangled like a storm had passed through. The other bed across the room was perfectly still. Too still. Blankets smoothed. Pillow untouched. Talah's gaze lingered there.

Mazin followed it with his own, then sat heavily on the edge of his bed, elbows on his knees. "They said he didn't make it," he said, voice flat.

Talah stayed near the door, as if crossing into the space fully would make it more real. "Did he...?"

"They said he broke," Mazin went on. "Mentally. From the Mirror. Just—snapped. The soldiers said he used his belt." His jaw tightened. "He went before... before whatever happened with you."

She moved toward the opposite bed, drawn despite herself, and stopped just shy of it. The silence around it was suffocating. No shoes lined up beneath it. No robe draped on the footboard.

Just absence.

He didn't break, Talah thought bitterly. *They killed him. They killed him and lied to cover it up.*

"I didn't know him that well," Mazin said, interrupting her thoughts. "He mostly kept to himself." His voice cracked slightly. "I didn't even notice he was gone until after I came back."

Talah sat on the edge of the tidy bed without thinking, staring at the indent of a head that would never rest there again.

"What did you see?" he asked, voice low. "What happened to you yesterday?"

Talah let out a bitter exhale, like the question had been waiting. "Nothing dramatic," she said. "No monsters. No bloody corpses. Just... me."

He frowned. But when she gave no further explanation, he went on. "I was afraid when it would be my turn," Mazin said, voice hoarse. "I was so afraid that it would show my worst fear. Standing on the sidelines. Watching everyone else do something that mattered. Watching you, Zayd, Adine—all of you survived because you had something I didn't." He glanced away, jaw tightening. "And every time I would try to fight—try to help—I would just be in the way."

Talah's chest ached. "That wouldn't have been true."

He gave a faint, crooked smile. "It would be if it was in the Mirror."

They sat in the quiet for a moment. Dust hung motionless in the air, catching stray shafts of light from the crack in the shutters. The room smelled faintly of cold ash, sweat, and the citrusy tang of the soap Mazin always used—sharp, clean, stubbornly persistent. The same scent that used to cling to the collars of his tunics back when they were kids.

Talah glanced down at her hands. They were clenched in her lap. Still scraped from where she'd caught herself on the arena floor. Still faintly stained from the Mirror. "I said I didn't need your protection. Before," she said finally, her voice low and uneven. "But I didn't mean that I didn't need you."

Mazin didn't look at her right away. He ran a hand through

his hair before letting it fall with a sigh. The sound that came from him was something between a breath and a hollow laugh. "I know," he murmured. "You were angry. But you weren't wrong."

She shifted beside him on the bed, the mattress creaking beneath their weight. The blanket between them was coarse under her palms, stiff with disuse. When she looked at him again, she saw the faint curve of a bruise just below his collarbone, the mottled bloom of a scrape along his jaw. For a moment, sitting there—shoulders brushing, silence stretching—it felt like it used to. Before the Trials. Before the weight of death. Before they both learned what it meant to survive.

Mazin moved slightly until their knees touched. "I wasn't trying to make you feel small," he said. "I just... didn't know what else to do. You were slipping away, and I thought maybe if I stepped in, I could prove myself to you."

Talah closed her eyes. The ache behind them hadn't gone since the Mirror. "I don't want you to throw yourself between me and the world," she said softly. "I don't need a shield. I need my best friend, Maz."

Mazin nodded and offered a quiet, tired smile—the kind that didn't quite reach his eyes. "That's what you'll have in me," he said. "Your best friend."

Their shoulders brushed again. This time, Talah didn't pull away. The warmth of him was steady. Human. Grounding. It cut through some of the cold still clinging to her from the Mirror, anchoring her to something solid, something real.

He looked over at her, but she kept her eyes forward, focused on the stillness of the room. On the bed across from her, too neat. Too silent. On the hollowness that had been echoing inside her chest since she'd touched that obsidian gate.

"You still don't really understand what you saw in there, do you?" he asked quietly.

She shook her head once, then stilled. "No. But I know it didn't lie." Her throat tightened. "I don't know if what I saw was me... or something I'm becoming."

Mazin said nothing, his hand extending into her line of sight—open, steady, waiting. Talah stared at it for a moment before placing her hand in his. His fingers gently closed around hers. Their hands stayed clasped for longer than she meant them to. The warmth of his skin seeped into hers, but it couldn't reach deep enough to melt the chill that still lingered beneath the surface, bone-deep, like something that had taken root since the Mirror.

Talah stared at the far wall, at nothing in particular. "There was a version of me in there," she said quietly, "and she wasn't angry. Or scared. Or trying to survive."

Mazin didn't speak. He just listened, the way he always did.

"She was powerful," Talah continued, voice barely above a whisper. "Unflinching. Certain. She looked at me like I was the weaker one. Like I was the version that needed to be erased." She let go of his hand slowly, curling her fingers back into her lap. Her palms felt too empty. "I didn't want to fight her," she said. "I didn't want to become her either."

The silence between them thickened. "I keep thinking about what she said. About how I keep pretending this is about proving something, when it's not. Not really."

Mazin shifted beside her, just slightly, but didn't interrupt.

"I don't even know who I am anymore," she admitted, blinking hard. "I thought I did. Before the maze. Before the second trial. Before the Mirror. But now..."

Her voice trailed off. All she could hear was the soft creak of the dormitory shifting around them, wind whispering through the cracked shutters.

"I don't know what I'm becoming," she finished.

Mazin looked at her for a long moment. She could feel the weight of it, even without turning her head. But she wasn't sure she could meet his eyes. Not when she was still afraid of what he might see in hers. Not when she was still afraid and angry. He would see it—all of it. Talah stood slowly, suddenly needing space. Mazin rose too, slower, rubbing the back of his neck as he glanced toward the shuttered window. Light filtered in through the slats, casting soft gold lines across the worn floor and the edge of his bed.

"You know," he said, his voice unusually quiet, "regardless of who you become, or who you were, I wouldn't trade a single version of you for anyone else."

Talah blinked. Her heart gave the smallest lurch, but her thoughts moved past it too quickly, still wrapped in the fog of everything else. The compliment slid over her like cool water. Kind. Safe.

She offered a faint, grateful smile. "You always know how to say the right thing."

Mazin didn't correct her. He just smiled back and looked down at his hands. Talah hesitated near the door. She could still feel the echo of his fingers in hers, the quiet warmth of their shared stillness. For a moment, she almost said something more. But instead, she murmured, "Thank you."

He looked up, brow furrowing just slightly. But he didn't ask what for. He only nodded once.

She stepped into the corridor, pulling the door softly shut behind her. The sound echoed faintly down the empty hallway, swallowed quickly by silence.

XXXVIII TALAH

The sky above Aphelion was clear the next night. No storm. No fog. Just stars—sharp and bright like someone had taken a blade to the dark and let the constellations bleed through. Their glow made the rooftop look colder, cleaner. Like the Trials hadn't stained her world in blood and fear.

Talah climbed the narrow stairwell past the top floor of the dormitories, muscles aching with each step. The sandstone under her bare feet was still warm from the day's heat, radiating faintly through her boots, reminding her cruelly that the world kept turning. They were already there, waiting for her.

Adine sat cross-legged on the low wall, her hair tied in a loose knot, chin tilted toward the sky as if daring the stars to fall. Zayd lounged on a pile of mismatched cushions, chewing on something that looked questionably stolen. Mazin leaned against one of the pillars, arms folded. He still looked tired in a way that sleep couldn't touch. But when he saw her, he gave the smallest nod.

The scent of baked citrus drifted up from the lower

orchards, tangled with ash and old dust—smoke in the bones of the building. The rooftop was half-lit by lanterns set in old brass bowls. They flickered in the breeze, casting long shadows across the stone, making the lines of her friends' faces look softer. Older. Like they'd all aged years in the span of a few weeks. And maybe they had. No one spoke as she joined them, dropping down beside Zayd, letting the cool air skim over her shoulders. The stone felt too cold under her thighs, and her breathing still caught when she wasn't thinking about it.

Zayd nudged her knee, offering her a silver flask. "You've got that 'freshly haunted' look. Mirror chew you up and spit you back out?"

Talah sniffed the flask before almost gagging. "I feel worse."

"Well, you don't look dead yet. Though it looks like something tried really hard to kill you off." Zayd shrugged, tipping the flask full of araq back against his lips.

"Are we not going to talk about what actually happened?" Adine looked around at the three of them. "Tal, you *broke* the Mirror. What in the stars happened?"

"I don't know," Talah whispered.

"How do—"

"Adine." Mazin's voice cut through the air.

They fell silent again. Just the wind and the stars above them, humming with things none of them dared say aloud. Adine's lips pursed, a look of frustration crossing her face. Talah knew she wouldn't let it go for long, but she was thankful it was let go for now. Zayd passed Mazin the flask, wiping the back of his hand against his mouth.

"It's almost over," Mazin murmured, breaking the silence. He sipped from the bottle, making a face as the araq burned down his throat.

"Or we are," Zayd added. "Depending on how tomorrow goes."

Adine flicked a crumb at him. "Not helping."

"It's true, though." Zayd leaned back on his elbows, gazing upward. "Think about it. One more trial. One more test. And then either we win, or we don't."

Talah reached across Zayd for the flask. Mazin silently handed it over to her without judgment for once.

"Do you even care anymore?" Talah asked quietly.

Zayd shrugged. "About winning? Sure. About what that even means anymore? Not really."

Mazin tilted his head toward the stars. "We came here to prove something."

Guilt pricked at Talah's conscience. *She'd* come here to prove something. But Mazin? He'd followed her across the sea just to support her. He had nothing to prove back then. He was perfectly fine living in Jawahra with her. It had been *her* who had dragged him here to this farce of a competition that might get him killed.

Talah's throat was dry, her voice nearly a rasp. "Why do they even still have the Trials?" All three sets of eyes turned toward her. "I mean, why can't they just give us one test to be admitted?"

"Because that would be too easy," Zayd joked.

"I'm being serious," Talah replied curtly. "Why do they do this? Why do they let people sacrifice themselves just to get into this university?"

Adine's mouth opened once before snapping shut. Mazin looked away, out over the roof's low walls. Zayd looked confused.

"There has to be a reason," Talah insisted.

"Maybe the reason is simple," Adine said finally. "Loyalty. I mean, is this not the greatest test of loyalty there is? To lay your life on the line? To sacrifice?"

"But for what?" Talah pressed.

"Why are you asking this now?" Mazin cut in, his gaze snapping to hers. "You didn't seem to have a problem with it before."

The guilt embedded itself deeper in her heart. "I was... just thinking about it. That's all."

"Is it?" Mazin's head tilted to the side.

Talah forced herself to hold Mazin's gaze, though her pulse drummed hard in her throat. "I just keep wondering if the Trials aren't really about loyalty at all. Maybe they're about... something else."

"Like what?" Zayd asked, leaning forward.

Her mouth felt dry. "Like finding people who don't... fit. Who aren't the way they're supposed to be."

Adine frowned. "You mean the weak ones. The ones who can't handle it."

"Or the different ones," Talah murmured, taking another sip of araq. It burned through her, giving her a false sense of strength.

Mazin's brow furrowed. Zayd tilted his head, studying her. But it was Adine who answered first.

"What do you mean by *different*?" Adine asked, her voice sharp with suspicion.

"You know what I mean."

"No," she snapped. "I don't. Please explain." When Talah fell silent, Adine scoffed. "Well, I'll say it if you won't. You mean the Ambigua, don't you?"

"And what if I am?" Talah challenged, lifting her chin.

"They're monsters, Talah. Abominations." Adine sneered. "They killed my brother."

"That doesn't—"

"My brother was stationed in the Earth Province," Adine said. Her hands had gone still in her lap. "A patrol went out. None of them returned."

The stars above Talah started to blur. "Adine, I—"

"Don't," Adine snapped. Her jaw tightened, but her voice cracked beneath it. "The Imperium tries to shield people from the truth, but those *things* don't just break the law. They destroy lives. Families. *My* family. If the Imperium is using the Trials to hunt for Ambigua, I say let them. Those of us who are innocent have nothing to hide."

Zayd finally spoke, his tone edged with conviction. "They've been attacking for years. Sabotaging caravans, poisoning wells, burning settlements. My father said they twist everything—turn villages against the Imperium with lies, stir rebellion in the provinces. If the Trials weed them out before they infiltrate Aphelion... maybe that's the point."

"Or maybe that's what they just want us to think," Talah said softly.

Adine's eyes narrowed. "You think the Imperium just makes this up? That my brother's death is just some story?"

"They're not misunderstood victims, Tal," Mazin said, shooting her a strange look. "They're killers that can hide in plain sight."

Talah's hands curled into the fabric of her robe. "But not all of them," she said. "Not every Ambigua is like that."

"You don't know that," Adine scoffed.

"Neither do you." Adine opened her mouth, but Talah didn't let her respond. "I just keep thinking... We're here risking our lives for a system that might not be entirely honest with us. Should we just blindly follow what the Imperium says without ever questioning it?"

"That's what loyalty means, in case you didn't already know," Adine replied. "And what you're talking about sounds dangerously close to sedition." She stood without waiting for an answer, sweeping from the rooftop without another word. They watched her go in silence.

"Why are you asking all this now?" Mazin asked again, voice tight.

"Because tomorrow," Talah said, "we'll either survive or we won't. And I'd like to know if we're still dying for the right reasons."

Silence pressed down on them. Even the stars seemed unwilling to bear witness.

Her throat burned as she tipped back the last of the araq, letting it scorch a path down to her stomach. The warmth settled heavily in her veins, a poor shield against the chill gnawing deeper inside her. She rose before anyone could answer, before anyone could look at her too closely.

She had believed the stories once, every word the Imperium fed them about loyalty and sacrifice and order. But that seemed like a century ago now. By the time Talah reached the stairs, the wind had picked up, tugging her hair loose, pulling at her like it wanted to strip her bare. It scraped across her skin like memory—coarse and sharp and cold. The warmth from her friends had faded too quickly, leaving only the press of their words behind.

She crept down the back stairwell, through the silent halls that always seemed too still the night before a trial, and past the mural of the Zodiac wheel etched in ancient lapis and gold. Past her own door. Past sleep she knew she probably needed. The araq still burned low in her stomach, her senses dulled by its toxicity. She staggered forward, every thought, every feeling, warring inside her.

Now that I know the truth… I can never go back.

That thought alone had her nearly gasping for air. Her lungs constricted, her hands shaking as she walked, the chill battling with the heat from the alcohol. The councilors, her *father*, perhaps other Starborn parents, were all complicit.

They were all murderers.

The corridor outside his quarters was darker than the rest—lit only by a single lantern burning low, its light flickering against the carved archway. Her pulse stuttered as she stood before it, the weight of what she was doing crashing in all at once.

Why am I here?

But her hand lifted anyway. Knuckles tapped against wood. The door opened a heartbeat later.

Iras stood shirtless, a thin linen wrap slung loose across his shoulders. His dark hair was damp, curling faintly at the ends. He didn't look surprised to see her. Only tired. And wary. Like something in him had already guessed this was coming.

"Talah."

His voice was lower than usual, rough from exhaustion, or drink, or something deeper she couldn't name. She opened her mouth. Closed it again. The world tilted slightly beneath her.

"I couldn't sleep," she said finally.

Iras stepped aside. "I couldn't either. Are you drunk?"

She slipped past him, and the door clicked shut behind her. "Of course not," she snapped.

The room was just as she remembered it: sandstone walls, bare floor, no personal items. The smell of parchment and myrrh lingered, threaded now with the faint trace of whatever he'd washed in—something sharp and clean and distinctly him. Talah stood in the center, arms crossed. Trying not to shake.

Iras watched her from the threshold for a long moment. "You smell like it," Iras noted.

"I didn't judge you before," Talah reminded him, leaning against his wall. The smooth surface steadied her, keeping the world beneath her feet. "I see it when I close my eyes," she whispered. "Everything. Rayen. Nadir. The Mirror."

Iras sighed, leaning one shoulder against the wall beside her, arms crossing. "I wish I could tell you that it gets better."

She shook her head, her breathing sharp. "What if I'm becoming something I hate? What if this is making me into a monster?"

His silence was worse than any answer. But then he spoke softly. So softly she almost didn't hear him. "Monsters don't worry about things like that."

Her eyes burned. She hated this. Hated feeling weak in front of him. But more than anything, she hated the fact that she didn't want to be alone right now. Not with her thoughts. Not with her memories.

Not with the truth.

"I don't know who I am anymore," she said, her voice breaking on the edges. "Or who I'll be tomorrow."

Iras stepped closer. Slowly. Carefully. He reached out—but didn't touch her. Not yet. Just let his hand hover beside her elbow. A silent offer. A gravity between them.

"Only you can decide who you become," he said.

Talah looked up. There was something in his eyes—something raw. Wounded. She didn't know what it was. Didn't want to name it. Didn't want to shatter this thin sliver of space between them with logic or fear. So she stepped forward. Not much. Just enough to feel the heat coming off him in waves.

Iras didn't move. Didn't speak.

And still—somehow—it felt like he was bracing for something far more dangerous than a fight. His breath hitched as she stopped just shy of his chest. Close enough to feel the frayed edges of his restraint, the taut coil in his shoulders, the way his pulse jumped just beneath his collarbone.

Talah's fingers trembled as they found the edge of his shirt. She didn't even realize she'd reached for it until her knuckles brushed the curve of his ribs, the fabric warm from his skin. She gripped it—lightly, then tighter. Just to keep her hands from shaking. Just to prove to herself that she was still here. That this was real.

Her voice cracked when she said it. "I don't want to die."

Iras's hand came up slowly, like he was afraid to spook her, and brushed a curl from her temple. His touch lingered, brief but electric.

"I won't let them kill you, Aasifati," he said, voice low and steady. "Not tomorrow. Not ever."

Her chest fractured around the words. And before she could stop herself, before the fear caught up to her, she rose onto her toes and kissed him. It wasn't soft. It was ragged and real and desperate, the kind of kiss born from everything they hadn't said, everything they couldn't name.

Talah poured all of it into that moment—the fire, the fear, the ache in her chest that hadn't stopped. The need to be touched without breaking, to be held without being protected, to feel something that wasn't pain or power or silence.

Iras froze for a breath, hesitating. Then his mouth moved against hers with a barely controlled desperation. His hands found her hips, pulled her in like he couldn't stand even an inch of distance. Her fingers slid into his hair, anchoring herself to him, breath hot between them as they moved together— uncertain and hungry and completely undone.

The room spun around them, light and shadows and starlight outside the narrow window, forgotten. Talah tilted her head, deepening the kiss. Iras responded in kind, and for a moment—just a moment—she wasn't afraid. He tasted of anise and resolve. Like something wild restrained.

When they finally broke apart, her lips tingled and her hands were still buried in his hair. Their foreheads pressed together, breath shallow and ragged between them. His gaze burned into hers—quiet, searching, like he was still trying to understand what she was becoming. Or what he already knew. Talah stared back, chest heaving, heart racing.

"I shouldn't have let you do that. Not when you're... like this," Iras said breathlessly. "I'm sorry."

"Don't." Talah shook her head slightly. "I'm not sorry. This might be the realest thing here so far."

For an instant, his eyes betrayed something she couldn't pin down, then shuttered closed again. He allowed her to stay there, caught between one heartbeat and the next, wondering if anything would ever feel this real again.

Talah let the steadiness of his breath anchor her frayed edges. But even as the warmth of his touch lingered on her skin, another feeling crept in beneath it—quiet and cold. A thread of doubt. There were still things he hadn't said. Secrets curled behind his eyes like smoke, and no matter how tightly she held on, she could feel the distance in him like a blade tucked behind his back.

She wanted to believe every word he said. Stars help her, she really wanted to. But trust was a fragile thing, and she couldn't shake the fear that letting him in might cut her deeper than keeping him out.

XXXIX FIRAS

They stood too close. Breathing the same air, sharing the same silence. Her hands slipped from his chest, but she hadn't stepped back just yet. And he... he hadn't moved at all.

The warmth lingered against his skin like an echo. Her breath still caught on his collarbone, ghosting hot through the fabric. He could feel the electricity still humming between them—raw, unfiltered, like a fraying wire in his ribs. He wanted to touch her again. Stars, he wanted to.

But worse, he wanted to tell her the truth. To tell her everything.

The weight of it pressed behind his teeth like iron despite knowing he couldn't—*shouldn't*—risk it. She was the daughter of a councilor, a part of the world that wanted to completely eradicate people like him. Despite how he was starting to feel about her now...she wasn't one of them. Yet.

He studied her; her lashes still damp, mouth slightly parted, chest rising in uneven pulls. Her whole body trembled with something between grief and fury. She'd kissed him like it might be the last thing she'd ever get to choose. And maybe it was. Maybe tomorrow would take that away, too.

Guilt plagued him. It seeped into every crevice, every blackened and bitter part of his soul. He could still smell the alcohol on her, knew this had been a terrible, terrible choice.

"I shouldn't have—" he started again, but she shook his head, cutting him off.

"No," she said, voice low. "You don't get to take that back."

Their eyes locked.

"I wish I could explain," Firas murmured, voice tighter now. "What this place does. What it's done to people like me. To people like—"

He stopped himself. Too close. Too soon.

Talah tilted her head slightly. Waiting.

He turned away from her before he cracked. Crossed the room in three sharp steps and braced both palms against the cedar shelf, its edges digging into the heels of his hands. The air in the room tasted dry—old parchment and ash, sweat and ghosted incense. A wind brushed in from the open slit in the stone, cool against the fire burning through him.

"I didn't come back to Aphelion just to play mentor," he said finally. "I didn't come here for favor or rank. I came back because I know what you, what all of you, are going through. And I just couldn't sit back and watch it destroy others like it almost destroyed me." He turned just enough to see her silhouette against the lamplight. "If you knew the truth…"

Talah had her arms wrapped around herself now, almost like armor. Her shoulders hunched slightly, but her chin was still high. Defiant even now.

"And what truth is that, exactly?"

His eyes caught hers as he gave a hollow laugh. "Every time I look at you, I see a reflection of what I used to be. Someone who might actually be worth saving. I've almost forgotten what that felt like."

Silence stretched between them, taut and waiting. Like a held breath. Firas took a step closer. Just one. "Whatever happens tomorrow," he said, "remember who you were before this place tried to define you. And remember that you don't owe them anything—not your loyalty, not your mercy."

Her gaze flicked over him, measured and uncertain. "You talk like you know what they're going to do to us tomorrow."

His mouth twitched. "I know exactly what they're capable of."

She stepped toward him then, the space between them charged again, like flint brushing steel. And for a second, he thought she'd ask. Ask what he meant. Ask what he was. Ask why he looked at her like he already knew the answer to a question she hadn't voiced.

But she didn't. Her breath hitched, shallow and uneven, as if her lungs no longer trusted the air. Her gaze locked on his, wide and burning, and he could almost feel the storm gathering behind it. Her hands curled tight at her sides, nails biting into her palms, shoulders rigid as though bracing against a blow only she could feel.

She looked carved from stone, unyielding—until he caught the tremor in her lip, the slight shake at the edge of her stance. Fury and fear warred in her eyes, glinting sharp as steel, but beneath it all he glimpsed the fracture lines splintering through her. She was holding herself together like a dam straining against the flood, every muscle taut, every thread pulled tight.

Firas knew exactly what she felt. He'd had his entire world ripped out from under him before. He reached for her hand, threading his fingers through hers—not just holding on, but anchoring her to the floor, to him, to something steadier than the chaos clawing at her chest.

"You'll make it through tomorrow," he said, voice low and unwavering.

Talah blinked, searching his face. "You don't know that."

His thumb brushed over her knuckles, slow, deliberate, as if the motion alone could steady her pulse. "No," he said. "You're right. I don't know what tomorrow holds. But I know this—I won't let them take you from me."

Her lips parted, breath catching, but no words came.

"They can drag us through blood and fire. They can strip everything else away." His voice roughened with something raw. "But they will not touch you. Not while I still draw breath."

"You shouldn't say things like that," she whispered, her voice breaking on the edge of the plea.

He didn't mean for the words to be loud. He meant them as a promise, a warning, a dark blessing. But the steadiness surprised even him — the fierceness that rose without asking permission. He realized, with that sudden, awful clarity, that the thought of someone breaking her again lit something like a brand inside his ribs.

"I don't care," he murmured, leaning closer until his forehead almost touched hers. "Let them hear me. Let them try. I'd burn their world to ash before I'd watch them break you."

Her fingers tightened in his. Then curled into a fist. Talah took a step back, not much, but enough to put space between them.

"Don't," she said sharply. "Don't say things like that."

Firas blinked, caught off guard. Her words left him raw. He'd expected gratitude, fear, maybe acceptance: anything but this neat, furious refusal.

"You're not the first person to say they'd protect me," she said, voice trembling now. "You won't be the last. But that's not what I need. I don't need someone to throw themselves in front of me like I'm fragile. Like I'm something to be saved." Her voice rose just slightly—tight and cracking at the edges. "That's what people always try to do. Step in. Intervene. Tell me I'm strong but treat me like I'm weak."

Anger flared—at himself, at the world that kept forcing choices on them both—but under the anger there was something worse: a hot, private shame. Of all the reasons he'd wanted to keep her close, most of them were selfish. She steadied him; when she broke, he broke. He was prone to making promises because the alternative, the thought of failing her, felt like a burden he couldn't bear.

She stepped closer again, jabbing the words between them like stakes. "I know how to fight. I have fought. I've bled. I've *killed*. I've survived things people said I couldn't. So don't stand there and tell me you'll protect me like I can't protect myself."

Firas stayed quiet for a breath. He let her spit the words like shrapnel, even if some of them hit him, too. He let her burn. And, stars help him, it was glorious.

"I'm not saying it because I think you need me," he said quietly. She stilled. "I know you can fight. I've seen it. You've survived more in these Trials than most ever will. You don't need a protector."

He took a slow step forward again, closing the distance. "I don't want to protect you because you're weak, Talah. I want to stand beside you because I can't bear the thought of you doing this alone."

Talah's breath hitched. Her throat worked, but no sound came.

"You don't need my protection," he continued. "But I'm still going to fight with you."

Something cracked behind her eyes then, something silent and old and fragile. She looked away, trying to blink it back. Her fists were still clenched.

"You don't know me," she said quietly. "And I don't know you. Not really."

Firas reached out slowly. Let his fingers brush the inside of her wrist. "Do you really believe that?"

"I should go," she whispered. Her voice was unsteady—not cold, not regretful, but full of something far more dangerous. Something that threatened to root itself in the hollow parts of his chest if he let it.

Firas didn't try to stop her. He didn't trust himself to speak. Instead, he simply nodded. As if anything louder might shatter whatever fragile, breath-held truce that existed between them.

She stepped back. The sound of her boots on the stone barely registered as he watched her walk away, heart thudding like distant hooves. Her silhouette flickered across the floor, swallowed by the soft torchlight beyond the corridor. Her braid swayed behind her shoulder like a trailing breath of ink, and she didn't look back.

He watched her until the shadows took her entirely.

And just like that—she was gone. The room felt emptier in her absence. Not just in presence, but in pressure, in heat, in gravity. As if her leaving had undone some quiet tension holding everything together. Firas stood motionless, the air cooling rapidly where her body had warmed the space between them.

Her scent still lingered. Smoke. And lavender. And that faint electric edge of power she didn't yet know how to control. The kind of power that lived just beneath the surface of her skin— bright and wild and terrifyingly beautiful.

His hand still tingled. The one that had held hers. It remembered the shape of her fingers. The way they'd curled, not in weakness, but in defiance of her own fear.

He flexed it once, then let it fall to his side.

Do not follow her.

She needed space. Distance. Time.

But stars, part of him ached to chase her. To drag her back just to hear her breathing again in the same room. To ask all the questions he couldn't afford to answer. To touch her, not because he was bracing her from breaking, but because he was already breaking himself. He let out a slow breath and started to close his door.

A shadow snapped from above the archway—black silk and steel, silent as death. Firas ducked just in time, the blade meant for his throat slicing the edge of his shoulder instead. He hissed in pain and rolled, crashing into a low shelf stacked with ancient tomes. Wood splintered. Books thudded around him like falling stones.

Hasha.

Assassins. Imperium-trained. Cloaked in silence. Masked in bone and ink. Eyes like knives.

The first attacker dropped low, flickering into motion like

smoke. Firas barely blocked the second strike, twisting to his feet. Blood trickled down his arm, hot against his skin. His pulse thundered as the second Hasha slipped through the doorway behind the first, moving with unnatural grace with no armor, with only shadows and the curve of a hooked blade. Her mouth was covered, but her eyes gleamed with feverish purpose.

He dove low, sliding across the sandstone floor to the edge of his bed, hand shooting beneath the frame. His fingers brushed the familiar leather strap of the satchel tucked into the hollow space, then curled around cold hilts. Twin daggers, curved and blackened steel, obsidian-inlaid, balanced for speed more than power. He yanked them free in one swift motion.

Dust clung to his skin as he spun to meet the next strike. One blade blocked high, metal shrieking against metal, as the other slashed low, slicing across cloth and skin. The assassin hissed, staggering back a step, but not enough.

Firas was already moving again. He rolled to his feet, blades flashing, blood slick on his arm and pooling fast where the first strike had caught him. His pulse pounded in his ears, faster now. He hadn't been attacked like this since the ambush in the Earth Province.

Back then, he'd made a mistake.

Not this time.

Another figure darted through the shadows—a third assassin, this one wielding twin daggers curved like scorpion stingers. Firas grabbed a heavy book from the wreckage beside him and hurled it. It slammed into the man's face, staggering him, but not downing him.

Three against one, with more shadows moving in the hallway.

Stars, he thought grimly, *they sent the whole godsdamned cell.*

He crouched, blades ready. His blood dripped to the floor, trailing behind him like splattered stars. His lungs burned. His shoulder ached where the first blade had torn through muscle. His fingers were starting to cramp from how tightly he gripped the hilts.

And still—he didn't run. Because running would've meant

dying slower.

The Hasha came again. This time, two at once—one from the front, another circling to flank. Firas met them with a roar and a blur of steel. He caught the first assassin's wrist mid-swing, twisting brutally until he heard the joint pop, then slammed the pommel of his dagger into the man's jaw. Blood sprayed. But the second attacker was faster. A blade caught him across the ribs, shallow, but deep enough to draw fire through his nerves.

He staggered, reeling toward the wall. A third figure appeared in the doorway.

Kamaria's staff spun in a deadly arc, catching the flanking assassin square in the side. Bone crunched. He collapsed with a strangled gasp, and Kam didn't hesitate. She planted a boot on his chest and brought the end of her staff down like a war drum.

"Couldn't wait five minutes before pissing someone off?" she snapped at Firas.

Another Hasha lunged from the side, but a flicker of movement caught him mid-air. Raven appeared like a ghost made of smoke, her hands glowing faintly with shimmering light. The assassin turned just in time to see the illusion of three figures converging on him—too late to register the real one. The illusion collapsed as Raven sent a dagger whistling into the man's side.

"Next time," she hissed, appearing beside Firas, "maybe scream or something."

"I was about to," he grunted, swiping blood from his brow.

Rami followed last—he didn't have the blistering power of Raven or Kamaria, but he moved with the desperation of someone who knew how close survival always was to slipping away. His control over water was limited, being a Crossborn, but he used what he could—pulling moisture from the air just enough to send the man skidding. Then Rami was on him.

He slammed the Hasha into the wall with a shoulder-check, raw force and weight behind the hit. The plaster cracked. He kneed the man in the gut, then drove an elbow into his throat with a grunt that came from somewhere deep. The assassin dropped.

For a breath, there was silence. The only sounds were the ragged panting of four fugitives and the slow drip of Firas's blood onto the floor. Until they heard more boots. More movement.

Kamaria's head snapped up. "They're regrouping."

"They won't let us out of here alive," Rami said, voice hoarse. "They were waiting for this."

"We need to leave," Raven snapped, already turning toward Firas. "You're bleeding out."

Firas staggered. His vision blurred for a breath, black edging the corners of his sight.

"I'm fine," he muttered, but his knees disagreed. "We can't leave..." His words slurred together.

Raven ignored him, grabbing his arm and pulling him toward her.

"I can get us out," she said, "but it's going to hurt."

"Just do it," Kamaria barked.

Raven's eyes flared. The air around them warped, the torchlight stuttering like a blown flame. Firas felt a cold wind coil around his spine, threading up through his ribs like ice—and then he was weightless. A tearing sensation dragged across his body like his skin was trying to separate from his bones.

They hit the floor. Hard.

Raven collapsed to one knee, clutching her side. Her skin was pale, damp with sweat. The teleport had nearly drained her. Firas coughed, blood sticking in his throat.

The scent hit him first—charcoal and leather, rosewater and brass. Then the familiar creak of iron hinges. The warmth of firelight licking low across sandstone walls. They were in the safe house. One of their oldest. One of their last. It lay hidden deep within the heart of Astrome's lowest quarter, hidden behind the façade of a closed apothecary. The floor was layered with threadbare rugs. Shelves full of bottles and wrapped satchels lined the walls. The windows were sealed.

Kamaria dropped her staff with a grunt and strode toward the front door. "I'm going to check to see if it's clear. Just in case."

Rami sank to the floor beside Firas, chest heaving. "What the hell was that?"

"The Hasha. They knew where I was," Firas said hoarsely. "They know what I am. They have to." He touched his side, winced. Blood soaked his wrap.

Firas's head dropped back against the wall. He could still feel Talah's fingers in his. Still smell her perfume on the burned edges of his clothes. If the Hasha had come for him tonight… how long before they went after her?

He exhaled hard.

"We need a new plan," he said.

Raven tossed a bloodied towel toward Firas and crossed her arms. "You're not going back there."

He didn't answer.

She stepped closer. "Firas. You almost died. You think they won't try again? You think that was the only squad?"

"They won't go for me again tonight," he said. "Not while they're still cleaning up their own mess. But they will go for her."

Raven nearly snarled. "So that's it now?" she asked, voice quiet and bitter. "You bleed out on your floor, we drag your half-dead body to safety, and all you can think about is *her*?"

"I'm thinking about what they'll do if they realize what she is before she does," he said.

"That's not your problem," Raven snapped. "She's not one of us. She could turn on us if she thinks it'll save her skin."

"She won't."

"You don't *know* that."

"I do." His voice cracked like stone.

Raven scoffed and crossed the room to the shelves—pretending to dig for something among the satchels. "You're making this too personal."

He didn't answer right away. Because she wasn't wrong. Firas stood, the towel clutched in one fist, stained red.

"This *is* personal," he said. "Because if you think I'll let the Imperium tear her apart while we sit here safe in the dark, then you don't know me at all. We still have a mission to complete. What is it we always say? For the lost, for the hunted, for those who refuse to fall. That includes her."

No one dared to say another word. And when Firas turned toward the door, the silence trailed behind him like a blade.

TALAH
XL

A sharp, biting wind met them the moment the carriage gates opened. It knifed through the thin fabric of their clothes, turned breath into mist, and sent goosebumps prickling up Talah's arms. She stepped onto the worn stone path with the others, blinking into the pale gray light.

They'd traveled to the edge of the forest. Not the gentle kind sung about in old lullabies. This one loomed. Massive trees, gnarled and overgrown, stretched high into a sky so overcast it looked carved from pewter. The trunks were thick as temple pillars, their bark split with age and black with old moss. Vines hung like nooses from the branches. Roots jutted from the soil in jagged veins. And through it all, a fortress rose from the trees like a scar—dark stone, spiked walls, watchtowers half-lost in the drifting fog.

Talah's boots crunched over the gravel, every step with too much finality. If she had to guess, they were north of Astrome and Aphelion. It had taken them hours to get here, with the sun starting to fade beyond the horizon.

Her fingers flexed, trying to ignore the tremor in them. Her body still hadn't recovered from the last trial. Neither had her mind. Even now, every so often, she caught the phantom flickers out of the corners of her eyes, reflections that moved just a second too late. A blur of her own face looking back at her.

Her powers hadn't stabilized since then. It was almost as if the Mirror hadn't just broken; it had broken something within *her*. Her illusions sometimes came uncalled, flashing like nerves misfiring—brief sparks of power that vanished before she could control them.

What if it happens again?
What if someone sees?

"You okay?"

Mazin appeared at her side, his steps quiet despite the gravel beneath their feet. He tucked his hands into his sleeves for warmth, his face pale from the cold. Despite shadowed eyes, he still gave her a small, tired smile.

"I'm not sure," she admitted. "Are you?"

Mazin huffed softly. "I stopped being sure around the first trial."

The others marched in a loose cluster in front of them, their movement subdued. Even Zayd kept his mouth shut. No one knew what the final trial would be, only that it was the end. That tomorrow some of them would no longer be competitors. They would be students.

Or dead.

"None of the other trials were outside of Aphelion," Talah murmured. "Let alone outside the city."

Mazin's brow furrowed. "Maybe it's something that can't be done within the walls of the school."

"Or maybe it's something they don't want the public to see."

Her breath came shorter now, each inhale tight with nerves. She glanced toward the front of the line where Khalias walked alongside several guards, all in black. His steps were smooth and confident. Like he knew exactly how this would end. Her thoughts drifted unbidden to Iras.

None of the mentors were present. At least not on their seemingly long walk to the fortress. Maybe they were already there.

She could still feel his hand in hers, his breath at her cheek. *I'd burn their world to ash before I'd watch them break you.*

Talah shook the memory away. She couldn't afford to be distracted now. Not when their final trial loomed ahead of her like a bad omen.

Ahead, the fortress gates creaked open with the sound of a hundred bones breaking at once. The wind picked up, the mist curling like fingers across the tree roots. Talah's heart beat faster, making it harder for her to breathe.

They were corralled into the main courtyard of the fortress like cattle, each step forward layered in dread. The trees surrounding the high walls loomed like silent sentinels, dark and ancient, their knotted trunks swallowing what was left of the morning light.

Around her, the others settled into place. Some were silent. Others whispered fervent prayers to the stars. Mazin stood beside her, face drawn, eyes distant. His shoulder brushed hers—whether for support or reassurance, she didn't know.

It didn't feel real. Not really.

But just as she saw them, the illusion cracked entirely.

The councilors stood on a raised arch above the gate, flanked by the guards in the Imperium's black and gold. Their abayas and thobes glinted like armor. Their eyes missed nothing. And among them...

Her heart ached.

Her father stood in his full regalia, ocean-blue silk banded with silver at the shoulder. The Pisces sigil shimmered. Regal. Composed.

Complicit.

He didn't look at her. Not once.

"Tal?" Mazin whispered.

She shook her head sharply. She was too focused on her father to register Kaed Soulinus had moved to his side. She had never met him personally, but she knew who he was. Everyone did.

He stood a full head taller than those around him, his frame lean but imposing, carved from angles and control. He wore no ostentatious robes like the councilors, only a dark tunic lined with silver thread, clean and severe. His black cloak hung straight as a blade down his back, unruffled even by the wind.

His hair, thick and dark as oil, was streaked at the temples with early gray. His beard was closely trimmed, jaw set like stone. But it was his eyes that caught her attention—the same dark color as Iras, only colder. Emptier. Eyes that didn't need to speak to command a room.

Kaed Soulinus radiated authority with every measured step, every glance that seemed to pin people in place. Like he could read the very shape of your fear before you'd even felt it yourself.

She forced her gaze from the Kaed, sweeping it along the elevated wall beside them where the mentors waited. Rows of black and gold uniforms, their faces half-obscured by shadows. But Iras wasn't there.

She checked again.

A cold needle slid between her ribs as her eyes raked over the row of mentors one last time. He said he'd stand beside her. That they'd face the storm together.

But he wasn't here.

Talah didn't know what twisted worse in her chest—the fear that something had happened to him or the fear that nothing had. That he'd chosen not to come. That his words had meant nothing. Her fingers curled into her sleeves, trying to hide the tremble.

Saahira Khatri stepped forward, her robes nearly translucent and stitched with gold thread that caught the minimum light like broken glass. Her white hair was coiled into an intricate knot, her expression as smooth and symmetrical as a sculpture carved by wind over time. Her voice rang out, cold and commanding.

"Competitors," she began, "you have proven yourselves in

combat, in cunning, in endurance. But strength of body and will are not enough."

Talah's body tensed, coiled with fear and foreboding.

Saahira lifted a pale hand, motioning around the courtyard. "The final trial is one of discernment. Of loyalty."

Behind them, a gate creaked open—low and metallic. The sound crawled under Talah's skin, wrong in the stillness. From the far side of the courtyard, soldiers emerged in black, dragging figures in chains. Talah's breath caught in her throat. The world seemed to narrow, sound folding in on itself until all she could hear was the dull scrape of chains across stone.

Some were bloodied. Some bruised. Most looked too dazed to stand. Their wrists were bound. Some had brands seared into their skin; others bore none. There were young ones. Older ones. A few barely older than her. She knew what they were. Her stomach twisted, a sharp, hollow ache. The smell of iron hit next—blood, sweat, smoke—turning her mouth dry.

Ambigua.

The word crashed through her like thunder. Her pulse roared in her ears, a hot, sick rush of disbelief and dread. Her fingers trembled where they hung at her sides, but she forced them still. She couldn't move, couldn't speak. Every instinct screamed to look away, yet she couldn't—because looking away would mean pretending she didn't know what was coming.

"These," Saahira continued, gesturing to the prisoners, "are traitors. Individuals who have hidden what they are. Who were marked for destruction the moment their gifts grew beyond control." Her voice didn't change. It never did. But her words cut deep. "They will be released into the forest with a two-minute lead."

Murmurs broke out in the crowd. Talah barely heard them.

"You will hunt them," Saahira said. "One for each competitor. If your quarry escapes... you will take their place."

Silence. The words hung in the air like the snap of a noose.

"None of them has the ability to teleport," Saahira assured them. "If you hesitate, if you fail, you will be deemed unfit. One life exchanged for another."

Talah's body went cold. Not just cold—frozen. Hollowed out, like someone had reached inside her chest and scraped everything clean.

Zayd gave a low, incredulous whistle. "She really said 'kill or die' with a smile on her face." His voice was dry, but there was no spark in his eyes. He kept glancing toward the tree line, fingers twitching as if they were already weighing how fast he could run—or fight.

Mazin said nothing. His arms were locked tight across his chest, face pale. But his throat moved as he swallowed, and the shadows under his eyes deepened. Adine's jaw was clenched, her posture rigid, arms folded like armor.

"They know what they are," she said at last. "They know what they've done."

Talah turned toward her, voice low, stunned. "They're not competitors. They're prisoners. You're acting like they had any choice in this."

Adine's expression hardened. "They're Ambigua."

"They're people," Talah snapped, louder this time.

"They're dangerous."

The words landed between them like a blade.

Zayd tried for levity again, his mouth tugging at the corners. "We've all killed to get here," he said, rolling a pebble beneath his sandal. "Just think of it like… one more fight." But his tone was forced. A little too light. A little too fast.

Talah's pulse pounded in her ears. She looked at Mazin.

He stepped closer, his voice low and almost gentle. "If you can't do it, I will," he said. "For you."

Talah stared at him—at all of them. Zayd, hiding his fear behind humor. Adine, refusing to meet her eyes now, gaze fixedly on the forest like she'd already made her decision. Mazin, whose mouth was a firm line but whose fingers trembled slightly against his sleeve. They would go through with it. Because they were terrified. Because they had no choice.

But she did.

"I won't kill them," she said, stepping back.

Adine spun toward her. "If you don't, you'll die."

Talah shook her head, her voice shaking. "There has to be another way."

"There isn't." Mazin's voice cracked. "You think I want this? You think I like this?"

"No," Talah said. "But you accept it. And that's just as bad."

Zayd exhaled, rubbing a hand over his face. "Look—no one's asking you to enjoy it. Just... survive it."

Her heart slammed against her ribs. Each beat sounded like a countdown. Talah turned her face to the trees beyond the wall. The shadows beneath the canopy stretched long, thick with waiting silence. The forest smelled of pine and moss and blood yet to be spilled. And somewhere in that fading afternoon light, people would be running for their lives.

Not threats. Not rebels.

People.

"I've already killed," she whispered, taking a step back. "I've already watched people die because of this place. I can't—" Her breath hitched. "I can't do it again. Not when they didn't choose this."

"You can," Mazin said, eyes wild. "You have to." He reached for her, hand outstretched.

Talah watched in disbelief as the prisoners were led toward the gate. Thin. Mud-streaked. Faces drawn. One stumbled, caught by another before hitting the ground. A woman with what looked like a broken wrist limped along, flinching as a soldier started for her. A boy—he couldn't have been older than fifteen—glanced back once.

Just once.

None of them had weapons. None of them had a chance. Every single one of them looked terrified. Because they knew.

They knew they were already dead.

Talah barely had time to draw breath before the walls began to tremble. The earth shook beneath their feet, rumbling throughout the fortress. Screams and cries rose up as stone splintered from the walls and rained down like jagged hail. Lanterns swung wildly on their chains, shadows jerking across the courtyard as if the night itself had teeth.

Figures tore through the darkness—shadows with fire in their veins and fury in their eyes. Some drove their hands into the earth and wrenched it apart, stone buckling as if it had turned to sand beneath their will. Others appeared in bursts of smoke and crackling light, teleporting past the iron gates with the weight of companions clutched to their arms, dragging the less able into the fight.

The rebels.

Their war cries echoed across the courtyard.

For the lost.

For the hunted.

For those who refuse to fall.

The soldiers guarding the prisoners barely had time to raise their swords before the first wave struck. Fire roared across the courtyard, swallowing men whole and leaving only ash where they had stood. Water surged in sudden walls, crashing against armored lines and tossing bodies like driftwood. A shriek of wind cut through the night, sharper than steel, slicing through spears and flesh alike.

Chains rattled and then shattered, the sound splitting the air like thunder. Prisoners stumbled forward, bloodied wrists still raw, until hands caught them—pulling, pushing, hurling them toward freedom.

The fortress dissolved into chaos.

Sand whipped up from nowhere, stinging Talah's skin like glass. Stone shards flew as the ground split wider, swallowing screaming soldiers into the black maw below. Flames clawed at the sky, painting the walls red and gold, turning the fortress into a furnace.

Talah could not move. She could only watch as the world tore itself apart, as power—unfettered, merciless—collided in every direction. Her ears rang with the clash of steel, the crack of lightning, the roar of fire, and the cries of the dying. Every breath was smoke and blood.

A voice broke through the violence, sharp and commanding. "For the Imperium!" Asad roared, raising his blade to the sky. The Aries Councilor vaulted from the walls, landing with a crack into the courtyard. "Competitors! Wield your blades and prove your loyalty. Desert us, and you will die as one of them."

The rest of the councilors stood elevated atop their arch, robes gleaming in the shifting light. The Sagittarius Councilor grabbed the three councilors closest to her and promptly disappeared, most likely teleporting to a safer location. The Capricorn Councilor vanished into thin air, using their invisibility to escape.

But Saahira and Musa stayed, watching over the chaos below them with eyes like cold steel.

TALAH
XLI

A round Talah, the others hesitated only a breath. Then steel scraped from sheaths, a chilling chorus that made her skin prickle, and the courtyard erupted with motion. Competitors threw themselves into the fray beside the soldiers, faces contorted in terror, rage, or the hollow hunger to prove themselves.

Adine was the first of them to move. Her braid snapped behind her as she charged, eyes blazing with a fury that had nothing to do with glory and everything to do with vengeance. She slammed her palms to the ground, and the cobblestones rippled like water before spearing upward in jagged walls of stone. The nearest Ambigua screamed as rock impaled their leg, blood slicking the stones before fire consumed the body whole.

Zayd split into two, then three, his copies surging forward with blades flashing silver. One was swallowed by a wall of fire, another cut down by a whip of water, but the real Zayd pressed on, his illusions scattering confusion in his wake. Air curled around him, sharp and fast, and he swung his sword with a snarl that made him look older than his years.

And Mazin—her Mazin—stepped in front of her. Shadows curled around him like a second skin, dark illusions taking form with teeth and claws. Competitors and soldiers alike flinched as the creatures lunged, snarling specters that tore into the Ambigua line. His twin curved blades gleamed in the firelight as he slashed through an enemy's side, his face twisted into something Talah barely recognized.

Her friends fought like their lives depended on it—because they did—while she could only watch as chaos swallowed the fortress whole.

"Tal!"

Talah threw herself sideways as a blast of fire split the air, roaring toward her. The heat seared her skin as it collided with the wall behind her, stone cracking and dust spilling around her. She coughed, vision swimming through the smoke, as another shape lunged from the haze, blade raised high.

Her body reacted before her mind could. She dragged the water from the air, a slick whip that snapped around the rebel's wrist, wrenching his blade aside. The Ambigua rebel snarled, but before he could attack her again, there was a flash of silver at his throat. Blood sprayed across the stones, warm and sharp-smelling. Talah staggered back, her heart hammering against her ribs as she stared at Mazin.

His chest heaved, arms shaking as blood ran down his blade, dripping to the ground. There was no remorse in his eyes, no sorrow or grief. Only relief.

"Are you alright?" he asked, reaching for her. "Are you hurt?"

Talah was about to answer when movement over his shoulder caught her eye. At first, it was only a figure in the chaos, moving with the Ambigua, cutting down soldiers with deadly precision. But when he turned, firelight struck his face—and her chest caved in.

The man who had helped her survive the Trials. Who had whispered those words in the dark, calming the storm raging inside of her. He was here, fighting *with them*. Every breath came like shards of glass.

"Iras!" The word tore from her throat, raw and disbelieving.

He froze, his eyes locking onto hers through the chaos. For a heartbeat, something flickered in his face—pain, hesitation—but it only fed the fury ripping through her.

"You—" Her voice broke, and she hated it, hated the crack that betrayed the storm inside. She shouldered past Mazin, anger surging through her veins. "You lied to me. You used me!" She hurled the accusation like a blade, her hand snapping out. Water surged from the shattered fountain beside her, crashing toward him in a torrent.

He raised his arm, fire blooming in answer, steam exploding between them as elements collided. The force rattled through her bones.

"I never lied to you!" he shouted back, straining against her attack. "I—"

"Don't you dare!" Her voice rang like steel, trembling with fury. She stepped forward, her power slamming harder, fueled by the betrayal tearing her apart. "You said you cared. You said—" Her throat burned. "And all this time, you were one of *them*?"

"I am not your enemy, Talah!" His words broke against the roar of the battle, desperate and ragged. He tried to step toward her, but she struck again, illusions spilling from her fingertips—snapping jaws of shadow and water, driving him back.

"You almost had me," she said, giving a bitter laugh. "You told me all of that... but you were hiding the truth this entire time."

His eyes burned in the smoke, dark and pleading. "No. Stars, Talah, no—"

But the word barely reached her. The world had narrowed to him—his face, his betrayal, and the gaping wound it had carved through her chest. The fortress was burning, soldiers and rebels screaming around them, but all Talah could hear was her own breaking heart.

Did he know about me? Why wouldn't he tell me the truth?

Talah's dagger was in her hand before she realized it, her

body moving as if it had always waited for this moment. She slashed at him, water coiling around the blade to sharpen its edge. Sparks flew when steel met steel, the clash ringing in her ears louder than the battle all around them.

"Was it all a game to you?" she spat, forcing him back with a vicious strike. The courtyard blurred—smoke, flame, shadows—only his face clear before her, a face she had trusted, leaned on, almost loved.

His eyes flinched at her words, but his hands did not falter. Fire licked his blade, his strikes fast and desperate, as if he were fighting her and himself all at once. "Talah, listen to me!"

"I *did* listen." She pressed harder, their blades locking. Her voice cracked, thick with fury and grief. "Every word. Every promise. And you—" She shoved him back, power exploding outward, a whip of water snapping against his chest. He staggered, his tunic blackening where it struck. "You lied!"

"I didn't lie!" His shout was raw, almost breaking, but she didn't care. She couldn't care.

"Did you know? About me?" Her dagger flashed again, fueled by the storm tearing inside her. Tears burned her eyes, hot against the smoke, but she blinked them away, refusing to let them fall. "*Did you know?* Or were you just waiting to use me?"

Was he going to use me against my father?

His fire met her water, steam engulfing them in a choking shroud. The heat singed her skin, her lungs burning as she coughed, but she didn't stop. Couldn't stop. Her fury was the only thing keeping her upright.

He surged through the haze, knocking her blade aside. His hand caught her wrist, grip bruising, his face inches from hers. His voice cracked, ragged with something more than desperation. "I was never going to use you, Talah. Stars, I—"

She wrenched free, fury igniting like a second heartbeat. Her power erupted—water slamming into him, illusions rising like shadows with teeth. They clawed at him, her anguish bleeding into every strike. "Don't you dare say you care. Not when you were hiding things from me."

The ground trembled beneath them, dust raining from the fortress walls as if the stones themselves recoiled from their war. A shadow fell across them. Heavy. Cold. A presence that made the air itself curdle.

The Kaed stepped through the smoke like a blade through flesh, towering, monstrous, the chaos bending around him as though even the elements bowed to his will. His voice carried above the roar, low and thunderous, cutting straight through her fury. But he wasn't looking at her.

"Firas." The Kaed's voice was iron, cold and unyielding, and the weight of that single name cracked the air around them.

The name slammed into her like a strike to the chest. She turned, blood roaring in her ears, to look at Iras—*Firas*—and in that heartbeat, she understood nothing at all except the shattering in her chest. Talah's blade faltered. Her chest clenched so tightly it hurt.

Firas.

She turned on him, fury and grief blurring her vision. "Firas?" Her voice broke, jagged as shattered glass. "That's who you are? That's who you've been this whole time?"

His face twisted, as if the word itself cut deeper than her blade. "Talah—"

The Kaed surged forward with the gravity of a storm, soldiers parting in terror as his cloak whipped behind him. His eyes—dark as obsidian, gleaming with command—fixed on the man Talah thought she knew. "You shame my blood every moment you draw breath," he hissed.

Firas's knuckles whitened around his sword hilt. He squared his shoulders, fire flickering along his blade as though daring to match the inferno in his father's gaze. "You lost the right to claim me the day you tried to kill me."

The Kaed's laugh was a thing of ash and cruelty. "I should have let you rot in the desert with your mother. Instead, you crawl back here to betray your blood and side with filth."

The truth snapped into place. His name echoed like a curse within her mind, a memory torn from whispers in shadowed corridors. The Kaed's son. The prodigy who should have won his Trials two years ago, the boy spoken of in hushed tones by apprentices and soldiers alike. He was meant to be unstoppable, the pride of his line—until he vanished. Some said he had been killed. Others claimed he had run. None knew for certain, only that the Kaed's heir had disappeared without a trace, leaving his legacy rotting like an open wound.

And here he was. Not dead. Not lost.

Her pulse thundered in her ears. Her vision blurred. She wanted to deny it, to shove the pieces away, but they fit too cleanly. *He was the Kaed's son. He had always been the Kaed's son.*

Bile rose at the back of her throat. All those moments she desperately wanted to let herself believe his words, his touch, those nights she'd wanted to trust him—poison.

The Kaed's roar dragged her back to the present, the sound more beast than human. His blade swung in a brutal arc, the ground shuddering beneath his strike as water exploded outward. Firas staggered but held, his face a mirror of defiance and pain. Father against son. Legacy against rebellion. And Talah stood frozen between them, the weight of betrayal crushing her chest.

The Kaed struck again, his blade coming down like a hammer, forcing Firas back to his knees. Sparks lit the air as steel ground against steel, Firas's sword trembling beneath the weight of his father's wrath. His fire guttered, sputtering weakly against the wave pressing down on him.

Talah's breath caught, but not from fear of the Kaed. Her chest ached with a deeper, sharper pain.

He knew.

Firas had always known what she was—what she wasn't. The way his eyes lingered when her power flickered out of control, the words he had left unsaid when she asked about Ambigua, the way he pushed her to see herself as more than Pisces. He hadn't been guiding her. He had been *measuring* her. Waiting.

And he hadn't told her the truth. Not once.

Because he wanted to use her. Against them. Against her father. Against the Imperium.

Every word he'd whispered, every touch that had steadied her blade, every flicker of tenderness—it had all been a game to him. A weapon honed in secret until he could place it in the rebels' hands.

The Kaed's roar shook her from the spiral. His sword angled, teeth bared in triumph as he drove his blade toward Firas's chest. Firas strained beneath him, muscles quivering, his fire no match for the storm bearing down.

"No!"

The word ripped from her throat as she surged forward. Her body moved before her mind could stop it, her fury breaking its chains. Power erupted, not the cool pull of water, not the shifting veil of illusion—but fire, searing and blinding. Air shrieked around her, tearing at the stones, and the ground itself buckled as jagged spears of earth split the courtyard.

The Kaed staggered back, his killing blow thrown wide. Soldiers and rebels alike froze, eyes turning toward the impossible storm rising from Talah's skin. Fire coiled with water, wind howled with stone, elements twisting into a single burst that threw both men apart. Her vision seared white, every nerve alight. The courtyard reeked of smoke and scorched stone, her ears ringing with the echo of her own scream.

For a single heartbeat, silence fell. The battle raged around them, but here—inside the shattered ring of her power—everything stilled. Smoke curled from the ruptured stones. Firas dragged himself to his feet, eyes locking on hers with something she couldn't name. And the Kaed... the Kaed's face twisted into a smile, slow and cruel.

"Seize her." His voice was low thunder, carrying over screams, over steel, over fire. "The girl is Ambigua."

Soldiers broke from their lines, turning toward her. Some stumbled, hesitant, but the Kaed's command drove them forward, their boots pounding against the fractured stones. Spears lowered. Chains glinted in the firelight.

"No!"

Mazin's voice cracked like a whip through the chaos. He

pushed through the ranks of competitors, his curved blades flashing as he cut down a soldier who reached for her. Shadows writhed at his feet, illusions snapping with teeth and claws, sending others scattering back. His face was pale, streaked with sweat and ash, but his eyes burned with something fierce, unshakable.

"Talah!" A soldier yanked him back, forcing Mazin to his knees.

"Enough!" the Kaed bellowed, his power surging. The air thickened as water burst from the cracked stones, sluicing in black rivulets across the courtyard. The soldiers faltered, but the Kaed raised his hand, and their hesitation vanished as if ripped away. Their eyes glazed with obedience, their grips tightening on chains and spears as they advanced—not by choice, but by his will.

Talah's chest constricted, every instinct screaming to move, to run, but her limbs felt bound by invisible cords. Even her own thoughts threatened to twist under his command, whispers pressing against her mind, urging her to *submit, kneel, obey.*

Mazin's shadows clawed at the ground, illusions striking out at the soldiers, but there were too many. Their boots pounded closer, water rippling around their ankles as if the Kaed himself drove the tide. Talah's breath came shallow and sharp, her heart battering like a trapped bird.

Her father carved through the press of bodies like a desert wind cutting through sand. One moment she was drowning beneath the Kaed's shadow; the next she was staring at her father, cloak whipping in the damp heat, his face set in a mask of fury and defiance.

Khalid stood like a wall of stone, shoulders squared, arms spread wide. Every line of him radiated the authority of a councilor, but more than that—of a father standing over his child. The torchlight caught in his eyes, sharp and unyielding, and when he spoke, his voice was a roar that cut through the Kaed's whispers clawing at her mind.

"Enough!" he thundered, his words striking like a hammer

across the courtyard. "You'll not touch her. She is my daughter."

The soldiers froze, caught between the Kaed's command and Khalid's fury. Even the Kaed's influence seemed to waver for a breath, the tide pausing mid-surge as if the fortress itself listened. And for the first time since the battle had erupted, Talah's lungs filled with air again.

The Kaed's head tilted, water streaming in rivulets at his feet, dark as spilled ink. His eyes—obsidian and fathomless—locked on Khalid with a glint of something colder than fury: disdain.

"Stand aside," the Kaed said, his voice smooth and venomous, a serpent's hiss beneath the roar of battle. "She is your daughter no longer. She is Ambigua. A weapon. And she belongs to the Imperium."

"You won't touch her," Khalid snapped back, his voice carrying like a strike of thunder. "Not while I still draw breath."

A low, humorless laugh rumbled from the Kaed's chest. "Then your breath will be cut short."

The air thickened, heavy with pressure that pressed on Talah's chest and clawed at her mind. Whispers slid into her skull—cold, insidious, demanding: *Kneel. Obey. Give yourself up.* She staggered, teeth grinding, fingernails biting into her palms as if pain could hold her steady.

"Stay out of her head!" Khalid roared, his voice cracking through the fog in her mind like lightning through storm clouds. With a sweep of his arm, the water at his feet surged upward into a wall, slamming between the soldiers and Talah.

But the Kaed only smiled, stepping forward through the spray. "Illusions and waves, Khalid? Do you think your parlor tricks will stop me?" His eyes gleamed, and for a breath the world wavered, tilting sideways. Talah blinked as soldiers multiplied, blades raised, eyes blank.

The Kaed's laugh was a rattle of bones. He thrust his hand outward, and Khalid stiffened, staggering as invisible fingers closed around his mind. Talah saw it—the twitch in his jaw, the sudden glaze in his eyes—as the Kaed pressed, bending him toward submission.

"No!" Talah's cry tore raw from her throat, her whole body shaking. She could *feel* it, the Kaed's power crawling toward her through the tether that bound her to her father. Her breath came fast, sharp, her chest burning with dread.

Khalid forced himself upright, his voice rough with strain but still unbroken. Illusions flickered from his body—shimmering doubles, a dozen Khalids rushing forward at once, crashing into the Kaed in a blur of water and shadow.

The courtyard shuddered with their collision. Soldiers stumbled back, competitors froze, and Talah clutched her dagger with trembling hands, caught between terror and the dawning realization that her father could not hold out forever.

The illusions struck like a tide—Khalid's figures flooding the courtyard, blades raised, water shimmering in their hands. For a heartbeat, the Kaed faltered, his soldiers recoiling as a dozen Khalids surrounded them.

Then the Kaed's eyes narrowed, black and sharp as glass. He raised one hand and clenched his fist.

The illusions burst like bubbles in the sun. One by one they shattered, dissolving into mist until only Khalid remained, gasping, his knees buckling under the weight pressing into his mind. The Kaed's voice coiled through the air, rich with venom.

"You are weak. Always hiding behind that title of yours. But titles cannot save you from me now." He stepped closer, the water surging at his feet, rising into a spear that gleamed in the torchlight. His eyes burned with triumph as he leveled it at Khalid's chest. "You harbored the enemy, Khalid. That makes you a traitor."

"Baba!" Talah's scream echoed around them, but her father was already faltering, his shield of water collapsing, his body bowing under the Kaed's will.

The blade drew back. The Kaed's arm tensed.

Talah's fury and terror snapped loose, shredding whatever fragile control she still clung to. Power surged—something vast, unbearable.

Light tore through her. Brilliant, searing white, bursting from her skin in a flood that split the night wide open. It seared across the courtyard, swallowing stone, soldier, and shadow alike. The Kaed's water-spear dissolved to mist; his soldiers stumbled back, blinded, clutching their faces.

Talah felt herself unraveling, every nerve alight, her body trembling on the edge of breaking. The light poured outward in an endless wave, drowning everything. Firas's voice rose through the chaos, calling her name—but it was already fading, already slipping away. The fortress vanished in brilliance.

Everything went white.

Then, the darkness consumed her.

JUST A SNEAK PEAK OF...

BOOK II
BOUND BY THE STARS

PROLOGUE
TALAH

Darkness folded in on itself. Shadows twisting and writhing like lost things in the sands of time. It was nothing and yet…it was everything.

But the light—the light. It blinded her, filling the space so completely. Heat pressed from every side, rippling off stone and sand, licking at her skin until her breath tasted of smoke. She could hear drums, the stamping of a thousand feet, the hiss of wind that smelled of iron and ash. Torches spit along arena walls. Shadows tower like pillars.

Her name.

Talah.

She turned toward the voice and the world fractured—a ring of faces, banners painted with each Sign, the ground scrawling with sigils that flared and died as if they were alive. As if they were breathing. Her hands were slick. Blood—or water? It gleamed black in the heat, streaking the lines of her palms.

Talah.

The word brushed her cheek. She couldn't see his face. He stood in the mouth of shadow, a darker shape amongst the night, and when he reached for her, she felt the cool edge of the night stealing across her fever. The boy smelled like rain and stone. His fingers were callused, steady. The whole arena leaned toward the space between their hands.

Don't let go.

Fire rolled across the sand, licking the hems of robes, swallowing banners. A wall of heat roared up and the crowd's voices broke into a hundred pieces—fear, triumph, a chant of something she couldn't bear to hear. The ground trembled. A flash of steel. A hand. A mask.

The man's outline faltered.

Talah's breath snagged. She reached.

Everything shattered. Something invisible and cold slid behind her eyes, a blade through water, and the memory she was holding split cleanly in two. Faces blurred. The man's hand, the one she almost caught, fractured into a dozen shards of movement and swam away.

"Stay with me," he said through the crack in the world. "Talah, stay—"

Everything tilted. The arena buckled into a corridor that stank of smoke and char; the corridor spilled into a courtyard where stars reeled so close she could touch them; the stars collapsed into a dark warehouse lit by a single lamp, a circle of figures around a map, a voice low and urgent as tidewater.

Then the knife of cold returned, and the warehouse scattered like a flock of birds.

She was running. She was falling. She was kneeling with blood on her knees and sand in her mouth, and someone was calling for a medic, calling for the Council, calling for the Twelve to witness. She tasted copper. She tasted salt. She thought, *this is important*, and clamped both hands around the thought like a lid. The boy's voice was a thread. She wound it around her wrist.

Remember me.

She would have sworn she did. The word remembered her back, shaking through her bones, anchoring her in the roar. She saw an outline where his face should have been—a jaw cut like a promise, eyes that caught torchlight and held it, a mouth that almost smiled even when the world was burning.

Talah reached again.

The cold slid deeper.

This time it was not a blade but a hand, gentle and inexorable, pressing against her brow. A murmur at her ear—words shaped in a language she knew and did not. The pressure built, sweet as sleep, heavy as stone. Beneath it, everything went quiet: the drums, the heat, the boy's breath. Even her own name loosened and began to float away.

Fire withdrew into embers. Blood dried to rust. The arena folded into darkness.

She woke to the scrape of a door and the low spill of lamplight.

The air was cool here, washed with the faint scents of jasmine and cardamom. The ceiling above her was painted night-blue, a procession of silver constellations marching from corner to corner. They looked familiar.

"Habibti?" a woman whispered.

Talah turned her head and found a face—the kind of beauty that belonged to sculptures and coins, hair threaded with gray, worry carved fine at the eyes. The woman took her hand and pressed it to her mouth, and only then did Talah realize the hand was hers.

"What...?" The word scraped out like a stone. "What happened?"

"You're home," the woman said, as if that were the whole story. "The physicians say the fever has broken."

A second shape hovered at the foot of the bed: a tall man, shoulders squared beneath a dark robe, his signet flashing in the lamplight. His gaze was steady and guarded at once, like a door with a lock already turned.

"The Trials are over," he said. "You're safe."

The Trials. The words sat in her mouth like a date pit—smooth, hard, tasteless. When she tried to bite down on it, it gave her nothing. She searched the painted constellations for a thread she could pull free. Somewhere, heat rose in waves. Somewhere, banners snapped. Somewhere, a boy with rain in his voice said her name.

"What Trials?" she asked softly.

Her mother's fingers flinched around hers. Her father's jaw tightened. A shadow crossed the lamp as the wick guttered and steadied.

"You were injured," her father said at last, tone ironed flat. "Rest now. We can speak tomorrow."

Tomorrow.

Talah nodded because nodding was easier than thinking. The motion made her skull throb. She closed her eyes and the darkness rolled close, cool and clean. But behind her lids, the stars rearranged themselves into unfamiliar patterns, and for an instant a hand reached toward her from the edge of a memory that wouldn't hold still.

"Don't," she heard from very far away. Or maybe she said it herself.

The grip on her hand tightened. Her mother murmured, "Hush."

The last things she knew before sleep took her was the cool weight of a blanket drawn to her chin, the thread of her mother's thumb stroking the back of her hand, the way the lamplight turned the signet on her father's finger into a small, steady star.

When morning came, they would call her clever, dutiful, recovered. They would tell her a story about Trials and triumph, about enemies and heroes. They would give her a dozen words to set like stones across the river of whatever she had lost.

And the boy with rain in his voice would be gone with the night.

Talah slept.

She woke to daylight, a soft wind, the quiet of a villa that had never been touched by fire, and the simple certainty that her name was Talah bint Khalid.

Everything else was nothing at all.

OTHER BOOKS
BY MICHELE KHALIL

THE STARBOUND TRILOGY

CURSED BY THE STARS
BOUND BY THE STARS
FREED BY THE STARS

AUTHORS NOTE

Cursed by the Stars was shaped during a formative chapter of my life—my time living in Egypt.

Although this story is not set in Egypt, much of its soul was born there. Living in a land layered with history, mythology, resilience, and beauty reshaped the way I understand the world and my place within it, and in turn transformed the way I tell stories. Egypt is a place where the past is never distant. Ancient stones rise beside modern streets, centuries coexist in a single glance, and history is not confined to books but felt—underfoot, overhead, and in the silences between daily moments.

During my time there, I fell deeply in love with the warmth of the people and the generosity woven into everyday life; with conversations that linger, laughter that survives hardship, and a culture rooted in enduring bonds of family, community, and shared memory. I was struck by the rhythm of daily life, steady and resilient, shaped by both tradition and necessity. There was beauty in the contrast between ancient and modern—between the immovable and the ever-changing—and in the sense that the land itself carries memory, as though it remembers everything that has ever passed over it.

The colors, the heat, the endless skies, the devotion to family and community, the humor sharpened by survival, the quiet strength required to endure—these elements stayed with me long after I left. They settled into me, influencing how I imagine worlds and characters, how I understand conflict, and how I write hope. You'll find their echoes woven throughout this book: in the textured worldbuilding, in the fierce and tender emotional bonds between characters, in the reverence for the past and its weight on the present, and in the quiet insistence that survival, hope, and love can coexist—even in the harshest, most unforgiving circumstances.

Aphelion University—and the rest of this world—was inspired not by Egypt directly, but by another ancient civilization that once stood at the heart of ancient civilizations. Often called the cradle of civilization, Mesopotamia was home to some of humanity's earliest cities, laws, sciences, and written records. Babylon, rising along the banks of the Euphrates, became not only a political and cultural center, but a celestial one. It was here that scholars began systematically observing the night sky—recording planetary movements, identifying recurring patterns, and dividing the heavens into recognizable constellations. These early astronomer–priests laid the foundations of astrology as we know it today, creating zodiac systems and celestial calendars that influenced Greek, Roman, and eventually modern astrological thought.

To the Babylonians, the stars were not distant or decorative. They were messages. Omens. Warnings and promises written across the sky by the gods themselves. Planetary alignments were consulted before wars were waged, rulers were crowned, or laws were upheld. Eclipses could signal disaster. Favorable constellations could justify the rise of kings. The heavens and the earth were inseparable—what happened above was believed to echo below.

That belief—that the cosmos carries weight, consequence, and authority over human lives—became a foundational pillar of *Cursed by the Stars*. In this world, astrology is not symbolism; it is power. The stars shape identity, hierarchy, and destiny. Fate is debated, feared, manipulated, and resisted, much as it was in the ancient world, where celestial knowledge could elevate empires—or rationalize cruelty in the name of divine order.

Mesopotamian cultures viewed history as cyclical rather than linear, the past as something alive rather than buried. Cities, like people, rose and fell. Knowledge was preserved because it mattered, because memory was survival. That reverence—for record, ritual, and remembrance—influenced how this world understands history, authority, and legacy. Aphelion is built on the idea that knowledge itself is sacred, dangerous, and deeply political.

While this story is fictional, it draws deep inspiration from real histories and cultures that treated the land as memory and the sky as something to be listened to rather than conquered. Egypt taught me reverence—for endurance, for heritage, for people whose lives are shaped by forces both visible and unseen. Babylon taught me that humanity has always looked upward in times of uncertainty, searching for order in chaos, meaning in movement, and guidance written among the stars.

It is here that the story becomes explicitly political—because knowledge has always been political. Who is permitted access to information, who is believed, who is deemed worthy of power, and who is sacrificed in the name of stability are not abstract questions; they are decisions made by systems. In Mesopotamian cultures, astronomical knowledge was guarded, interpreted, and weaponized by those in authority. The same is true in this world. Control over the stars becomes control over people. Law, faith, education, and power intertwine—often at the expense of those already made vulnerable.

Reading itself is political for the same reason history is political. Stories decide whose lives are centered, whose suffering is legitimized, and whose resistance is framed as necessary—or dangerous. *Cursed by the Stars* does not shy away from this truth. It asks questions about fate versus free will, about institutional power masquerading as destiny, and about what happens when systems built to create order instead perpetuate harm. It challenges the idea that cruelty becomes righteous when it is sanctioned by tradition, prophecy, or authority.

Mesopotamian cultures viewed history as cyclical rather than linear, the past as something alive rather than buried. Cities, like people, rose and fell. Knowledge was preserved because it mattered—because memory was survival. That reverence for record, ritual, and remembrance deeply influenced how this world understands history, authority, and legacy. Aphelion is built on the idea that knowledge itself is sacred, dangerous, and profoundly powerful.

While this story is fictional, it draws deep inspiration from real histories and cultures that treated the land as memory and the sky as something to be listened to rather than conquered. Egypt taught me reverence—for endurance, for heritage, for people whose lives are shaped by forces both visible and unseen. Babylon taught me that humanity has always looked upward in times of uncertainty, searching for order in chaos, meaning in movement, and guidance written among the stars.

This story exists because of that time in my life, and because of the people and places that inspired it. Any beauty you find within these pages was shaped by real moments, real lessons, and cultures that left an indelible mark on my heart.

With deep gratitude and respect,

Michele Khalil

ACKNOWLEDGMENTS

This book might have existed previously, but it wouldn't be what it is today without the support of many loving and talented people. This is my attempt to thank all of them.

To my partner, Nick—thank you for believing in me when I couldn't believe in myself. For reminding me that love doesn't have to hurt, that it can be steady, kind, and healing. You helped me find my way back to writing when I thought I'd lost it forever. You showed me what true love is supposed to be like, and because of you, I learned how to create again. This book exists because you reminded me I could still dream.

To my friends in the STL Writing Gals—Yaya, Kayla, Riley, Amanda, Pooja, and Stephanie—thank you for being the most supportive, inspiring community of women I could ask for. You've cheered me on through every draft, every doubt, every 5pm virtual coffee. You made this journey joyful and inspiring. And Kate—thank you for pointing out that we don't have to *smell* every chapter. You saved more scenes than you know.

To my beta readers and my incredible editor, Victoria Jane—thank you for your sharp eyes, your honesty, and your patience.

You helped me shape this story into what it was always meant to be. To Lucia—thank you for your early insight, and for letting me revel in all the witty banter. You helped me fall in love with my characters all over again.

I want to thank my incredible artists who brought my characters to life—to Jessica (@zelyphia) and Jessica (@lampofblob). You two created some of the most precious and most beautiful artwork of my characters and I cannot praise nor thank either of you enough.

I also want to thank the newest addition--my PA, Jaz. Without her, I wouldn't have continued to have the spoons to market this book or keep writing the next. Thank you for your endless support. I am so glad I met you!

The last five years have been some of the hardest and most transformative years of my life. There were times I couldn't write, couldn't create, couldn't even imagine finishing a story again. But now I'm finally in a safe space—one that allows me to grow, to learn, and to breathe as a writer. I couldn't have finished this book, or found my voice again, without the love, encouragement, and faith of these incredible people.

And I cannot have any sort of acknowledgments without my family. Thank you to my mother for continuously believing in me. I couldn't do this without the endless "You're such a beautiful writer" to boost my ego every now and then.

Thank you for holding space for me, for believing in me, and for helping me find the light again.

ABOUT THE AUTHOR

When Michele Khalil isn't lost in fictional worlds of rebellion and slow-burn romance, they're hoarding books like a dragon, cheering on fellow authors, and daydreaming about more stories than they could ever possibly write. Inspired by ancient cultures, sweeping romances, and the belief that stories can change us, Michele writes fantasy worlds where love and survival collide. Cursed by the Stars is their debut novel, and the first book in The Starbound Trilogy.

authormichelekhalil.com
@authormichelekhalil
www.facebook.com/michelejkhalil

www.ingramcontent.com/pod-product-compliance
Lightning Source LLC
LaVergne TN
LVHW040036080526
838202LV00045B/3356